YOU
BELONG
to ME

YOU BELONG to ME

A Novel

ELIZABETH COOKE

WRITING AS ELIZABETH McGREGOR

Cover design by Kat JK Lee

ISBN: 978-1-5040-1933-0

Distributed in 2015 by Open Road Distribution
345 Hudson Street
New York, NY 10014
www.openroadmedia.com

YOU
BELONG
to ME

PROLOGUE

THERE WERE LILIES AT THE DOOR OF THE CHURCH. Funeral flowers, arranged for a wedding, with thin yellow tongues at their heart. She had a violent urge to tear them to pieces, there in the shadows of the porch.

But she was surprised at how calm she actually managed to be. She walked into the church, packed with its two hundred guests, and a rustle went through the congregation as she turned towards the altar. Heads turned from every direction, whispering. She heard her name repeated again and again.

Struggling to maintain control, she walked steadily up the aisle. Acknowledging people. Nodding at them. Smiling. Just as if she hadn't a care in the world.

Just as if she *wanted* Thomas to marry someone else.

She knew, without looking, that Randolph and Ruth had turned to look at her; perhaps her parents were, even now, beckoning for her to join them.

But she chose a seat at the end of a crowded pew, waiting calmly while the others moved up to let her in. She stared down at them, daring them to suggest, even by a look, that her large size was too much to accommodate. Sitting down, she rested her forehead on her hands as though she were praying. And, in a minute or so, she managed to get her breathing under control.

She would not look at Thomas, either. She dared not. She glanced away: at the side chapel, at the posies on the end of the pew. Gardenias and pinks. *Christ.* If she caught so much as a glimpse of him, she would shriek her misery. She clasped her hands in her lap until her knuckles whitened.

Hands.

All that morning, since the first sickening certainty of waking, she had been thinking of hands. Fingers clutching at an open frame; smaller hands enclosed by an adult fist. A child's hands hiding a face of bruised longing. Something else, then, worse. Trees behind glass, and the descent from steps into a garden, and past that, Randolph's voice.

Steps and an open door . . .

She frowned. The air was being compressed out of her. And she had no idea what it meant, except, after the door, came a garden. The images were important, she felt their weight and texture, but she could not place them. As with a forgotten name, leaning at the edge of a memory, falling away; so the stairs, the doorway, the green garden . . .

The organ began to play the *Wedding March.*

And it was then that something huge rose up and filled her throat, her eyes. She knew at once that she was going to be sick. It was as though her body rebelled and failed, where all her mental strength had succeeded. The organ music was beginning to build; there was a murmur at the back of the church, a hurried rustling of paper, of clothes.

Joz knew exactly what Anna would look like. A Victorian dress, too large for Anna's skinny frame. Her grandmother's, and totally wrong. But Anna didn't care. She wasn't capable of looking decent even on her wedding day. And this colourless, bloodless, dry stick was going to be in his bed, in his bed, in his bed . . .

Oh my God . . .

The church around her rolled and tilted; the colours faded in and out. Panic washed over her. She got up from the pew and rushed down the aisle.

Anna was standing, ready to begin. Joz bore down on her, her hand clapped across her own mouth, bile rising in her throat. The sight of Anna made her stop—just for a second—as the filthy feeling temporarily receded. It was replaced by something infinitely more terrible, infinitely more cold.

She got outside somehow.

She leaned against the wall of the church, watching the trees dancing above the graves. The sky was brilliant between their branches: the blue of Fabergé, almost turquoise.

She ran down the path, and up the narrow village street, oblivious to the turning heads of passers-by. She was dressed in a violent lime green, with hat and shoes and bag to match. *Colour me envy.* She got to the car, wrenched the driver's door, took off her hat, threw it on to the back seat, and stumbled in.

She sat, staring through the windscreen.

Very gradually, a semblance of control came back to her, and the reflection of the woman in the driving mirror ceased to have the wide-eyed wretchedness of a few minutes ago, and began to be *her* again. She reached up and touched the edge of her mouth, where the lipstick had begun to bleed. She pulled a strand of hair into place across her forehead. *Just wait*, she thought. *Just wait.*

And she knew then that Randolph was right. Revenge was by far the sweetest taste; outranking love by light years. He had taught her that well. She had learned it over and over, all her life.

Thomas used to tell her, when they were children together and very small, that the world would come right. They would have a little island, he used to say. With sand around it like a skirt. He *said* that. He *promised* that . . .

She watched people go by, saw them glance in at her. Eventually, by an enormous effort of will, she managed to start the engine, put the car into gear, and release the handbrake. Even then, her foot juddered on the clutch as she sat waiting for the traffic lights to change. The Mercedes glittered in the summer sunlight; she sat with one hand on the gearstick, her face rigid. It was as if both she and the car were carved from ice.

The lilies, the pinks, the silk ribbons.

5

Anna in that sickly cream.

The trees . . .

The lights changed; the car sprang forward. Joz shoved the accelerator down to the floor.

Nobody took Thomas away from her.

Nobody.

She gripped the wheel and stared straight ahead. After all, Thomas was her brother. And he was hers *first*.

ONE

*T*HE PHONE RINGS, as it always does, at night.

'What are you doing?'

'I can't speak to you. Not any more.'

'Of course you can. Nothing has changed. What are you doing?'

There is a moment while she sits, swallowing some gagging obstruction that has suddenly choked her. Fear. 'I'm . . . the lights are off . . . I'm just sitting . . .' The words bolt from her throat. 'Why did you let them—?'

'Looking where?'

'Out . . . on to . . .'

'*Concentrate.*'

'How can I?' She is almost hysterical. 'How can I think of *any-thing . . .*'

She can't play the game tonight. It is breaking her heart. 'I don't know why you let her do it,' she says. 'Why you let him do it. I don't understand.'

His reply is matter-of-fact. 'You will see. I'll show you. I'll explain. You can do what I do. It's easy. Remember?'

'I can't think, I don't know what to do . . .' She wants to tell him about the trees and the steps. But a small voice inside her is warning against it.

'It doesn't matter. It can't touch you,' he is telling her softly. 'What is she? No one. You belong to me. Did you hear me?'

'Yes.'

'Tell me. Nice and slowly.'

'I belong . . .' Whispers inside. Ghosts. *It is a lie, a lie* . . . With every repetition, her heart becomes more numb, her thoughts more distant. In the end, they cease to be hers at all.

'Nothing has changed.'

'I wish I could believe that,' she murmurs, thinking aloud.

His voice hardens. 'Listen. *Listen.*'

'I . . . I'm listening.'

'I want you to ring her up. Belong. I want you to write to her. Belong. You understand? It's the same as all the rest. You want him back?'

She trembles from head to foot, filled with a terror that has pushed everything else from her mind. 'I don't know . . .'

'It's your choice. It was always that *you* wanted *him* . . .'

'I wish . . .' She can't say it. She is confused now. It isn't true that it was only her wanting. Thomas wanted them together. He used to say so, all the time. When they were little. At nine, they sent him to boarding school, to separate them. But bonds like that could never be broken. She *could* get back there, to the only time she had been loved. Thomas said . . . but she can't remember, now, *what* he said. Her stepfather's words get in the way. She wishes she were small. A long time ago. Four, three. Before he came into their lives.

'You're not listening.'

'But I don't want to any more. Oh, please . . .'

There is a silence.

'You don't want to belong any more?'

'You promised! You said I had to wait. Was it a lie?' This, more to herself than to him. Breathed. 'I keep thinking it must be a story. Did you make up a story? I don't know any more. It's *you* that has left *me* . . .' She is crying now. She only ever cries when he speaks to her.

'Write her a letter,' he is saying, his voice slow and measured. 'It will bring him back. He's only a little lamb, strayed from the fold. A little lamb. Call him back. Do you think I would have abandoned you? Do you think I would do that? It's only your mother's will. You can break that, can't you? It's such a little thing. Do you think he really wanted all this? It's just your mother's pushing. Get a pen . . . write this down . . .'

In the dark, she fumbles for a pen and a sheet of paper. She wants to believe him. She wants to believe every word he tells her. She *needs* to. There is nothing else.

She puts her face close to the paper so that she can see something in the gloom. She will never put the light on.

All these conversations belong to the dark.

TWO

*S*HE SAT WITH HER HANDS ON THE TABLE, on top of her portfolio. The conference room of the TV agency was huge, and extraordinarily dead. It was one of her little triumphs. Last week, just last week... only last week... it would have amused her. But not today.

Joz caught sight of herself, picked out by sunlight, in the glass of the window. She was a black blur topped with wide blonde hair, a triangle on top of a circle. Nothing out of place; nothing to suggest she had just spent the most miserable weekend of her life. Nothing to suggest the pain raging inside her. She glanced at her watch.

Mark Estwood was precisely eight minutes late. She gave a tight smile. It was *perfectly* OK; she was good at waiting. Superb, in fact. It was the one thing that she knew how to do flawlessly. The smile flickered, twitched. A little tic of bitterness that she did not yet know she possessed.

She would take it out on someone today. Monday. Work day. Thomas somewhere with ... She crushed the feeling. *That's the way they pay.* That's what Randolph said. Someone... it didn't matter who. Probably Mark Estwood.

Her eyes strayed back to the room: grey and black, with grey blinds.

She'd been the interior designer for this place three years ago; it had been one of her first assignments. Now she had been called back. The agency had a new director, and they wanted the place refurbished. Joz considered her previous work with calm approval.

An air-conditioner froze the blood. One wall was a complete bank of television monitors and VCRs, whose screens ticked and blurred constantly. She had brought in a thick grey carpet that made the floor look as if it were covered in the ashes of a thousand cremations. Grey carpet, grey gravestone plinth table, grey hissing screens, white walls.

'It will look so clean,' she'd told Tremain. '*Sanitised.*' And he had laughed, finally wrenching himself clear of her direct gaze. Ben Tremain was not sure, even when she'd finished the job, if he had been ripped off or not. She saw it in the way that he wrote the last cheque. She had furnished every other inch of this place in the same ash-grey, with black metal sculpture in the reception, and great grey ceramic bowls and grey-sprayed partitions.

Sometimes she lay awake at night, grinning at the nightmares she persuaded her clients to live in. Sometimes the horrors that she devised, subtle and beautiful, took her breath away. Sometimes . . . she hesitated . . . something else—not quite guilt. The flickering at the edge of her sight.

Take the ambassadress. It was six months since Joz had stood in the embassy, surrounded by strewn wallpapers. The woman had frowned at the colours she suggested, the green-and-red trellis-pattern. Said it was too much.

'Really?' Joz had asked, feigning boredom. 'In the *Beaux Saisons . . .*'

The implication that some arts charity had chosen the same pattern finally pushed the woman to accept it. Snobbery won out. That terrible trellised hallucination was now vaulting up and down her staircase, and the cold bitch probably had to wear Raybans just to get down to breakfast. Serve her damned right for giving her that *I'm more refined than you* crap the whole time.

Got you back, got you back.

The childhood phrase rattled round her head.

She glanced down at the agency books of actors, laid, as if for amusement, on the grey tabletop before her. Hundreds of faces, serious or boyish or whimsical or artfully rugged, packed together. Everything from hopeful grins to serious determination—and all the expressions in between. Anything to command the attention.

Bored with the paper faces, she turned her head, and stared at the painting that took up most of the inner wall. *That* was far more deserving of her attention. It was nothing short of stupendous. Sixteen feet by twenty, if it was an inch. A masterful copy of Signorelli's *Last Judgement.*

'Who painted you?' she asked the silent mural. It had been brought in some time after she'd left. It must have been Tremain's idea. The kind of thing he liked. She'd known that weakness in him from his first limp handshake. Ben's first touch had been full of flesh.

And here it was, in the painting. Mountains of the stuff: round thighs and high breasts and agonised faces gazing back at the paradise that was retreating from them. She narrowed her eyes, assessing the copy. Gloriously cruel. Devils clutched at knees and hands, drawing their human victims to the soil. Demons carried unconscious women on their backs, or sank their thumbs into their necks. Joz wondered how many of the hopeful-serious actors had sat, with their hopeful-serious managers, and been forced to stare at those fingers searching for the throats of their victims. *Nice one, Ben*, she thought. *Frighten the shit out of the opposition before you even come in the room.*

That's the style. That's Step-Daddy's way.

Still, Ben had vanished now. He had been replaced by the infamous Sandy Merrion-Walsh, who spoke with a mock-American accent, reeked of Guerlain, and had two teeth at the front that overlapped each other and drew the eye. The woman was absolutely fascinating, a study in primal power. Joz had wanted, when she met her at Randolph's last party, to taste the palm of Sandy's bloated little hand. Snuggle up to her, and breathe in the blood she'd spilt.

Joz concentrated on the picture. Tried to gauge which of the fakemasters painters had done the copy. There were only half a dozen in the country with such talent. A remarkable stillness flowed over her as she stared at the horns and wings and expressions of terror.

Her hands settled almost voluptuously on the cardboard folder on the table in front of her. It had horrors of its own, inside that maroon cover: stone heads from churches, green men with vines crawling from their mouths. The stark childish realism of the New England grave-stones. The *cloisonné* faces of Oriental dogs; blacks and reds; insects and monsters. She had second-guessed what the agency wanted this time. More of the same.

Well, she'd soon see if she was right or wrong. Maybe the new boss, her of the crossed teeth and bloody palms, would amaze them all and go for the country look. Maybe she'd give Joz a brief for mock-fireplaces and baskets of logs and aromatic balls of thyme. You never knew with these bastards. They ate up image, swallowed it, then gulped about, like fish, for more.

She would soon see.

And, as if on cue, the door opened.

She did not stand. Cecily Joscelyne never stood. She sat immobile and watched him, without giving him a twitch of greeting.

That'll teach you not to make me wait.

Mark Estwood wouldn't be much of a challenge, it was obvious. He stopped on the threshold, this—what did he call himself?—this *executive director's administrative assistant*, expecting a word from her, and getting none. Even as he was walking towards her now, he was waiting for her to jolt into life, to start fawning and babbling. Poor little soldier. She fought down an urge to laugh.

He was about twenty-five, with a crop of curly blond hair. Blue eyes. Very pretty. When he opened his mouth, he brayed *public school*, and she knew he'd be an easy mark, and was deeply disappointed.

'Ms Joscelyne? Mark Estwood.'

She didn't move or speak.

'I—er—I've been detailed, as it were.'

She closed her eyes momentarily, her forefinger running down the spine of the binder in front of her. At last, she spoke. 'I'm *terribly* disappointed that Sandy isn't here to see me.'

He twitched. 'I'm fully briefed with what Sandy wants,' he said. 'She does send her apologies.'

She put her head on one side, then extended her hand at last, like Royalty conferring recognition on a subject. 'Before you tell me all about it,' she murmured. 'Who was commissioned to paint the Signorelli? It's arrived since I was last here.'

'The . . . ?' He looked a little stunned, possibly at the rigid strength of her hand gripping his.

She raised an eyebrow at the wall. 'The copy Signorelli.' She released him.

'Ah. Isn't it a horror? We call it the Beasties.'

'Do you indeed.'

'Well—er—I believe the artist was Faith Collins.'

'Oh.' She considered. 'Faith *Mary* Collins, you mean? She's always called by the three names.'

'Yes—I—yes, quite. Now, as for the design here . . .' He had backed off, until he stood alongside the demons, looking like an angelic child stranded in the underworld.

'Have you any drawings?' she asked. 'Anything I can look at? Colours; rooms that Sandy likes? Painters? Countries; moods?' *Oh, he's blushing*, she thought triumphantly. *How horrible for him.*

'She wondered if you knew . . .' Mark Estwood searched his brain for the exact words. He'd learned them in the train. 'She wondered,' he said, '*A La Mie*, and the brothel pictures of Lautrec?'

'She wants a brothel?' Joz asked.

'No. No. She was quite definite. Not the red plush and gilt, she said. She said, oranges and blues. She asked if you knew *Lucie Bellanger* . . .'

'Erotica?'

'Subdued. Possibly. Probably.'

'Furniture?'

'I don't know. It's just preliminary sketches.'

'I don't do those,' Joz replied equably. 'Sandy knows that. We'll come up with some ideas, some motifs perhaps, today. She wants that turn-of-the-century thing, that baroque? An *unfinished* look. You'll want to take the flooring up . . . I'll ring her.'

'But, I—'

She smiled. 'I don't compete, Mark. Either I'm hired or not. I don't waste time. I don't sketch. I don't have a chintzy shop off the Park where I sell curtains. I don't sew little cushions. I'm not an upholsterer or a shopfitter. When you hire me, it's a meeting of minds. A creative experience.'

He looked suitably chastened.

And so you should, she thought. *That speech has hamstrung greater men than you. That's why it'll cost you a fortune, darling. It's the case of the Emperor's New Clothes. You'll never quite know if you've been duped or not. Only in the worst moments will you look around and get that terrible sick feeling that it's some grotesque joke on you . . . But the beauty is, you'll never know. I'm famous, you see? It's a licence to deceive.*

'Of course, if you just want a painter and decorator . . .' she said, picking up her portfolio slowly with one hand.

'No, no—she wants you, I—'

'Naturally, I'll execute proper plans in time. Sandy will see them. But this is an *artistic venture*, you see? You understand? I expect a free hand.' Her voice hadn't altered from it's rolling, low pattern. She appeared absolutely unhurried.

This time he blushed an awful shade of red. Sheer embarrassment. She took pity on him at last, rose to her feet, and advanced on him, until, in Mark Estwood's mind, he could only think of her nickname— the Serpent. Others in the agency had laughingly warned him about her, and he could now see why. Cecily Joscelyne was a sixteen-stone, immaculately dressed, blonde python dropping from a tree. And she was unrolling towards him.

She laid a hand on his arm. 'Shall we put our heads together? Perhaps we'll surprise even Sandy.'

She smelled of acid, Mark thought vacantly. Etching acid. Pewter. Brass. And, suffocatingly, sex.

'And where shall we have lunch?' she asked.

THREE

$\mathcal{A}$s DISASTERS GO, it rated pretty high.

Faith Mary Collins stood in the small white loo, the sloping ceiling almost touching her head, and stared at the plastic stick in her hand. Perhaps she hadn't washed the container properly; perhaps *that* was it. Perhaps there was limescale or chlorine or fluoride in the water, enough to alter the result. *Could* that alter it? Her mind scrabbled about wildly for excuses. Perhaps this was the .001 per cent they said went wrong, gave a wrong reading.

Perhaps *nothing*.

Perhaps she was pregnant.

She sat down on the closed seat of the loo, shoving the door tight with her free hand. She had a sudden urge to lock herself in and never come out. To hide.

'Oh God,' she whispered. 'No . . . no . . .'

There was no one else in the house, and she was right at the very top—the attic of her home that overlooked the grey and brown roofs of Notting Hill. And yet the closed door didn't seem enough to conceal her. It was as though, if she could get far enough away, or roll herself into the tightest of balls, the problem would go away. She would squeeze her eyes shut, and, when she opened them, it would have gone. The little blue circle in the stick.

She squeezed out another glance at the pregnancy test. It stared back: one small disc of colour, roaring significance.

She would never be alone again for a long time. If ever. From now on, there would always be someone else.

She sat there holding a separate, different life inside her. It already had its own heartbeat; it had already settled in her, drawing from her without her knowing until now. An unexpected, unplanned life. It was unbelievable. It was shocking. She had thought that such accidents only happened to other women. Not her—so precise, so detailed in everything she did. So careful.

She looked once more at the tiny fabric window, now showing the evidence in a deeper and more irrevocable shade of blue.

And then she put her head in her hands, and started to laugh. It was so ironic, for God's sake.

'Oh, you've done it *now*,' she whispered.

Guy had never wanted children. They had argued about it wildly in the beginning. But she'd always thought there would be a time— some time in the vague future—when she would be able to bring him around to the idea, and so she had silently let it drop.

Guy turned his nose up at the offspring of friends: charming little angels, who smeared their biscuity fingers along his carefully pressed chinos; crying just at the comfortable moment when the adults had settled into chairs after a good dinner.

'Look at what that little bastard's done to my phone,' he had gasped once, wiping paint from his hands.

She had laughed, and said, 'They're just ordinary kids. All kids do that.'

'*Kids*?' he'd yelled. 'They're not children. They're bloody anarchists. They all want locking up till they're twenty. All that sick and Marmite. Look at Charlie,' he'd said, naming a friend's two-year-old as if it proved his argument. 'Why does he *have* all that snot?'

The laughter bubbled up almost hysterically now; Faith sat back on the loo and rested her head on the white wall, and wiped the first tear from the corner of her eye. Guy, a father. She, a mother. A baby made from them, the most unsuited pair in the history of the world.

So unsuited that they had split up six months ago.

The laughter stopped abruptly.

On the opposite wall, above the cramped little basin, she saw herself—just her face—reflected. Pale face, dark chin-length hair, large brown eyes. In the last few months those lines at the edges of her eyes, at the edges of her mouth, had considerably deepened, drawing down her normally cheerful face into a pout. Shock did that. And grief, at being told that your husband's latest affair was no affair at all, but true love, the real thing, what he had been waiting for all his life. Guy's own words.

His clichés had revolted her. *All his life . . . the real thing.* He, the master of the lie. Now, and only now—in the last few empty months— she had heard the weakness in his voice, the failure to accept responsibility.

Yet she'd hoped, for a long time, that he would come back, changed and remorseful. Held out that last faint and ridiculous hope. One night, about two months ago, he *had* come. Drunk, at half past eleven. He told her some shambling, incoherent story on the doorstep about a row with Chloe, and she'd—fool, *fool*—taken him in, made him coffee, listened for an hour, until, as he rose to leave . . .

Oh, God. She'd been so sure that it meant something. His arms, his kisses. Yet the moment he rolled away from her in bed, she knew that it was over. The last, the final, time. After the frantic coupling, the room had felt as cold as the grave. He had sat up, his back to her, and said, 'Faith, I'm sorry. I'm so sorry.'

Eight weeks ago . . .

'Oh boy,' she whispered now. 'What a shock you're going to have.'

She was seeing him today, at twelve. They were collecting their cheques from the solicitor's, the proceeds of the sale of their house. She had already decided that she would say nothing, there would be no rehashing of the past. Not the long past, the first days. Nor the recent past.

Most of all, she would say nothing about the afternoon he left— that terrible Sunday last August, when Chloe's car drew up outside, and Guy got out, and she had stared in disbelief as he stripped their home of what he wanted. No warning, no explanation. And she had run up and down the stairs after him, saying, 'What are you doing? Won't you at least tell me? Haven't I got a right to know? Where are you going? Please, *please* . . .'

And she would say nothing about sitting on the carpet of the hall after he had gone, feeling—not surprised, not that—but feeling winded, as if he had punched her. Winded and disorientated. Sick, at the sheer cruelty of his silence as he had packed his suitcases on their bed, an expression like a grin—an embarrassed grin—never leaving his face.

Guy loved his games. Just as he used to love standing her up when they first met, and then bombarding her with calls and flowers until she relented, and then leaving her again—at a rail station once, in the rush hour, even at an airport once, the flight tickets sticky in her hand as they welded themselves to her skin out of unadulterated panic. Guy, to the last—wrongfooting and worrying her, making her ask, making her beg to be looked at and spoken to as an adult. Guy, black hair falling over his forehead, slamming the door in her face.

Outside, he had wrapped his arms around Chloe on the pavement, knowing that Faith would be watching. And she did watch; she did just what he wanted. She watched, despite knowing it was all done for her benefit. Watched as Guy kissed the girl hard in the Sunday afternoon drizzle. She saw that Chloe—younger by ten years, round-faced, triumphant—had that same dazed, confused, thrilled expression that *she* had worn when she first met him. Faith had stood in the bay window, her heart pounding with a kind of shameful horror.

She hated him for standing there in the road like that. Making such a show of it. Turning the knife. He was no better than a child . . .

The idea . . . *child* . . . jolted Faith back to the present. She bit her lip.

She would see him in about an hour's time. She would even raise a glass with him, for the idea of Guy without a drink in his hand was impossible. She would be bright, as if he had never hurt her, and could never hurt her . . . not even his memory. At least, not once she had left London. She had just bought a house on the coast, on a tiny windblown island, a shambling wreck of a place, because she was desperate to get away from him and from all the places they had been together—the familiar streets and bars and shops. *Desperate* . . .

When she was alone in the new place, and the taste and touch of him came back to haunt her in the dark, it would be a private pain that she would never admit to him. Today she would pretend she was over him, to his face. She would lie as much as that.

But . . . she would not tell him the most important thing of all.

She threw the pregnancy test into the washbasin sink, sure now. Convinced.

She would not tell Guy *this*.

FOUR

$\mathcal{I}$T WAS PITCH DARK by the time Joz got home. So dark that, after getting out of the car, she had to stand for a while on her step, fumbling for her keys, trying to register shape: the shape of the door and the lock. *I ought to get a porch light*, she thought, *one of those things that come on automatically. But then, I ought to do a lot of things, and I don't.*

The door opened on to a steep stairway. She had a Dockland terraced town house, four storeys high, overlooking a stretch of water seeping in from the Thames.

She had bought the place two years ago.

'Move *out*?' her step-father had said, astounded. Beside him, Ruth had been wringing her hands at Randolph's fury. 'Move out! But you won't last three minutes on your own!'

He had stalked across the room to where she trembled in the doorway, her chin raised in unaccustomed defiance. Then, he had started to laugh and stroke her hair.

'Oh, I see,' he'd murmured, so softly that it was impossible for Ruth to hear. 'Kicking against the traces? Yes?'

'I shall be fine,' she had said.

What had possessed her? The urges to get away from them both came like bolts from the blue, struck her dumb, made her head swim. They were dimly connected to strings of words, whispered as if in song . . .

But she had never before acted on these sudden desperations to break free. Randolph's hands on her hair froze her to the spot. He had begun to laugh.

'Go on,' he was saying. 'We shall see how you fly, little bird.'

'I will,' she had replied. 'I will fly.'

He had kissed her on the cheek. 'I will ring you every night,' he said. 'So that you feel you still belong somewhere.'

In the beginning, she had liked to stand in the luxury of the house, and stare out of the window at the rim of deserted dock, the red buses threading through other, lesser streets. She had liked to see the Cortinas prowling down the road, outside the brick-lined courtyards and patios and security systems. Kids came and hung on the railings of the renovated bridge, gazing at the apartments that had sprung up in the middle of desolation. But the novelty of being the princess in the castle had soon worn off.

She'd had great plans, at first, for how she'd decorate it. A dresser full of blue Delft in the kitchen, cream linen sofas in the sitting room, a yew desk, cream and gold and tan drapes. In the bedroom, Mediterranean yellows. The bathroom, green on green.

She locked the door now behind her, and felt for the light. It came on with a dull click. The house was revealed in its concrete drabness. Clothes were strewn on the landing banister, and the top was nearly blocked by a black plastic sack of rubbish. No paintings, no carpet on the stair, no flowers. The phone sat on the Yellow Pages by the door. No table, no mirror. A sheaf of scribbled notes—taxi numbers, client numbers, takeaways—littered the floor.

Joz looked at the phone for a moment, then unplugged it and carried it upstairs. And it was only half-way up that the smell hit her. Bilious and vile. She stopped a second, looking towards the dark living room, then turned away, and went into the kitchen, where the fluorescent light revealed more sluttish mayhem. Wrappers, half-cooked food in a pan, the door of the dishwasher open, stacked with dirty plates.

She made herself tea and looked in the fridge. A packet of wafer ham, a box of Belgian chocolates, a bottle of Jagermeister. No milk for the tea. She snatched up the chocolates and ate them, standing all the while. Half a pound or more, swallowed almost without tasting, and without pleasure.

She drifted out of the kitchen and stood on the landing.

'Maxy,' she called. 'Maxi-*mil*-i-an . . .'

The dog in the living room whined. She heard him scrabble, trying to get to her. Then a small stifled groan as he lay back down. He was only a young dog, no more than a puppy, really. Yet for the last few days he'd groaned like an old man.

She knew that she ought to do something about him. She ought to take him to someone, someone who would put him to sleep. Or find him a home. She ought to find a better way than this. Some way to get rid of him that wouldn't concern her; that would be clean. It was all so untidy, so complicated. She'd never had a pet before. Now she knew why. They were such a bloody fuss.

Max had been awfully nice when she'd picked him up. A friend of one of her clients had been going abroad, and she'd offered—it was on the spur of the moment—to look after him. His owners lived in Camden, an arty house in outdated ethnic. The woman was a sculptress, of all things. She wafted about in chinos and oversized shirts. She constantly bemoaned the fact of going to France, following her husband's work.

'But I simply can't take Maxy there,' she'd explained to Joz. 'It's only an apartment, in Lyons, *so* small, he would fret so much, and then, rabies, you know . . .'

The terrier's blackcurrant eyes had pierced Joz, almost as if he knew what lay in store for him. He had been brushed furiously, until his fur stood up as though he'd had an electric shock. He was like a furry pompom, not a dog at all. He whined when Joz held out her arms. She had wanted to grab him, to squeeze him.

'Isn't he a love?' she had said.

She imagined him wriggling about next to her, looking devoted and making her laugh, like the Highland Terriers in the dog-food adverts on TV. It had seemed a great idea. At the time.

'I've got his dear little brush—it's bristle, look, with Rupert the Bear on the back—oh, here, and yes, his toy and blanket,' his owner said, as she tearfully arranged his belongings for Joz to put in the car. 'He likes a walk before breakfast and one after lunch and one again in the evening. Don't go too far. Just a mile at most.'

The woman had ruffled his head as Joz turned away. The dog had a tartan collar and lead, a tartan basket and blanket. His toy was a grey rubber mouse.

Joz *had* wanted him. She really had. She thought it would be nice—a novelty—to look after the little chap. People did that, didn't they? They had pets. They had hobbies and collections and preferences. That was how it worked. Those were the things that occupied you, when you were grown-up and lived alone. She *watched*, so she knew. She could be like that too, if she tried.

She went out with him obligingly the first day, and that night when she got home, and everything was all right, and he was quite sweet when he tugged and pulled at his toy, and snuffled around under the beds, exploring. She fed him pieces of tikka masala chicken, and whipped up two eggs and sugar in milk. He was sick about midnight, and she grudgingly cleared it up. He came and slept on the bed, because he was used to it. She had to lock him out, shoving him down the stairs, because she was not.

'I don't want you. Get out,' she'd told him, and he scrabbled for purchase on each step and she pushed him down with her foot.

Of course, there was no alternative but to tie him up. He bit things. Chewed things. He chewed the corner of the sofa on the first day he didn't get a walk. She took the basket and blanket away because they reeked. She got a piece of nylon washing line and tied him to the lock of the patio door, by threading the line through the handle. He thought it was a game, and rolled and chewed at the line, pulling at it, and then staring at the lock, defeated and puzzled. But at least, that way, there was no damage to her furniture at night.

'Just be a little petal and lie down until tonight,' she'd said in the morning. 'I've got to *dash* to Canterbury, it's hours, I *must go*.' She glanced back at him, standing four-square on the discoloured carpet, begging her with his eyes to take him too.

On the fourth day, she came home to find he'd peed on the floor. She realised that she'd not walked him at all that day, but still the sight of it infuriated her. 'You little bastard,' she'd yelled, incensed. 'You *filthy thing*.'

Rolling up a newspaper, she'd frightened the hell out of him, slamming it down all around him, catching him from time to time across his back and head. He started to bark at her, and she yanked at the line and hauled him off his feet, until he hung, half-strangled in her grasp, his legs weakly kicking. Out of disgust, she had dropped him. He fell to the floor silently, like a bag of washing, and lay there motionless, only his eyes following her as she went out of the room.

She didn't even look in there the next morning. She closed the door and shut him out of her mind. If she didn't think about him, he wouldn't exist.

On the sixth night, however, she took pity on him. She stood at the threshold of the room, gagging at the smell, and yet feeling surprisingly sorry for the wet little bundle, that shivered in the darkness as she walked towards him. He had tried biting through the line, and had cut his jaw. 'Oh . . . look at you,' she had murmured.

She had picked him up and taken him to the downstairs utility-room sink, and shampooed him and combed him, and dried him with a hairdryer. She had put antiseptic on the mouth, fixing him tight as he struggled, feeling his bony little rib cage and spiny—so tiny, so fragile. *You could snap it with one hand*, she thought, intrigued.

I wonder if I could.

I could, if I liked.

He had gnawed on her thumb as she dried him, like a baby, sucking at her as if she were able to feed him through her skin. And, babylike, she'd wrapped him in a towel until only his face showed. He panted heavily as she clutched him to her chest.

She used to be carried like this once. All wrapped up after bathtime. Suffocating. Difficult to breathe. When she was good, she was very very good . . . Randolph's friends at a party. What was she . . . seven, or eight? She was sat, purposefully, on someone's knee. When the man touched her, she bit him.

You mustn't do that. That was your step-father's friend. He is a very

*important man. You mustn't upset an important man. You must be nice
to them all. You must listen to the things they tell you.*

And when she was good, she was very, very good.

And when she was bad, she was horrid.

She took the dog back upstairs, cradled in her arms, forgiving him
aloud for being so dirty, such a trouble, and stroking him all the while.
She had fed him a little bread and a half a biscuit and a small saucer of
milk, just a morsel at a time over the next hour or so.

'You poor thing,' she'd told him. 'What did I do, then? What did
I do?'

She had to tie him up again, so that he wouldn't come in the bedroom.

He didn't whine. He just stared at her with those small coal-black
shining eyes, and he pulled on the nylon line until she could hear him
choking, panting desperately as she shut the door. She smiled as she
went out.

The trouble was, there wasn't enough time in the mornings. And
it was out of the question that she should ever come home for lunch.
And sometimes—like today—it was late when she got home. Impossible to go for *walks*. She never walked *anywhere* usually. She felt so
stupid, trolling along with this rat on a string, trying to look the other
way as he staggered about on one leg, or squatted on the grass. She felt
just *absurd*. 'For God's sake, hurry up,' she'd hiss at him.

She knew she should never have taken the wretched animal. He
had been amusing for about ten minutes.

She stood now, biting her lip at the door of the living room. 'Maxy?'
she whispered. 'Hello . . . Maximilian?'

She picked up the phone from where she had left it, and walked
upstairs. She heard the nylon line snap, and then slacken. She began to
sing softly to herself.

Her bedroom was unfurnished except for the double bed and the
fitted wardrobe with its mirror doors. There was a huge pile of fabric
in here: swatches she had brought home about a year ago, intending
to put up curtains and make a spread. Never had time. Couldn't, now,
be bothered. Those little things that you were supposed to do, to make
it right, to make it a home, seemed to escape her. She didn't seem to

fit inside a room: those cushioned, draped and coloured places were for others. Anyone else. But not for her. Not her. She glanced at her reflection. Big; blank. She turned this way and that in the light from the landing, her head on one side, looking at herself.

Dozens of diets had failed her. She didn't try any more. She didn't care. The whole subject bored her to death. Size was a sort of fascism, a girl had once said to her. Another *fat* girl. Joz liked that phrase; she repeated it if anyone dared to mention her weight. 'Size is fascism,' she would say, in the violin-string pitch she could muster, her best Thatcher-in-Cabinet voice. Then she would lean forward. 'Are you a fascist, darling?' They would sometimes deny it.

'Of course you're not,' she'd reply, gently. If the odd one retorted, 'Yes, of course I am, what d'you bloody think?' she'd say, smiling, 'I couldn't agree more. Size is important. Don't believe it when they say size doesn't matter. And so, darling, exactly how big are *you*?'

And she had a trick—it never failed, it was a hoot—that, as she leaned back, she would run one hand down a breast, lightly, no more than a hint. Tilt her head back slightly, momentarily close her eyes, as if luxuriating in the feel of her own body. She never wore tent clothes: oversized tops, or voluminous skirts. She had her clothes made, even her underwear, and, as a result, looked sculpted, generous, full-blown. Nothing too skimpy or too tight; everything expensive. She wore a size twenty dress and a size eight shoe. The fact was, she was big all over: big hands and fingers, large head, large mouth, broad hips, thick legs, thick ankles. She knew she was overpowering.

Strange, wasn't it?

She frightened them all. And yet, she was ruled by *him*.

Slowly, she began to undress, putting the phone down alongside the bed. The mirror revealed a mountainous Venus, a Botticelli face on top of a Rubens body. She started to laugh, remembering Mark Estwood.

She'd bought him a fabulous lunch. He said he never had sea bass or scallops, and she'd ordered both to tease him, and a roulade and salad and cheese and pastries and coffee. Two bottles of Sancerre, one of Burgundy. Brandy, of course. The tablecloths had been white damask with yellow napkins, silverware, fresh flowers. Pure as the driven, a white and floral landscape, under which she wreaked her private havoc. She'd put her hand under the table and squeezed him. His face turned puce. She had begun to fondle and massage him, as he sat, petrified, with the ice around the sea bass melting and the glass half-way to his mouth.

In the hotel, she'd had the most godawful job with him. It was more like fifteen rounds with a flyweight; he kept slipping under her, gorging himself on her, exclaiming at her. They liked to be smothered, these schoolboys. They liked to be fed and watered. Shampooed, like the Highland terrier. It was such an effort not to laugh at him gaping and gasping, his hands fumbling about as if he were trying to find where she began and he ended. When it was over, she had looked out of the window at the Thames and thought how bored she was.

It was always like that. She could stand and watch herself in a man's embrace. *Outside.* Always, always . . . *outside* . . .

'You must meet my step-father,' she had said.

He had brightened a little, flattered.

'Do you know him at all?' she had asked.

He had smiled. 'There isn't a person in London who doesn't know Randolph Joscelyne.'

She had nodded, satisfied. 'He would like to meet you,' she had murmured. 'He likes me to bring him fresh people.'

She took a shower, wrapped herself in a dressing gown, and laid down on the bed, the phone next to her.

FIVE

_F_AITH SAW GUY AT ONCE, at lunchtime in the crowded bistro.

He was sitting at the bar, leaning on it with one elbow in an attitude of absolute boredom. The two girls—the barmaids—were intent on putting up Christmas decorations, and he was watching them, occasionally murmuring something to them that made them turn round, exclaiming, laughing. They were on a stepladder, taping twisted red crepe to the fake holly. Guy speared an olive and rolled it round his mouth, staring frankly at the vision of black-stockinged thighs.

Faith, standing watching him in the shadows of the doorway, took a deep breath. Guy could be sweet, and Guy could be childish and savage. She wondered which Guy was meeting her today.

'Faith!' he cried. He stood up and held out his arms, as if they hadn't seen each other for years, and she were a long-lost sister. She walked forward.

He kissed her on both cheeks; she caught that unforgettable taste and smell, that mixture of aftershave and soap. He was always immaculate, fastidious, really, about himself. She stepped back from him, smiling, wondering if her smile looked as false and strained as it felt. Her true reaction, if she were honest, if she were braver, was not to smile at all, but to take out some heavy, blunt object and swing it into the side of his head. She had a fleeting vision of Guy reeling under the impact of a blacksmith's anvil, staggering backwards in a spray of gore, the smug expression wiped off his face forever.

Take a grip, she told herself, looking down at the floor as she pulled out the stool.

But the association of Guy and feeling murderous was too strong. It was exactly like the old fantasy she used to have: sitting across from him in the flat at night, when he was in one of his silent moods.

She would have the urge to reach over and cut him—swiftly, cleanly, with a surgical knife—just to see if the blood flowed. For he played the stranger so well, smirking if she lost her temper, mouth clamped shut if she demanded an explanation. And it was then that she would get this feeling—as he sat flicking through the paper, or cleaning invisible dirt from under his nails, or watching the TV without comment or movement—it was then that her hands itched in the desire to lean over and run the blade down his arm, revealing the tendons and blood vessels and bones. Just to convince herself that he was real, made of the same fragile stuff of life, actual flesh and blood, as she was.

'Sweetheart,' he said now as at last she settled back and looked around her. 'What are you drinking?'

'White wine, please.'

'Glass of something extra nice,' he told the barmaid. 'No muck, darling. So.' He turned back to grin at her, taking in the red dress, the coat, the red shoes. 'How *are* you? You look *fabulous*.'

I'm pregnant. That's how fine I am, you shit. That's what she wanted to say. But she didn't.

Even now, after everything, Guy was intimidating. He had a dazzling quality that he was quite well aware of, a boyish, enthusiastic expression that disarmed every female within fifty feet, a way of getting too close and speaking very low, and smiling. Those lovely blue eyes, ringed with grey. That north-country burr he had almost dropped, and then revived when he thought working-class was back in vogue.

Perhaps *she* was part of that package, she thought. Very Eighties, wasn't it, to have an Essex girl on your arm, and in your bed? Now that that time had gone, the Essex girl was out and the seriously, old-money rich girl was in. Faith out, Chloe in.

'Big day,' he said.

'Yes.'

'When are we due at the solicitor's?'

'Don't you remember?'

'I left my mobile somewhere, or I'd have rung to check.'

She shook her head. Guy was careless with his belongings, not just people. There was a time when she used to pick up after him, and go through a checklist every morning. 'Half past one,' she told him.

'Right, right . . .' This whole thing, this ludicrous, impossible meeting, had been Guy's idea—a sort of wake to celebrate their parting. She still didn't know if it would work, if either of them could be that magnanimous. The atmosphere was embarrassingly frigid. It was as if they had never been lovers, let alone married.

She glanced down at the ring on her left third finger. She ought to take it off, she knew. She imagined throwing it away. Wondered if she could just put it into a rubbish bin somewhere. She looked at Guy's profile as he smiled at the barmaids. What did people do with their wedding rings, anyway? When they divorced? It was one of those unanswerable questions, like *Where do flies go in the winter?* or *Why do toenails grow more slowly than fingernails?* or *Where do birds go when they die?* She smiled, and lifted her head.

The wine arrived, and she promptly grabbed it and drank half of it in one go, saying 'Cheers' in the sort of bright voice she supposed was required. Guy raised his glass to her. She looked away at once, fixing her eyes on the copper-effect bar, and the polished brass footrest underneath them, in which their two images writhed.

'Have you had your hair done?' he asked.

She put her hand to her head. 'Just a cut yesterday, an inch.'

'And the colour . . .'

'I bought a packet in the chemist's.' She laughed, trying to make a joke of it. 'It's the same thing I used to buy when I was fourteen and wanted to be seductive. Fades to the colour of diluted raspberry ice cream.'

He said nothing for a moment. Then, 'It works. You look wonderful.'

He hitched his stool a little closer to her, stroked her hand. She felt

31

mesmerised by his touch, a fly in a web, watching the spider drawing out silk.

'I wanted to say something,' he said. 'Look, I've got this little speech. I must say it; will you hear me out?' She said nothing. 'I wanted to say . . . darling Faith . . . that I'm sorry I hurt you. I can't bear to think—'

She interrupted him. 'Can we talk about something else?' she said. 'Anything else. You always wanted to go, right? Now you've got what you always wanted.'

'Look Faith. Fay . . .'

His old nickname for her cut. She drank the last half of the glass of wine, signalled for another. Her throat felt as if it were closing up.

'Fay, don't be angry.'

'*Moi?*' She grinned. 'I'm not angry, *sweetheart.*'

'Ah, but you are. I know you are.'

'OK. So I'm *furious.*' Her Dad's East End accent climbed out of her. She always did sound like Dad when she was losing her temper. She took a long breath. 'What good will it do?' she asked out loud.

He looked at her—his best, his very best, hurt child expression. Perhaps he didn't really know when he was acting. Couldn't tell the difference any more. His voice had that poor-baby inflection: slightly hammy, slightly pitiful. Freddie Bartholomew in *Captains Courageous. I'll be all right, really I will, if I could just . . .*

'Faith, I can't bear to sit here, with you so close, and think I might never touch you again,' he said.

The barmaid, grinning slightly and casting a raised eyebrow in Guy's direction, delivered the second glass. She took an extortionately long time to wipe away the spilled ring of the previous glass, tidy up the coasters into a regular line and polish the handle of the beer pump. More people came in the door, talking nineteen to the dozen, shaking the slight rain off their coats, laughing.

'How is dear Chloe?' Faith asked.

'Oh, Faith,' he replied. 'That's really cheap.'

'Me? *I'm* cheap.'

She looked at him, fighting down a grieving contempt. She had aged ten thousand years since she met him. It was no exaggeration. She had been naive, immature—but he had been worse. He had been cynical and loud and sharp, and *spoiled*. Spoiled the world for her. Really. Made it ugly. She had been nineteen, and he twenty-two, when they met. She had believed everything he said, was impressed by him, was dragged along into accountant-and-broker-filled parties. Those long, terrible Friday evenings in The Grapes, watching him get steadily drunker. He used to tell her stories of how he had set people up: clients, colleagues. *Pulled a flanker, worked a blinder, cut them off, left them gasping*. All those sadistic phrases he had. He'd roar with laughter. And she thought that's the way the world was, and had been dazzled.

The world still didn't look right to her even now, even though they had lived apart for six months. It wasn't the world her parents had left her. Not the world full of stories and fun and kindness, knights and princesses, rollercoasters and lights. *This* world was wrinkled and shoddy. It was tacky. It was still Guy's world, still slewed and cock-eyed and tilted.

'Well,' she said now, 'I think you're right.' She nodded slowly. 'Yes . . . Remember how your boss used to mimic me? Frank the Bullshit Williams. He used to get me to say something, read a piece from a newspaper. You would start nodding and saying, "Go on Fay, go on Fay." I was a good old party piece, wasn't I? Friday nights. Yes, it was all so *very jolly funny . . .*'

She sighed, looking him in the eye, while a great wave of sadness, of dispiritedness, threatened to drown her. That familiar *Guy* feeling. 'Got the wrong accent now,' she said. 'Not jolly funny any more. You need a Chloe. More subtle. More money.'

'Don't talk such fucking rubbish,' he retorted. 'You know what's wrong with you, don't you? What's always been wrong with you— since—day—one.' And to labour his point he stabbed his index finger on the bar in front of her. 'You've got this bloody great chip on your shoulder.'

She coloured up. 'I have not,' she said.

He nodded. 'That's why we get the old Romford girl after a couple of drinks, isn't it? That's why we get the *one-Christmas-I-didn't-get-any-presents* routine, isn't it?' He leaned forward, until his face was an inch from hers. 'A snob,' he said.

'No!'

'No? Well, sorry. Sorry if it's not true.'

She seethed inwardly for another minute, staring at him. Then she looked away. 'Let's just change the subject, for Christ's sake,' she said.

He leaned forward, and put his hand on her knee. He had control of himself again. She looked at the hand, willing it to shrivel and turn to sand, but couldn't bring herself to lift it off. He was touching her, and the irony of this, possibly the last touch, burned through her skin.

'I'm going to tell you something,' he said, 'one last time. We're chained together, you know. Like this.' He held up one hand, the first two fingers twined round each other. 'You'll never get over me, Faith. I'll still come to see you when we're ninety, and you'll still love me.'

She stared at him. The noise of the bar boomed, getting louder by the minute. More people came in the door, shouting to a group across the room.

'Tell me,' she said softly. 'How rich *is* Chloe?'

'Ha fucking ha,' he retorted.

Then he faced his drink and resolutely finished it, twirling his finger in it. Sulky. It was almost funny. If she had passed her arms around his neck when he spouted all those lies about love, and cried on his shoulder, and told him about the baby, she could have probably cemented a terrific triangle. Guy swanning backwards and forwards between her and Chloe, telling each he had given up the other.

And the pity of it all was that he would probably make a wonderful father. She could visualise him now, in the maternity ward, clutching his enormous bunch of flowers, standing teary-eyed and totally useless over the cot, and telling everyone *It's my son, it's my daughter* . . .

'By the way . . . I got that Rendells thing,' he said. 'If you're interested.'

She looked up at him. He had pitched his voice a little higher, as though broadcasting for the rest of the bar. The change of subject didn't surprise her; Guy's intensity had a limited shelf-life.

'The commission?'

'Yes.'

This was a promotion. Something he'd been angling for for nearly two years. She saw that he was trying desperately hard to be casual about it.

'Congratulations.'

Faith started to drink her wine, and then suddenly remembered, and stopped. She oughtn't to drink. Wasn't that right? You weren't supposed to drink.

'Listen . . .' Guy began. The look she gave him was acute; he actually started to laugh. 'No, it's not us,' he said. 'It's you. I've been thinking.'

'About what?'

Could he know? He couldn't possibly know. Did it show? Did she look pregnant—did it show in the way she walked, the way she sat? She felt her face go suddenly hot with embarrassment.

'I've been thinking about this new place of yours,' he said.

'What about it?' Relief.

'It's too remote,' he told her. 'Some dump in the middle of nowhere. You're not used to it, are you? It's not as if you've ever lived in the country . . .'

'Guy, don't tell me what's good for me. And it is *not* a dump.'

'Don't get on your high horse.'

'But it's nothing to do with you. It's *my* house—'

'I know, I know.' He actually patted her knee. 'I just don't think you realise what you're taking on. Your agent told me it needs some *attention*. Agentese for fucking falling down. Am I right, or am I right, lover? And it's going to be incredibly lonely. I know you—'

That really did it. She stood up. 'Don't tell me what's going to happen to me,' she retorted. 'My God. You *don't* know me. Haven't you got it yet? Hasn't it registered? You don't know me. That's what this is all about.'

She sat down again abruptly, damning him inwardly for making her lose her temper. She realised that he was staring at her profile, drilling his gaze into the side of her head, willing her to glance back at him. She did not.

She sat with her fingers tracing the edge of the glass stem. She dared not say another word. She was afraid that she'd release the long years of pent-up, clamped-down fury she thought she'd successfully conquered.

She wondered if divorcing couples ever got rid of that primitive rage. So nameless, so formless. The rage of rejection, the feeling of being subtly down-graded. And she'd been doing so well, too: being so *calm*.

Damn. Don't blow it now, she thought. Just another hour.

Guy stood up. 'Drink up,' he said. He paid the bill, gathered up his coat. 'One twenty,' he told her. 'Time to go.'

Faith did as she was told.

This was it. This was the goodbye: not the later one outside the solicitor's, when they would both have to rush elsewhere and be surrounded by strangers. This was the real goodbye: leaving a bar, as they'd done a thousand times, she on his arm, adrift in a nightmare relationship and yet still searching his face for a tremor of feeling. This was the goodbye. Here it comes, now . . . do it well, she told herself. Don't let yourself down.

They had reached the outside street. Slow wet flakes of sleet were falling. They rested in his hair, on his shoulders. Her heart rose into her throat, and she wildly imagined one last afternoon in bed with him; an afternoon, still and perfect, when there would not be any doubt about his love for her.

She recalled standing at the window of that first flat in Putney, picking off the flaking paint from the window, waiting for him to come down the street. Watching a corner of hedge, and the grey wing of someone's parked car, the very spot where he would appear, walking, from the station. When it got dark, she could only see the strip of pavement under the streetlight. That was Guy. Not the face, not the body, not the voice, not the man. Guy was the waiting: the anxious strain of looking for his movement in an empty street. That summed him up as succinctly as any photograph.

'Come and see me sometimes,' she said. 'Will you?'

He turned a look of triumph on her, as if this proved what he had been saying: that she would welcome him back forever into the future.

She added quickly, 'Bring Chloe.'

Guy looked at her for what seemed like an age. He lifted his hand, very slowly, and picked a disintegrating flake of sleet from her collar.

And then he put his arms around her and kissed her, whispering, 'Oh Faith, oh Faith . . .'

SIX

'YOU TOOK TOO LONG.'

'I was downstairs . . .'

'You should be waiting.'

She sits, looking at her foot, swinging it from side to side. She is curiously impervious to him tonight. At least, until he begins to speak. His pressure pours down the line. Five thousand miles.

'Where are you?'

'I'm not playing.'

'Ah, little Martian . . .'

'I'm *not*.'

'You must calm down.'

'I *am* calm. I am *perfectly* calm.'

'Good. What have you been doing? Did you see Sandy?'

'She wasn't there. She had to go to Dublin.'

'No, no, no . . .'

'There was someone called Mark Estwood.'

'And?'

Her calm leaves her. Last night's dream is coming back in a flood: all day it has been scratching at the corner of her mind. Hands scrabbling for purchase in thin air. The trees. The feeling of overwhelming guilt. Randolph's soothing, smothering, monotone voice. 'I can't do any more,' she whispers.

'Who is he? You know that you belong—'

'His father is in the Select Committee.'

'On trade? Timothy Estwood?'

'Yes.'

'Oh, wonderful. *Wonderful.*' Down the line, down the thousands of miles from America, she hears him actually clap his hands. 'What timing! Fat from the fire. You've done very well. Ah, you're such a clever little Martian, aren't you? When will I see him?'

'Please give Thomas back.'

'He's never left you.'

'Please give him back.'

There was a pain in her chest as if her heart were tearing itself slowly in two. She would have to offer Thomas more, if she ever had any hope of bringing him home to her. She would have to find somewhere, away from Randolph, somewhere secret.

You belong to me.

She crushed one hand against the side of her head. She tried to clamp it there, to block Randolph's voice, to clear a path for her own thoughts that struggled inside her head like snakes, crawling over each other in total darkness.

'What would you like?'

'What?'

'How about a nice holiday? You could come out here. California would suit you. I could extend the suite. We could look at the ocean . . .'

'Oh, please . . .'

'You ought to go shopping,' he says. 'It always cheers you up. Charge it. Prezzie, darling. You'd like that? You always do.'

'You won't do anything to him?'

'To whom?'

'Mark Estwood. He's just a boy. He's twenty-five.'

'Why should I do anything to Mark Estwood?'

She raises her fist to the phone, presses it against the head of the receiver.

'Now. More cheerful things. Did you write the letter?'

'Yes.'

'Good. And posted it?'

'Yes, yes.'

'Not from London?'

'*No.*'

She can hear him stretch and sigh. She imagines him lying on the big bed staring at the breakers on the beach below.

'I don't want to do this any more,' she says.

But he ignores her. 'Dear girl. What a clever, what an obedient, what a very very good little girl. *When she is good, she is very very good!* Now dear. Tell me exactly where you are sitting . . .'

SEVEN

*F*AITH LEFT LONDON THE NEXT DAY.

And there, standing at the entrance to the causeway, she looked around her, feeling disorientated and cold. Well . . . she'd done it. She'd gone. She was out of it all. She was tempted to pinch herself. She was free. She belonged to no one. And no one belonged to her . . . it was a dizzying sensation.

She had driven down that morning, leaving the old house at five. Dropping the key in its envelope through the estate agents' door—a strange experience, in the sulphur streetlight, with no one about—and driving away had not been the wrench she might have expected. Just as closing the door on the house had not been what she had expected.

In fact, it had been something of an anti-climax. The sky did not fall in as she unplugged her kettle from the familiar shelf, wrapped her jar of coffee and teaspoon in a teatowel, and stowed them in a box in the back of the car. No avenging angel of doom appeared as she checked the bedroom for the last time; no sickness, no plunging inside occurred at the sight of the faintly paler outline against the wall where the double bed had been.

The darkness gave way to dawn as she came down through Hampshire, through the New Forest. It was a purposeful detour, just to see the heaths, the trees, the first strange glimmer of a different light, the arch of high colour over the sea.

When she was little, her Mum and Dad liked to go on day trips. Through the Dartford Tunnel, into Kent. Great overloaded orange coaches, crammed with kids and carrier bags and buckets and spades. Day trips out, free because her Dad worked for the Bus Company. From London to Ramsgate and Margate. Brilliant days.

The lure of that unusual sea-light was fantastic. Faith would hang out of the window and wait for that vastness of sky. 'I can smell the salt!' she'd yell. And her mother would pull her down again, hauling at the hem of her dress. Faith wound down the windows now, until the car was icy and damp with that blessed foreign air.

And now, here at last, at the silent entrance to the island, in the daylight, she stood perfectly still. It was a cold day; nearly nine. Early frost, bright sun. December, and the sea.

The new house stood above the bay: a sickle of heath falling to a pebbly beach. It was hidden behind a bank of hawthorn trees. From the top of the hill, you could see that it stood upon one of perhaps twenty small islands, linked together by bridges or causeways at the mouth of the river estuary. The view from the top was comprehensive; the land was so flat here that, on a good day, more than twenty miles of coast could be seen, a complicated series of inlets and larger islands, and the deep grey line of the deeper water, where the boats went in and out from Villard harbour.

Faith leaned on the bonnet of the car, drawing her coat around her. There was an arc of sand and gravel and rushes here, and black-and-white markers at the roadside showed the height of high tide.

Couldn't see the house. Perhaps just as well. It would spoil the view.

The island was a mile long and half a mile wide; little more than a slip of silt and gravel and sandstone, covered with low-growing hawthorn and gorse. It boasted half a dozen houses, a decrepit boatyard, and a line of wooden huts, rented out as beach huts to summer visitors. It wasn't really *land* at all; it was so close to the sea, so much a part of it, a castaway from the shoreline, striking out for the ocean, and only tethered to the real world by the merest strip of soil.

Faith's house was the furthest back, up the single-track lane. Stunted trees disguised it, as if the road had burrowed itself down into the ground for shelter, making a scooped-out shape. Two drives, belonging to neighbours she had not yet met, branched out to left and right.

'Home,' she said, to no one in particular. The wind washed in, salt and water. That smell. That smell.

She got back in the car, only reluctantly, and drove on.

Her car complained, grinding in second gear as it bumped over the potholes. She started laughing to herself. Guy was right. It was stupid to come here. And it was not only he who had said so. In fact, she had had a lecture on the very subject just a week ago.

'I can understand you making the break from the house,' the man at the wholesaler's had said. She hadn't asked for his opinion, but he was evidently dying to give it. 'But Villard Porcorum? It sounds like a disease. Where the hell is it, anyway?'

She had told him. No one had lived in the single-storey house since the owner had died two years before. She told him it was stone, with no central heating, no TV, no mains drainage. Told him she'd dreamed of living here ever since they came to this coast when she was about ten—come for the shingly, sandy arc of beach and the castle ruin that was back along the main road. 'I've even got a septic tank,' she'd said, starting to laugh.

'Where does all the gunge go, then?'

'Down the bottom of the garden. It rots away. Apparently.' And she had winced with him.

'Bloody hellfire.' He'd lit a cigarette, narrowing his eyes at her as if considering a lunatic. 'Where's your shops, then?'

'Eight miles away, on the mainland.'

He gave a great sigh; he'd lived in the city all his life and saw no earthly reason to move out of it. 'I always had you down as straight,' he said. 'Not one of these ones that goes down to Wiltshire at weekends. Bloody green wellies in the boot.'

'It's not Wiltshire. It's on the coast. And it's not a weekend—it's permanent. I should have done it years ago.'

'All the same. You wait till your tapwater tastes of cow muck. You'll come back.' He'd loaded the last of the canvas into her car, leaned on the open hatchback, and said, 'Course, it's understandable. But it's too big a leap.'

She smiled. She'd been coming to this same supplier for five years now, passing the time of day with him. Once she'd burst into tears— uncharacteristically—on a bad day over Guy, and he'd sat her down in his office with a mug of hot chocolate and a Kit-Kat, and watched her like a hawk until she drank and ate both. She hadn't had the heart to tell him she, didn't want either. He was a kind man, though: he had four kids, a talent of his own now long neglected, a house in Tottenham, a passion for Spurs. He guarded her jealously. She had once heard him say, as she was coming into the warehouse, 'Faith Mary Collins is one of mine, so put that in your pipe and soddin' smoke it, mate.' She'd had to hide, laughing, behind a pallet of stock until the unfortunate salesman disappeared.

He liked to hear how a job was going. Knew everything there was to know about pigment, about oils; knew the world's most obscure suppliers; knew how Faith herself made up experimental colours. But he didn't know how much, and for how long, she'd wanted to leave London.

'You'll take care?' he had asked.

'It's only three hours away. And that's driving slowly . . .'

'Women want to be careful on their own.'

She had bitten her lip to stop herself retorting that she could come to no more harm on her own then she had suffered being married. Instead, she gave him a fleeting, smiling kiss on his cheek. 'I'll still order from you.'

'I'm not delivering to the back of beyond.'

She'd laughed. 'I'll pick stuff up whenever I'm in town.'

Her car came up the last hundred yards of the drive. Over the top of the hedge, she could see the roof of the removals lorry. As she got closer, the house was revealed: a long, low stone block, looking rather miserable and abandoned behind its stunted trees and the long tawny grass of what used to be a lawn.

The van was parked on the flat stone yard in the front, and the two men were leaning on the door, smoking.

'Hello,' she called, getting out. 'You got here all right, then?'

'Morning.'

She strode up to them. 'Well, what d'you think?'

'We had a hell of a job coming up that lane.'

'I know. I did warn you, didn't I? I'm sorry.'

'Couldn't have made more of a change, could you?' the driver asked. Just yesterday afternoon he had been struggling with her furniture past the parked cars on her London street.

'View's lovely, though,' she said, unlocking the door. 'Lots of light. It gets the sun all day, the big room.' She was already visualising her work occupying most of the space, with a sofa to one side near the fire.

'Make a start, OK?' said the driver, totally unimpressed. She heard him say, 'Knacker your axle in no time, cost a fortune,' under his breath as he made for the van.

She smiled, and walked forward into the house.

It was cold, but not piercingly so. She would make a fire in the hearth straight away, then clean the windows: the sea was nothing more than a blue haze through them now. She dashed back to the car, and dragged out her survival kit: coffee, mugs, biscuits. She carried them back to the kitchen.

Faith looked about herself with pride. Here would go the large pine table, in the centre, and surrounding it her four mismatched chairs, all ancient, picked up in different auctions and shops. She squinted, imagining too her cushions on the seats, her china on the shelves. Going to the window, she drew an experimental F, then an exclamation mark, on the misty glass.

She'd be safe. Quiet, and safe, as she used to be at home—an only child alone in her bedroom, with the bedspread wrapped round her and her drawing pad propped on her knees . . .

Picking up the kettle, she turned on the tap. It hissed a second, a dribble of water came out, then stopped. She frowned, then went to the bathroom—on the same floor, along the hall. The same thing: no water in the taps.

The removal men were just carrying a box in.

'I can't make us a drink,' she said. 'There's no water.'

They trooped after her, checked under the sink, and in the airing cupboard. All the stoptaps were turned on.

'You're cut off. Dry,' said the driver. "Sfunny."

'Oh, yeah, hilarious,' Faith muttered. There was a short silence.

'What're we doing for a brew, then?' asked the driver's mate. 'Got to have something hot, right? 'Snever the middle of summer, is it?'

Grimacing, Faith gathered up her jacket.

She went back in the car to the point in the lane where the two other drives forked off to left and right. The left-hand house could be seen only a hundred yards in: an almost new building, with an antiseptically neat garden. It looked back in at the mainland, the sea hidden from it by the rising bulk of the hill. Faith saw that the windows had metal shutters, securely down, and the driveway was cleanly swept and empty. Weekenders; and obviously not at home.

She turned to the alternative.

A sandy track skirted the hill, cut into its side and running out of sight. There was a five-bar gate, held together more by luck than mechanics. She moved the loop of orange nylon rope over the top, opened it, and drove warily in. The track was little more than two ruts in the grass, but, as she went along, it gave a long, sloping outlook on the sea. The shoreline was black here, and about a hundred feet below. Another three hundred yards, and she saw the house.

It wasn't what she was expecting; she supposed, because her own house was so run-down, she had subconsciously imagined the others to be the same. But this was a total contrast: a picture-book house, flint-and-cob, built into the side of the hill with what must surely be an 180-degree panorama of the ocean. As she drew closer, she could see that the house was probably not more than two or three years old, but had been built meticulously to *look* old. The slate roof was low, the windows broad and Victorianly square; the doorway was arched and complimented by a wooden porch, thatched, with its canopy on stilts, in Dorset style.

There were no roses around the door, though. Whoever had built it was missing something. Perhaps it was just that the house was new, and in the face of the Channel wind, the garden had not had time to establish itself. Or perhaps . . . Faith stopped for a second, head on one side, considering, with an eye that habitually sought out detail.

It was a postcard house, probably all beams and inglenooks inside. Made to be pretty. Prettier, really, than the stark cliff it occupied. She noticed, with a curious pang, that there were no curtains at the downstairs windows, and the ones upstairs, their glass shut against the cold day, were hanging in low loops, as if they had not been fitted properly.

'I wonder,' she said, in the strangled tones of a TV game-show host, 'who lives in a house like *this*?' Smiling, she got out, and knocked on the door.

There was perfect silence. She walked round to the side. Here in the perfect brick-patterned driveway, a grey Range Rover was parked.

'Hello?' she called.

Then she noticed the workshop. Its corrugated-iron roof showed only as a red oblong in the grass below, and the path that led down to it was several winding hairpins. She realised that, very faintly, she could hear a radio.

'Hello?' she called. No response. She negotiated the pathway with difficulty, gravel and sand and small stones rolling down with every footstep. *I expect I'll find some ruddy gorgon in here*, she thought. *Some escapee from the WI brewing damson wine . . . some exhippie making kites . . .* 'Jesus!' she snapped, slithering the last ten feet. And then she stopped absolutely short, holding her breath, remembering the baby. Her hand passed speculatively across her stomach. It was hard to believe anything at all was there, let alone another human being. Eight weeks. The tenuous, improbable grip on life; the impossibility of it. The sensation, the experience, still seemed to have nothing at all to do with her.

She knocked on the door.

It sounded as if something heavy had been dropped. 'Shit,' said a male voice.

'Hello?'

'Who the hell is that?'

'I did call, from your house . . .' She stayed on the outside, not exactly attracted to the voice within. 'I'm Faith Collins. I moved in today. I wondered . . .'

The door was wrenched open. On the threshold stood a man in his late forties. He looked as if he had crawled out from under a stone. His clothes were filthy, his greying hair uncombed. He was about six foot three. The first thing that Faith registered was that he had a beard (and she had never liked them), and the thought crossed her mind that she had moved in next to some freak, and that she'd be at war with him for a thousand years, and that *everyone in London had been right.*

'Faith . . .' she said, hesitantly holding out her hand.

He didn't take it. 'You just made me drop my bloody stuff,' he said. 'It's a difficult finish, that . . .'

She resisted the temptation to peer round him, to see what he was doing. The phrase hadn't endeared him to her, either—the implication that he was a craftsman or artist of some kind. She was not the sociable type when it came to work: she had never attended work groups, and had even hated the crowded sensation of her own art-school days, much preferring to be on her own. Enlisted in her first life class, she'd taken her board to the far corner of the room, with her back to the window, her arm cupped over the sheet of paper like a child afraid of being copied. The thought of having an artist neighbour didn't appeal at all. *Don't tell me I've joined some godawful St Ives creative clique,* she thought instead. *It'll be all bare feet and poetry readings at the pub. I'm going back.* She tried holding this line of thought in check, only partially successfully.

'Sorry, but I've got a problem too,' she said. 'My phone hasn't been connected yet, and I've got no water in the taps.'

The man grunted. 'They're always turning it off,' he said. 'You're in the old Rawlings house?'

'Yes, I—'

'Bloody place, I'm afraid. Had a fracture in the main, you know.'

Faith felt her mouth drop open. She snapped it shut again when she realised that she was gaping like a landed fish. 'Nobody told me,' she said.

He laughed. 'They wouldn't,' he replied, wiping his hands on his trousers.

'Oh, God. But they mended it?'

'Doesn't sound much like it, does it?'

She put her hand to her forehead. 'I wonder if I could be done for murder,' she whispered. 'The estate agent. He *couldn't* just . . .'

'I suppose, theoretically, it's connected to the mains supply. That's all they ever say, isn't it?'

'But the *surveyor* . . .'

'Paid for the expensive survey, did you?'

'No,' she admitted. 'But *surely* . . .'

He gave a great sigh. 'Look, why don't you speak to the Water Company? Come up to the house and ring them.'

She attempted a smile. 'If you're sure,' she said. 'Thanks.'

'Spoilt it now anyway,' he muttered, jerking his thumb back towards the workbench.

She pulled a face at him as he passed. Her mouth was still stretched in the expression when he abruptly turned, stuck out his hand, and said, 'Sorry. Alex Hurley.'

She bit her lip, mumbled a reply. He watched her closely for a second, then a curious expression—something like relief—came over his face.

'Expect I deserved that look.'

'Well, no. I—'

He actually laughed. 'Don't worry about it.'

'Bloody *hell*,' she muttered, following him up the slope to the house.

EIGHT

*J*OZ ARRIVED AT HER PARENTS' HOUSE precisely on time: it was eight o'clock on a winter's night, ten days after Thomas's wedding. The place was, as usual, beautiful.

She stood on the opposite side of the London square, staring at it through the dark and leafless lime trees. The stone facade was faultlessly cream; broad steps led up to a great red Edwardian door. On either side, the reception rooms were bright, the drapes held back as if to disclose the fairyland within.

Joz closed her eyes momentarily.

She couldn't go through with it. She couldn't. Not even if it *was* Randolph's birthday.

The enchanted castle. White upon white in the downstairs rooms, with massive mirrors and a host of tiny golden lights. The Chinese rugs, the Chinese spirit houses, the Gothic chandeliers, the Georgian wing armchairs upholstered in shantung silk, the lacquered chests, the Blue Room dominated by the bronze horses . . . She struggled with an instinct to scream. Like a sulky child called in to tea, she began to cross the road.

As she got to their pavement, a car pulled up at the kerb, and a couple got out, who glanced towards her.

'Cecily!' said the woman, reaching for her, and kissing the air to either side of her head. 'How perfectly marvellous. I hear you're so sought-after these days, darling. Super congrats.'

'Thanks . . .'

All this as they walked up the steps. The man—some minor Treasury face—came in their wake, pulling at his cuffs. The castle intimidated even people like him—the perfection of it. The ineffable charm of their hosts, their accomplishments, their consideration, their wealth, their taste in art, their *contacts*, their power. The downstairs rooms where Thomas and Joz had been banned as children always made her flesh crawl. She felt as if she were suffocating every time she stepped into them. It was like drowning slowly in double cream.

The door was already open, and Joz could see her mother in the hall.

I can't do it, she thought. *I can't even be polite to her.*

Ruth Joscelyne was dressed in black. Five foot five inches tall. Very petite and French-looking. Floor-length gown. A discreet single strand of twisted gold at her throat. Her black hair cut as close as a cap, revealing a slim neck, small shoulders. Curved arms, delicate hands. *Eight stone*, Joz thought. *Not an ounce more.*

She could see that Ruth was listening to one of the guests, her head bent forward at an impossibly deferential angle. She was nodding and smiling. The guest obviously finished some joke or other, and those around laughed. All except for Joz's mother. She screwed her face to a semblance of humour that scored anxiety into every pore. She was far too tense. As always.

Joz, stepping forward, felt overwhelmingly irritated with her. *This is your house. You don't have to crawl to people.* But, of course, her mother *would* crawl. Just as she crawled, on her hands and knees, to her husband.

The moment she noticed Joz, her mother left the group she was with, ignored the couple at Joz's side who were already making cooing noises, and opened her arms to her daughter. She held her at arm's length, smiling, saying, 'Oh, Cecily, I'm so glad you could come. How lovely. You look wonderful.'

Stop it, mother.

'Randolph told me you've got the Merrion-Walsh contract. Congratulations. And the galleries. I'm so proud of you.' She turned to the couple, kissed them both, and said, 'Isn't my daughter clever?'

'Absolutely, absolutely,' they agreed.

'You must come and tell me what to do with my flat,' the woman said.

'I'll give you my number,' Joz said. And thought, *It'll be my pleasure.*

She was feeling sick. Someone came up with a tray of champagne; she asked for claret.

'Do you know, you're right,' her mother said. 'Red wine is actually good for you. There is some University research—'

'I like to do the right thing,' Joz said.

Her mother's smile froze just a little. Joz noticed that her mother's eyes hadn't strayed below Joz's neckline. Her mother scrupulously avoided referring to or looking at Joz's size. She never talked about diets; she treated her daughter as if she were one of her own stick-thin friends. She gushed over how nicely Joz put colours together, how lovely a fabric was, but never, *never never never*, letting those nervous green eyes stray below Joz's shoulders. It was as if Joz were invisible from the throat down. 'You've got *such* a pretty face,' her mother used to say, when she was fourteen and fifteen.

'Darling, go and find Randolph,' she said now.

'OK,' Joz said. She walked away.

She looked around for her step-father. The room was only moderately full; the Joscelynes never crowded their guest list. Music played softly in the background and there was a comforting drone of conversation. She couldn't see him; he wasn't there. A single glance was enough to determine this, as her step-father was always head and shoulders above everyone else. At six foot five, he dominated every room.

When they were younger, and they used to ask what he did, as all children do, he would laugh and say, 'Oh, I throw money at empty stages.' Their mother would demur gently: 'Darling, the children can't possibly understand that.' Joz remembered being taken on his knee, aged probably about six, and his arms fastening around her for the cuddle he said he must have because she was so round and nice.

As a small child, Randolph would often take her to the theatres in London, and she would sit in the cavernous red plush wastes in the dark, listening to his voice, always soft, reassuring, placating—until someone opposed him. Then it would either become low—exceptionally low, so that you had to strain to catch his words—or he would thunder. God and the elements. Storm and the eye of the storm. Battering and unnatural peace. She didn't know what she feared more: the rage or the silence.

Still, he reserved his most secret rages for her alone.

Sometimes they let her up on to the stage. Wood boards in her earliest memories, but that flat, smooth surface in the later ones: that ice-rink shine. The immense curtains; the open-mouth darkness of the wings.

She understood that none of it was real. This was an artfully manufactured world, where hundreds of strangers could be made to weep, or laugh, or feel horror. People you had never met, and never would meet, there beyond the light, waiting to be moved by invisible strings. Her step-father came into that; stood in its wings, setting it up. Feted and fawned over, his eye for the right touch was unerring. He was the master of the dance.

He had a lifelong fascination with the theatre. Not film—not the tacky celluloid stuff that rots on tape. But *shows*. He first saw Joz's mother in a show, playing the violin in an orchestra pit. It was a performance of *La Traviata*. He went to the side of the pit and called down to her (they were below the body of the hall). He leaned forward, and said, 'You must stop playing. You are outshining them all.'

It was a great story. Joz had heard it a thousand times. The princess emerged from the dark prison, and the shining prince took her hand.

Mother had been alone, and trying to earn her living through playing and teaching. Her husband—Joz and Thomas's father—had died when Joz was four. Ruth and Randolph married when she was six. Joz had nothing left of that other man, only the faintest remembrance of sweetness and slightness. He had been small, like Ruth. In Ruth's dressing table, Joz knew, in a jewellery box, there was a photograph of him, screwing up his face at a joke in the exact way that Ruth still did. Joz thought that he used to play with both her and Thomas, crawling under tables, lying on the floor laughing. But perhaps this was a fantasy: of a man whom she longed for as a father, rather than the man she had actually had.

Ruth and Randolph had moved to London, where Randolph knew a man who had just bought a cinema in Surrey, and wanted to turn it back into a theatre. Randolph was the only one willing to help him, and they formed The Hollis Francis. Never looked back. Brilliant success. Bought a house in this square. The fairy-castle house. Began their parties. Raised a beautiful fairytale family.

Oh God.

Mother still played the violin. Quietly, in the evenings, before Randolph came home. There would be unutterable melancholy in those pieces played in the dusk.

The very first time that Joz had seen Randolph, he had come striding down the garden, where she was playing with a toy truck and her dolls. She had taken one look at him and dropped the toys, as if their future relationship in all its adult horror had transmitted itself to her in those first three or four seconds, and she had known that the toys were obsolete already in his company. He had lifted her up—so high up that fear knocked in her throat, and she could see over the fence, out to the street—and he had pinioned her in his bear-like arms.

The quiet house had never been the same again. He was always talking. Talking, talking, talking. When he had first walked into Thomas's room, Randolph had frowned at the Superman posters, the strewn clothes, the Lego castle, the toy cars underfoot. For his next birthday, he bought Thomas leather-bound complete works: Milton, Shakespeare, Wordsworth. Thomas was eight. It was as if Randolph, rather than simply not understanding childhood, could not even *connect* with it. Thomas had taken down his posters and retreated, over those first few months, into stony silence, pulling up the tenuous drawbridge of what relationship there might have been. Joz admired him for that: his silence and immobility in Randolph's presence. It was just as if Thomas could sublimate the desire to move, to blink, even to breathe. He became a motionless waxwork of a child while Joz, frightened and nervous, became ever more frantic. Laughing and smiling in an effort to please, and listening . . . even then. She tried to listen, to understand. And there was never any peace any more.

Joz stood still, her eyes drawn to the fire.

And Randolph, as if summoned by thoughts, materialised before her.

'Jozzy, darling,' he said.

She immediately stepped into his embrace. Her head came just to his shoulder. He pressed her cheek to the expensive, dense material of his dinner jacket. She obeyed wordlessly. He kissed her, lingeringly, on top of her head, squeezing her shoulder, and then stroking her back, up and down the silvery silk. 'Oh, you're so lovely and warm,' he said.

She looked up into his face. He had a tan from his recent trip to California. There were half a dozen people at his side, and he spoke in that stagy voice that he always used in company. 'Where have you been hiding?' he asked. 'We haven't seen you since the wedding. Goodness, how I miss you. My favourite Martian.'

It was a nickname. He'd called her that since the TV programme, years ago. He told her that she was so beautiful, so *unlike* a Martian, that it was funny.

'Oh, you know,' she said, playing the game. 'Busy.' Talking down the suddenly leaping leaves, behind glass. A stranger's questioning voice. *Oh, God. Where were these pictures coming from?* She tried hard to fix on his face. He liked her to look at him, *only* him, when they were in company.

He smiled down at her, gauging her.

'Did you get what you wanted in America?' she asked.

He laughed again, and nodded. 'They are really very cute when you get to know them,' he said.

They smiled at each other. They were alike in their easy, low opinion of others.

He held her out from him, his eyes ranging over her. 'Oh, you are good enough to eat,' he said. 'Guess what I've been doing all afternoon. Your mother can't understand it. But you will, Martian.'

'What?'

'Playing with my birthday toy. I've bought a C-type Jag.'

'Ooooh,' said Joz, making a disappointed sound, and pouting. 'I want one too.'

The people at his elbow laughed self-consciously. Father and daughter's regular little show. She knew her lines by heart. The right faces to make. Randolph himself threw his head back and laughed. 'Jozzy, they're rare. They're *old*. You can't go and buy one like a packet of peas. I've been chasing this one for months. Isn't she priceless?' he asked the assembled audience. 'The Martian.'

She increased her pout, smirking. 'Want one like yours.'

'What's up with the Merc?' he asked.

'Nothing.'

'You're incorrigible,' he said.

Across the room, they heard Ruth's voice. They turned.

'Darling!' she was calling. 'Darling!'

Something fell into the pit of Joz's stomach, something violent and heavy.

Across the acre of velvet carpet, under the softly glowing lamps, Thomas was standing next to his mother.

The dinner was over before she spoke to him. All night she had watched him—he had come alone, without Anna—talking to the women on either side of him at the long table. The room was dim, cream, gold, shedding a veil over every face, so that everyone looked beautiful. The Joscelyne theatrical dinners. Joz's eyes ranged over the director, the dancer, the politician, the actress, dotted among the guests like trophies. She studied for a long time the actress positioned next to Thomas: a wraith dressed in what looked like an underslip—just a piece of satin with shoestring straps. Her mother had done it on purpose.

Randolph was deep in hurried conversation with the Treasury man. Heads together, their chairs pulled back slightly from the table, they turned away from the others. The Government official was looking at the floor, Randolph's hand on his shoulder. Joz could see the whites of his knuckles. The man shook his head. The hand tightened . . .

Occasionally Thomas would glance at Joz: that dry, expressionless look that anyone else might interpret as mild disapproval. Thomas was self-employed, a computer designer. He regularly sealed himself up in his study. He looked very serious, rather distinguished, with those alluring touches of early grey. It was the first time she'd seen him since the wedding, and now her stomach knotted and her throat closed up. Nothing in Thomas's demeanour suggested that she was more than an acquaintance. She put down her knife and fork and looked at him uncompromisingly, longing screaming from every pore.

What's she like, Thomas?

Not like me.

He turned his head away.

It was afterwards, in the hall, that he came up to her.

'Hello, Cecily,' he said. He didn't kiss her. He never kissed her. When he put his hand on her arm, to steer her towards the drawing room, his touch was feather-light. He was always terribly formal with her in public.

'How's work?' she asked.

'Intricate.'

He had this way of implying that his life was far too complicated to explain. Far too important, too cerebral for her. She forced the next question out.

'And Anna?'

His back straightened slightly. 'Not too good,' he said.

'Oh—I'm sorry to hear that.'

He gave a little smile, as if he didn't believe her.

'She's not still getting those awful calls?'

Thomas shook his head. 'We only had two or three,' he said. 'But . . . we had a letter this week. From Lincolnshire.'

Joz affected interest. 'Who do you know in Lincolnshire?'

His faced darkened. 'We don't know *anyone* in Lincolnshire, of course,' he said.

'Oh dear,' Joz sighed. 'What do they say?'

'You can guess.'

'Can I?' she asked. 'Why can I?'

He let it pass. They stood barely an inch apart. She laid a hand on his arm. He looked down at it.

'Tell me about it,' she said.

His eyes ranged over her face for a second, trying to read her.

'Well . . . It goes on about the way Anna's mother died. Details. Dreadful details.'

'Oh! It must have upset Anna?'

'Yes.'

'What do the police say?'

'We haven't told them.'

'But shouldn't you?'

'I think it best just to ignore it.'

Joz smiled. 'You think it's the same person who broke in that day?'

'I suppose it must be . . . the details . . .' he murmured.

'But then you really *must*.'

'Anna says not to.'

'But why?'

'I don't think she wants to talk about it. She won't tell me.'

'Oh, dear . . .'

Six months previously, soon after Thomas and Anna had met, Anna's house had been broken into. She lived with her elderly mother, a terrible gorgon of a woman who ruled her daughter with a rod of iron. When Anna had come home—she taught at the University—her mother was dead on the carpet in the living room, curled into a foetal position as though protecting herself from blows. But the coroner had said she had died from natural causes: a heart attack, probably caused by the shock and ferocity of the burglary. Anna had never forgiven herself for not being at home that day. A day that she had spent with Thomas, at a seminar sixty miles away.

Thomas drained the last of his drink. 'This week, she can't work *at all*.'

Anna contributed to a rather obtuse literary magazine: indulgently long, academic articles on indulgently long, academic books. She was a part-time lecturer at a women's college. She had published three books. *The Female in Seventeenth Century Religion and Politics and Her Relationship to Rural and Domestic Life* was one. Joz had once read the first two pages and thrown it down, infuriated by the tone of the thing, at the dense typeset of the pages, at the fact that the woman who had written it was supposedly in love with her brother, and pouring this extinct prose into his ear morning, noon and night.

'Should she be working?' Joz asked. 'On your honeymoon?'

He flashed her a look. 'Don't be ridiculous,' he said.

'Ridiculous? Me? *I'm* not the one who got married.'

Thomas was looking away. Joz considered his profile. She began to stroke his arm, just as her step-father had stroked her before dinner, lingeringly and smoothly, as you would stroke the fur of a cat. And, like a cat, Thomas seemed to straighten for a moment, arching his neck towards her touch.

'Oh, she's not looking after you,' she said.

'Why don't you come up and see us?' he asked.

'You're not *serious*.'

'Of course I am.'

She dropped her hand. 'Why should I want to see *her*?' she demanded. She stuck out her bottom lip in the pout that always appealed to their step-father. 'Why don't you come down and see *me*?' she asked him.

He smiled. 'Anna isn't fit to travel.'

'I didn't ask her, I asked you.' She put her head on his shoulder and looked up at him with the innocent expression of a four-year-old. 'It's ages since you came to see me,' she whispered.

He stepped abruptly to one side, shrugging her off. He looked around himself, as if to check whether anyone had been watching them. Then, in a louder voice, he said, 'You and Dad are like two peas in a pod.'

'So?'

'Nothing,' he said. 'Forget it.'

'Tom . . .'

'You're like this,' he said. And he raised his arms to shoulder height at either side, and tipped back his head, and rolled it from side to side with closed eyes and a large smirk on his face, mimicking someone revelling in hot sunshine, or receiving thunderous applause.

'*So?*' she repeated.

He stepped forward, dropped his voice. 'I'm not *like* that,' he told her. 'Please . . . stop it.'

'Stop what?'

'For God's sake . . . you know. It's all different now.'

She brought up both hands swiftly, held each side of his face. 'No,' she said softly. 'I never give up hope, Tom. One day you'll realise.'

He stared at her, then laughed. He raised his arms to duplicate the applause-receiving gesture of a moment ago. 'That's all it is,' he said.

'I *mean* it,' she said.

'For heaven's sake,' he muttered. 'It's beyond a joke. Grow up.'

She flinched as if he had hit her. Staring at his averted face, her mouth moved wordlessly. *He didn't mean it. They wouldn't grow up. They couldn't grow up.* Childhood was the only place of any pleasure, an unspoken sanctuary.

The party was breaking up.

People were standing up, brushing down their clothes, gathering handbags, shaking hands. Ruth had disappeared behind a phalanx of thankyou-givers. Their step-father stood with one hand on the mantelpiece, looking over at them.

'When will I see you again?' she asked.

'When I'm back in town,' Thomas said. 'I don't know exactly.'

She squeezed his hand and he gave a little smile and turned away, trying to extricate himself. She laced their fingers tightly.

'Let go, idiot,' he told her.

'No,' she said. 'Never. You'll see.'

She got home about midnight. She kicked the door closed, went up the stairs, and flicked on the answering machine. She stood looking out of the kitchen window, not bothering to turn the lights on, listening to the messages.

'This is Faith,' said a woman's voice.

Joz turned and looked hard at the phone.

'I've got your letter about Lautrec copies for the TV agency. I see it was posted last week. Look, I'm sorry, but I've just moved house.' The voice gave the address: somewhere in Dorset. Faith was laughing. 'I'm just all disorientated here. It's an island, and . . . oh, the problems, you wouldn't believe . . . I wouldn't know where to start . . . Mind if I ring back? Will you be in on Sunday morning? I'll phone then . . .'

Joz stopped the machine.

She rewound it, and listened again.

Then she rewound it and listened again.

NINE

*F*AITH WOKE EARLY; she lay in bed for a second, wondering where on earth she was, seeing an unaccustomed light in the room, an unaccustomed shape to the window.

Then, *I'm home*, she thought.

Home.

She could feel that the air in the bedroom was icy; realised that, unconsciously, she had been waiting for the familiar click and roar of the gas boiler in the London house. No sound came here. She drew her arms back inside the bed and curled up, burying her head into the pillow and looking at the room with one eye.

The roof sloped. The wardrobe she'd brought from town didn't fit in the corner as she'd planned; it stood mid-room, packing cases around it. The enormous wall mirror she'd salvaged from a house sale—black and gold, six foot by ten—was behind the wardrobe, reflecting only the unglamorous plywood back.

Turning on to her back, she looked up at the ceiling. There was a crack running from one side to the other, with a network of finer plaster lines that resembled a stretched hand. She'd had a ceiling like that at home, when she was small; her Dad used to come upstairs and reassure her that no dragons could come crawling from the cracks. No goblins, none of the leprechauns in her book, with their polished hazelnut faces and little green suits with pointed collars that looked like knives dangling around their necks . . .

Smiling, Faith drew up a mental worklist while she savoured the last of the bed's warmth. Bad as this place was, she couldn't fight down the feeling of excitement. It was the first house that she had owned alone. Her *own*. She would re-plaster in here. Paint. A bar across the ceiling: she was going to hang white muslin and make a ship's-bed, a cabin-bed, with a thick mass of layered, opaque curtains. Her own paintings in here—the ones she wouldn't let anyone see. The yellow and blue. The blue and white. The ones she wasn't sure of . . . With these pieces she was feeling her way, past the copies, past someone else's view of the world, and letting herself explore. There had never really been time for that before. Guy was always at her back insisting she take the next contract. She would take her own studies out at night and pace up and down before them, still not convinced they had any merit.

'You're a *commercial* artist,' Guy would say. 'I mean, you make money at it. Thank God for small mercies, Faith. Not many do. Don't bite the hand that feeds.'

'I know, I know,' she would reply. Could see herself now, sitting at their basement kitchen table, chewing the ends of her hair, his hand slapping it away, ticking her off like a baby.

She sat up in the bed, drawing up her knees. That was years ago, when they first lived together. That was not her any more. That was not Guy any more.

'Enough of this,' she muttered, and stepped out of bed. She ran around gasping for a minute or two, hopping about, pulling on sweat-shirt, leggings, socks, an extra sweater from last night's discarded pile on the floor.

She ran out to the kitchen, dodging more boxes, a pile of shoes, a pile of magazines that had slithered over. She could see her breath in the room, which was in shadow, the window nothing but a sheet of grey-blue. The sea. Far out, a tanker was ploughing the horizon. It looked like the cardboard silhouettes on *Captain Pugwash*.

Too cold for orange juice, grapefruit. Too cold for *anything* from the fridge. Still hopping, she turned on the hob, wrinkled her nose at the new smell coming off it, took down a pan, and managed to unearth a packet of instant porridge from the box on the table.

She turned on the taps suspiciously, watching as a brownish glug came through them, which slowly accelerated into a clear stream. She let it run for a full three minutes.

Alex Hurley had got the water turned back on. The Water Company had arrived and explained—as though to a sub-normal child, in words of one syllable, which instead of making her furious, by that time merely etched a bleak smile on her face—that Mr Rawlings had experienced pressure supply difficulties, blah blah . . .

They had all sat down on the bonnet of the Water Company's car while the engineer drew a little map for them. This was the last house on the loop supply, which ran round . . . here (scribble) . . . and *here* (scribble) and came from Hurley's house along the contour of the hill and down Faith's back garden. The supply was in cast-iron pipes. 'Rust,' said Alex Hurley.

'Rust?' she echoed.

'In the bath. Everywhere. I had to get mine changed.'

'But yours is a new house, isn't it?'

'Not entirely. There was a ramshackle place like yours before I started on it.' Then, realising what he had just said, he grinned, and added, 'Sorry.'

'Oh, bloody marvellous. Bloody *marvellous*,' she had murmured.

'What you want,' said the engineer, his face brightening with enthusiasm at the thought, 'is to hook on to the main at the front. Down your lane. The new house was hooked up there; it'd cut off the loop; we ran a new main to within two hundred yards of you; it'd be plastic—'

'Any nearer to a cup of tea?' the van driver had said, looking over their shoulders.

Faith had taken a deep breath. 'How much?' she asked the water engineer.

'Well, I'll get the Inspector to come down, we might join you up. Course, you know that any pipe inside your land is your responsibility. Your expense.'

'But *you* own the pipes!'

He'd grinned at her, held up an admonishing finger. 'Ah. Now, not many people know this,' he said, 'but the householder owns the pipes. *We* just own the water. What we'll do is, turn you back on today, might be a bit discoloured, but—'

Alex Hurley had been gazing down at the gravel drive. 'You'll have to get a trench dug to the main,' he said. 'Right through the garden. Bit of a mess.'

'A trench,' she said. She was beginning to feel like a parrot.

'Two foot six deep. Regulation. Chalky here, mind,' said the water man.

'Noisy business,' muttered Alex. 'Sleeve the pipe with another one all the length. Need a plumber, need an excavator. Your floors look solid. Might have to dig them up, cross the kitchen.' He sighed and shrugged. 'Just the same as mine.'

Faith resisted the temptation to demand why Alex Hurley rarely spoke in whole sentences. He stood pulling on his beard thoughtfully, never quite meeting her eyes. She had an urge to walk in front of him, lift his chin with her hand, and say, 'What's your problem? Are you talking to me, or the ruddy gravel? For God's sake *look* at people when you talk to them!' Instead, she asked again, 'How much?'

'Oh, maybe a couple of thousand. Two and a half or three if the pipes inside need doing,' he replied equably.

They all looked at her, waiting for her to scream.

'Oh God, God,' she breathed, running her hands through her hair. 'Isn't that just *dandy*. I need that like a hole in the head. Just *brilliant*.'

Alex Hurley had smiled sympathetically, at last raising his head, and glancing momentarily at her. She saw, with a mild interest, that he had green, *very* green eyes, with flecks of white in them.

'On your first day,' he said.

She smiled bleakly. 'Bingo.'

The telephone van had arrived at that very moment. A large spotty boy got out, whistling. He walked over to Faith, and said, 'Found yu, my lover. Nice spot. Lovely spot. Not on the way to anywhere, mind. Any tea going?'

'No,' she had said. 'Good, isn't it?'

* * *

The phone rang as she was eating breakfast.

She was sitting with the plate on her lap, and reached down to find the phone behind the sofa.

'Faith Mary Collins.' Then, under her breath, 'Sod,' as the porridge slid to the edge of the plate and honey ran off the top and on to her hands.

'Hello. This is Cecily Joscelyne.'

'Oh . . .' Faith hastily swallowed her food, sucked on her sticky fingers. 'Hello. Sorry I wasn't with it last night. I've just moved in here—'

'That's *perfectly* OK. We haven't met, have we?'

'No, I don't think so. Of course, I have heard of you. The Palmersville house off Chelsea Bridge—'

'I wonder if you'd be interested in a commission?'

Faith thought of the two pictures she still had left to do, and of all the other things she wanted to spend time doing in this house. Then, at once, the words *two or three thousand to get you fixed to the main* came rolling back to her. She couldn't be picky just now. 'What size?' she asked, sighing.

'Six Monets for a Japanese bank.'

Faith began to laugh. The voice on the other end of the line responded, throaty and full. 'There's the other one, too. For the TV agency. You've done a Signorelli for them. I can't think why we haven't met before.'

Faith opened her mouth to reply, but was beaten to it.

'Look, I know it's a terrible imposition, but I'm down your way today. Might I just call in, for a chat?'

'Well, I don't think—'

'*Just* a chat. Perhaps I can buy you lunch; I don't suppose you've found a thing yet in your kitchen. Awful to have to cook! I have some ideas with me.'

'You're around here?'

'I'm in somewhere called Winterwell.'

'You're just five miles away . . . ?'

'Yes.'

Faith held the receiver away from her ear, raised an eyebrow at it, then returned it to her ear. 'Well, all right,' she said.

'Oh, *lovely*. Are you hard to find?'

Faith gave her directions.

'Sounds wonderful,' said the voice. Cecily Joscelyne sounded genuinely excited. 'Twenty minutes or so?' They hung up.

Faith gazed round at the freezing, littered house. 'Oh, it is,' she said, aloud. Her voice fell to an impersonation of Joz's plummy tones. 'It's all absolutely *super*, darling.'

She saw the Mercedes coming up the lane a half-hour later, and caught her breath.

Some car; red, and a soft-top. Gleaming. Thousands upon thousands of pounds lurched drunkenly over her potholes, and turned into the drive.

She wiped her hands down her trousers. She had hurriedly made a fire in the wide stone fireplace, and it was now cracking at her back: a lot of noise, a damp smell, smoke. But no heat.

She bit her lip. Ever since the call, she'd been trying to think what she knew about Cecily Joscelyne. She knew that she was very wealthy. She had heard some gossip last year about an affair with—who was it now?—some minor celebrity. An actor who was in one of Randolph Joscelyne's plays. The one that nosedived at the box office. And she had seen Cecily Joscelyne's picture in the *Tatler* (read in the hairdresser's), looking huge and glittery and shiny in taffeta . . .

But her thoughts didn't get much further. Joz was stepping out from the car.

She went to the porch feeling curiously *unready*. And the woman coming towards her looked formidable. Glamorous. And—boy, was she big! Faith went down the couple of steps, her feet crunched on the gravelly stone of the yard, and Joz extended a soft, square hand.

'Hello!' said Joz. 'It's wonderful, *wonderful* . . .'

Whenever Faith met anyone, she found herself doing a lightning inventory; her eye for detail was accurate, and she retained those details, sometimes, for years. Joz was smiling broadly, and held on to Faith's hand for just a fraction too long. In those few seconds, Faith took rapid stock of a mass of blonde hair, teased out, baby fine, heavily lacquered. Blue eyes; a perfect coral-coloured expensive mouth. Immaculate skin with a layer of fine powder. A blue suit. Several intricate, broad rings. On the feet, a pair of blue court shoes with an elaborate leather bow. Polished and shiny, like the rest of her. *New.* Everything looked impossibly *new.*

Joz was certainly a vision. She looked as though she had stepped off a television set. She even *smelled* expensive: of opiate jasmine, so thick you could have stirred the air with a spoon.

'What dreadful timing,' Joz was saying. 'Arriving when you're all at sixes and sevens.'

'No, no,' Faith murmured, turning, and indicating that they should go in the house. She looked at her own slippered, socked feet and grinned to herself. Talk about a contrast.

'What a *tremendous* view.'

Joz was standing at the very edge of the lawn, from where one could see the coast. A smile of utter delight had come to her face. She turned quickly back to Faith. 'I can see the sea,' she said.

'Well, yes, of course . . .'

'Is it a sandy beach?'

'Sand? I don't know, I—'

'Here, at the bottom of your garden? Marvellous.'

Joz's voice was distant, breathy. A peculiar light had come into her eyes, like someone who had undergone some sudden religious conversion. Faith gave her an *are you crazy, or what?* look behind her back.

Joz turned back, smiled, and laughed. 'You must forgive me,' she said, all charm. 'I just adore islands. This is . . . quite *perfect.*'

Faith indicated the steps. Joz followed her. In the living room, the newspaper under the wood had caught: sparks rushed up the chimney.

'Oh yes,' said Joz. 'Yes.'

She went to the centre of the room and looked all around herself. She carried a leather portfolio, and now opened it, and laid it on the sofa. She spread out prints.

'Do you remember the Creation Agency?' she was asking.

'The devils?'

Joz smiled. 'Yes, the devils.'

'It was a very grey place. Grey everywhere.'

'That's the one.'

Faith had rolled a strand of hair around a finger and was unconsciously pulling at it. 'I remember the man who hired me.'

'Tremain?'

'I've got a blank with names. He was very short, with . . .' She mimed a moustache, drooping at the corners of her mouth.

'Oily little bastard?'

Faith hesitated, then laughed. 'Same man.'

'Did he try and touch you up in the lift? He had a thing about lifts.'

Faith stared at her. 'No . . .'

Joz pointed at the Lautrecs she had brought. 'Now, how do you feel about these? I don't ask you just to manufacture, you know. I don't mind if you say "No can do". I realise you aren't *simply* a copier.'

Faith had come round to the side of the sofa, and now she looked up abruptly into Joz's face.

Joz gave her a fantastically wide smile. 'I can tell an artist from a reproducer,' she said. 'There's a little something in your paintings, isn't there? There's a little stencil of yourself over the top of the idea. There's a difference in that Signorelli. It is the painting, and it is *not* the painting.'

Faith sat down on the sofa arm. No one—not even Guy—had ever remarked on this. She herself could not have put it into words. 'Are you an artist?' she asked.

'No. But—' Joz put her fingertip close to—not resting on—her cheek. 'I have an eye. I do see. I see the whole thing in my mind. I always see wholes, I see completes . . .'

Something passed over Joz's face in that moment. She registered a second of concern, looking slightly over Faith's shoulder. Briefly, Faith wondered if there was something wrong in the room behind them. Then, she saw quite clearly that Joz was considering some inner picture. Something that troubled her. She glanced back at Faith. 'Do you know what I like so much about this house?' she asked.

Faith did a double-take for a second. She thought they had been talking about work. 'No . . .' she said. 'What?'

'There are no trees.'

Faith was completely baffled. She didn't know what to say. Joz gave her a dazzling smile, and asked, just as if the last sentence had never been spoken, 'Is your husband here with you?'

'Er . . . no . . . No.'

'This is just a workplace? Out of London?'

'No. This is my home. I don't live with my husband any more.'

'I see.'

No formal expression of sympathy had been given. Faith had expected a little flutter of embarrassment. There was none. Instead, Faith found herself under that direct, scrutinising gaze. 'Which leaves you free to work.'

'Yes, it leaves me . . . free.'

Joz insisted on taking Faith to lunch as she had promised. Faith changed her clothes, made her face up hastily—two smudged lines of eye pencil and a quick bit of mascara—and sat in the Mercedes while Joz talked, driving unusually slowly through lanes where the hedges had just been cut and the splinters still littered the road.

Faith stole glances at her companion. Joz was telling her about her work. She had, it appeared, an almost photographic memory for places, for people, reeling off names and addresses like a phone book, with poisonous personal asides. 'Of course, their son stole his father's credit cards, cost them *twelve* thousand,' she said, turning the car into a parking space. 'It was *wonderful.*'

The pub was on a hill, looking out over neatly fenced fields of pasture, dotted with seemingly picture-book sheep in immense winter fleeces.

'Are you going anywhere for Christmas?' Joz asked, as they got out.

'Doubt it.'

'Just snuggle up in your hideaway?'

They went in the door. *Am I hiding away?* thought Faith. She felt disgruntled and off-balance. She wanted very much to go home and unpack. She felt a twitching desire to paint, a kind of withdrawal symptom. Painting, she would forget houses and water and neighbours and Guy's bloody interfering memory. His face kept cropping up in front of her, an index finger raised in amused *I told-you-so* admonishment. The finger, the hand behind it, would swim towards her face so clearly she almost waited for it to connect. If she were just left alone a moment, to get her bearings, to stand still . . . They approached the bar.

Faith noticed a couple of male locals—one waxed jacket, one green tweed, one pair green wellies, one pair muddy brogues—look frankly across at them both, and their gaze fixed on Joz in mingled, rapt astonishment.

'White wine and . . .' Joz turned to Faith.

'Tomato juice. Thanks.'

Joz took down a menu. 'Here, or in the restaurant?'

'Here? The fire looks good.'

They took their drinks to it, sitting down in wonderful padded armchairs. Faith stretched out her legs, holding up her feet luxuriously to the flames. 'I guess I'll get the knack of building these things so they actually warm you up,' she said, smiling.

Joz, with finger and thumb, picked at the upholstery of the chair. 'Shoddy,' she remarked. Then, suddenly, she looked up. 'Do we have an arrangement?' she asked.

For a second, Faith thought she was talking about paying for the meal. 'Well, I—'

'Are you doing the paintings?'

It was quite an aggressive question. Joz sat perfectly still, a blue stone Buddha.

'How soon?' Faith asked.

Joz named the time, and the fee. It was so large that Faith sat stunned, her glass gripped in her hand. She didn't come cheap, but the figure that Joz named was twice the usual.

'That's very generous,' she said.

Joz smiled. 'Not really,' she replied. 'You see . . . I intend to take up *all* your time.'

'Do you want them individually?'

'Not at all. I want you to finish the six. Then the three for the Agency. In a group.'

'It will be next year . . .'

'Of course.'

'Well, then . . . thanks.'

'Good. I'll write you a cheque. An advance.'

To Faith's amazement, Joz got up, crouched down by her chair, and squeezed her hands in a soft, warm, paw-like grip. Faith saw a little thread of lipstick bleeding from the bottom lip, and noticed, with it, the first signs of pursed-mouth vertical lines running down from Joz's mouth. In time, Joz would have one of those old-woman's mouths that refused to stay still, that made a permanent chewing motion. A tip of a front tooth sat on that lower lip, as though too large to fit inside. Imperfections under the shine.

'I feel we shall be tremendous friends,' Joz said. 'Don't you think so? I'm never wrong about these things.'

Faith didn't feel anything of the sort. All she did feel was an enormous embarrassment. She saw the wellies-and-brogues turn, leaning on the bar, looking frankly at the two women by the fire. Kneeling on the floor gripping another person's hand was obviously tantamount to high drama here.

'Oh yes,' Faith gabbled, tortured by the locals' inspection. 'Yes . . . but, you know, you ought to get up. Your lovely clothes . . .'

Joz laughed, straightened, and went back to her seat. As she sat down, she said, 'I have another thing to ask of you.'

'Ask away.'

'How much would you like for your house?'

Faith's mouth dropped open in astonishment. 'My—house? But it's not for sale. I just moved in two days ago!'

'Yes,' said Joz, perfectly calm. 'But you've so many problems up there, haven't you? Not conducive to work. How much would you sell it for?'

Faith had a stirring of the stubbornness that Guy claimed was one of her many faults. She knew the house was awful, but it was *hers*. She'd done it all by herself, for the first time. Made a pig's ear of it, of course, but what the hell. It would get better.

And there was something else, equally important. *It felt like home.* Not just her home now, but the home she used to have, all make-do-and-mend: her parents' house. The rickety doors that never shut properly. The cold. The pantry door with its ancient handle, the flagstone floor. The scullery with its Belfast stone sink. It was *home*.

It might have been ramshackle, as Alex Hurley had put it, but it felt good. She had been blessed with a secure, happy childhood. Coming to this house was like re-entering a time of contentment.

'I'll never sell it,' she told Joz.

'Do you mind me asking how much you paid for it?'

'Actually, I do.'

Joz smiled broadly, unflustered. It seemed that she rather relished confrontation. 'I should say about ninety? For the land and the view. Awful house but marvellous location. Ninety, or eighty-eight, perhaps?'

Faith said nothing.

'I'll give you two hundred thousand for it.'

'Two—!' Faith started to laugh. 'You're joking.'

Joz merely smiled at her. She continued smiling as the food arrived. Shaking her head, Faith looked down at her plate, and grinned up at the barmaid who had brought it. 'Thanks,' she said. 'I'm *starving*.'

She tucked into her plate of steak and kidney pie at once. In fact, she couldn't remember ever being so desperately hungry, and hadn't known it until the food was placed in front of her. It smelt like heaven. She sat hunched forward, shovelling obliviously, the fire toasting her face. She dismissed the talk of the house. It was obviously Cecily Joscelyne's idea of a joke.

'Is it . . . nice?' Joz asked.

Faith glanced up. Joz was sitting back in the chair, her food almost untouched. She was balancing a green salad precariously on her knee, with a sachet of mayonnaise hanging from finger and thumb.

Faith started to laugh. 'Oh God, you must excuse me,' she said. 'I haven't had a proper meal for about three days.'

Joz shook her head. Faith scrupulously finished every scrap. Joz ate a little salad, then found herself watching this slight, brown-haired woman, with her fragile, bone-thin wrists, her small squirrel's face, her crossed legs encased in thick wool tights below a short black skirt, her body invisible in layers of T-shirt and sweater and scarf.

'There,' Faith announced, putting down her knife and fork. 'Finished.'

'Would you like a dessert?'

'What do you think there is?'

'They have a selection—'

'Oh, it's not cheesecakes and things, is it? Is there anything hot?'

This time, Joz smiled. 'My step-father always says he loves to see a woman with an appetite.'

'Does he? Sounds like we'd get on.' And Faith gave her a mock shame-faced smile.

Joz sat back, folding her arms across her. 'Are *your* parents alive?' she asked.

'No.'

'Both mine are. At least . . . my mother and stepfather.'

Faith waited for something else, but it didn't come. Joz had emphasised the word 'both' as if it were some kind of affliction.

'Your father is Randolph Francis Joscelyne, isn't he? The theatre man.'

'Yes.'

'Exciting.'

Joz gazed into the fire for a second, then glanced up. 'Where are you from?' she asked.

'From?'

'Yes. Where were you born?'

'Paddington.'

'Paddington.' Joz repeated the word as if she hadn't heard it before.

'We moved out to Essex when I was four.'

'Oh . . . of course.'

Faith bit the inside of her lip. She looked Joz straight in the eye. *Come on then*, she thought. *Come on and make your stupid joke about Essex girls.*

But Joz did not. 'Why move down here?' she asked.

'It was a place we came to in the summer. On trips,' Faith said. 'It was supposed to be the place my Mum and Dad would retire to. I always wanted to live here.'

'Ah, I see. Were your parents artistic?'

'God, no.'

'Oh?'

'Dad worked on the buses. He always said he couldn't draw a breath, never mind anything else. It was a joke, you see . . .'

Evidently, Joz didn't see. Faith ploughed on. 'Mum worked in a shop. She could paint things like rabbits on Christmas cards, or a picture of me building a snowman, she would do those little drawings in the margin of a letter, but . . . nothing else. She worked in the shop for eighteen years.'

'Her own?'

'No, no.' Faith named a high-street chemist. 'Eighteen years.'

Joz inclined her head, her eyes ranging over Faith as if seeing her anew. 'So how did you get into art?' she asked.

'I don't know. From nowhere.'

'It doesn't come from nowhere,' Joz said. 'Everything is *made*.'

'Made?'

'Manufactured. It doesn't float out of the ether. It is constructed, by effort, by work.'

Faith shook her head. 'It was the only thing that interested me at school,' she murmured. 'But it isn't manufactured. It's a pleasure.'

'I don't believe that, I'm afraid.'

'You said you weren't an artist—'

'And I'm not. But I see how artists work. If you become absorbed, and you feel it's a pleasure, then fine for you. *Great* for you. But, from the outside, I see everything the artist excludes. They exclude their families, their children . . . they are heartless. They really are fiends, you know . . .' This was delivered in a flat calm voice.

'I don't think that's true.'

'Don't you? I know that it is. I don't mean to be personal. It's simply a fact.' Cecily smiled slowly. 'Look at you, for instance. Aren't you here alone? To work?'

Faith bridled at that. 'That's not my choice. My husband left me.'

'I see.'

'For someone else.'

'And you don't think you excluded him?'

Faith stared at Joz. She was wounded at the lack of sympathy. Shocked, too, at how much she wanted that sympathy. She shrieked inside to be petted, to be cuddled, to be touched. Cecily Joscelyne spoke as if she were referring to some species of laboratory animal; not a human being at all. Faith wondered who it was that she had known, or knew, that had prompted this low opinion. 'No,' she replied, swallowing her fury. 'That had nothing to do with it.'

There was a momentary silence, in which Faith privately fumed. This damned woman, coming here and wading in with her size eight feet . . . Despite herself, Faith looked down at Joz's blue court shoes. They *were* big, too. Everything about her was enormous. Including her outrageous rudeness. And that stupid joke about buying the house. So pointless. She looked back up.

Joz's face wore a straight, unemotional smile. 'Do you have any children?' she asked.

'No,' Faith said. 'Not yet.'

'Oh?'

'I'm pregnant.'

Oh, Jesus, Faith thought. I've said it! My secret. And I've said it to *her*. She raged inwardly with an extraordinary disappointment. She had been saving it, she realised, holding it in, a possession, something for herself alone. Now she had given it away . . . to this . . . gargantuan *witch* of a woman . . .

Joz leaned forward. 'Are you, really?'

'Yes . . . yes . . .'

'Much?'

'Eight, nine weeks.'

'Eight weeks. Just a bunch of cells.' Joz repeated this, while she looked Faith frankly up and down. Then, 'Are you going to get rid of it?' she asked.

TEN

$\mathcal{M}$ARK ESTWOOD WAITED NERVOUSLY at the lift for Sandy Merrion-Walsh.

He knew what his boss would be like: he'd seen her fury at meetings before now, when some brief hadn't been meticulously prepared. She liked perfection. Nothing less.

She'd been in Eire until last night; six days. In those six days, the builders had started re-fitting the agency. All he had for reassurance was Cecily Joscelyne's word that she had spoken to Sandy and got her approval; and he didn't like to question that *We all move in the same circles, darling, you couldn't possibly understand* tone that Joz gave him when he suggested they ought to wait.

'Sandy will be delighted we've moved so quickly,' she had said. She'd squeezed his leg, which brought him out in an immediate cold sweat. 'She *knows* me, don't worry.'

But he did worry. Five days ago Joz had disappeared from the face of the earth; five days ago they'd moved the office into half the available space, and watched in horror as walls were ripped down and flooring taken up. Everyone had to get in and out through the Fire Stairs.

Two days ago, some kind of filthy stripper had been put on the foyer, and it became impossible to work. Mark was forced to hire the upper floor of a nearby pub; the staff had complained of being asphyxiated. It was a nightmare.

The lift doors opened.

Sandy already had a handkerchief pressed to her face. She stepped out.

'Christ, Mark. What the *hell* is that smell?'

'It's some kind of glue,' he said. 'Look, we'd better go back down. I've got some rooms in The Red Admiral . . .'

'The Red Admiral! What the fuck are you talking about?'

Mark felt about one inch tall. 'Cecily Joscelyne didn't tell me,' he said.

'Tell you what?'

'How quick it would all be. When she said she was coming in on Monday, I thought *she* was, for drawings—'

'She faxed me the drawings last week, Mark.'

'I know, but, she never *said* it was builders, she said—'

Sandy stabbed the Door Open button furiously. 'You stupid little shit,' she said.

They got in; the doors closed. Mark shrivelled against the wall as Sandy fixed him with a truly terrible smile. 'Cecily Joscelyne is a *professional*,' she said. 'She moves fast. She's the best there is. The *best*.' She pointed a red-tipped finger at Mark. It reminded him of the bloody point of a knife. 'D'you think I'd hire her, after all this crap I've had with her step-father over the rights to *Dancing In The Wind*, if she wasn't the absolute best? You put feelings aside in business, boy. You don't start whining about being picked on. It's your job to keep up with her.'

'But she didn't even warn me . . .'

The lift stopped. They stepped into a downstairs entrance that still reeked.

Sandy was staring venomously across the road, at the gilt-and-blue frontage of the pub that now housed her entire operation. 'I'm supposed to impress Sebastian in *that*,' she muttered. 'For God's sake, ring the Inn On The Park or somebody. Get me a suite.'

'Yes, OK. Sure. Right . . .'

She turned on her heel and shot him a look that turned his bowels to water. *Hot* water. 'Listen to me, Mark,' she said slowly. 'My patience is this—' and she held up her index finger and thumb, a millimetre apart '—*this* thin. All right? I've been kept up half the night by some lunatic who thinks it's funny to ring me and then not say a single word. So I'm not in the *best temper*, OK?'

Mark's face had paled. He nodded.

'So I don't want to hear what you *can't* do. I want to hear what you *can* do. Am I making myself quite plain?'

'Yes,' he whispered.

She stormed across the road, pale cashmere coat thrown over her shoulders and blowing in the wind, her portfolio case clutched to her side.

He watched her with two thoughts uppermost in his mind and fighting each other for supremacy.

One was that he *despised* Cecily Joscelyne. He shoved his hands into his pockets and followed his boss with a feeling of desolation.

The other thought was strange. So strange it hardly seemed likely to be a coincidence.

Both he *and* Sandy had suffered a freak caller on the same night.

ELEVEN

$\mathscr{S}$ATURDAY SILENCE. Saturday stillness.

So unlike the old street, where Saturday meant noise and movement. Faith could hear seagulls, the keening cry, only a few yards down the ragged grass behind the house. She could hear the sea today, whipped up by the wind that was like a low voice continually whispering.

She stood in the bathroom, staring fixedly at the loo, trying to listen to the new sounds, and wondering desperately if she was going to be sick.

Think of something else.

Not Guy again. Think of . . . painting. Just the first swift strokes, pencil on paper, this morning. It was all she had been able to manage before being gripped by this foreign sensation.

She looked at herself in the mirror, and smiled grimly. She was the most delicate shade of green.

She'd always been a hypochondriac, that was the trouble. She dwelled on anything that diverted from the norm. Listened to her body with ripe misgiving. In her time she'd had an imaginary stroke, imaginary multiple sclerosis, and a heart attack. As an adolescent, she'd been convinced *she'd* be the one to catch AIDS, *she'd* be the one with herpes, *she'd* catch malaria abroad. The fact that she'd reached thirty and was as fit as a butcher's dog rarely knocked these old opinions off course. Occasionally, in the grip of a head cold, she'd rewrite the wording on her headstone, and wonder hopefully if she'd rate an obit in the *Telegraph.*

But that was all child's play compared to this.

Child's play. Yes.

She looked about, trying to concentrate on anything other than the terrible travel-sickness feeling rolling around inside her. Think about . . . Cecily Joscelyne. Fury momentarily gripped her, then subsided. People sometimes didn't realise how cruel an offhand remark could be. And her initial outrage at Joz's question about termination— she'd had to turn away and finish her drink, staring at the fire—had probably been unfair. Cecily had no idea about children, or wanting them, had obviously never felt that bone-deep need. So Faith hadn't even attempted a reply. Explaining her sudden and overwhelming longing for this child would have been pointless, meaningless. Like explaining the four-minute mile to a tortoise.

When Joz had gone, Faith exorcised her company with four hours of concentrated clearing up. The kitchen was first to surrender, followed by the bathroom. Here, a big Wadeheath vase held her half-dozen children's windmills; there was a bowl of shells, their inner blue-silver contrasting with ceramic white. A blind at the window instead of the plastic curtains. It had become a sea room. The previous owner had left Brylcreem boxes and old razor cases and a crinoline crocheted poodle on the window ledge, all encrusted with damp and dust. She had swept them off into a bin bag, making disgusted noises to herself.

Here it came again.

Wrong to think about blue and green, and being at sea. Here came the lurching motion of the water, rolling and tipping. A mild private earthquake, her stomach dancing to the beat.

Just at the last moment she remembered the steak and kidney pie. That did it.

Coming out of the bathroom ten minutes later, her mind fixed on an old girlfriend's advice, which ran something like, *Don't panic, think about it objectively, think, Isn't this a very interesting pain?*, she heard a knock on the porch door.

'I'm never going to be allowed to work in this house,' she muttered, going to answer it.

It was Alex Hurley.

'Oh, it's you,' she said.

He said nothing at first; he looked her up and down, and gave a brief smile.

'Look,' she said. 'I don't want to be rude, but—'

'Something you ate?' he asked.

'No. Nothing to do with it.'

'I see. In that case, have you tried soda water and a bit of orange juice in it?'

She put her hand on one hip, holding on to the door frame with the other. 'Just what is it that you're talking about? Have I come in halfway through this conversation?'

He smiled. 'Can I come in?'

'Oh, sure.' She stepped back and waved her hand. 'Sure, sure. Be my guest.'

'I came about the trench.'

'I hired someone. They're coming Monday.'

He put his hands in his pockets, looking faintly embarrassed. 'Oh,' he said. 'The thing is, I've got a mini excavator. I thought I could save you some money.'

'Save?' She digested this for a second. 'You mean you'd do it for nothing?'

'Yes.'

'Why?'

He raised his eyebrows, turned, and said, 'All right, fine.'

She caught his arm. 'No, no. Look . . . I'm sorry.' She shook her head. He crossed his arms, and waited.

'Let's go back a bit,' Faith said. 'Rewind. Knock knock. I open the door. I say, Oh, how awfully nice to see you. *Do* come in. Mr Hurley says, How terribly *lovely*, and politely makes no reference at all to the lady of the house looking like death warmed up.'

He laughed.

'All right?'

'All right.'

He walked into the house, and she mimed sweeping dust from his path and pointed to the sofa. He sat down obediently, pulling on the ribbed hem of his sweater like a small boy tidying himself up. She grinned at him.

'I always was a rotten hostess,' she said. '*Hello* magazine never calls any more. Tea or coffee?'

'Coffee. Lots of milk and two sugars.'

'And just a dash of caffeine?'

He smiled, but had already turned his attention to the corner of the room. He was looking frankly at the stripped area where she had set up her tables and easel.

'OK,' Faith said. 'Hold on.'

She looked at the back of his head, from the kitchen where she made the drinks, thinking that he seemed different today. She soon realised it was because he was tidy: washed, combed, clean. A thick white sweater, cords, leather hiking boots. His hair was silver with threads of black, combed back from his forehead, heavy and straight.

She came in, bearing the tray. 'It's been one of those mornings. I promised myself to start work today, and—'

'Just as you get straight, some swine interrupts you.' He took his cup.

'To be honest?' she said. 'Yes.'

'Are you always?'

'What, honest?'

'Yes.'

'I think so.'

He sipped his tea, 'You paint,' he said.

'Yes. Copies.'

'Sorry?'

'Copies. Fakes.' He still looked as if he didn't understand, so she added, 'For people who either own the real thing, and can't afford to take it out of the bank, or for people or companies who'd like you to *think* they own the real thing . . .'

'. . . and can't afford to take it out of the bank. Ah. I see. Good job you *are* honest, then.'

'I've had my offers,' she admitted.

'What, and never been tempted?'

She smiled frankly. 'Oh yes. I've been tempted.'

He looked at the empty easel. 'And your own work?'

'I don't sell that.'

'Why?'

She shrugged. 'Not yet.'

He regarded her for a moment. She was sipping her tea carefully, waiting for the next lurch, wondering if she could possibly dash across the room *casually*. She decided she couldn't.

He finished his drink, and sat forward. 'This digger,' he said. 'It's a small one, but it'll do the job. I bought it last year. I excavated a deeper channel at the beach. For the boats.'

'You've got boats?'

'I build them.'

'Oh.' Faith had no interest at all in boats, and offered no further comment.

'Well, to be honest, I've only built two. I don't think I want a trade, but then things take off in odd directions . . .' Alex seemed to jolt himself back to the present, and to her. 'Still, that's by the by,' he said. 'The point is, d'you want me to dig this trench for you? Take a day or two, that's all.'

'It's good of you,' she said. 'But I've got to pay you for it. Then there's the time . . .'

'That doesn't matter. Tell your husband. See if it's OK with him.'

'I don't need to. He doesn't live here.'

'Oh . . .' He glanced down at her finger, where she still wore the wedding ring. 'All right . . . look, work it out with me next week.' He stood up. 'If you must know, I thought you were right the other day. I was putting salt in the wound. I'm sorry—bad temper. Call this easing my conscience . . . You'll still need the plumber, though. I can't do that.'

'OK. I'll get on to it. Thanks.'

Glancing back at the easel, Alex suddenly asked, 'What is it you're doing?'

'Monet.'

'*Monet* . . . blimey. Do you let people see?'

'Sometimes. F'rinstance. I *might* let someone digging me a thousand-pound trench see.'

'You really make it exactly like Monet?'

She laughed. 'I'd be out of business if I didn't.'

'Amazing.'

'That's me.'

They walked to the door.

On the step, he asked her, 'Do you sail?'

'No.' She shook her head furiously, then wished she hadn't, and gripped the back of a wooden chair for support. 'No, I get seasick in a pedalo, ten feet from the beach.'

He seemed taken aback by this, hesitated, then stepped down from the porch.

'Oh, listen,' he added, looking over his shoulder as he walked away. 'Remember: soda and orange juice. Or grapefruit juice. Works . . .'

TWELVE

SATURDAY MORNING. Early. Thomas's wife sat on the stairs, the letter in her hand.

It was postmarked Sittingbourne, Kent.

Anna had opened it five minutes ago. Now she sat, turning it over and over in her hands. The funny thing was, she remembered Sittingbourne. She'd had an interview there once for a college place. A long time ago. She remembered a dusty train out of London on a hot afternoon; a long station platform, the haze rippling over the tracks. A small college hidden behind an estate of houses. It had been nice: the interview board, nice. But she had another offer, and never went there again.

Now, from Sittingbourne, of all places on earth, came another letter.

The first from Lincolnshire, the next from Kent. It made no sense at all. But then, she felt beyond sense. Way beyond sense.

They were the same. A sheet of A4 white printer paper. Some letters from newspapers and the rest filled in with a thick blue felt-tip pen. This one called her by her married name.

She read it again.

Dear Mrs JOsceLyNe,

The last one had called her Anna.

Did*n*'t youR MUM be *sick*. **SHE** was *OK* til the picTuRE *was* BROKE.

Anna Joscelyne let the paper fall, covering her face with both hands, and weeping silently. Her mother had been sixty-one; she had arthritis. The picture had been her father, in his wartime uniform, taken in the Libyan desert.

Her mother *had* been sick that day, and the picture was lying next to her body, speckled with that . . . that terrible last seizure of her mother's. Her swollen knuckles were pressed to the glass, miraculously whole where the frame was splintered. Her knees were scratched and her stockings torn. The police thought she might have crawled to the spot on the carpet where the photograph had been thrown.

Anna had dreamed of it again and again: reconstructing her mother's unknown last hour in her head. She ought to have been with her. She blamed herself constantly that she was not. She and Thomas should not have gone away that day.

It had been in the first month of their relationship. They had bumped into each other many times before it blossomed, so suddenly, last year. And she—who'd only had a handful of boyfriends, and no one that remotely moved her at all—was suddenly schoolgirlish, and silly, and wildly happy. Thomas's hand in hers. Thomas, who looked like some sort of elder statesman, in her arms, telling her his ponderous jokes, asking her advice about work. It was as if she had been caught in a glorious emotional sandstorm.

Of course, Thomas was not like that with her now. He'd reverted to his silences. He went visiting his family, leaving her behind. A fleeting game was over. She had been the toy, and the game was togetherness. But Thomas had grown tired of it. He liked to be left alone, sometimes for days. He liked his own company. Absolute solitude. The only people he ever talked to at length were his family. They were a closed society, that group. The overwhelming step-father, the silent mother, the flashy, gluttonish sister. They talked a language between them that she didn't understand. And only the mother seemed to be on her side; sometimes she thought that the other two actually hated her.

On that terrible, fateful day last year, they'd driven in Thomas's car all the way to Leicester. She couldn't remember a single detail about the seminar. All she remembered was that it was a spring day, and everything had seemed perfectly right. Until she came home. Until she opened the door. And that first agonising wash of guilt had never left her.

Someone had come in and terrified Mother, vandalised the house, perhaps even stood over her as she died gasping on the floor next to father's picture, her fingers clutching for his image to hold next to her. Perhaps they had even stood over her, laughing.

That was the idea that wouldn't leave her. That some stranger had stood over Mother laughing while she died, *and while her daughter was away.*

Until Thomas came into her life, she and Mother had been so close. She had accepted that she would probably never marry—she was so particular, no man ever measured up to Mother's high standards—and then Thomas came: silent, straight, self-controlled, just as *they* were, and they seemed like three pieces of a puzzle fitting together . . .

Thomas had been very good to Mother. Understood that Anna had to visit every day, sometimes to stay overnight if Mother was not feeling well; their relationship was not one of high passion, anyway. Despite the fact that she would have secretly *liked* it to be. No, they were more two minds meeting rather than two bodies. Thomas didn't mind if she left his bed and went to Mother instead. He understood all that.

In the grey light of the winter morning, Anna Joscelyne stood up. She looked like an invalid struggling to get upright, worn down with an invisible burden. She eventually got to the front door.

The glass was cold: she rested her head against it. Through this door, the letters came.

The wedding was only a fortnight ago. A fortnight ago, she'd got ready, stepped through this door, gambling that in marrying Thomas she'd be able to erase mother's death. Start again. But she had known almost at once that it wouldn't work. There had been a lot of talk at the reception about Cecily walking out of the church, which seemed to worry Thomas's stepfather greatly, as if Cecily's disturbance was all that mattered, and not Anna's feelings at all . . . and then the night away, at a local hotel, had been so *staged* somehow, and empty, and lifeless, with Thomas lying on the bed staring into space, and the champagne left unopened, and her dress hanging bleached over the back of the chair like a shroud . . . And the drive back in the morning, in silence. The moment Thomas got in, he'd rung his mother.

She had no mother.

He couldn't *see* how much that phone call, the very act of lifting the receiver to talk to her, when she herself felt so utterly alone, had wounded her . . .

The way that Mother died, and the letters and phone calls afterwards, had destroyed everything that went before. All the peaceful, pleasant years alone with Mother. All their evenings together. All their little trips out, even the innocuous shopping trips to town at the weekends. All those touching small memories. They were overshadowed completely by one monstrous day. A day that had grown ever larger, ever more significant in her mind, until it edged everything else out. Mother was now the woman on the floor on the old red carpet; no longer the round-faced, arms-crossed woman of the years that went before. Mother was the woman grovelling on the worn red pile begging, perhaps, for help. Her image shattered as neatly as the photograph. All composure gone.

And what the letters said was right.

That was the unbearable thing about them.

They were right.

It was all her fault.

She glanced up, at the dark stairs above her. Thomas was still asleep. She imagined going to wake him, showing him the letter. He would frown; he would sit up in bed, take his glasses carefully from the bedside cabinet, and read the message. Then he would say nothing, except look at her with that level, interrogating gaze. He would not kiss her or put an arm around her.

She took down the car keys from the hook alongside the front door.

Of course . . . she hadn't *wanted* that kind of marriage. She had chosen him for that quality: that silence, that measured, slow approach to everything.

If only, though . . . if only *once in a while*, like these times, like the last few weeks in the lead-up to the wedding when all those annoying details seemed to go wrong, and he never helped her, like when the letters came . . . if only he could have shown that he could be angry. It would have helped her to unfreeze this desperate coldness she carried inside. Just to stroke her hair, as other men might do, and tell her that he would find an answer . . .

But no, that was not Thomas.

That would never be Thomas.

She opened the front door. She walked over the drive, opened the car door, and got in. The interior was breathtakingly cold; the leather seats stung her bare flesh. She was still just wearing the thin nightdress. No dressing gown. No slippers on her feet.

She turned the key in the ignition, put the car into reverse. The gravel spun a little: she heard it spatter against the underside of the car. She changed to first, and second, steering out of the drive, turning left into the road.

It took her five minutes to reach the right road. A piece of dual carriageway, only a half mile long.

Half-way down was a bridge, a footbridge that spanned the road. Children sometimes hung from here, waving at traffic.

On each side were concrete pillars, the span supports. They were quite pretty, really. Arches above concrete. They made a nice pattern above the grey road. Sometimes in the morning, driving this way, she would see the sun shining through the spaces of the arches, casting a pattern on the grass of the embankment.

She put the car into fifth, thinking, *my fault* . . .

She hit the bridge at almost seventy miles an hour.

And died instantly.

THIRTEEN

$\mathcal{G}$UY SAW FAITH as soon as he started driving up the bumpy lane. She was standing at a wooden gate, and looking around her, and back up the drive. She was holding a pair of gardening shears that looked wildly inappropriate in her hands. She wore a big brown anorak that he recognised as being very old. She heard his car, looked up, looked again, and her hands fell to her sides. He stopped, wound down his window.

She walked to the car, glanced in at the passenger seat.

'I've come to see you,' he said, smiling broadly.

'Obviously. Where's Chloe?'

'Working.'

'On a *Sunday*?'

'The agency's got an exhibition tomorrow. You know what it's like. Running around after plastics factories, this time. Showcards of cable insulation and grommets, I shouldn't wonder.'

'How very down-market for her,' Faith said. 'I thought her lot only organised catwalks and supermodels.' She looked at him intently, biting her bottom lip.

'Don't be bitchy. Say hello.'

'Hello.'

'What are you doing?'

'I'm trying—' She glanced back at the gate. 'I'm trying to cut back the hedge. Make the gate wider . . .' Then she stopped, turned back, glaring at him. 'Never mind that,' she said. 'What the hell are you doing here?'

'Get in,' he said.

'No. I'm busy.'

'Oh, for Christ's bloody sake, just get in, Faith.'

She came reluctantly round to the passenger side, still glaring furiously at him. She got in, slamming the door hard.

'Straight up here?'

'Yes.'

When he first saw the house, he had to tell himself not to laugh. It looked like one of those terrible playhouses to him, all one storey, as if it had been made out of a railway carriage and cladded on the outside with mock-stone. It looked like he could knock it down with one hand.

'Holy shit, you've got a job on with this place,' he said, pulling on the handbrake.

'Tell me about it,' she replied.

She took him in, and stood in the big room while he inspected the house. After a while, he came back in to her, stared at her.

'You're sick of it already, aren't you?' he said.

'No.'

He started to laugh. She threw down the shears. 'There's nothing wrong here that can't be put right,' she said. 'It's just neglected.'

He nodded. 'Faith Collins, handywoman.'

'I've got a list,' she said. 'I'm getting it all done.'

'Why didn't you get it fixed before you moved in?' he asked her. 'You could have stayed in London a bit longer. A month or two, what's the difference? Move in when it's spring.'

She looked directly at him. 'If you don't know the answer to that, you're more a bloody fool than I thought,' she said.

It was his turn to stare at his feet. He saw the old carpet they had bought when they first moved in together, and a reflex reaction crossed his face, an expression somewhere between dismay and guilt.

Faith saw that look. Her heart shrank: paper curling fast in fire. They had made love on this carpet, and laughed afterwards as they hunched before the old electric heater that hummed and crackled as its bars grew hot . . .

Oh Lord, this *ache*.

She wished there were a cure for him. Imagined walking into a chemist's. 'Have you got anything for . . . ?' A packet, a pill, a powder. Take one in the morning and one at night. Flush longing from the system. She frowned, and looked up at him.

'Have you had an argument with her?' Faith asked.

'No . . . no. She's really working. It's in Penbold Street. Very important, big show . . . you know.'

'And you're all right?'

'Yes, we're all right.'

'Does she know you're here today?'

He made a face, a schoolboy's naughty face that didn't amuse her one bit. 'No,' he said.

'Oh, Guy . . .'

'No, it's all right. I just came to make sure you're OK. Thought you might be lonely. You *said* to come.'

She merely shook her head.

'Let me take you out somewhere,' he offered, after a moment. 'Sunday lunch. Your favourite. Roast beef and Yorkshire pudding.'

Faith went suddenly pale. 'No thanks,' she said.

'Just a drive, then.'

'No.'

'Let's go down to Bournemouth and play all the slot machines.'

She began to smile.

'You like those things,' he said. 'You could play push-the-penny all afternoon. Go down the slides. Put 10p in the plastic parrot. All the wiggly mirrors . . .'

She was laughing now.

'Come on, Fay,' he coaxed. 'Peace offering. No big deal. Come and talk to me. I miss you talking to me.'

'You're bored, aren't you?' she said. 'You had a whole Sunday and you were bored.'

He looked like a little boy, standing there. She knew it was an act. An old, old act. A script they had played out a thousand times. An indifferent scene. Still, just today, just at this moment, she wanted the old. Wanted to pull on the old like a shoe and feel its familiar contours, worn by years of use. Even if it didn't fit right, even if it pinched her and hurt.

She closed her eyes for a second, turning her head away from him.

They arrived in the town at one o'clock, parked at the edge of the sea. When they got out, Faith walked apart from Guy purposefully, her hands deep in her pockets. They agreed to walk for a while, and set out along the broad promenade, shoulder to shoulder with dog-walking, skateboarding, child-busy crowds, until they had gone a mile or more, and the people thinned out, and they were eventually alone. They went down the last of the steps and on to the beach: a wide, white scoop of sand, punctuated by breakers.

It was very cold. The wind that blew in was so icy that it took Faith's breath away. They didn't talk for some time; time in which Faith repeatedly bent down to pick up shells, or pieces of curiously marked, smoothed stone. The tide was out, and the sand was rippled by the withdrawing waves.

'You didn't really mind me coming, did you?' Guy asked.

'I'd rather you visited with Chloe.'

He looked for some time at her profile, bent over a stone in the palm of her hand. 'I want to see you sometimes, as a friend,' he said.

She let the stone fall to the ground. 'I don't think that's possible.'

'Yes, it is. It's possible.'

'No.' She walked on, saying, 'Come with Chloe.'

'Look—can't you stop talking about Chloe for a minute? This is about us.'

She stopped, and faced him. 'Why?'

'Why what?'

'Why can't you just stay away? It would be easier. It would be kinder.'

'But I don't *want* to stay away. I want to see you sometimes.'

She gave a short laugh. 'But, don't you see? You can't *do* that. We split up!'

He caught hold of her arm. 'That's the whole point. Now that we've split, we can be closer. Don't laugh . . . I mean it. Look, I can tell you things that I couldn't before.'

'Like what?'

'Well . . .' He looked at his feet. 'Things that happened when we were together, I can tell you now. Things I never explained before. I can tell you.'

'What things?'

He smiled. 'Things we argued about. Lies. Whatever.'

'Oh, I get it, I get it. Things that'll make you feel better.'

'That's it.'

'*You*. Not me, necessarily.'

'You want me to be honest, don't you?'

She winced. 'I never wanted you to lie to me. But you always did it.'

'Now I can *un*do it. For instance . . . remember that argument we had over my training course?'

She frowned. It was four years ago. 'Yes . . .'

'I was late home.'

'I rang the hotel and they said you'd left at two, and you came home at ten.'

'And the time I said I was at work . . .'

She stared at him. 'You said that a lot of times. Look—what has this to do with anything? It's all finished with. Don't rake it all up. For Christ's sake.'

'I was thinking about it this morning, driving down. I thought, just to make it right . . .'

An incident had already sprung to Faith's mind. A day when she'd been trying to get in touch with Guy, and rang a firm where he was supposed to be carrying out an audit, found that he had never turned up, rang his office, and discovered he had a day's leave . . . And when he had come home, he'd been furious with her. Yelling that she was checking up on him. Denying everything. Insisting that he had been working.

There had been the most terrible row over that. She recalled standing in the kitchen of their first flat, grabbing a vegetable knife in an absolute paroxysm of exasperation and frustration, waving it in front of his face. She recalled her hands grabbing at his sleeve as he turned away, and her fingers skittering along the seam of the material, and the crooked smile of triumph he had given her as he walked up the stairs to the bedroom.

'I was right,' she said. 'Wasn't I?'

Guy picked up her gloved hand and held it between his two. 'That's what I mean about now,' he said. 'Now that we've split, we can be honest. Set the record straight. I never meant to lie to you, Faith. I hated lying to you. Got myself into a corner and tried to bluff my way out of it. I can apologise now, now there's nothing at stake . . . I can tell you things . . .'

'To salve your conscience.'

'No, just make things . . . just *straight* . . . between us.'

She had a feeling that Guy's honesty was going to make her sicker than she had ever felt before. 'I knew I was right,' she whispered. 'I knew there was someone.'

He shrugged. A little heartless shrug. 'She wasn't important.'

'I *knew* I was right.'

'It was *nothing*.'

'Who was it?' Her voice was now level, and as icy as the wind that sliced across them.

'It doesn't matter.'

'Yes, it does. Who?'

'It was Jennifer Bailey.'

In the silence, she stared at him. Jennifer Bailey had been so friendly towards her. At those Friday night drinks at the pub, Jennifer Bailey used to be the first to come across. Jennifer Bailey, with that pinched up, wizened little pixie face, those thin pencilled eyebrows. Jennifer Bailey was a braying bore; worse still, she was an ambitious, greedy, braying bore. Jennifer Bailey drank Bacardi, in those dim, loud Friday evenings. Bacardi and Coke, leaning over the bar, insisting on real Coke, the real bottle, demanding to see that she wasn't given a mixer from a pump . . . boring, boring, boring Jennifer Bailey, who thought it hysterically funny to flash her stockings when she'd had three or four of those drinks . . .

'Oh, God . . .' *Jennifer Sodding Bailey. It couldn't even be someone nice.* And the lunatic irrationality of this thought forced a wry smile out of her. He misinterpreted it as approval to go on.

'Look, and in Liverpool—'

'Guy. Enough.'

'In Liverpool—'

'The girl in the computer room.'

His eyes widened in genuine surprise. 'You knew about her?'

Faith's heart seemed to be beating heavily in her throat. 'We went to a dance, a Christmas dance. She was sitting at the next table.'

'I never said a word to her. I never even looked at her!'

Oh God, Guy. You are such a child. 'No . . . you looked away.'

The humiliation of that glance was fresh. Faith had sat down, just out of reach and earshot of Guy, and had seen how deliberately he gazed everywhere but at the next table. And there she sat: the tall brunette with those knowing, reptilian eyes. Thin and glamorous. Long curly hair. Long nails. She kept pulling her skirt back down across her knees. And that glance, that look, that smile she directed at Faith had been full of *pity* . . .

'Good God. You've got some memory,' he said now.

Faith's hand was still encased in Guy's grasp. She was glad she couldn't feel his skin against hers. She had a memory, she wanted to say, because it had hurt. He would have a *memory* too, if he had felt anything like the same sinking grief.

'Well,' she said, at last. 'Isn't it nice we can be so honest now?'

The sarcasm was utterly lost on him. He put his arm around her shoulders. She stepped sideways, letting his arm fall. For a second, she was able to look at him totally objectively, seeing the beginnings of the extra fold of flesh under his chin, the redness of his face. Chloe must be feeding him well. Heart-attack food. Lots to drink. He needed a haircut . . .

She imagined him, in the throes of a coronary, maybe fifteen, maybe twenty years from now, this self-indulgent man. The thought of him tearing at his neck for air, clutching at his chest to press away the pain, gave her a small but acute sense of pleasure.

She closed her eyes.

What you make me think . . .

'Faith?' He was looking at her, half-smiling. 'I could always talk to you. That's all I wanted back. I can't do without that.'

'Talk to Chloe.'

'I can't.'

'Well . . . that's your problem, chum,' she said, and began to walk on. He followed her.

'Faith . . . Faith!'

She stopped. 'You know your trouble? You really are a complete *shit.*'

He started to laugh. 'You've told me that a hundred times.'

She punched him in the chest, so that he stepped backwards with a look of wounded surprise.

'A *shit,*' she repeated. 'I could tell you a thousand times. Chloe will probably tell you a thousand times, and you will just bloody well go on, laughing at us, and not realising how low, how crass, how *stupid* that makes you.' She stood looking at him furiously. 'You've got something missing, you know?' she said. 'Some component. Some *essential part.* You think you haven't done any *real, serious* damage. You think, when it's all said and done, it can be wiped clean, like a blackboard. Faith will stand up again, grinning like a monkey, *just like you do . . .'*

He started making his face, his *Oh dear, is it that time of the month?* face.

'Look at you,' she said softly. 'You sick, stupid, witless apology for a man.'

She turned, and began stamping back to the car, head down. For a moment, he watched her go, smiling vaguely to himself. Then he walked after her. He caught her up after a few seconds, pulled on her arm until she faced him.

'You're right,' he said.

She said nothing.

'No, no, you're really right. I wasted us.' He looked at her with his innocent-seeming smile, the one that was so honest, so disarming, the one that melted opposition. Hard to believe life with him was so bad. And *that* was what the look was saying . . .

Am I really so bad?

'I'm just thinking about the future,' he continued. 'I want us all to be friends.'

Faith started to laugh. 'Oh yes? I wonder what Chloe thinks. Have you run this past her at all? The poor cow.'

He shook his head disapprovingly. 'No, no . . .' he told her. 'But it doesn't *have* to be World War Three, does it? Can't we find a way, call a peace? I mean, when Chloe and I start a family, I still want to know you, have us meet, all together. It could be nice, d'you see? I don't want to have this great shadow in the back of me, the big mistake . . . I want us all to be friends, everything out in the open . . . what're you looking at me like that for?'

'Is Chloe pregnant?'

'No.'

'But you're trying?'

'It's just that we both want children, and if—'

'You want children?' she echoed, amazed. 'She might *be* pregnant, then. Now. This minute. Theoretically.'

'It's possible, I suppose. But it'd be a shock.'

She smiled wanly. 'Yes, it would be,' she said. 'I didn't think you ever wanted a family.'

He grinned, shrugging his shoulders. 'Neither did I. But it's growing on me.'

'With Chloe.'

'Yes . . . what is it?'

'Nothing. Nothing at all.'

He lifted her chin with his hand. 'You don't mind, surely?'

'What if I did?' she said.

'But Faith . . .' He saw her stricken expression, and, not understanding it, tried unsuccessfully to hug her. She stiffened in his arms while he spoke over her shoulder. 'I mean, it was never seriously an issue with us, was it?' he said, almost dreamily.

Faith broke out of his embrace. 'Wasn't it?' she asked. To his amazement, he saw that her eyes were full of tears.

'Fay, what *is* the matter?' he repeated.

'Forget it. Nothing.'

He stood, perplexed, as the wind drew long strands of hair around her face. She looked utterly miserable.

'I don't know what I've done,' he said. 'I just wanted to make every-thing right.'

She laughed, wiped her nose on the back of her glove, and then fumbled about in her pocket for a tissue.

'Oh God, you bloody fool,' she said.

'Me? You mean *me*?'

'Is there anyone else about?'

'Why? I thought you'd be happy now.'

She pressed the tissue momentarily to her eyes, sighed, drew an arc in the soft sand with the edge of her shoe.

'I would be,' she said. 'If I weren't pregnant myself.'

They went for a meal in one of the seafront hotels. Guy had barely said half a dozen words after her revelation, and he sat now, his back to the large plate-glass window that faced the sea, staring aimlessly down at his place setting, a glass of Scotch in one hand. He had ordered steak for them both, without asking her what she wanted. She hadn't strength enough to argue. It didn't seem to matter. She felt empty and drained and curiously weightless, as though she didn't quite belong to the world. She watched him fiddling with the cuffs of his shirt, frown-ing. He looked about for a clock.

'Where is your watch?' she asked.

'I forgot it.'

She considered him, while his gaze flickered down again at his empty wrist, and over the place settings and the other tables. Any-where but at her.

Just as she saw the waiter coming with the food, he blurted out, 'What are you going to do?'

'Nothing,' she said.

The trolley was rolled to their side; they sat in silence while the meat, the vegetables, the potatoes, were served. Guy had ordered a bottle of Burgundy; their glasses were filled.

'Another wake,' said Faith.

'What?'

'A wake,' she repeated. 'You said our meeting before the solicitor's was a wake, a burial. But this feels worse.'

'Yes,' he said.

'Are you going to eat any of this?'

'Yes,' he said.

And he did. She watched him devour the lot, systematically, while she toyed with most of hers. The morning sickness had receded, leaving her feeling as if she were on the top deck of some luxury liner, the motions transmitting themselves to her only faintly. Guy said nothing else. He chewed his food slowly, making a visible effort to swallow, to digest it, never once looking up at her. In fact, she thought, he hadn't looked at her directly at all since she had told him about the baby.

He finished. The plates were taken away. He drank the second glass of wine in one go, and poured a third. She put her hand over the top of her own glass when he held the bottle over it. He looked at that hand steadfastly, obviously registering why it was there.

At last, after dessert, he spoke.

'You must get an abortion,' he said.

There was a long silence. After looking intently at every contour on his closed, sulky face, she said, 'Why? Why must I?'

'Because it's the only sensible thing to do.'

'I see.'

'I hope you do. You can't bring a child up alone, in that horrible house. A child needs a father.'

'It has one.'

'I mean a father who's going to be there.'

'Ah . . .' She took up a teaspoon and began tracing the pattern on the tablecloth.

'Well?' he asked.

'I'm thinking.'

'About what?'

'About you.'

He leaned forward. 'I'll find out the best place. The absolute best.'

She said nothing.

'You'll thank me for it in a year's time,' he said. 'You're not motherly at all, Faith. If I had to name one woman in the world who was totally unsuited to motherhood, you'd be it.'

'But Chloe *is*?'

'If you want the truth, yes.'

'Pity no one told my body that.'

'Stop joking.'

She glanced at him. 'It's no joke.'

'You . . . you're just not a mother, that's all. Not made for it. And what about your work?'

'I know,' she replied.

'Well, there you are then. There you are.'

'Yes . . . here I am.'

The coffee came. Guy, looking more relaxed now, ordered a brandy. He evidently thought some sort of agreement had been reached. A minute passed; and, as if to mark it, a clock in the foyer chimed.

'We thought we might go away in the New Year,' Guy said, suddenly. His tone was cheery. 'We thought about skiing. In Switzerland.'

She looked at him.

'Yes, Chloe's parents know this place where they always go. Sounds quite nice. My skiing's rusty, though. I booked some dry-slope sessions . . .'

Faith looked out of the window. Seagulls were wheeling about in the wind. Across the dining room, only one other couple sat, deep in conversation, laughing occasionally, reaching out across the table to hold each other's hands.

The bill came. Guy paid it.

He helped her into her coat, and they walked out into the biting air. The sun was slanting almost horizontally across the bay, casting a brilliant theatrical blue and gold light, picking out colours, giving the outlines of buildings and of land and the edge of the sea an effect almost like a hologram. Faith felt that she could reach out and pick up the far headland, glowing in sandy contrast to the water.

'I'll run you back,' Guy said. 'And look—I'll get the name of someone, ring you up tomorrow, get this all fixed. There's no need to mention it all to Chloe, is there? I mean, it must be just that one time, and that was all a big mistake,' he said.

She put her hands into her coat pockets. 'Thank you for lunch,' she said.

'It's nothing. No trouble.'

'But when we get back, I don't want you to come in the house,' she continued, cutting over the last word of his sentence. 'I don't want you to phone me in the morning, either. I don't want you *ever* to phone me, do you understand? There isn't any need. Because I'm having this baby.'

She stepped down, reached the pavement, and looked back at him. He was staring at her, stunned.

'In fact,' she said, 'after today, I'd be grateful if you got this one fact into your head. Try to remember it, Guy, will you? *Remember*: after today, I *never* want to see you again.'

FOURTEEN

THERE WERE NOT MANY PEOPLE AT THE FUNERAL.

On one side sat the Joscelyne family: Thomas, Ruth, Randolph and Cecily. On the other, a few of Anna's colleagues and students.

Joz stole a look at Anna's friends: frowsy, colourless types, she thought. Earnest and dull. In the last row before the door sat four girls from one of her classes, four Identikit souls with hair plaited or pony-tailed back, pale skins, nervous hands. Anna clones. Joz looked back, into her own lap, resisting a smile.

How different to *them*. That proved it. Anna had never, could never have been one of *them*, one of this family. She considered their quartet with something approaching pride: even Mother had managed to do it right today. She looked chic in charcoal grey, with a severely tailored jacket and pencil skirt, and a matching grey coat, grey gloves and shoes. The colour deepened the slightly Latin look of her face. And Randolph, beautiful and still in a dark suit, his hair swept back, an expression of solemnity on his face. Utterly right. They *breathed* superiority.

Thomas had chosen 'All Things Bright And Beautiful' as a hymn; Joz stood to sing. How funny . . . what a choice. Perhaps he'd done it to show up what a childish farce the whole marriage had been. After all, he *couldn't* be serious, picking this child's hymn for his wife, a woman who had been sixty since the day she was *born*.

Joz glanced to her left. Thomas was standing next to the aisle. Then came mother, Randolph, and her. She could only see Thomas's sleeve. He had a herringbone-pattern coat in grey and black. She longed to reach forward, that denied hand's breadth, and touch the grey coat and the white cuff beneath it.

You're rid of her now.

She's gone.

Isn't that much *better?*

She saw Ruth's hand take Thomas's and squeeze it tight.

Small fingers.

Small fingers clasped in Thomas's hand. Small hand scraping against brick, and an upturned face. And the trees beyond the window . . .

'Cecily . . . are you feeling comfortable?'

She had said nothing.

The room had been very spare, and had that horrible hospital smell. Why was it that, even in the most expensive private clinics, that tart caustic smell still seeped in, still swam up from the upholstery, still tainted the teacup just before you drank?

There was an aluminium window opposite. Through it, she could see three tall ash trees. She fixed on them so hard every day that she could probably have drawn each branch, each twig, each leaf from memory. Just the very idea of trees, now . . . lately . . . makes her sweat. Gives her a feeling of slowly drowning, of being submerged. Silenced.

'Cecily . . . are you comfortable?'

'Yes.'

The therapist had an irritating voice. At least, that's what she had thought when he first started. He pitched up at the end of sentences, as if he were asking a question. He finished on a small squeak. He wore a suit. No white coat. That had surprised her.

'Cecily . . . I want you to imagine you are on a journey. I want you to imagine you are stepping down a flight of stairs in a house. A big, comfortable, pleasant house that holds no fears for you. The stairs are wide and easy and sweeping, and they lead towards some doors that go into a garden. There are ten steps. With every step you will become more relaxed. You are on the first step . . .'

No, I'm not!

Who are you, anyway? You're not a proper doctor.

'You are on the second step. With every step you are becoming more relaxed, happier, sleepier. You will hear my voice, follow my voice as you become more relaxed still. You are on the fourth step . . .'

You stupid man.

'The fifth, the sixth . . .'

I'm still on this chair. I'm still here.

'The seventh, eighth, ninth . . .'

She gripped the arm of the chair, feeling its woodenness, feeling with her other hand the blanket that had been stretched over her knees. She was not asleep. She was still here.

'Ten. And you're stepping forward, through the doors to the garden . . . Cecily, you are fourteen now, but I'm going to take you back in time as you walk down this garden. You are twelve years old now, you are ten years old now. You are much smaller now, you are nine. You are a little girl now, you are eight years old now . . .'

It was Bellisande in summer. The summer that Randolph had rented Bellisande while the Chichester season was on. She was seven . . . eight. She played in the maze behind the yew hedges. She went to the greenhouses with a boy who belonged to the gardener, and they trapped lizards in the sandy grit of the benches.

They trapped frogs in the Shasta daisies, up against the fence, where there was nowhere for them to go. She could see them panting in the shadow and they built a line of bricks to trap them properly.

'You can kill 'em, with stones,' said the boy.

Thomas had come home from boarding school for the weekend. He sat at her side on the warm soil, in the evening, staring with her at the two frogs, at their speckled skin.

'You shouldn't do that,' said Thomas.

She curled her hand round his wrist. It was damp.

'Let's see if they jump,' she said.

She picked up a stick, and prodded the nearest. It did nothing for a second or two, then leapt at the line of bricks and struggled for purchase. It fell back, its sides heaving. She pushed the tip of the stick under until she lifted its back legs off the ground.

The boy got up, came back with a stone. A flint, with murderous, sharp sides. 'Look,' he said.

He stood up and aimed the stone at the frog, and it hit it foursquare. There was a sound like an old balloon being punctured: a sigh, a sense of defeat. The frog wriggled desperately, and Thomas jumped backwards, too, a guttural sound of disgust in his throat. She held on to him, though, with her spare hand. His wrist slipped in her grasp. She fastened her fingers tighter.

She helped to kill both the frogs, with stones.

The most disappointing thing was that they didn't make a noise. No pop, no bangs. They just died. And after a while they weren't frogs any more but grey, thin sacks on the soil. There were no explosions, no dramas. There was no cramp in her chest, no guilt, no God's hand on her shoulder. No question. One moment they were there, and the next they were not. They had gone. They were just fragments on the ground.

It was all over so quickly.

Randolph was proved right. Things died in silent, unsurprising ways. No God came down to save them. He did not exist.

Not as exciting as she'd hoped.

Thomas walked away and went and stood by the yews, kicking a clod of earth with one shoe, his hands in his pockets. 'You're getting like him,' he said.

She put one hand, trembling, on his back. 'No, I'm not,' she told him. 'I'm like you. We're just the same.'

Thomas turned to look at her. 'Why'd you let him?' he asked.

'Let him—'

'Let him talk to you, on and on. He wouldn't talk to *me* like that. I'd punch him.' And he raised two small, white fists.

She smiled, and he blushed furiously, advancing on her with all the authority of his twelve years.

'I saw you, carrying his shoes.'

'He tells me. I clean them.'

'Other people do that. They pay other people.'

Tears had begun to form, catching in her throat. 'He says I do it best. If I don't do it . . . I don't like him shouting . . .'

Frustration creased Thomas's face. 'It's not right.'

'Mother says it is.'

'She . . . ?' Words failed him. He began walking, very quickly. She followed him back to the house, the house where the windows were open, and they could hear Mother playing. Randolph stood at the window sill, leaning on it, his hand outside the room, touching the bushes whose leaves lay sleepily on the wide stone sill. He was holding a brandy glass.

She put her arms round Thomas's waist from behind. They were at the edge of the lawn.

'Thomas, come back,' she said. She blew on his neck, and he twitched, although he didn't disengage her.

'Come on,' she whispered. 'I'll show you it's still the same. They don't matter. *He* doesn't. I'll show you where the island is.'

He allowed himself to be taken, down through the yews, into the dense cover of the rhododendrons, where she had dug a shallow bowl in the sandy ground, and filled it with grass clippings. She crawled down into it, looking up at him. The very last sunlight pierced the cover of the trees, touching his shoulders, the side of his face. Two bright spots of colour marked each cheek beneath the eye; he bit on his lip until his mouth almost disappeared in a taut line.

She was eight, and he was twelve.

She wriggled in the sweet grass.

'Look . . .' she said.

And, afterwards, she ran across the lawn, and it was getting dark, and Randolph reached down over the sill and picked her up, exclaiming at the sight of her, all green-marked on her dress, clippings in her hair, and lifted her up through the window, like God lifting an angel up through clouds, and he let her stay up, long after Thomas had come in and gone sulking up to bed, refusing to sit with them, and she curled in the corner of the settee, eating chocolate, and dipping her finger in Randolph's brandy, smearing the glass . . .

'Coming back down the garden now . . .'

No.

'Coming back to the door of the house, Cecily . . .'

No.

Here is another day.

There are so many, *so many*, like it . . .

She is standing in her bedroom. She is eight, she is ten, she is eleven, twelve. Randolph, sitting in a chair, is talking. He always comes to her room to talk. Nothing more. And yet it is indescribable purgatory. She dreads it from the second she wakes. She is so frightened of him, of his threats and stories. One of his favourite things is to make her learn parts from plays. She has to recite them, word for perfect word, while he beats the rhythm on the arm of the chair. One spring, he makes her learn Spenser's *The Bower of Bliss*. She doesn't understand it—she is nine—and yet she repeats it . . .

> With a new lover, whom through sorceree
> And witchcraft she from farre did thither bring . . .

His gaze would become fixed, his breath ragged. She hates it when she hears that altered cadence, and, forbidden to look away, tries to let her gaze blur, as if there is something prettier to see if she concentrates *through* him. Sometimes he would leap up and leave the room, crashing the door open and leaving it propped ajar, and, for some unfathomable reason she could not grasp, he would stand down the corridor of the large house, two floors above the white and light reception rooms, in the darkness. His voice would filter along the shadows. 'Carry on! Carry on . . .'

> Quite molten into lust and pleasure lewd . . .

One day, at school, she summons enough courage to tell her form mistress that her father comes to talk to her every night.

But the woman misunderstands. She is preoccupied with packing her briefcase, and does not look up. She says, 'How nice.' Joz stands before the scarred wooden desk and longs to reach across it, and beg to be allowed to stay in the school. To sleep in the school, and never go home.

Randolph also comes to tell her secrets. Adult secrets that she does not want to hear. Her mother's failings, for instance. He says, with curdled fury in his tone, that her mother is too demanding; that she is greedy; that she cannot be satisfied. And Joz is confused and worried and misunderstands; after all, the mother she sees—now ever more distant, her protective arms and the cuddle at night now just a memory—is weak and silent. Joz wonders, helplessly, what it is that her mother needs from her step-father and is denied.

Still . . . Randolph's opinions of others are always savage: he is not the smiling giant of the day. Clients' and rivals' weaknesses and faults come rolling out. And he tells her unpleasant jokes. And from him, she learns the facts of life. Afterwards, she is physically ill.

His voice changes at night. It becomes low, rapid, seething, conspiring. She realises, dimly, far down inside, that he is a very sick man. But by the time she knows that, he has already infected her. She will never scrub his pictures from her mind. Worse, they have become part of her.

She wants a Daddy.

Just a Daddy.

But she has *him*.

'Travelling back up the steps, and with every step you will become more aware of where you are, and my voice, and the room you are sitting in, and you will awake perfectly relaxed and calm, and all the bad memories will fade . . .'

She didn't want to come back to the wood arm of the chair, and the blanket, and the window and the ash trees that waved and waved.

But they're not bad memories with Thomas.

They're nice.

Somebody really liked me.

He might be cold. The coldest man in the world. Now. But he liked her, once. He loved her. And she must get that back.

She wanted to stay . . .

'Count to three, and you will wake.'

I will not.

'One . . . two . . .'

Leave me alone.

'Three.'

Grudgingly, she opened her eyes, and stared at him. Rain had begun to pitter against the ash tree windows. The doctor neither smiled nor frowned. He regarded her levelly, coolly.

She stood up, and the blanket fell to the ground. All she could think of was her father's hands, prising each scrabbling fingertip away.

'I'm not sick,' she said.

'All right,' he told her.

'But don't you see? It's not *me* that's sick . . .'

The vicar was telling them about Anna, reassuring them, in the hushed tones of someone who fears he might be found out by his betters, that Anna's death did not mean she would not be admitted to the sight of God. *To the sight of God.*

Joz looked up, to where a solitary rectangle of sun rested across the ceiling and part of the flower display next to the coffin. Winter sun, dry colour.

But there isn't any God, she thought. That's the joke. Ask Randolph. HE knows.

And her eyes rested back on Thomas and her mother, on Thomas's hand, now clasped in her mother's lap.

Ask her, my mother.

She knows.

Anna's coffin had been tastefully decorated with white lilies. The wedding flowers. It seemed incredible that Anna should be lying under them, tidied up and made up, everything that Anna had never been.

Ruth and Randolph had been to see Anna at the undertaker's, the evening before. Ruth wouldn't speak to her daughter about it at all, saying merely that Joz should have made the effort to come earlier, and not on the funeral day itself. Joz didn't tell her that the reason she couldn't come earlier was not that she hadn't set out from London in good time; on the contrary. It was that, as she drove up the M11, she kept *laughing.*

She kept on laughing as she drove round Cambridge, and eventually she had had to drive into a lay-by and pull herself together, to make sure there were no more smiles left, to arrange her face in a semblance of regret.

She found that her hands had clenched in her lap. Carefully, she extended them, her black calfskin gloves shining softly against her wool coat. She would like to get up *now*, and prise open that lid. She would like to watch as the box rolled towards the flames . . .

Thomas put his head down, resting it in one hand, leaning on the pew. The vicar—a trendy-looking chap, with spiky blond hair, whose corduroy trousers showed under the hem of his robe—was saying that Thomas and Anna had been married only a matter of days, but their relationship had been full of application and study, mutual understanding and support.

Joz pursed her lips and looked at the quarry-tiled floor in disgust. *What rubbish . . .* One of the girls at the back was weeping. Loud.

The curtains closed, and the organ huffed into life, playing *Ave Maria*. Ave Maria! Christ! It was too terrible for words.

They heard a clunk of other doors, and Thomas stiffened and looked away, into Ruth's face.

Joz leaned forward, to look at him.

There was a mole at the side of her mother's mouth.

There was a mole at the corner of Thomas's eye.

Joz's glance flickered from one to the other, absorbing the imperfections, while in her mind's eye her mother's fingers bent backwards, backwards, until the skin broke, and the bone showed through.

FIFTEEN

$\mathcal{G}$UY STOOD BEHIND CHLOE and watched her dress. She looked very pretty, pulling on the frothy pink slip.

'Can you do the hook and eye at the top?'

He did, planting a kiss on her shoulder mechanically. In response, she turned and enveloped him.

'Are you all right?'

'Me?'

She smiled. 'Yes.'

'I'm fine.'

She went to the bed and started to put on stockings. A little thrill of affection ran through him; *Faith* never wore stockings. She said they were uncomfortable. But Chloe wore them because he liked them. *That's what a woman ought to be like*, he thought.

And he sat in the chair opposite and watched, and Chloe smiled to herself as he watched, and arched her foot, and played up to him.

After a while, he felt rather sick.

He went to the window and looked out, at the London square with its dusty cars, an overcast sky and litter blowing in the road.

Don't ever ... ever ... come near me again.

'You don't want to go, do you?' Chloe said. 'That's what it is.'

He turned to look at her. She was swinging one shoe in her hand.

'Of course I do.'

'No, you don't. You've got that look. Why is it that whenever it's *my* work you don't want to go? We went to that terrible thing at *yours* last week. Why don't you want to come tonight? It's *ever* so unfair of you.'

And, without waiting for an answer, she started to pick up his work clothes, lying where he had dropped them an hour ago.

'I do want to come.'

'No . .'

'Oh, for Christ's sake. We're ready and we're going. OK?' He spread his arms. 'I've been ready here for twenty minutes.'

She stuffed his shirt and socks into the laundry basket. 'You've been funny all week,' she muttered.

He looked for his keys on the dressing table.

She advanced on him.

'All week,' she repeated.

'Give it a rest, sweetheart.'

'What is it?'

'Nothing.'

She caught his lapel. 'Come on, tell me.'

He stopped, and considered her. She was very young, eleven years his junior. Very rich and very pretty. He had read in the paper that the *gels* of London society were much prettier than they had been forty years ago, because the upper classes married their secretaries now, and the inbreeding was dying out. So the children were all glamorous, with the aristocratic high foreheads and aquiline noses of their fathers, and the egalitarian beauty of their mothers. He had smiled at that, and had looked over the top of his paper at Chloe at the breakfast table.

Blonde and smooth, with a pertly childish mouth and a slightly long face, and wide-apart eyes, she had looked back at him. Their children would be very beautiful, he thought. He had imagined a line of two sons and two daughters, two dark and two fair. It was all very picture-book and clean, with doting in-laws in the background. They fanned out in his mind like a double-page spread in the *Tatler*.

And then Faith had walked into the fantasy. Straight across the tightly clipped lawns of the *Tatler* picture, kicking the photographer out of the way, towing a dark-haired child.

'What *is* it?' Chloe asked now. She slipped her arms around his waist, under his jacket. 'You can tell me.'

He sat down. She knelt at his feet, and began twisting one shoelace lazily around her index finger, and pretending to tickle his ankle.

'Faith is pregnant,' he said.

It was interesting to see how quickly every single bit of colour drained out of her face.

'What?'

'Faith is two months' pregnant.'

'By who?'

'By me.'

He saw her do the calculation in her head.

'She's going to keep it,' he added.

Chloe said nothing for a while. Disbelief rapidly chased over her face, then pain. 'It's yours,' she said. It wasn't a question, but a statement.

The lace was by now firmly knotted around her finger; he reached down and disentangled it, and tried lifting her from the floor so that she could sit next to him. She responded about as much as a stuffed doll.

'Chloe—darling. Listen to me. Please.' He lifted her hair back and stroked it on to her shoulder. 'It was a terrible mistake,' he said. 'Just the one time, a mistake. Just *once*. I've never seen her since. I'll never see her again.'

She wasn't looking at him, but at the door across the room.

'It wasn't planned,' he went on. 'There's been nothing going on behind your back. You believe me, don't you? I wouldn't do that to you. It was a one-off thing, one night . . .'

She stood up, walked a couple of paces. Spoke with her back to him.

'We had already moved in here two months ago,' she said. 'We were choosing the sofas. We were choosing the curtains for downstairs. We were going up to Angela's after work and looking at samples.'

'I know. I *know*. I'm really sorry.'

She turned to look at him. 'Why can't she have an abortion?'

'She won't.'

'Why not?'

'She just won't.'

'You've discussed it?'

'I wouldn't call it a discussion.'

'You've met her?'

'No. She phoned.' *God preserve me in this lie,* he thought.

Chloe's mouth trembled. She was trying to absorb what was, to her, the greatest bolt ever to fall out of her bright blue sky. Her lip wobbled like a child's. 'She's going to spoil everything,' she murmured.

Hope flared in Guy for a second. She was blaming Faith. That was good. But his hope only lasted a moment. Chloe suddenly ran at him, and slapped him. It took him utterly by surprise, and was so ineffectual that he began to laugh.

'While we were *here!*' she shouted.

He tried to make his face contrite. 'It's a mess,' he said. 'You can't know what a mess it is.'

'Oh, can't I? Oh, can't I?' she demanded. All the nice pink ruffles down the neck of her frock fluttered. 'You'll want to see it, won't you? You'll want to have it here.'

'No.'

'Yes! You will.'

He stared at her.

Yes . . . he would.

His son or daughter.

Chloe began to cry. 'Oh, you've spoiled it,' she said, and sat down in the middle of the floor. Sobs began to rack her, and she started to sway backwards and forwards.

'It was so nice,' she said. 'And now it's all *spoiled.*'

SIXTEEN

THEY WENT BACK TO THE HOUSE AFTER THE FUNERAL.
Randolph and Ruth had a première that night.

'I'll stay with you,' Ruth said, as they all cleared the last of the glasses and plates. It was a quarter to six; Randolph stood by the door, shifting from foot to foot.

Thomas shook his head. 'No, Mother.'

'I *must*.'

'No. You go back.'

Ruth stroked his face. 'Is that what you want? I shall only do what you want.'

Randolph was pulling on his gloves, stretching his fingers in them, considering the backs of his hands.

All this time, Joz had been standing at the sink, dreamily washing the cups and plates, her back to the three of them. She was thinking of how she'd taken the place of Anna here, had her hands inside Anna's worn rubber gloves, in Anna's sink, turning Anna's ancient mixer tap off and on. It gave her a little thrill of pleasure, of excitement. *She was in Anna's place*, in the very place where habitually she had stood, in the very rooms.

Anna had looked out of this window, at a beech hedge and a slice of Cambridge street, where a woman was now walking her dog in the winter twilight. Here were Anna's ornaments: a china dog with a navy blue ribbon round its neck; a blue vase; a trinket box, for putting rings in. A kirby grip was wedged between shelf and window frame. That was more pathetic, in its way, than the flower-stacked coffin of the afternoon.

'Cecily,' said her mother.

She looked over her shoulder. 'What?'

'I said, Are you coming?'

'No.'

'Thomas wants to be left alone.'

Joz glanced at her brother. He was stacking glasses in a cabinet, his face hidden from them all.

'I know.'

Ruth was drawing on her coat. 'I wish we didn't have to go,' Ruth was saying. 'I feel so dreadful about it.'

Thomas saw them out. Joz heard the fading footsteps, the click of the front-door latch. She moved away from the sink and sat at the table, so that she was relieved of waving goodbye to the Daimler as it drew away.

For some time, Thomas didn't move from the hallway. Joz heard him open a couple of letters, and then throw them down on the hall table. She listened, and then, seeing that he was not about to come in to her, she got up, and went out.

He was by the pegs for the coats, taking off Anna's things, looping them over his arm, in extreme slow motion.

It was almost dark; the hall was lit by the streetlamps outside. Thomas looked as though he were standing in an orange pool of light, his body outlined in the same strange and luminous shade. The house was silent.

'Oh, Thomas,' she said.

She walked up to him, and put her arms around him. His body was spare, and straight, and hard. She rested her head in the crook of his shoulder, stroking his back rhythmically from centre to waist.

He said nothing.

'You don't need to worry now,' she whispered. 'It'll all be fine now. I can make you a meal. I can make up a fire.' She stood slightly away from him, raised her head, tried to see into his eyes though his face was all shadow. 'Do you remember,' she asked, 'when we used to make cocoa, in the kitchen?'

He said nothing.

She put her head back into the comfortable, almost forgotten hollow beneath his neck, sighing at its long-abandoned familiarity.

She took his hand, and led him into the sitting room, where she sat him on the couch facing the empty fireplace. Someone had already laid a fire: kindling, paper and coal. She put a match to it, and it took immediately, spurting yellow flames high into the chimney. She sat down at Thomas's feet, and carefully unlaced his shoes—so tight, double-knotted—then went and found his slippers, and eased them on. All the time he let himself be lifted and placed; he sat with his hands clasped, staring at the flames.

'We can just be cosy,' Joz told him. 'D'you remember how Mother would never let us sit by the fires? We had that electric one upstairs; it wasn't the same. Just the fires at Christmas . . . that was the only time.'

She looked up at him. 'Just you and me. You wouldn't have to do anything, Tom. I'd get everything in. I'll look after you.'

He shook his head, and then closed his eyes, resting his elbow on the arm of the couch and propping his head on his hand. 'Cecily,' he said. It was hard to distinguish what he meant: whether the *Cecily* was a breath of endearment, or objection, or weariness.

Joz edged closer to him. 'Remember how it used to be when Mother had her Christmas party coming up?' she said softly. 'Remember how we used to say, at Christmas, that we wished all the other people would just go away, and that we had a quiet house, where the phone didn't ring, and no one knocked, and the hall wasn't like Charing Cross Station?' She laughed, but Thomas didn't respond.

'There won't be any fuss this time,' she continued. 'When Christmas comes, we won't even go to church; we won't go anywhere. We'll stay in.' And she laid her hand, softly, on his knee.

Thomas shifted slightly.

At once, she pulled the cushions from the neighbouring chairs and propped them in a pile close to his resting elbow. Gently she pressed on his shoulder, until he fell sideways, his head on the pile, his legs tucked under him, his arms crossed. He was not asleep, though; when she moved his arms and hands, she felt the rigidity still in them, and his breathing was still fast. She stroked his face. 'Would you like a rug?' she asked.

He said nothing.

She looked at the fire.

Christmas . . . other Novembers and Decembers. They had a Victorian evening one year, Randolph joking in a maroon frock coat with a silver waistcoat and bow tie. A Santa Claus at the door on the way out, giving little red-satin-bow tied parcels to departing guests; professional singers at the piano in the drawing room. Handbell ringers, a string quartet, games of charades, a giant spruce festooned with silver and maroon.

Thomas had been dressed in a suit to match his stepfather, with a wing collar and a maroon silk stock. Mother had looked breathtaking in a maroon and blue chiffon dress, with a cartwheel hat on her head. Not especially Victorian, but stunning nevertheless. She still fluttered under that hat, in that dress, unsure of herself under Randolph's periodic gaze. Joz wore a maroon and silver dress with a hooped underskirt that forced her to stand all night, and a white-lined, lace-trimmed mob-cap from which her setting-lotioned ringlets hung down like shiny blonde sausages. She had felt enormous: like a bag of bread dough expanding inside a warm plastic bag.

Randolph would whisper to her every time he passed: sometimes praise; sometimes to tell her what she was doing wrong.

She must have been thirteen that Christmas. Sometimes, looking back, she was convinced that thirteen was the worst of all.

Mother seemed to dislike her more as her body took shape. She seemed deeply embarrassed by her own daughter's growth. She refused to believe that Joz needed a bra until the girls at school told their own mothers that Joz shamed them in games lessons. Joz was dragged to a lingerie shop—Mother wouldn't allow her to buy something anonymously from M&S.

'She's nagging me for a brassière,' her mother announced, the moment they were over the threshold. She began to laugh breathily. 'She doesn't need it, but you know what these girls are like . . .'

In a curtained cubicle, Joz was measured. It was terrible. Like being examined by a doctor for some unmentionable disease. She turned her face away as the woman came close, passing the measure under her armpits.

'She does, you know,' the stranger said. 'She's a 34A already.'

Joz's mother had pulled a face. 'I can't believe there's anything made to fit her,' she said.

'Oh, there's lots,' the woman responded, grinning at Joz, up close.

God, the humiliation.

It was a time of arguments. Adolescent-and-mother arguments were normal enough; but these were not *normal* disagreements. They were battles, fights. Her mother had once taken a walking stick of Randolph's to Joz's back, beating her into a corner of the beautiful arching hall. It had been because Joz did not want to go out to a birthday party.

As she beat her, Ruth wept: little choking, dog-like sounds. Joz did not retaliate. She curled into a ball on the floor, and hoped the blows would stop. Fury turned inwards and burned right down, through every muscle and nerve. Somewhere on the stairs, an *outside* Joz lingered, smiling quizzically at the lump in the corner, the frail demon above it with the stick. The shadow on the stairs wondered why the girl didn't get up and grab the stick and beat the living daylights out of the woman. She *could*, if she wanted. Perhaps she was saving it. Saving it all up, the days, the evenings, the afternoons, the words, the looks; saving them, boiling them down inside her into that unforgiving rock she carried welded into her gut. Storing, saving . . .

'You bring out the worst in me,' Ruth had once admitted. 'No one knows how I have to suffer your silence in this house . . .'

Ruth wanted a daughter who talked. She wanted a bright, chatty girl; a *thin*, clever, bright, chatty girl. A girl who wanted to ski and dance and ride. A girl with energy.

But I don't talk.

You must know that.

I . . . listen.

'Oh, she's so . . . *winsome*,' Ruth had once said, to Joz, about one of her friend's daughters. 'You never hear that word any more. Do you know what it means, Cecily? *Winsome*. So clever and entertaining about people, such a chatterbox . . .'

Joz would sit and stare at the teacups, a feeling of bile in her throat. She wanted to leap up and scream. 'Why don't you beat *him*? Why don't you stop *him*? It isn't my fault he talks to me. I don't want him to talk to me! Why don't you *leave* him?'

But she never did.

She wanted to know why all the fury that her mother bottled up came surging out whenever they were alone.

Why doesn't he talk to you?

Why won't you let him?

I wish he would.

Why doesn't he sleep with you?

What is the matter with you both?

Thomas . . . Thomas understood. Thomas could withdraw inside himself too. So far inside that it sometimes became hard to reach him.

'Thomas,' she said now. He had done that since ten, twelve.

Made himself stone whenever he came home. Locked the door of his room.

She looked back at him. He was not asleep: he was looking up at the ceiling, having turned on to his back. She suddenly felt desperately sorry for them both, cold behind their private barricades, where they had retreated, each, from Randolph.

'Thomas,' she repeated. 'Christmas . . . What shall we do, at Christmas?'

She leaned forward and kissed his face gently. His skin felt ragged under her lips—torn, almost. She regarded his face with her head on one side, smoothing the lines under his eyes with her fingers. He submitted to it all without a flicker of response.

'We'll be together, anyway. That's all that matters, Tom.'

He looked directly at her, then sat up. He gave a great sigh. Shadows played over his face.

'Sit up here, next to me,' he said. 'Off the floor.'

She did as he asked, smiling.

'Cecily . . .' he said. 'When did you last see Lewis Brown?'

She reacted as though she had been stung. 'Brown?' she echoed. '*Brown?*'

'You heard me well enough. When did you last see him?'

She felt her stomach tighten, her throat begin to close. 'Not in ages. Why should I?'

'What did he say to you—how did you leave it at your last appointment?'

She tried to reach for his hand. 'Thomas, Thomas, Tom—'

'You're not talking to Randolph now. When did you last see Lewis Brown?'

'But why *should* I see him? I don't want to see him. I don't *need* to see him!'

'How *long!*'

She made a face, and looked at her feet. 'About twoish. Two-ish, three-ish.'

'Months?'

She shook her head and laughed. 'Don't be silly, Tom,' she said, at last. 'Years.'

Horror registered on his face. 'Christ,' he muttered. There was a long silence, in which he took three or four deep breaths, painstakingly. Then, very slowly, he said, 'You told mother you were.'

'*Mother,*' Joz said, venomously. '*Her.*'

Eventually, unable to look into his desperate face any longer, she sprang up and paced round the room. At the mirror, she started pulling her hair this way and that, fluffing it out, smoothing it, holding it back. She pulled it into a pony tail at the back of her head and stared at the resulting reflection, the skin pulled tight.

'Cecily,' said Thomas.

'No.'

'Cecily . . .'

She let the hair go, and ran across to him, throwing herself into his reluctant arms. He slipped back in the chair, thrown by sheer weight. She put her arms round his neck and held him in a vice-like grip, her head pressed to that comforting depression of his shoulder. The sensation of her jaws moving against his skin as she spoke was revolting. He tried to lift his head up. She held him even tighter.

'You remember the island?' she was saying. 'The island, Tom. Remember the island. You said it had a road that we could flood to stop people coming on to it. You said it had a house on a hill, and sand all round it, and rocks, and a path that went down to a cove that only belonged to us . . .'

'Oh, Christ,' Thomas whispered.

'We made a house out of bricks and branches and stones and from the window all you could see was the ocean.'

He tried, in vain, to release the lock of her fingers behind his head.

'D'you remember, that day we made soup?' she was asking. 'Out of leaves and water and mud and flowers. Wasn't it awful? Wasn't it *dreadful*?' She was laughing now. 'Thomas . . .'

He finally succeeded in getting her hands down. He held them in front of her.

'Listen to me,' he told her. Very quietly. 'Are you listening to me, Cecily?'

'Yes,' she said. 'Of course.'

'I want you to ring Lewis. If you don't want to see him, see his partner. You've met Andrew, haven't you? I want you to ring them, in the morning. I want you to go home now and ring them *in the morning* . . .'

She gazed at him. 'But I'm not going home,' she said. 'Am I?'

'Yes, you are.'

'No. No, no, no, no . . .' She grinned at him. Thomas had a peculiar idea of jokes. This was one of them, she thought. 'No . . . Tom . . . I'm not going home, am I? I'm staying here with you. Now Anna's not here. I'm staying here with you.'

He got to his feet, lifting her. She stood in front of him, hands clasped in unconscious supplication.

'Cecily, I want to be on my own right now.'

'But . . . *why*?'

'Oh, God,' he whispered. It was a prayer.

'I don't understand!'

He seemed to try very hard to get himself under control. It unnerved her terribly. Thomas was *always* in control. Thomas always knew the right thing to do. Thomas was always calm.

He passed a hand across his forehead; held it there, pinching the bridge of his nose. 'My wife has just died,' he said.

'I *know* that.'

'Cecily, my *wife* . . .'

'But you didn't need her. You're so much better without her! I knew you would be.'

He shot her a look. His hand dropped from his face. 'What did you say?'

'Don't be angry, Tom.'

He gripped one arm, hurting her. '*What* did you say?'

'You're hurting. And I found the island.'

'What? What bloody island?'

She smiled triumphantly. 'Found it. Found the island. Found our house. Just like you always said. It really exists, Tom! A real island and a real house. I've got to get there, Tom. Really soon. It will all come right when we get there. It will, won't it? And it's got *sand round the bottom, like toes peeping out from under my skirt.*'

She delivered this last piece of information with absolute delight, a *fait accompli*, her trump card. 'Like you said!' she added, so excited now that a flush was making two perfectly round, almost scarlet, drops of colour in her face. 'Just like you always *said!*'

He stared back at her, dropped his hand. For a moment, she thought he swayed slightly.

'It was just play,' he said, very faint. 'We were just children.'

'But it's real, Tom. I found it.'

He put both hands to his face, turned his back on her, went to the fire. It was sputtering in the grate, dying for lack of attention. A blue tongue of gas wriggled in the embers.

'I love you,' she said.

He turned round.

She was in the centre of the room, holding out her arms.

'Please . . . get out,' he said.

'What . . . ?'

'Get out. Get out of my house. Go away, Cecily. I want you to go away.'

'But, Tom, it's *me.*'

He walked round the back of the couch, where Joz's coat was slung across a chair. He picked it up, and threw it at her.

'I don't want to see you again until you've been to Lewis Brown.'

The coat fell short of her. Her arms were still extended, and her mouth dropped open, shocked, as if she had been slapped. In two strides, he was next to her, picking up the coat in his fist, pushing it into her grasp. 'I want you to go home now, Cecily,' he said. 'D'you hear me? Go home.'

'I love you,' she repeated. 'We must go. We *must.* I won't . . . see these things . . . any more, if we do . . . not when we're there, will I?'

Quite suddenly, Thomas's body sagged. The weight of the day, and now this added burden, crowded on him. 'Please go away, I can't bear it,' he said.

And, hearing the abrupt crack in his voice, Joz began to weep. 'I would look after you; it would be nice; I can love you better than her . . .' she started to say.

'What? *What?*'

'Better, better. Better than Anna.'

Something terrible gripped him. It seemed to pass over his body like a giant hand squeezing and compressing him; it looked, for one awful second, as if his flesh were shrinking in on itself, off the bones, off the planes of his face.

He pushed her backwards. She stumbled, but regained her balance in time to be virtually manhandled through the door of the sitting room, out into the hall, to the front door. Thomas hauled it open, and the cold night came rushing in. He was shaking. He shoved her out on to the step, picked up her handbag from where it lay by the coatstand, and threw it out. It bounced, almost comically, on the three broad steps, and landed on the gravel path, where the catch sprang open, and credit cards and cosmetics and a hairbrush rolled out into the dirt.

He brought his face to within an inch of hers. She felt his breath on her skin.

'You—stay—you stay *away* from me,' he said. The words tumbled one over the other, the note in his voice rising almost hysterically. Joz was gazing at him, startled but not shocked; surprised, rather than hurt. At one corner of her mouth, her lips tweaked upwards in the beginning of a smile.

'If you just saw it, you would like it,' she said. 'You would love it. All of him would go away. We can get away, you see? At last. It's ours.'

Blood almost blinded him: for the first time in his life, he actually saw red. Saw it coursing down his vision, in a violent curtain.

He went back into the house, and slammed the door hard in her face.

She stood for a long time, in the dark, looking up at the knocker on the shiny black wood.

'You haven't even seen it,' she said.

She picked up her bag, forgetting the brush, which lay in the soil.

She began to walk to her car.

'If you just gave it a chance,' she said, to herself. 'You haven't even given it a chance. That's not fair. Not fair. It would all come right. Just wait. I'll prove it to you. Just wait and see.'

Her fingers fumbled for the lock. She dropped the key.

All she could see now was hands. Small hands, reaching for hers. Little hands dancing in the blackness.

And then—quite suddenly—she remembered whose they were.

SEVENTEEN

As FAITH CAME INTO THE ROOM, she turned on the radio. A Christmas advertising jingle was playing fortissimo.

'Save me,' she said, switching it off.

She walked to the easel, crossing her arms and staring critically at the drawing. She wet the edge of her thumb and began experimentally to change the first outline, already absorbed, although she had promised herself a break.

It was almost eleven in the morning now. She had been working since six.

It was not just the sickness that had awoken her so early, but some charging dream . . . *charging, leaping, racing*. Horses thundering down a racecourse, and she on their backs, blinded by sunlight, the necks of the horses straining and sweating, tendons knotting and flickering with tension in the burning light. Veiny brown shining flesh under her.

It was sexual in the extreme, and she had sat up in bed, breathing heavily. It was still dark. She had got up, sighing, rubbing her face, dragged on a thick towelling robe, and gone out into the empty house. There were no curtains at the window of the main room, and she could see a light horizon far out, over the Channel. Lights on some moving ship, two candle-like specks, wavering in the gloom.

She had got down on her hands and knees, swept out the fireplace, and made up the fire. She was getting better at it now. In two or three minutes, the flames took hold. She went to the kitchen, made toast and tea, and brought it to the hearth, eating voraciously, trying to stave off the lurching sensations that she was now *almost* getting used to.

Alex Hurley was coming today.

He was starting on the trench.

Eight o'clock.

Suddenly, the dream came back to her in every detail. The sun hot on her back, the smell of crushed grass, the heat from the horses themselves. The movement between her legs. She had only ridden once or twice, and never at speed, and yet the whole thing was utterly, breathtakingly vivid. The connection of Alex and the dream flashed on her like a neon sign lighting inside her head. Alex under her. Alex *over* her. Suddenly, from out of thin air, *there*, that sensation, summoned up by some spell, blocking out the sight of the fire and the before-dawn room. Oh, *God* . . . Alex Hurley, his thumbs working on her thighs, *her* hands guiding him quickly into her, the abrupt rocking motion as she sank on to him . . . All at once, her heart stuttered, as if slipping, and gave a double beat, knocked off its customary rhythm. She had a real, living, three-dimensional image of herself lying back on the floor, whispering, begging, and Alex taking off her clothes in frenzied haste . . .

The light came stealing into the room. She watched it picking out the outline of chair, rug, window frame. She had never thought of Alex that way. He was so different to Guy. Almost-white hair, much older, taller. *Shaped* differently. Funny, how people—the same species—could be *shaped* differently. Different hands and fingers, different shape of face, different in colouring; the bunched-up way Alex held his shoulders, and Guy drooped them down as if tired of life . . .

She stopped, in the act of gathering up the cup and the plate.

Hell. When would the connections to Guy fade? She willed them to vanish, and here they came, rolling back of their own accord. Like a fever that struck you in the centre of recovery. She covered his image with another man, and yet still he surfaced.

You'll never get over me.

She shook her head. 'Yes, I will,' she whispered. 'Watch me. I *will*.'

She looked at the reflection of herself, caught in the window of the room. She saw that she was slightly heavier, slightly thicker around the shoulders and waist. *Flesh under her.* It wouldn't go away, that erotic connection that had come out of *nowhere.* Guy . . . Alex. Alex . . . Guy. She tried forcibly to superimpose the dream Alex on the image of Guy, smiling, in her head. Now Alex was there indelibly, his hands slipping down her skin . . .

'Oh Lordy,' she said to herself, walking quickly to the kitchen, and clattering the plate and cup into the kitchen sink. 'Hormones, hormones. Yes, siree.'

She smiled to herself, as she walked to the bathroom and turned on the shower.

There was a knock at the door.

She turned now, drawn back to the present, wiping her hands. Alex was at the door. She hadn't even registered that the excavator's industrious noise had stopped.

She went and opened it.

'Come and look,' he said.

She squinted at the brightness of the day as she followed him out. He walked down the drive, and stopped, where the excavator hung poised on the edge of the three-foot-wide scar in the soil. Three foot wide, three foot deep. At the bottom of the trench the rock was blindingly white, like new snow packed tight. But there was at least two feet of ordinary soil above it, greyish and fine.

He caught her elbow as she edged to look down. 'Careful,' he said. And pointed into the earth.

Her hand flew to her mouth in shock; then, narrowing her eyes, she saw that it wasn't a child at all. It was a doll, the size of a six-month-old baby, its porcelain face staring up at them. One moulded hand was upright, as if the toy were calling for help, asking to be pulled up from its grave. She could see that it was wrapped in something: a wool shawl, hand-knitted, brown with decay.

She looked at Alex, her eyes still wide, her hand at her throat. 'I thought it was—'

'Yes, me too. My stomach turned over.'

They stared down together.

'Whose is it?' Faith murmured.

Alex hunched down, and then jumped into the trench. His boots sent up a fine spray of the dusty soil. He leaned over the doll, picking at it gingerly with one hand.

'There's things all around it,' he said. 'There's a doll's dress and a glass jar, and . . . a box . . .'

'What kind of box?'

'A biscuit tin.' He showed her. It was rusty, but a decoration of red roses could still be deciphered on the lid. 'Shall I open it?'

'All right.'

He did so. Inside, there was an empty toy plastic feeding bottle, and a handkerchief. Nothing else.

Alex levered himself back up, standing beside her.

'Somebody buried it,' Faith said.

'Probably a child,' Alex replied. 'It looks as if they decided the doll had died. A game. Perhaps they couldn't find it again.'

Faith didn't touch the box. It gave her a strange, creeping sensation just looking at it. She imagined a little girl, dutifully enacting a funeral here, interring her favourite toy with long solemnity, and then—afterwards—desperately trying to find it again in the soil. Or perhaps there had never been an effort to find it. Maybe this doll was the burial of something else—some affection, some chapter that was finished. She thought of all the years that the doll must have lain in the ground with one arm reaching upwards, its face smothered in soil, the wool blanket still tenderly wrapped about its body.

Without knowing that she did it, her hand went to her stomach. *Buried babies . . . buried babies.*

And at that moment, an awful premonition swept over her. She thought she felt a dragging sensation, thought she felt the baby—it was *impossible*—but she thought she felt the baby twist and turn, as though distressed, pressing against her cervix in an urgent motion to be released. A feeling of closing doom bore down as violently as the imagined movement.

Her heart began to thud. Her stomach tied itself into a rigid knot.

'What's the matter?' Alex asked.

She sat down, abruptly, on one of the piles of turf and chalk. She closed her eyes for a second; when she opened them he was bending over her solicitously, and the feeling of some terror sweeping towards her mingled with the sensation of the night's erotic dream. She shrank back from him, although the expression on his face was of nothing but kindness.

'Are you all right?' he asked.

'Yes . . . yes.'

He looked embarrassedly down at the box which was still in his hands. 'I'm sorry,' he said. 'I just thought it was interesting.'

'Yes . . .'

He frowned. 'You're really ill,' he said.

'I feel peculiar,' she admitted.

'What can I do?'

'Nothing.'

'A cup of tea.'

She smiled thinly.

'Yes, I know,' he said. 'The cure-all. Hold on.'

And he went off, up the path to the house. She watched him go.

Five minutes later he was back, with a tray and two cups of tea, and a packet of crackers. He sat down next to her and gave her the cup rather as one would feed an invalid: gently, firmly.

'You must keep eating things like this, dry things, snacks, every couple of hours or so,' he said. 'Even if you don't feel like it. It's the blood sugar.'

She pursed her lips. 'There you go again,' she said. 'Making me feel as if I've come in half-way through a conversation.'

He smiled. 'It stops the morning sickness,' he replied.

She was so shocked for a moment that an uncharacteristic blush spread down from her face like hotly draining water, turning her neck red. In the silence, a small pile of loose stones gave up teetering on the edge of the trench and fell into it, with a faintly musical diminuendo.

'How did you know?' she said.

'My wife was the same.'

'Oh. You have children?'

He shook his head. 'No,' he said. 'There were twins. Stillborn. There was no more after that.'

With the extraordinary reactions that this pregnancy seemed to have bestowed on her, Faith felt a rush of tears threaten. Stop it, she told herself. *Don't act that way, it's embarrassing.*

'Oh, I'm very sorry,' she said.

He gave a fleeting shrug. 'A long time ago,' he said. 'Twenty-something years, you know.'

'I'm still sorry.'

He looked down into his cup. 'Yes,' he said. 'So am I.'

She took a sip of the tea. The blackness of the *buried baby* feeling was receding. 'Is your wife here?' she asked. 'I didn't realise you were married. I'd have asked permission to borrow you for this.' And she nodded in the direction of the excavator, smiling.

'No need,' he said. 'My wife died eight years ago.'

'Oh Christ,' she said.

He put his cup back on the tray and stood. 'Look,' he told her, 'I don't know how we got on this tack . . .'

She got up too. 'It's my fault,' she said. 'I wouldn't have said that if I knew. Nobody told me. Christ, I really am sorry . . .'

'Can we just change the subject?'

'Course we can. Course.' She picked up the tray, still swearing at herself under her breath at having put her foot in it. Alex went to the edge of the trench, looked at it, looked up at the house, as though calculating the distance, and then went back to the cab, putting his foot on the first step.

'You better get back to Monet,' he told her.

'Yes.'

Faith started out for the house, tray in hands. Then, abruptly, she stopped, and turned back to him.

'Somebody told me last week that I came here to hide,' she said.

He said nothing.

She turned away. 'Never mind,' she muttered.

* * *

It began to rain late in the winter afternoon; dark clouds crushed out the horizon and seemed to merge with the sea, and Faith stood for a while at the window, staring almost absently at the changes of light. Then, throwing down a cloth spattered with paint, she walked to the back of the house, and watched as the green-sand colour of the causeway and the low hills beyond were swallowed up in the same encroaching grey.

Alex was about twenty yards from the house. As the rain began in earnest, he stopped the excavator and came running up the drive, a shapeless black hat pulled down over his eyes. She opened the door to him immediately.

'It was forecast,' he said, coming in and shaking off the drops from his hands. 'I've only another hour or so to do.'

'I rang the plumber,' Faith said. 'He's coming on Friday, and the water company, to check the trench.'

They moved into the large living room, and Alex stopped, looking at the easel.

Faith had begun work on *The Bridge At Argenteuil*; the heat of its colour possessed the room. It was as if a summer afternoon were running out of the canvas.

'You work quickly,' he said.

'Sometimes,' she responded, and made a face, walking from one side of the painting to the other, looking at it from all angles.

'Wrong?' he asked.

She shook her head. 'They're always wrong.'

'Why?'

Sighing, she sat down on the sofa, drawing up her legs underneath her, and crossing her arms over her chest, resting her hands on each shoulder. 'I've got this, and *The Thames Below Westminster*, and *The Water Lily Pond* to do for these people.' She gave a short laugh. 'They build bridges, apparently. A construction company. Steel. Asian or Japanese . . . I forget. They build bridges, so they wanted some paintings with bridges in them. And the Chairman spent a loose-end lunch hour in the National one day and saw the Japanese bridge at Giverny, and said, "I'll have a couple of those."'

She laughed. Alex sat down opposite her.

'Do you know how long Monet spent painting that particular

bridge?' she asked. She leaned forward. 'He could work on several canvases at once. Trying to get the changes of light. The water lilies, for instance . . . he built an enormous studio, and had easels specially made alongside the water, and gardeners moved them around for him as the light altered.'

She waved ineffectually at her own canvas.

'This is just one, one of the hundreds he did just to get it completely *right*,' she said. 'But the bridge people don't want right, they want *pretty much the same*. What would Monet think, d'you suppose? Me with my order book, three bridges, two Westminster At Dawns, and a couple of Cezannes . . .' She began to smile broadly. 'I have this nightmare. Picasso is chasing me down the alleys of Horta del Ebro, machete in hand. He's screaming, *Cheat!*'

Alex smiled with her. 'So all these industrialists, all philistines trying to be cultured, are destroying today's Picasso?'

Faith actually laughed out loud at that. 'Me, Picasso?' she said. 'I don't cheat *myself*.' In the icy blue light he saw the red shades in the hair that fell over her face, and glimpsed them ripple through the brown, next to a skin muted by other colours. She was right. Things fleeting were acute, touching silent strings. That's what Monet had been trying to capture. Then they were gone.

She gave a great sigh. 'I'm not an artist. I'm a . . .' and she searched for the right word. 'A technician.'

Alex frowned. 'That's the most outrageous arrogance I've ever heard.'

She blinked twice, double-taking. 'What?'

'Arrogance. *I'm just a simple artisan* . . . all that crap. You don't really believe that?'

'How the hell would you know!'

'You can draw and paint. That makes an artist. All the rest is artyfarty-speak.'

She gazed at him, weighing up the depth of this remark, and decided he was serious. But not aggressive. 'You're the second person I've met recently who thinks anyone creative is a sort of liar,' she said.

He nodded. 'Painting *is* a lie,' he said. 'Just like stories. Or plays, or films. Real things wrapped up.'

She looked back at him perfectly levelly in the almost-darkness. 'Real things wrapped up,' she repeated. 'I see. Real things like . . .'

He shrugged. 'Eating. Drinking. Business. Working.'

'Oh, right,' she remarked, acidly. 'You mean, the City kind of business? Stocks and shares? Politics, maybe? Trade, all that? Those kind of real worlds, run by honest men who can't lie. Everything *unwrapped*?'

Alex stared at her for a second. Then colour invaded his face. He looked away, but she continued to gaze at him, wondering what she had said in the last sentence or so that had touched so deep a nerve.

She started to smile. She *liked* puzzles. Russian dolls, one inside the other; complicated anagrams and word games; tortuously unreadable books. She liked to handle them in her head. And here *he* was. A living enigma. He looked up, at last.

'You're right,' he said. 'I don't know what I'm talking about. Life is full of secrets. Pictures we draw to deceive.' He looked back at the painting. The composition of the boats and the bridge and the river banks was laid out in blue pigment. 'I've offended you,' he said.

'No.'

'I'm sorry.'

'I'm really not offended at all,' she told him. 'It's an honour to meet a real person.' He flinched a little at that, but in a charming fashion, as if he knew it were coming.

'Tell me . . .' Faith stood up. 'What real things did you do until you came here?'

He stood up too.

The darkness seemed incredibly intimate: secret, as soothing as the womb. In just a second, perhaps two, she could kiss him, put her lips to that mouth. Desire seemed to roll round them like an incoming tide, making the air between them almost solid with promise.

'I was the kind of man who orders six Monets for the boardroom wall,' he said. 'I ran a company called Robertson Hall Construction. I started out thirty years ago digging trenches.' And he inclined his head, fractionally, towards the garden outside.

She made no move. 'Are you famous?' she asked.

'Only to other philistines,' he replied.

EIGHTEEN

*J*OZ GOT HOME AT THREE A.M.

She slammed the front door behind her and sat down on the steps, staring into space. The world was racing, tipping and jumbling. She was in a kaleidoscope, sliced by succeeding lenses. For more than half an hour she sat with her arms wrapped tightly around herself, waiting for the pieces to stop in some coherent pattern.

But nothing happened.

She only sank a little deeper into the storm.

At last, she pressed the Messages button of the answerphone.

The first voice was hesitant.

'Miss Joscelyne? It's Marjorie Carver.'

It was the woman who had owned the dog.

'We've just moved in. How is he? Would you mind ringing me? I know it's an imposition . . .' She gave a telephone number in France.

Joz looked at it, silently.

The second voice was Mark Estwood.

'Er . . . hi. Just a feeler about the work really. We have a problem, the construction people . . .' He, too, gave a home number.

The third was a friend of her mother's, asking her to a gallery showing. Fourth, a woman employed to make curtains. She was in tears.

'Miss Joscelyne, the widths . . .'

Slowly and methodically, Joz erased them all. She got up and walked upstairs, up the two flights to her bedroom, pulled a suitcase from the wardrobe and began packing it. It took a quarter of an hour. Dragging it downstairs, she kicked open the door of the living room and stared at the dog.

As she went out of the house five minutes later, she stopped to make two calls.

During the first one to Mark Estwood, she didn't speak at all, merely held the receiver away from her face as his bleary, sleep-filled questions filled the line.

'Who is it? Look, I mean it's twenty to four in the morning . . .'

She cut him off.

Then she dialled France.

That was another answerphone. She kicked the front door as she waited for the tone.

'Listen,' she said, at last. 'He's *dead*, all right? So don't phone me any more.'

As she got to the car, in the pitch darkness of the courtyard, it struck her that what she had said was ludicrously funny. She began laughing, and could not stop.

She was on the motorway by five, and heading for the coast.

NINETEEN

$\mathcal{A}$NOTHER PHONE CALL IN THE DARKNESS.

Guy was sitting in the kitchen, without the light on, nursing a large brandy. Moonlight spilled over the Smallbone units, the Italian tiles. They had paid a fortune to have the flat customised to Chloe's fantasy requirements, and, as a result, he was sitting here now in a Tuscan farmhouse, with all its terracotta and baskets and copper pans that they hardly used, looking over a grey stretch of the river.

The water out there looked luminous tonight.

He ran his hand through his hair, drained the glass, and thought of Faith. He had been looking at the phone for nearly an hour now, and was sizeably drunk.

Fumbling, he dialled her number.

She answered, evidently not asleep yet, although it was almost one o'clock.

'Hello?'

'Hello Fay.'

She didn't reply.

'Hello, Fay, why aren't you asleep?'

'Ringing to wake me? How nice.'

'Don't be touchy, love. It's me.'

'I'm not your love. What time is it?' And he heard her turn away from the phone, as if looking for a clock. She came back on. 'Get off the line, Guy.'

He coughed. 'Want to know secret? Little secret?'

'You're drunk,' she said.

He wanted to weep, quite suddenly. 'I want to see you. *Got* to.'

'*Smashed.*' A long exhalation of breath.

'Look, f'get all that. That I just said. F'get it, all right. All right? I've got—' he gestured about himself, as if she could see him '—all this. Waterside, this is. *Very* nice.'

Silence on the other end.

'But I keep thinking.' His voice cracked, and he felt abruptly and deeply sorry for himself, hearing that tremble in it. 'Look—' He tried to get a grip on this conversation. He had a desperate urge to make her feel what he was feeling, through the complicated, night-hours, drink-charged chaos. 'The baby, that's what it's about, OK? I want to talk about the baby.'

'Jesus *wept.*'

'Fay . . .'

'I *told* you—'

'Listen, listen, listen. I've been thinking. I keep thinking of you all alone.' He paused for breath. She still said nothing. He held the phone close to his mouth, his lips touching the receiver. 'Look, if you want this baby, I mean, it's not just you, I'm the father, I've been thinking, can't I buy you something, shouldn't we sort out something, if we just met . . .'

He balled his free hand into a fist, willing her to agree. Then, he realised. He realised what the sound was running relentlessly over his own voice.

Faith had hung up.

TWENTY

THE MORNING DAWNED STEELY GREY; the first few flakes of snow were falling, melting as soon as they touched the street. Thomas arrived at his parents' house at ten minutes to eight.

Randolph and Ruth were not up. Margaritha, the maid, was setting the breakfast table. He went on up the stairs and heard them talking in Ruth's room. He knocked on the door.

Ruth was dressed, and brushing her hair. Randolph was sitting, still in a dressing gown, reading the morning paper.

'Thomas!' Ruth exclaimed, turning.

He brushed her forehead with his lips, turning to Randolph.

'What is it?' said his step-father. 'You look ghastly.'

Ruth gave him a surprised glance. 'Of *course* he looks terrible,' she said. She turned the chair under the window so that it faced her, and indicated that Thomas should sit down. 'Darling, you haven't slept, have you?' he said.

'I couldn't.'

'Oh, Tom. Poor love.'

'It's not Anna. It's Cecily.'

There was tangible silence in the room, so solid it could almost be cut. Randolph slowly lowered the paper, folded it, and laid it on his lap.

'Mother, something must be done about Cecily.'

Ruth looked at her husband. His face was set.

'She hasn't been seeing anyone,' Thomas continued. 'Not *anyone*.'

Ruth smiled. 'But she sees Lewis.'

'She doesn't see Lewis. No one. She told me last night. She doesn't take any medication any more.'

Ruth shook her head, confused.

'She's all right.' It was the first time that Randolph had spoken. Thomas sprang to his feet. He walked a pace or two, controlling his temper. 'How can you possibly say that?' he asked. 'What was she like at the wedding? What was she like yesterday? Can't you *see*?'

Randolph shrugged.

'Oh, Jesus *Christ!*'

Randolph stood up. 'Don't swear at me, Tom.'

Thomas walked up to him, within an inch or two. 'Do you want it to happen again?' he asked. 'Because it will. She's going the same way, again. Last night . . .' His face creased at the memory. 'She implied, something about Anna . . .'

Ruth froze, brush in mid-air. Then, very slowly, she replaced it on the dressing table. 'You surely don't think she had something to do with it? Oh, Thomas. You must be mistaken, darling.'

He looked at her helplessly. Then he turned his attention back to Randolph.

The older man gazed down at him—with his six-inch advantage in height—like a stone god glaring down at some lowly disciple. His face was totally expressionless. 'I really think you're exaggerating,' he said.

Thomas failed to hold his look. As always, he dropped his eyes from that unfathomable vacancy deep in his step-father's gaze. Like Ruth, he preferred not to confront it. He preferred to turn away, and always had.

Ruth stood up now, and came between them. She placed a hand on both their arms. 'Don't you think . . . if we rang Lewis?' she asked.

Randolph put both hands in his pockets. 'I shall do no such thing,' he said, perfectly calm. 'There's nothing wrong with her.'

'Oh, Ran*dolph*!' This from Ruth.

'Last night—'

Randolph held up his hand. 'I don't want to hear it,' he said. 'You and your mother—and I don't say this lightly, Tom, I know you're distressed, we all are—but really, you and your mother have been paranoid about this thing, and I want her to be left alone. I don't want either of you interfering—'

'Oh, *darling*,' Ruth protested. 'The clinic . . . the reports . . . the doctor . . .' She smoothed both hands back across her hair, a trick she had whenever she was thinking, or under strain. 'Let's see, let's see . . .'

Randolph got up, walked to the door of his dressing room.

'Randolph,' said Ruth, 'will you talk to her?'

'Yes,' he said. He closed the door behind him. Ruth sat down again, staring at her reflection, and at Thomas, who hesitated behind her, his face pale in the glass, and dark rings showing beneath his eyes.

'It's happening again,' he told her. 'All over again.'

Ruth lifted her powder compact, snapped it open, and proceeded, very carefully, to make up her face. 'No it isn't,' she replied. 'It can't. Randolph will see to it. She only ever listens to him, anyway. He goes to the study every night specifically to telephone her . . .' She did not look up to meet his gaze. 'Perhaps you didn't understand, last night,' she murmured.

Thomas shook his head. He sat down heavily on the bed, and stared down at his own clasped hands. 'Mother,' he asked quietly. 'What does Randolph tell her to do?'

Ruth glanced up; she began faintly to colour as she looked at him. 'Nothing,' she responded. Then, so softly that it was hard to catch the words, she added, 'She was always such a peculiar little girl, and he always had a knack of calming her . . .'

'Mother—'

'No,' she said. She tilted her head defensively. 'I don't know. I don't want to know.' Her eyes narrowed, and she began to twist the braid fastening on the handle of the brush. 'Neither do you,' she said.

They regarded each other silently, across the lie of more than twenty years.

TWENTY-ONE

*F*AITH SLEPT IN THE NEXT MORNING. She woke, at nine, to the sound of the excavator starting up.

She turned on her side, and looked at the window, and saw to her surprise that it was snowing. She got up, pulling on a towelling robe, and went to the glass, rubbing a hole in the fretwork of frost.

Alex was in the cab of the digger. He rubbed a hand across his eyes and yawned.

She was washed and dressed in five minutes. Not since childhood, before her Mum and Dad had got central heating in the house, had she felt this cold. It took her breath away as she scrubbed at her face and under her arms. She experienced a moment of acute, terrible loneliness. And, brushing her hair furiously as she looked in the mirror, she realised with a pang that she wanted to go home and see her mother.

Except Mum had died in 1979.

She put the brush down and stared into the sudsy remains of the sink.

All because of you, Guy.

Oh . . . not her mother's death. Not that. But being here, alone, in this decayed house. Just to get away from Guy. Just to erase him.

And it wasn't as if she had succeeded. The phone call last night, the visit last week. She was no less accessible here. And she'd had this stupid idea that she'd vanish into the back of beyond, and be completely free. Furiously, she rinsed out the sink and rubbed the mirror clean.

As she walked into the kitchen, she told herself, 'For Christ's sake, stop acting like a wet rag.'

She had to smile then. Talking to herself was one of her favourite occupations, and, as long as she was still doing it, she was sane. This nice bit of cock-eyed logic cheered her considerably.

She made hot chocolate, and toasted thick chunks of bread. Putting them on a tray, she went out to Alex. The snow was light and dry, and was settling. There was hardly a breath of wind.

He turned off the engine, and took the tray, and she climbed up in the cab next to him, laughing at the lack of space.

'Alex,' she said, holding her cup with both hands, 'do you think I'm a bit crazy? I think I'm a bit crazy.'

'He smiled. Why?'

She pulled a face. 'I mean, *look* at that place.'

Together, they regarded the house through the steamed-up window. White was beginning to trace the ridge tiles; beyond, the sea was almost as grey as the sky. Smoke was trailing, one dark thread, from the chimney.

'Why don't you call it *The Shambles*?' he said.

'I thought of *The Millstone*.'

'It's not so bad. It's solid enough.'

'Guess what? Guy rang last night.'

She had told him a little about Guy yesterday. Described him more like a vaudeville act than a husband. What other way was there? She couldn't sit down and put into words what Guy had done to her: it was so intense that it was almost comical. A round hole in her stomach, like Goldie Hawn in *Death Becomes Her*. A cartoon. She had told him the story of Guy's departure, hamming up the part where she ran after him.

'What did he say?'

'He was drunk.'

'But what did he say?'

'He wants to see me.'

'Ah.'

She put down her cup, wiping the dust from the dashboard, drawing a stick man on the windscreen.

'Do you want to see him?'

'No.' She glanced at Alex. He was picking a small and solid drip of blue paint from the side of his cup. 'Do you think I should?'

'It's your life.'

'It's just a case of him wanting what he can't have.' She gave a pained smile. 'If I wanted him, if I gave in to him now, he would just leave again,' she said. 'You see . . .' And she starting twisting the belt of her jacket round and round her wrist, frowning in concentration. 'Once he *has* something, he doesn't want it. Once he loses something . . .' She glanced up at Alex. 'I don't suppose he thought that I would leave London. He could leave *me*, you see. And I would stay in the house, neatly, where he knew where to find me. That was the game plan, that was the pattern. But now . . . I've spoiled it. You see? I've gone away, and I've got to be pursued. Put back in place. And when I'm *back*—'

'He'll leave.'

'Yes.'

'But you are still married.'

'So I should take him back? After everything . . . after Chloe?'

Alex winced a little. 'I'm trying to say the right thing here.'

She bit her lip. 'It's so crazy,' she murmured. She was talking more to herself than to him. 'Even now, I have this stupid picture in my head, of Guy coming home and wanting to do ordinary things, family things, washing up, watching TV . . . being kind. That's my fantasy, do you know? Guy being kind. Pathetic.'

She turned to look at him.

'Here's a funny thing,' she said. The tone of her voice, brittle and over-bright, belied the look in her eyes. 'We had neighbours in London. Oh, this is . . . maybe, four years ago. A young couple. They moved in and they started to knock the back yard about, making a patio, planting a tree, making flowerbeds. They used to giggle, have fights, talk . . . I could hear them. I'd be working upstairs, and Guy would be out.' She smiled thinly. 'And I would sit and listen to them, and it was like—like listening to Shakespeare in Greek. You know the phrases but they sound different.' She laughed softly. 'I mean . . . Guy and I never talked like that. We never chatted, we never gossiped. We struck poses. Like this.'

And she made an attempt at a joke, holding up both fists like a prize fighter. Alex did not respond. He was watching her intently.

'One day I went down, and the neighbours saw me, and invited me over for a drink. They were . . .' She tried to find the words. 'A couple. Do you understand? They wanted the same things. They helped each other to get those things. Guy thought they were boring . . . he called them *Mr and Mrs Austin Allegro*. But I liked them.'

She sat forward, staring past the stick man.

'This particular day, it was hot, I had just finished a painting, I went over, and the girl told me she was pregnant. All *smiles*. Thrilled. Him too. He was telling her not to get up. Spoiling her. And she said she'd been feeling ill in the mornings, and having to dash to the loo as soon as she got up—' Faith's face clouded '—and she said how her husband would come in and rub her back.'

There was a momentary silence. Alex was looking at Faith's rapt profile, a frown of concern on his face.

'And he said, "I can't do much, but I can rub her back." Like that. "I can rub her back." And I thought, well, isn't that nice? Isn't that kind of him? He didn't mind her being sick down the loo. He just wanted to help her . . . he rubbed her back . . .'

And, slowly, softly, Faith began to cry.

'Oh, Faith,' said Alex.

He reached out and took her gently in his arms, rather ham-fistedly, as if wondering whether he should. For a second, he held her awkwardly at arm's length, difficult in the cramped cab; then, he pulled her tightly to him. They sat, he in the driver's seat and she wedged between him and the ridge of the window, she on her knees, snuffling into his thick sweater. Outside the snow began lying on the windscreen in lacy scrawls. Faith suddenly felt very hot and foolish. She started searching for a tissue or a handkerchief that she knew full well she had not got.

'God, I'm sorry,' she said.

He edged to one side. 'Look, sit here a minute.'

'There isn't room.'

'I know there isn't room. There wasn't room for you in the first place.'

She grinned, wiping her face with the palms of both hands. He stopped her, taking one hand and looking at it. There was colour smeared down the wrist: red, as livid as a scar.

'Faith,' he said.

For a split second before he kissed her, she thought, *Isn't that funny, being kissed by someone else.* Then she forgot about Guy completely.

It was like being submerged in something intensely peaceful, almost silent. Alex's kiss was very slow, his lips soft and warm and dry. He smelled *good*. Quite suddenly, desire flooded her. She was fifteen again, in the back of a boy's car, willing him to touch her.

He felt it, too. They struggled for a second against the confines of the ridiculous seat. Then he pulled away.

She gazed at him, feeling still that she must have him: *must*, like thirst, like addiction. Then she realised with horror that he might have someone else, might even be gay for all she knew.

She tried to twist round to get out. 'Oh, look, forget it,' she said. 'Sorry.'

He caught her arm. 'Let's just get out of here,' he said. 'I want to talk to you.'

'You don't have to,' she replied, blushing now furiously.

'Oh, for God's sake,' he said.

She paused, looking back over her shoulder, then got down from the cab, shivering at the sudden drop in temperature as she opened the door. Flakes of snow swirled in. He leaned over, caught her wrist.

He got out behind her, holding her like this for a moment, a small smile on his face. Then, he took her in his arms and stroked her hair back from her face. She leaned back into his embrace, almost letting herself be held up. He drew back enough to look in her eyes.

'There's a few things you ought to know,' he said. 'And the first of them is, this isn't fair on you. Not with all your problems right now.'

'Why?' She was smiling at him.

'Baggage,' he said.

'Sorry?'

'From the past. Baggage. What I was before—'

'You're a drugs baron?'

He started to smile. 'No, no.'

'You weren't a VAT inspector?' She made a sign of the cross. 'Or Inland Revenue?'

His smile faded slightly as he looked at her, tracing the line of her forehead, cheek, chin.

'You're serious,' she said. 'What is it? It can't be so bad.'

She put a hand on either side of his head—he was handsome, in a bear-like way, with those green eyes, his hair wiry and thick—and, pulling him towards her, she kissed him lightly on the mouth. 'You sold those fluffy dogs that go over loo rolls?' she said. 'You liked watching game shows? Never mind. You can get counselling. I'll even come with you.'

He put a fingertip on her lips. 'Can we go inside?' he asked.

There was a flicker of movement to one side; they both turned to look.

Guy was standing by the gate.

For a moment, Faith did a double-take. She thought she must be hallucinating. Guy was in London. Guy was at work.

Yet Guy was *here*. He stood, in his Aquascutum American-tourist mac that she had so often teased him about, one hand shoved in its pocket, and the other clutching his black leather Filofax. He looked, absurdly, like an estate agent out on call. Out of context, as if he had been lifted straight from the front steps of Lloyd's and set down in this deserted place for no reason. He hesitated a second, as if he too sensed the disorientation. Then he began walking very quickly towards them.

Alex stepped back, though he still kept hold of Faith's hand.

The snow blew across them all like grainy monochrome scratches on an ancient film. Guy's face wore his childish look of betrayal: that spoilt, demanding look. As he got closer she saw that he looked positively ill: grey, his hair unwashed, his skin scraped-looking and raw.

'Who the hell is this? What the hell is this?' he shouted, ten yards away.

'Guy—'

At her side, she felt Alex give something like a reflex leap: his hand swung upwards a little in hers, then he tightened his grip.

'What the *fucking* hell is this?'

The irrationality of it shocked her, and she felt, equally irrationally, that she had done something morally wrong. She began to shake.

'Go in the house,' Alex said.

A paroxysm flashed over Guy's face. 'Oh, it's *go in the house*, is it?' he demanded.

The snow flew. The day had closed right down to this grey, flecked box of soil. The sky pressed down on them.

Guy promptly launched himself at Alex, missed him, and came turning back with his arms flailing. Faith saw that he must still be drunk: it was only eight hours since the phone call. Perhaps he had been drinking all night.

The thought flashed through her mind, *Chloe?*

Alex was saying, 'Look, calm down, look—'

Guy's fist at last connected with his face. In a second, Guy was on Alex as he staggered backwards, thumping him in the body. She saw Alex trying to cover up.

Why don't you hit him back?

'You bastard,' Guy was grunting. Each word connecting with a blow. 'You bastard!'

She felt suddenly, hugely, angry.

She walked to where Guy stood hunched over Alex, and, with a feeling of heavy calm, struck Guy hard between the shoulder-blades. She probably didn't hurt him, but he swung round.

'I could kill you,' she said.

'Go on, then,' he replied.

It was absurd. Alex got to his feet; he shot Faith a glance. She looked back at him. *You see what I mean, now.*

'Are you all right?' she asked. 'I'm really sorry . . .'

Alex wiped down his clothes. He didn't answer.

'Go home,' she said to Guy.

Then her hand flew to her stomach. A pain, bright and vivid, had shot down through her, from waist to thigh. It felt as if a wire were being twisted, the connection buried somewhere in her stomach, and linked, like a jointed doll, to her knees. She pressed her fist into her side, sighing, 'Oh . . .'

'What is it?' said Alex.

'What's the matter?' Guy stepped forward and got his hand under her arm a fraction before Alex. They stood glaring at each other.

The pain flashed brilliantly for another second; then it was replaced with a low, dragging ache.

'I've got to go in,' she said.

She lay down on the couch inside, in front of the fire. Alex put more wood on, but the atmosphere in the room was still piercingly cold. The two men stood on either side of the chimney.

'Guy, what're you doing here?'

'I'm not talking to you with *him* in here.'

'I don't want to talk to you anyway,' she said.

'Look, I'll leave you to it,' Alex offered, moving away.

She caught his hand. 'Don't,' she said. 'Please.'

Guy reddened.

'Don't start,' she said. 'You've behaved like a fool already. Just say whatever it is.'

'You're my *wife*.'

She put her face in her hands, grimacing and laughing at the same time. 'Oh God, oh God.'

'Don't laugh at me. It's true.'

'Oh, please, for God's sake, *what is it* . . . ?'

'It's the baby.'

Alex stiffened. He pulled himself very straight. It telegraphed outrage, and Guy's glance flickered to him, and back at Faith.

'This is—my business,' Guy faltered.

'No it isn't. You walked out on your business. Go home,' Faith said.

'It's my business!' he shouted.

She crossed her arms where she lay. The ache was deepening, broadening.

'Can't you see she's not well?' Alex said.

'She never lets me have what I want,' Guy said.

It was so ridiculous, so childish, that Alex laughed. Guy ignited at once. He was across the room in two strides, shouting, 'Don't you—'

But Alex wasn't letting it happen again. He caught Guy's wrist and gave it a flick, a sudden twist. Guy sprang back with a small, grunting cry. He looked down at his arm and rubbed it.

'Oh, *please*,' said Faith.

Alex walked away. He went to the kitchen and began loudly filling the kettle, rattling cups, opening cupboards. Guy watched him go, listened to the sounds for a moment, and stood over Faith, saying, 'It didn't take long for you to get *him* trained.'

She closed her eyes fleetingly. A hand inside her was pressing down hard, pulling, shifting.

Guy sat down on the floor next to the couch. Seeing him there within a hand's reach, Faith recalled acutely how, in their early days, she would stroke his hair when he sat in this position. His hair grew low on his neck. He had a little widow's peak at the front. She used to have an urge to pull the hair this way and that, trying to make it lie flat. Now, the urge was no longer there. It was curious to look at him, and to feel the conflict of knowing him yet feeling there was something fundamental missing—something like the need to stroke that wayward piece of hair.

'Faith, this is a mess,' he was saying.

'Yes, isn't it.'

He said nothing for a minute.

'Don't you love Chloe?' she asked.

'Yes,' he said. 'I love you both.'

The pain suddenly clicked off. The inner hand vanished. The wire line from waist to thigh. She felt sick and sad.

'It's too late,' she said. 'You can't always have what you want.'

He gripped her hand. 'Yes you can,' he said. 'You can have whatever you want. What do you want? Do you want me to come and live here? I will.'

'And then what? You'll be going to Chloe, at night, at weekends, saying the same thing.' She prised his fingers off her. 'You're so selfish,' she said. 'You can't split yourself in two. You can't have both. In fact, you can't have me. Go back to Chloe.'

He tried to turn her face to look at his and she slapped his hand away. 'There must be something we can do,' he said. 'There's the baby.'
'It's nothing to do with you.'

'Oh.' He looked stagily affronted. 'Oh, right. So, when it's born, you won't ask for a penny, I won't have to give you any maintenance, I won't get the fucking Child Support Agency on my fucking back . . .'

'Well . . .' She hesitated. She hadn't thought this through. 'You . . . I suppose you'll have a right to support . . .'

'Ah!' He slammed his fist on the couch next to her. His ill temper, which he had never learned to control, flared up. 'Oh, yes, I'll have to shell out. I'll have to give you thirty pieces of silver, even if I went to a bloody solicitor, they'd tell me, even if I signed a piece of paper saying I never wanted this child, I'd *still* have to support it, even if you lock the doors on me and never let me see the little bastard! That's bloody fair, isn't it?' he demanded, really furious now, and stuttering slightly. 'That's rich, I should say! You can lock me out of your whole life, and some shit from the Government will still be after me with a begging bowl. *Go away, Guy. Go home, Guy.* But don't forget to leave the money on the side before you go!'

She genuinely hadn't considered this at all. But it was obvious that he had.

'You've talked to Alan Percival,' she said. Percival had once been their mutual friend; now, he was Guy's solicitor.

Guy had got up, and now paced up and down, then stopped in front of her. 'Yes, I have,' he said. 'And you know what rights I've got?' He snapped his fingers in her face. 'That!' he shouted. 'That! See? Nothing at all!'

'And you tried to . . . sign this . . . sign something saying it was none of your business?' Faith's voice was very low.

Guy blushed. 'Well, you won't talk to me,' he said. He turned away, facing the latest picture, the Bridge.

She began to shake her head. 'God, you're priceless.'

'I just don't want to lose you,' he said.

At that second, Alex came back into the room. He was carrying a teapot, and three mugs in the other hand. Faith glanced up at him, and he made a face, apologetic.

In the same moment, she was already repeating, 'This is nothing to do with you.'

Guy turned round. His face was almost laughably pleased. He had misunderstood her. He had thought she was speaking to Alex; in a flash, however, he saw that she was speaking to him. 'It's nothing to do with you.'

His glance shot from Faith to Alex. Alex to Faith. Then he looked at the hand that Faith had stretched across her stomach.

A light dawned in his face.

'Well, you bitch,' he said.

Faith got up on one elbow.

'You bitch,' he repeated. 'It's not mine.'

'Yes, it—'

'It's not *mine!*'

He struck his forehead with the flat of his hand. 'Well, I must be fucking blind. Am I blind or *what?*' he said. 'It's not mine. It's *his.*'

'Guy—' Faith swung her legs off the couch.

Guy backed away. 'I've got to hand it to you, I really thought—'

Alex, having swiftly put the pot and cups down, was moving round the side of the couch. 'Just a minute,' he was saying.

'Alex is a friend. He's my neighbour.'

Guy pulled at the peak of hair on his forehead, and a kind of furious, twisted, sentimental agony pierced Faith.

'You saw this house—what?' Guy muttered. He was trying desperately to work out the time scale. 'Three months ago? Five months ago? When did Chloe and I . . .'

'It's not that,' Faith said.

'Five . . . four and a half months . . .'

'Guy, you're wrong—'

'Listen—' said Alex.

'Guy—'

'Oh, that's very nice; oh, you stick me with child support; oh, that's *good*, that's a nice touch.' Guy was fuming, ranting now. 'You put me through seven kinds of hell. Why not? Get your own back. Pay me back. The two of you got it worked out nicely. Nicely. That's clever—'

'Guy, *please* . . .'

Guy wheeled back, towards the picture.

None of them heard the door open behind them.

He smashed his fist into the canvas, tore it from the easel, and tried, unsuccessfully, to wrench the frame apart. Eventually, he threw it on the floor. He turned back to them.

'You're going to fry for this. You fucking wait,' he said.

The door slammed shut. Footsteps on the floor.

All three turned round.

Cecily Joscelyne stood with one hand on the back of the rocking chair, her eyebrows raised, smiling broadly.

'Is this a private party, or can anyone join in?' she said.

TWENTY-TWO

*F*OR A MOMENT, NO ONE MOVED.

Faith sat, hunched over.

Joz stepped forward. She held out to her hand to Alex. 'Hello again,' she said. 'Fancy seeing you, and all that stuff.'

He doesn't know you, Faith thought.

You've never met.

For a moment, she saw the look of total horror that appeared on Alex's face. He stepped back, to avoid Joz's hand, and she, in turn, smiled at him, and shrugged.

Faith got up rapidly, and, as she did so, there was an abrupt, and painless, popping sensation. It was just as if a small paper bag had burst inside her. Almost immediately, a warm rush of fluid soaked her. She clenched both hands on her thighs. 'Oh, God,' she whispered. 'Oh no.'

Alex grabbed her arm.

'Can you call a doctor,' she said.

'Who is it?'

'What?'

'Who's your GP?'

She looked at him, stricken. 'I haven't got one. I haven't registered yet.'

'You haven't . . .' He shook his head in disbelief for a second. Then, 'I'll call mine,' he told her. 'It's Harret, in Milborne.'

'Milborne?' said Joz. 'I just drove through a Milborne. It's ten miles away.'

Alex gave her a filthy look. 'It's not ten,' he said. 'It's six.'

'But the hospital's six miles, isn't it?'

'*Nine*. What the hell is it to you anyway?' Alex was trying to support Faith as she sank backwards to the couch.

Joz looked from Faith to Alex, and then upwards at Guy. She smiled at him sweetly. 'Well, none of my business, of course,' she said. 'You'll be the husband, I expect? But it seems to me that a hospital would be more use.'

Guy seemed to jolt to life at that. 'That's right, you've got to go to hospital,' he said to Faith. 'Get up.'

Alex pushed him back. '*Get up?*' he said, aghast. 'Are you bloody serious?' He stared at Joz. 'And *you* . . .' He gave her a furious look. 'You keep out of this.'

Joz hardly batted an eyelid. 'But he's right,' she said, smiling. 'Absolutely right. She ought to get to hospital.' Her gaze bounced from one man to the other. 'I must say, this seems awfully interesting,' she murmured.

'Oh Christ,' moaned Faith. 'Somebody *please* do something. *Anything.*'

She lay on the trolley in Casualty, staring at the green curtains. It was midday.

Outside, she could hear a curious weave of sounds. It seemed to be made up principally of Guy's voice, low and insistent and persistent. Around and over him the noise of the hospital surged and retreated: other voices; the rattle of wheels; the slap of shoes against polished floors; the ringing of telephones.

She was in a cream-coloured cubicle. A nurse had been to take her blood pressure and to give her a sanitary towel, after the Casualty doctor had given her a quick once-over. 'The gynae man will want to look at that,' she said.

Faith had fought down an urge to laugh. 'He must be some kind of freak, then,' she was tempted to reply.

There was no pain at all. That was the strangest thing. She lay with her hands crossed over her stomach, pressing down, as if she were trying to reach inside and hold on to the baby. She had an idea that, providing she laid absolutely still, she could stop whatever was happening. Even reverse it.

She turned her head.

The next-door cubicle was occupied. It sounded like an elderly man, who huffed complainingly as he was hoisted on to the bed. 'Ah now, that's it, see?' he said. 'Look. I told you.'

'When did you last see Mr Elthwaite?'

'Friday.'

'Ah. They *do* come loose, sometimes.'

The old man's voice dropped to a confidential whisper of which Faith could hear every syllable. 'I can't piss, love,' he said.

Faith looked away, not knowing if she should laugh or cry. There was that smell—not just the hospital one, which was bad enough—but now the unmistakable smell of old age. A jumble-sale smell: liniment and wet paper.

She bit her lip helplessly. When was anyone going to come?

'We've bleeped the doctor,' the nurse had said. 'He'll be here shortly.'

How long was *shortly*? she wondered.

Five minutes?

Evidently not.

Not even ten minutes. She could see the grey and black face of the clock on the opposite wall, just the top half showing. It read 12.10. She had been here twenty minutes.

'Is there anybody there?' she called.

As she shifted on to her elbow, something seeped from her. Grimacing and fastidious and afraid, she lifted the sheet and gently prised back the waistband of the briefs she was wearing. *Don't let there be anything*, she thought.

It was soaked and pinkish.

She dropped the sheet, feeling sick.

Another commotion on the other side. Someone was being brought in, groaning deeply, another man. 'It's just a nasty gash,' the nurse was saying.

Faith put her hand up to her head, smiling, feeling a bubble of hysterical laughter threatening. She put her hand to her mouth, whispering, 'Please come and see my baby.' She lay there, repeating it soundlessly, her lips moving constantly over the words. *Please come and see. Please come now and see. Please come here quickly and see.* Somewhere down the corridor, there was the sudden splintering clatter of cups and saucers and spoons. Voices swooped on each other. 'That was my tea!' 'Oh—shit and double shit!'

A doctor had come to the man opposite. She heard the curtains pulled back. The doctor had an Indian accent.

'What have we here?'

'He fell at work, doctor. Injury to the knee, and—'

'Aargh! Bloody hell, doc!'

'Sorry, sorry. You fell from where?'

'Ducting.'

'Sorry?'

'*Ducting.*'

'What is ducking?'

'It's like a pipe,' said the nurse.

'And where is this pipe?'

'In the factory.' This from the patient, in a voice of disbelief.

'Yes, I know in the factory. What I am trying to establish is the height from which you fell. And what on to you fell.'

'Forty feet. On to a pallet.'

'This is a wood pallet?'

'That's it, mate. You got it.' A great sigh, followed by another 'Ouch! Fucking *hell*, doc!'

'Is there anywhere else that you're hurting now?'

'On m'head. Here.'

'Mmm. Anywhere else?'

Faith's patience snapped. 'Here!' she yelled. 'I'm hurting over *here*!'

A momentary and very complete silence settled.

'My baby!' she yelled.

The curtains opened. The nurse smiled at her. 'Don't worry,' she said.

'I *am* worried. I'm bleeding.'

'Doctor is coming in a minute.'

'What's he doing? Playing golf? Having it off with his secretary? What?'

'Doctor won't be a moment.'

'I want him now.'

'Yes, he—'

Faith slammed her hand on the bed. 'Look, not in a minute. For Christ's sake! *Please*. What do I have to say? I've been bleeding for over an hour, it's everywhere, please. You see to people with cut legs and you get people catheters . . .'

The nurse came into the cubicle, making a shushing noise. 'You won't do yourself any good getting into a state,' she murmured.

Words strangled Faith. She lay gazing at this fresh-faced, vivid-blue-eyelinered girl with her hair scraped back with two kirby grips under her cap, and felt an overpowering desire to kill her on the spot.

'You'll just get yourself all het up for nothing,' the girl was continuing.

Faith bit back a repetition of the *for nothing*. Nothing! She really had said *for nothing*. The room seemed to swirl and jolt. She gripped the nurse's wrist. 'I want to see my husband.'

'OK—fine.' Very saccharine and soothing. 'I'll pop along and get him.'

Faith lay with both hands clenched until Guy strode in.

'Look, you just do something, Guy,' she said, at once. She didn't allow him even to say hello. 'OK? *Now*. Just do something. Get someone here *now*.'

He looked at her for a moment, flushed, obviously torn. Then he turned on his heel. 'Right,' he muttered.

She slumped back. Whatever she thought of Guy, whatever mess they were in, he was no slouch at causing havoc. Now that he'd been pointed in a direction, he'd go after his target like a Scud missile. She'd seen him tear his staff off at work: reduce them to piles of sand. His voice could carry a hundred metres when he felt like it. It was just those little inconsequential things—tenderness, honesty, fidelity—that he was so hopelessly bad at.

Faith heard him stride down the corridor, and a fire door whooshed open and slammed again. She wondered desperately where Alex was, and realised that to hold his hand, just for a moment, would be immensely comforting.

She pressed her hands to her head and began to sob, more out of frustration and immobility than anything.

Life is what happens while you're doing something else.

The doctor was doing something else. Guy and Alex and the rest of the people in this place, and all those people outside in the rest of the world, they were *doing something else.* And all the time a life, a real life, was draining silently away between Faith's legs; there was nothing she could do to stop it. Even a deep breath, the slightest motion of her hips, seemed to precipitate another flooding sensation. She rubbed her eyes furiously with the palms of her hands.

She turned over, and curled up, edging her hands under her cheek in an attitude of childish prayer. Two sluggish tears ran into the side of her mouth.

And, at that moment, the curtains opened.

The *gynae* was six foot four, handsome, and about thirty. He looked down at her with a broad, tanned, smiling face. She felt quite shocked, and absurdly embarrassed. She pressed her thighs together instinctively, while a voice at the back of her mind warned her not to open her legs to handsome strangers.

'This is our lady with the loss,' the nurse said.

'Hello, I'm Adam Martins,' he said. 'Bit of a prob?' He had an Australian accent.

'I'm afraid we're a little distressed,' the nurse added.

Faith shot her a look of loathing. 'No *we're* not,' she snapped. 'I'm eight weeks pregnant,' she continued, as loudly and as evenly as she could. 'This is my first baby and I don't want to lose it.' The calm gave way on the last two words. Her voice shot upwards and hovered somewhere over their heads.

'No, of course not,' said Adam Martins. 'And what makes you think you're losing it?'

'Oh, for Christ's sake!'

'Yes?'

'Why does everyone treat you like you're five years old here? I'm *bleeding*.'

'Actually, you're not. Not much. A miscarriage can get a lot messier than this. This is a bit of leakage at the moment.' He turned to the nurse. 'Have we any history?'

For an absurd second, Faith thought he was asking the nurse if the two of them had ever had an affair. Then, she realised he was asking about her own medical history. 'There isn't a GP,' the nurse said.

'No?'

'I just moved house,' Faith muttered. 'I can tell you my history. I ought to know it.'

'Right . . . right . . . let's see . . .' He had ignored her.

The nurse was hovering close by, stroking Faith's shoulder. 'Don't worry,' she said.

Faith gulped, her mouth trembling. She looked at a spot of grey plaster on the ceiling, trying not to register what the doctor was doing, trying to float out of herself. 'I thought no one was coming,' she whispered.

'Much pain?' This from the doctor.

'No.' She brought herself back to the bed. 'It was aching, like a period. Then . . . this pop.'

'A pop. I see.'

'Yes . . . then the water. The . . .'

'The fluid.'

'Yes.'

'Hmmm. I'm just going to examine you on the outside.' He pressed delicately and firmly for a minute or more. 'Have you felt at all ill in the last few days? Any pain in the shoulders?'

'No . . . just morning sickness.'

'Did you still have that this morning?'

'A little. It's wearing off.'

'Ah. Mmmmm.'

He stood back from her.

Faith gazed at him.

'I think we'll have you down for a scan.'

'A scan . . .'

Adam Martins leaned on the bed, smiling softly. His voice fell, and then he tapped her arm. Almost stroked it. 'We *might* be looking at a miscarriage here,' he said. 'But let's check.'

Alex stood at a window in the corridor, turning a newspaper over and over in his hands. Unconsciously, he had rolled it into a tube.

He was thinking how absurd they must have looked: Guy and Faith in one car, Joz in the Mercedes, he in the Range Rover. He'd had to run back to his house, panting and cursing, and then caught them up by the time they were almost at the hospital. He had a conviction that Faith was being kidnapped, abducted. That he couldn't let her out of his sight. If he did, he thought, this maniac husband, this terrible woman, would do something final, irrevocable, to Faith. Something murderous.

It didn't make a lot of sense. But he found himself believing it.

He'd seen Guy's car slow at the entrance, not sure where to turn. He'd overtaken both the Merc and Guy, and accelerated away, waving out of his window for them to follow. He'd pulled up right outside the Casualty doors, not bothering to park. The staff must have thought someone had at least been shot.

'Penny for them.'

He turned. Cecily Joscelyne was at his side, holding out a polystyrene cup full of coffee. He ignored it. She shrugged, and put it down on a table by their side.

A porter went past, pushing a man on a stretcher trolley. The porter was whistling and the man whimpering slightly, his hand clenched over his leg.

'Isn't she private?'

'What?'

'Faith. Isn't she BUPA or anything? This is quite ghastly.'

'I don't know. Ask her husband.'

Joz sat down on the plastic chair next to him, crossed her legs, and began swinging one foot. She was smiling broadly.

'What a turn up, seeing you.' He said nothing.

'It must be—what? Eight years?'

Slowly, he uncurled the newspaper. He bent it backwards. Headlines shouted up at him. Wars, politics, race winners. He tried to make sense of it.

'Oh—aren't you speaking to me?'

'I'd rather not.'

She made a little gasp of mock outrage. 'That's awfully ungallant of you.'

'*Ungallant* . . .' He gave her a withering look. 'There's nothing I want to discuss with you.'

'Now, now. Don't be tetchy.'

'I couldn't be gallant to you with a noose around my neck. With a pistol to my head. Take your pick.'

She smiled, pursing her lips lingeringly. 'The noose, I think. Yes . . . absolutely.'

He turned on his heel.

She got up and followed him down the hallway. Wards opened on each side. Signs jostled over their heads. Dental Laboratory. Administration. Obstetrics. He realised that he didn't know where he was, where he was headed. He eventually came to a door in a corridor, and found himself in a small courtyard, furnished very beautifully in Japanese style, with perfectly arranged rings of pebbles and a small fountain. A sign declared that it was a gift of the local Lions. On the black bench, he sat down, ignoring the layer of dry and undisturbed snow.

Joz stood over him.

He remembered her. That flesh pressing up to him in a crowded bar. Those heavily coloured lips. The gagging, sweet perfume. She was always talking about her brother and her father. She would compare him to them. Laugh about it.

They were all perfect, the Joscelynes. She had often told him so.

'Alex,' she said. 'I won't tell her if you'll do something for me.'

'Tell her what, exactly?'

Joz laughed. It bounced off the walls of the courtyard and made a slight, but definite, second and third echo. 'Don't be silly,' she said. 'You haven't told her, have you? I bet you haven't told anyone down here.'

'No one would care.'

'Oh, right.' She tapped her shiny black pump in the gravel and snow. 'Just like they didn't care in town? I hear no one on your board spoke to you. I heard all about it. That last Monday morning. Must have been dreadful for you. Just dreadful.'

'It wasn't like that.'

'Oh? Richard must have been lying, then.'

He flinched.

'Yes, Richard told me. Another ally bites the dust. He knows Randolph. To give him credit, Richard didn't stick the knife in as far as the rest. But after a drink or two he yatters away. *How are the mighty fallen.* That's what he said.'

'He wouldn't,' Alex said. 'I know Richard.'

She moved closer to him, bent down, and whispered in his ear. 'I know what it's like on the *outside*, Alex,' she said. 'I don't underestimate how *cold* it is, *outside*.'

He wiped the side of his face, as if her breath on his cheek had slimed it. She straightened, and looked up at the birch tree.

'You never feel quite the same again, do you?' she said. Her voice was far away. Soft. Almost puzzled. 'People are so fickle. They make all sorts of noises. They say how sorry they are and how it could happen to anyone. They say *they don't blame you*. Didn't they, Alex? To your face at least.' She looked away from the birch, and picked a frond from a juniper, and stroked it along the back of her hand.

'It's past,' he said.

'Oh yes, oh yes,' she agreed. 'The past. All those nasty little articles in the press and the court case. Oh dear.'

He leaned forward, dropping the paper, putting his head in his hands. 'You really are a bitch,' he whispered. 'I bet you both laughed yourselves stupid. You and that bastard you call a step-father.'

She blanched, and lifted her head. 'What exactly is Faith to you?' she asked.

He shook his head.

'You don't think the split will *last*, do you?' she asked. 'Can't you see her wavering? I could see it the first time I met her. Can't shake hubby free from in here.' And she tapped her temple with one large, red-polished fingertip. 'If you're interested in her, you'd better move *bloody* fast.'

He raised his head and thought, quite soberly, that if ever one person could be the personification of evil, it was Cecily Joscelyne.

He remembered their last argument. Before the company takeover and all the nightmare that followed. On the stairs of the Robertson Hall building off Cheapside. Across the rooftops, there was a glimpse of St Paul's. The river to the south, the rise towards Holborn before him. Cecily Joscelyne with her back to the plate-glass window on the stairwell. He remembered how he had longed to push her through the window. How many problems it would have solved. How much misery avoided . . . the trail of misery she always left behind her.

But he'd been so preoccupied. If only he'd seen it coming . . .

'How much?' she asked.

'What?' He was jolted back to the present.

'Or should I say, how *long*?'

'What are you talking about?'

'How long is it that you've loved her? Faith.'

He didn't reply, except to gaze at her mutely.

'Oh,' she said, reading his eyes. '*That* much. How very, very awkward for you.'

He stood up slowly. 'Cecily,' he said, 'what are you doing here?'

She smiled, swept an imaginary hair from her sleeve, straightened the sit of her jacket. 'Didn't she say? I've commissioned six pictures from her. For a Japanese bank.'

'You,' he said.

'Me.'

He caught her arm. 'Don't do this,' he said. 'What's Faith Collins to you? You don't have to ruin her life.'

'Ruin her life? I don't know *what* you mean.'

His grip tightened. 'Because that's what you do,' he said angrily. 'You step into lives and ruin them.' He looked down at his own hand, made a grimace of distaste, and dropped her.

They stood, an inch or two from each other, staring into each other's eyes.

'All right,' she replied equably. 'I'll leave her alone. Marry her, and get her out of that house.'

He took a step back as though she'd slapped him. 'Why?'

'I want the house,' she said.

'Faith's ... *Faith's* house?'

'That's the one.'

'You want ... but it's a wreck,' he said. 'You want a *house*? What next?'

'That's right,' she told him. 'I want *that* house.'

'But why?'

'That's my business.' A far-away look came into her face, rapidly replaced by something that made him recoil even further: an expression of lust. His skin prickled and shrank.

'You're crazy,' he said.

'Am I, darling?' she asked sweetly. 'Crazy, like you?'

Alex frowned, shook his head. His gaze dropped to his feet.

'You're an outcast,' she said.

He laughed bitterly. 'It takes one to know one.'

'I thought you looked very good in court,' she taunted. 'Very *distrait*.'

'For God's sake, leave me alone,' he said.

She nodded brightly. 'Yes, I think I will,' she said. 'If you just do this one thing.' She picked up his newspaper, dusted off the snow, and handed it back to him. 'Get her to move in with you and sell the house. I'll give her two hundred thousand for it. You understand? Is that clear? Tell her. Two hundred thousand.'

'Crazy,' he repeated, his voice tinged with sadness.

They took Faith in a wheelchair to the scan, and left her in a small, bright room with two other women. They appraised her with sideways looks for a moment or two. One was young, about twenty. The second was much older, probably forty-five, with a heavily swollen stomach and a weary expression on her face.

The younger girl was called in.

Watching her go, Faith and the older woman's eyes met.

'All this waiting,' she said.

'Yes,' Faith agreed.

The woman was wearing a dressing gown. 'Are you on a ward?' Faith asked.

'Mmmm.'

A silence. Faith felt desperately that she must make conversation. She was frightened, threatened, in a manner she had never experienced before. She realised quite suddenly that it was because she was afraid for someone other than herself, someone over whom she had the literal power of life and death.

'Have you many children?' she asked her companion.

'Yes, five.'

'Oh . . . that's nice.' She really didn't know if to have five children was *nice* or not. But to say anything else would have been wrong.

'Yes.'

'How old are they?'

The older woman smiled. 'The oldest's sixteen. The youngest is five.'

'Quite a handful.'

'They can be. How about you? This your first?'

'Yes. How can you tell?'

'You look a bit worried.'

'It's a . . . it might be a . . .' She tried to remember the euphemism the nurse had used. 'A loss.'

'Oh, I'm sorry.'

Faith's heart thudded. 'When is your new baby due?' She nodded at the woman's stomach.

'My baby? This?'

'Yes, I . . .'

'This isn't a baby, dear. It's a tumour.'

Horror washed over Faith like cold water. 'Oh . . . excuse me. I'm sorry,' she said.

'Don't worry about it.'

The woman crossed her hands across herself placidly. Either she was a wonderful actress, or she really didn't care. Her eyes had a vacant, beaten look.

Two or three minutes passed, and then the young girl came scurrying out in a rush, laughing, a Polaroid picture waving between her thumb and index finger to dry. 'Oh, I'm *dying*,' she said, pushing open the door of the loo, and putting the picture down on the empty seat between the two other women.

'Isn't he lovely?' she gasped. 'You can see his little willy and everything! Isn't he great? Wait till I show my Graham! God, I must go. Why d'you have to drink all that water? I'm desperate.'

Faith glanced at the photo.

A perfect child shone glossily back at them, a drawing in black and white, like a star map. Two fragile hands extended to the top of the image. From the toilet cubicle came the unmistakable sound of relief. 'Oh, talk loudly,' the young girl called. 'Isn't it awful? I was just dying. Don't laugh.'

We won't, thought Faith.

She tore her eyes away from the photograph.

The other woman was staring down at it. 'Ain't life grand?' she whispered.

Just as Faith was going in, Guy appeared. She was walking gingerly through the swing doors when he came round the corner.

'Go away,' she snapped.

'All right, all right,' he said. But he didn't budge. She let the door shut in his face.

She climbed on to the couch in the dim room. A folder of notes was handed across her. The radiographer sat down, pulling the television screen away so that Faith couldn't see it. Blue oil was spread over Faith's stomach, icy at first, rapidly warming. The black scanner was pressed down on her.

She looked away, into the corner, where she saw a supermarket carrier bag wedged unsuccessfully into the bottom drawer of a filing cabinet. Somebody's dinner, she thought absently. The radiographer was wearing L'Air Du Temps; its scent, full of flowers, reminded her of France. She closed her eyes and conjured up something else. Anything else, some other time. *I failed*, she kept thinking. *Poor baby*.

It seemed she had failed at a lot of things lately. This. Guy. The move. The only thing she was good at was painting. Perhaps Cecily

Joscelyne was right after all. *People like me are selfish.* We can't function in relation to other people.

And then she thought of Cecily's over-bright, piercing eye. Of her over-tended look. *People in glass houses . . .* she thought. There was something very scary about that woman.

She thought of Cecily's warm, dough-like hands on hers, and shuddered involuntarily. Cecily and Guy; criticising, probing. All so quick to tell her what she ought to do, and how wrong she had been up to now.

Were they right?

Were they?

Alex's face came rushing into her mind. Smiling, shaking his head. Squeezing her hand, giving her that rush of quick confidence. She felt warm next to him, she realised. She felt . . . she tried to put her finger on it. Equal . . . that was it. Not better, not worse. But *the same.*

Guy had held a picture up to her for years now: a reflection of herself that he had always insisted was real. In the picture, she always said slightly the wrong thing. Talked with a funny voice that was right enough to *be* funny, but wrong enough to embarrass him. And she never wore quite the right thing. Often when they would go out, he would stand at the door, looking her up and down, sometimes wordlessly, and, at other times, saying, 'You're wearing *that?*' or, 'Where did you get *that?*' She would look down at herself. 'Why?' she would say. 'What's the matter?' He would shrug. And all night she'd catch sight of herself in mirrors, in windows, and wonder if he was right.

Wrong-footing. The trip game. He would put something in her path—some invisible obstacle—and she would fall over it, and he would pick her up and dust her off, asking how on earth she could have missed that. He would trip her up in conversations; in showing how much more he knew than her. In saying she knew nothing of the world, that she was naive, that she was gullible. Trip her up in front of others. Trip her up over money, doing her tax returns and clicking his tongue against his teeth at her notes, guffawing now and again at her handwritten memos. Trip her up in bed, hinting at her ineptness.

And then, when she had tripped, when she had fallen, she would sometimes look back—much more often, in the latter months—and think, *But you put that there to MAKE me fall. It wasn't ME at all . . .*

It hadn't always been that way. It wasn't that way in the very beginning. With her head thrown back on the pillow, still looking at the far wall, Faith summoned up the past: opening the car window as she came down the motorway, turning east. Their first holiday, in Fréjus. Thyme and salt and sand and flowers. Guy's hand inching up her thigh as she drove, and her laughing and slapping it away. The restaurant in Cannes, in the back street, with its polished dark wood interior, its green-painted tables in the alleyway. A younger Guy, very young, flushed, sitting straighter than he did now, waving his arms about. The bill came and was left on a plate as they lingered over the last of the wine. As Guy tipped francs and centimes out on to the iron-topped table, he asked her casually to marry him.

The radiographer turned the screen around towards her.

'Mrs Collins?'

'Miss.'

'Look . . .'

She glanced at the screen. It was, at first, an impenetrable jungle of lines. The radiographer pointed with a pencil at the screen.

'See the little heart beating?'

'Heart?'

'Here's the back . . . Wait a minute . . . that's the spine. See the heart?'

'Yes,' Faith whispered. 'That's the heart.' And she began to laugh. It came out as a series of choked gurgles, and she put her hand to her mouth. The woman looked at her. 'I thought I'd miscarried,' Faith said.

'Well, you haven't,' came the reply. 'There's the proof. Good news, then? You're about ten weeks, a bit over. Perfectly OK.'

Faith couldn't speak. She did a rapid calculation. Yes, it could be ten weeks. She'd counted the months in four-week bites; but it was actually more than that.

I did something right, she thought wildly.

Oh boy! Oh boy, oh boy.

I did something RIGHT at last.

She couldn't help herself. She began to cry, gloriously releasing tears of plain joy. The radiographer, smiling, gave her a tissue. 'But what was all that this morning?' Faith managed to ask, at last.

The radiographer shrugged. 'You'd better ask the doctor. It might have been a twin pregnancy, and you've lost the twin. More likely though, it was just a little leak. Have you been overdoing it?'

'You could say that.'

'Well, don't.' The radiographer looked over her shoulder. 'Is that Dad at the door?' she asked. 'Shall we let him in?' She was already beckoning to Guy.

'No, no,' said Faith.

But it was too late. Guy walked over to the bed, glancing briefly at Faith but then fixing his attention on the screen.

'Here's your baby,' said the nurse.

He hesitated, wringing his hands in an uncharacteristic gesture. He leaned forward from the waist. 'Did it kick?' he said, suddenly. 'I saw a kick.'

'It's an involuntary reflex at the moment,' said the radiographer. 'Kicks won't come till later.'

'It looks like a fish.'

The woman laughed. 'Trust a man.'

'Is it a boy or a girl?'

'Pass.'

'Later?'

'Later. What do you want, a boy?'

She's already got you marked down as a chauvinist, thought Faith wryly.

He reached out and placed his fingertip on the screen, on the point where the vertebrae met the skull. 'I don't mind,' he said. 'I don't mind at all.'

When he turned to look down at Faith, his eyes were full of tears. It shook her totally.

'Will you tell me?' he asked softly. 'Is it mine?'

'Yes,' she replied. She was unable to say anything to him but the absolute truth. 'It's yours.'

TWENTY-THREE

*G*UY ARRIVED BACK IN LONDON AT SIX O'CLOCK.

As he unlocked the door, he saw Chloe in the hall. She had just come in from work and was unwinding a scarf from her neck. She paused, then murmured a hello.

She was waiting for him to come and kiss her. He took off his coat, taking a long time to shake it and hang it up.

'Busy day?' she asked.

'Some.'

'Meetings?'

'Yes.'

She hesitated, then smiled. 'I thought we could go out to dinner . . .'

'Why?'

She shrugged. 'Why not? We haven't been out in a fortnight.' She walked towards him, smiling rather forcedly. 'Why don't we go mad for once,' she said.

He felt weighed down, as if he would have trouble putting one foot in front of the other. A little twitch, a movement—a *reflex action*—kept skipping in and out of his mind, like a beckoning finger at the corner of his eye.

Chloe kissed him delicately. She picked up his hand and pressed it to her breast. 'Or we could stay in,' she said.

He stared at her as though she had begun speaking a foreign language. She caressed him through his clothes, then unbuckled his belt. When he made no response, she brought his hand down, lifting the hem of her black dress. She insinuated his hand inside her briefs, a thin slip of oyster-coloured silk, and tried to clamp it there with her thighs. She was so inexpert it almost made him laugh.

He shrugged away from her, almost tearing his hand away. Her eyes rounded in surprise.

He went to the stairs and bounded up them two at a time.

Chloe came to the bottom of the flight and stared after him. 'We can make babies, too!' she shouted.

He paused at the top, looking down at her. Did she know where he had been all day? Did she know?

'I can make babies, too,' she whispered.

She turned away and walked to the kitchen at the back of the house. He heard the sound of her heeled shoes, striking the tiled floor.

TWENTY-FOUR

$\mathcal{W}$HEN FAITH WOKE UP THE NEXT MORNING IN HOSPITAL, she sat up slowly, rubbing sleep from her eyes. Lifting her watch from the locker, she saw that it was a quarter to seven. She swung her legs out of bed just at the moment that a nurse arrived, waving what looked like a cardboard hat.

'Sample,' she said breezily.

Faith lifted it and looked at it. 'Delightful,' she muttered.

As the nurse pushed back the curtains, a woman came into the ward pushing a trolley. 'All right, lover?' she asked Faith. 'Tea?'

'Have you got any herbal?' Faith asked.

The auxiliary started to laugh. 'Oh yeah,' she said. '*And* champagne. *And* chocolate.'

After breakfast, Faith sat upright in bed, waiting for the doctor's rounds. As she did so, Alex appeared in the doorway of the ward, almost obscured by the bunch of white roses and gypsophilia that he was carrying.

'Oh God,' Faith said, holding out her arms as he walked towards her, grinning, 'whose funeral are you going to?'

'I'm not allowed in,' he replied. 'I just got told off.'

'The older nurse? Oh, ignore her. She's in the Womb Police,' Faith said.

'What's their motto? *They Shall Not Pass?*'

'No. It's *Spread 'Em.*'

Alex put the flowers down on the locker, considered her a second, and then kissed her. 'Language unbecoming in a mother,' he said.

'I am one, too.'

'I know.'

They smiled at each other, as if this were their personal, mutual achievement.

'The rumour is they're letting me out,' Faith said. 'I have to be prodded first. Then I'm free.'

'I know. The sister told me when I rang up.'

'When was that?'

'Dawn.'

She smiled wonderingly at him. 'Couldn't you sleep?'

He ran his finger down the side of the bed. 'Will you do me a favour?' he asked.

'Depends what it is.'

'Keep me company. I'm going to Cornwall for a few days.'

'Since when?'

'Since I decided.'

The ward was silent. The other women, heads studiously buried behind magazines and newspapers, were obviously not reading them, but waiting, instead, to see what she would say.

'I ought to work.'

'You ought to rest.'

'Where in Cornwall?'

'Does it matter?'

She met his look. 'No,' she said.

He leaned forward, taking her hand. 'No funny business, I promise. Just peace and quiet.'

'Shame,' said one of Faith's neighbours, from behind her *Woman's Own*.

It was eleven o'clock when they drove out from the hospital together, in bright sunshine.

White skein snow ridges dusted the fields; the sky was brilliant and cloudless. Faith slipped into the front seat of the Range Rover.

Alex had gone to the house and packed a bag for her, and it nestled between the front and back seats. He had already apologised for that: for walking into the house and going through her things, for making a decision without really consulting her. She had waved the comment aside. She didn't care if he took charge. Just so long as *someone* did. For the moment, she was weary with her own independence—being *stubborn*, as her mother would have said.

As they had left the hospital, she had taken Alex's offered arm. He felt secure; like a rock. As he had opened the car door, he was all attention, brushing down the seat, folding the hem of her coat in so that the door didn't catch on it.

'OK?' he asked.

'OK,' she murmured.

There was a nagging voice of conscience at the back of her mind. She *ought* to go home. She *ought* to carry on. Then, as Alex steered the car through the sparse traffic and out into the country, she leaned back into the seat and let the house and the work flood from her mind. Alex was right. A few days' peace was what she needed right now.

'Do you know that you left the back door open?' he asked.

'No . . . God, in all that panic it's a wonder I didn't do worse,' she commented. 'Only the back door? What about the front?'

'The front was locked.'

She paused a second. The front-door lock was ancient, an iron key on a round iron loop. 'Guy must have done it,' she murmured. 'Still, I've got a spare in my car.'

'Parked in the drive. So that's OK.'

'Where's the back-door key now?'

'Here,' he said. Driving, he fished the key out of his hip pocket, and gave it to her.

They drove for an hour, until midday.

By that time, they had left Dorset and were already into Devon, and they decided to stop at a roadside pub for lunch. It was a place that looked quaint from the outside and turned out to be surprisingly awful on the inside; but it at least had a roaring fire, around which a fifties-style tiled hearth had been polished to a shine. Fake strings of hops and vine leaves hung over the one-armed bandit. A framed newspaper clipping on the wall told how the place had been filled with mud during the rains of a lost winter. After a while, a black Labrador came and lay on Faith's feet, with a grunting sigh that was almost human.

'I'm sorry about this,' said Alex. 'I only hope the food's better than the decor.'

Faith smiled. 'So you've not been here before?'

'I've passed it sometimes. I drive down to Helford about three or four times a year. Thought it looked all right.'

'Have you got a house in Helford?'

'No. I made a boat for a man who lives there. Then I got to know someone who builds launches: hand-built, wood launches.'

Faith sipped her drink. 'I don't really fancy sailing,' she admitted. 'I don't like the herd of people you get.'

'What people?'

She wrinkled her nose. 'Oh, the kind that go to Cowes or Henley, that sort.'

'Half of them are just hangers-on. They're not proper sailors.'

'Can you separate them? The hangers-on, I mean? The ones at Henley look as if they've escaped from *Wind In The Willows*. Striped caps and blazers and Mr Toad stomachs. Then . . .' She was into her stride now, grinning at Alex, who had propped his chin in his hand in a mock attitude of enchantment. 'Well, then there's the *other* sort I don't like. *Proper* sailors. The ones that go out every weekend and are fanatical about it and go everywhere in Guernsey jumpers and always call themselves *yotties*, and prop up bars and sound so ruddy hearty about it.'

Alex was laughing by now. 'I don't know a single person like that!'

'Oh, come *on*. They're all over the south coast like a rash. Who are your buyers, then?'

'They're mostly Asian or Arab, actually.'

'Ah.'

'*Ah*. What does that mean—*ah*?'

'Nothing. But it's still people with money.'

'And you don't like people with money.'

'Not usually, no.'

He pointed an accusing finger at her. 'It's you then,' he said. '*You're* the last living socialist.'

'Oh, piss off.'

He nodded for a moment without saying anything. Then, 'It's appealing, really,' he said.

'Oh . . . right. We're back to *naive.*'

'Who called you that?'

'Guy. Guy always said I was stupid. So you're not the first. You can get in line.'

She stared down at the table top. The Labrador lifted its head and looked at her with a soulful expression.

Alex sighed. 'There's a difference between naive and stupid,' he said, quietly. 'You're *not* stupid, and you *are* naive. If you're naive, you're honest. Don't knock that quality. Don't trade it in for *cynical.* And don't get touchy and bitter,' he added. 'It makes your mouth an ugly shape.'

Their food came. Faith sat looking at Alex intently, hardly knowing how to take this last remark. She rapidly decided she didn't mind it half as much as she should. In fact, and very peculiarly, she found herself wanting to laugh. Conversations like that with Guy had always ended in a shouting match—by now, Guy would have started trading personal insults about Faith's parents and the council house she grew up in. He would have started saying things like, 'You and the *dish* people,' meaning, the satellite dishes that seemed to festoon the streets where she had been brought up. But, by contrast, Alex was still smiling, handing her the cutlery wrapped in its paper napkin, warning her that the plate in front of her was hot. *I'm having a conversation with an adult,* Faith thought. *How novel.*

'Thank goodness,' he said, indicating the plates with an inclination of his head.

He was right. The soup was thick, home-made, and looked delicious; the bread was soft and warm. Alongside the soup, the prawn and salad sandwiches were on Victorian plates with voluptuous painted wreaths of pink roses.

'Eat,' he said.

'Master, I obey,' she responded.

They continued in silence for some minutes. The Labrador rolled on to his side and held one front paw in the air, a patent party trick for scraps. Faith began to laugh, tickling him with the tip of her shoe.

'It's only four days till Christmas,' she said.

'It certainly is.'

'I'd nearly forgotten.'

'Congratulations. You must be one of the few women in the country who hasn't got a box of festive biscuits in the larder and six tins of ham.'

'Sexist.'

He smiled. 'All those lists. All those sorties to Waitrose. It's genetically programmed in me. Christmas equals woman in tears next to pile of Christmas cards.'

There was the slightest, momentary pause. 'Do you miss it?' Faith asked.

'Last December,' he said quietly, 'I remember coming in about nine o'clock one night, and I watched Morecambe and Wise on the TV and wondered why we were getting a decent week's programmes for a change. They showed that sketch . . . the one where all the newsreaders were singing the song from *South Pacific*?'

'I remember.'

'Dawned on me. Must be Christmas, then. On Christmas Day I went for a walk, and got to the pub, and listened to a lot of men in new sweaters talking about what a bloody day they were having. How much they'd spent on the kids' presents . . .'

'Didn't you feel low?'

'Yes . . . I wished I were having a bloody day, too.'

The honesty of this remark touched her deeply. She laid her hand over his. 'Well, I must do that Waitrose run,' she said. 'I'm going to buy crackers and pull them with myself and I'm going to cook a big dinner and get a plum pudding—the works. I haven't *not* had Christmas, and I'm not starting now just because I'm by myself.'

He saluted her with a raised glass. They had finished the food, and Alex leaned back now into the chair.

Something that had been scratching at the corner of Faith's mind, irritatedly scratching for attention like a fingernail on a window pane, now occurred to her. 'Listen . . . how do you know Cecily Joscelyne?' she asked.

She didn't expect the reaction she got. Alex's face drained of colour for a second: his body went rigid. Then he seemed to get himself in hand, brushing his hair back.

'Do I know her?' he asked.

She smiled. 'She said, "Fancy seeing you." Something like that.'

'Did she?'

'You *know* she did.'

'Maybe.'

'Well . . . yes, she did. Not *maybe*. She did.'

He said nothing.

She frowned at him. Then a horrible suspicion swept over her. 'Don't tell me . . . not *you and her*,' she said.

'And *me*? Christ save me.'

'Then what? What is it?'

'I just knew her in London. She . . . it's a long time ago. It's nothing.'

'I can see in your face it's not *nothing*.'

'I just wish . . . Look, it's none of my business, Faith. But it's best not to get involved with that woman.'

'But I'm already involved. She's given me this huge advance, and this contract . . .'

'Can't you get out of it?'

'But why should I?'

He paused, looking down at the fire and the dog, whose attention was still fixed rigidly on the rim of their table, expecting food to drop from it at any moment.

'I knew her in London,' he said, finally. 'She had an affair with a friend of mine. A married man. A weak man. Someone with one of those worthless titles and ancient debts and a house he couldn't afford, and four children . . .'

An expression of regret crossed his face. The memory was evidently painful.

'He was a dimwit really, old Piers,' he continued, in a soft, affectionate voice. 'He was one of those men who would say sorry if you stepped on him. D'you know, he once apologised to a lorry driver who'd cut him up and then got out of his cab when Piers hooted on the horn. Piers actually apologised and called him *sir*.' Alex smiled broadly.

Faith smiled, too. 'He sounds all right to me.'

Alex shook his head. 'He was good company. He and his wife used to support charities, go to theatre nights. At one of those nights, Cecily Joscelyne crossed his path.' He clasped his hands in his lap. 'She's the devil incarnate. And I'm *not* joking.'

Faith felt very still. Very calm, as if the room and the world beyond it had stopped. 'What happened?' she asked.

'Oh . . . the predictable. Affair. All her initiative. Piers was bloody useless. Like watching a spider with a fly. And it wasn't as if she really wanted him. She played with him; kind of bloodsport. I think she actually hates men. Every man, with the exception of her bloody brother and step-father. Piers knew her brother; they went to school together, apparently. And he had handled some money affairs for the father. Stocks and shares.' He raised his eyes to Faith. 'Has she told you about them?'

'No. What?'

He shook his head. 'Her step-father is far worse than her,' he said. He turned away for a second, reaching down to pet the dog, and to look across at the jukebox. He seemed to be collecting himself; calming himself. 'Cecily used to tell Piers how he wasn't a patch on him.' Alex gave a short, bitter laugh. 'Then, when she got bored with calling him a limp dick, she started the phone calls. Letters.'

'What phone calls?'

Alex took a long draught of his drink. 'Obscene things. Insults about Piers's family. Last one said that his children would never inherit because there would be nothing *left* to inherit because this . . . someone, whoever it was, would *see* to it that there was nothing left. Ruin them. See them thrown into the street . . .'

'My God,' whispered Faith. 'And this . . . this was *her*? This was *Cecily*?'

Alex finished his drink, lifted the car keys and spun them, reflectively, around his finger. 'Caroline always thought it was a man on the phone,' he said, thoughtfully. 'But I think that was just because it's what you would expect. *Expect* a nuisance caller to be a man. Most of them are. But then, she didn't know Cecily.'

'Did she ever find out about the affair?'

'Oh, yes. One of the letters spelled it out for her.'

'God, how terrible.'

Alex looked at Faith levelly. 'Yes,' he said. 'It was terrible. Piers committed suicide.'

'No . . .'

'He just couldn't stand it.'

'Did you ever . . . ask her? Confront her with it?'

He gave a grim smile. 'Yes,' he said. And the morning on the stairs at the Robertson Hall building flashed back to him. The longing to thrust Cecily Joscelyne through the plate-glass window and watch her fall the ten floors to the street below.

'And?'

He stood up. 'She denied it, of course.' He took Faith's arm. 'But Piers knew it was her,' he said. 'That's good enough for me.'

They reached the hotel late in the afternoon. Faith had fallen asleep over the last fifty miles or so, and, when she woke, it was with the sensation of the car being at a steep angle. They had been creeping along at ten miles an hour around a hairpin bend. On one side, grey rock formed a wall; on the other, the road could be seen threading down with a backdrop of sea.

She had squirmed upright. 'Where are we?'

'Nearly there. Postwithiel Trevarrack.'

'Post what?' She laughed, rubbing her eyes. 'That's some drop.'

'Smuggler country.'

'Daphne du Maurier?'

'South.'

She was almost getting used to his shorthand way of speaking. As she peered through the windscreen, the village had been suddenly revealed below them: a handful of square grey houses seemingly wedged into a V-shaped crack in the rocks. Roofs crowded each other above a shelf of pebbled beach about thirty yards long. Right in the centre, there was a pub, the light from its windows strengthening against the last of the afternoon light.

'Pretty,' Faith said.

'Yes.'

They parked at the back and walked into a lowceilinged bar. Faith looked around her as Alex signed the register. Everything seemed to have been designed for midgets: the door heights, the stairs. 'Seventeenth century,' Alex said, following her eyes. 'They didn't make thin, tall women like you then.'

'You might have said lissome and willowy,' she grumbled.

They were shown upstairs, and parted on the landing: Alex going left, she going right.

Her room was perfect.

It looked out over the knuckle of rock that stretched, like a protective arm, half way across the little bay. The sea went out in a dog-leg fashion between the rock and the headland. Snow still clung in neat little lines to each stony shelf of the cliff. It was a painting in grey and rose.

She looked around herself, smiling, feeling like a kid playing truant from school.

I ought to be somewhere else.

She didn't feel like caring.

Each house further up the road on the left had its oblong of light. Just for a second, Faith held her breath, jolted at the sight of what she thought were faces pressed to the glass porch of one of the top cottages. Then, smiling, she realised that the figures weren't human at all, but a collection of wooden figureheads from old sailing ships. An orange light was on in the porch, lighting them up like characters crowded to the edge of a stage, picked out by footlights. They looked so incongruous, like a group of goblin faces sardined into the flat-roofed box on the front of the terrace. The nearest figure was voluptuously female: swathed in a purple dress, with painted yellow hair falling like lazy boa constrictors over her shoulders and around her waist. She stared out at the sea with a fierce grin of triumph.

Cecily Joscelyne, thought Faith.

She leaned on the window frame, her arm unconsciously crossed over her stomach. She had thought Joz strange from the first moment she had seen her: out of place, polished, *perfected*, like an airbrushed photograph. Her image was too tight, too right, to be natural. She remembered how she had recoiled at Cecily's touch in the pub: the podginess of those manicured hands, the smell of her perfume. How smothering it had been. She was like a tide rolling in. They were all Canutes ordering the inevitable to go back.

Faith looked down at the sea. But *evil* . . . ? No. Surely not. Nobody was really evil, were they? Not like Alex had said . . .

She had a second of disorientation. Just for that second, she wondered why she was here, why she was with Alex. *Running all over the place*, she thought. *I've been running since the day Guy packed his things and kissed Chloe on the pavement* . . .

Running to some sort of netherworld. She glanced across again at the funny little house fifty feet above her on the hillside, with its figureheads staring into the gloom. It reminded her of a story from childhood: of a little girl who had stepped the wrong side of the shadow of the church spire, the *widdershins* side, and forever afterwards had been lost in a fairy world where the trees moved and the walls breathed and the path wound up the mountain to a palace of gold.

She had stepped *widdershins* of the spire.

'I'm all right,' she said out loud. 'I'm with Alex.'

Smiling and shaking her head at herself, she turned away from the window. Looking about her with approval, she noted really for the first time how comfortable it all was: the thick curtains, the soft towels, the white sheets turned back on the three-quarter bed, the tray with its tea and coffee and biscuits and chocolates. There was a spray of winter jasmine in a carnival glass vase; it shed an arc of refracted colour on the wall behind. She peeled off her coat and dress and stood in the luxurious comfort, waving her arms about. A *warm*, centrally-heated, clean, sweet-smelling, delicious, *warm warm* room. Wonderful! She jumped on the bed, spreadeagled herself, and wriggled in pagan delight on the thick feather duvet.

'Alex, you are a genius,' she said.

At that very moment, the phone rang. She picked it up.

'OK?' he said.

'I'm just thinking about you.'

'How's your view?'

'Lovely. *Lovely.*'

'Better than home?'

'I don't think I can face going back there. Not after this!'

There was a momentary pause. 'You don't have to, if you don't want to,' he said.

'Alex, I was joking.'

'Uh-huh. Hungry?'

'Maybe after a shower. Where are you?'

'The next floor up. Meet me in an hour? In the bar?'

'Yes.'

She replaced the receiver.

She took off the rest of her clothes, and caught sight of herself in the full-length mirror. There was a definite thickening across her hips. She turned this way and that. Her breasts were heavier by an inch or more; her bra had left red marks. *I must get myself proper clothes*, she thought. *I must start behaving sensibly. Stop running, stop running.* Register with a GP, and think about prams and eating regularly, and iron tablets, and baby books, and all those other things. She ran her hands across her body experimentally. The sensations seemed heightened—everything with a sharp edge now, everything technicoloured. She lifted her hair and took a long, critical look at the shape of her face: her high forehead, her angular cheekbones, chin, and shoulders.

Someone inside her carried these same imprints. They would emerge with some of them, carry them away. Part of her would go on in someone else's skin: hands, face, hair colour. The length of her fingers, the arch of her foot.

She had become immortal.

She slipped to the soft cream carpet and sat cross-legged, still staring at herself in the twilight. Beyond the window, the sea boomed on the beach. The tide had now reached the pebbles, and drew them back with a lingering, whispering voice. Pushing, sighing. She crossed her arms over her chest, resting each hand on the opposite shoulder, and sat there, looking, until it was quite dark.

When she came down to dinner, Alex was already in the bar, sitting on a stool and reading what looked like a very old copy of *Country Life*.

She caught sight of him the second she got to the bottom of the stairs, and he suddenly reminded her of a famous country-and-western singer: all beard and luxuriant white hair. She smiled. As she walked towards him, she said, 'Do you like country music?'

'Can't stand it,' he replied.

He did not ask where this topic of conversation had come from. Instead, he regarded her quietly for a moment, never taking his eyes off hers. She glowed under his intense inspection, and perched on the stool alongside him. 'Tell me what you do like,' she said.

'Genesis, Dylan, Pink Floyd, Cream.'

'You old rocker.'

'I stopped at punk and started regressing. You?'

She wrinkled her nose. 'Joni Mitchell and Tamla Motown. And if things get really bad, when I feel low, I put on Louis Armstrong. *Hotter Than That*, recorded 1927. If I'm not leaping about after that, it's probably flu.'

He smiled. 'Drink?'

'Orange juice.'

He ordered it.

'You look very pretty,' he said.

The compliment startled her. She fussed with the front of her loose shirt and the pleat in the leg of the black trousers.

'I hope you didn't think I rifled about in your cupboards,' Alex said. 'I just opened drawers and sort of ladled them wholesale into the suitcase. I hope you don't mind.'

'No, of course not,' she said. Although, if she were perfectly honest, the idea had slightly disturbed her when she had been dressing just now: Alex looking through her underwear, choosing things. It didn't sit right in her head. Yet she had brushed this feeling away.

'Good health,' he said, lifting his glass.

'Lots of it,' she responded.

The menus came. She let him order for her. He chose fresh salmon steaks, broccoli, baby carrots, salad, potatoes poached in cream. She pretended to sit by, marking him out of 10, holding up invisible cards with imaginary scores for each dish. Except for the wine—then she mimed tearing up the cards and throwing them away.

'No wine?'

'The baby.'

'Champagne. Champagne is good for babies.'

'It is not!'

'It's good for life. One glass.'

'It's thirty pounds a bottle!'

He ordered it.

She sat looking at him with her head on one side. 'Are you rich?' she asked.

'Filthy rich,' he said.

'Good,' she retorted.

They burst out laughing.

'What shall we do tomorrow?' he asked, as they were shown to their table, and settled down to a now black-and-gold portrait of the village and the sea.

'Not sail,' she said.

'Why not? I promise if you come with me, you won't be sick.'

'I get sick in the bath.'

'No, no . . . well, leave it. We'll see.'

'We could walk a little way,' she offered.

'Yes, we could walk.'

'Where to?'

'Anywhere,' he said. He took her hand. Conflicting emotions took hold of her: confusion, desire, a subliminal fear that dotted the rim of her feelings, like Morse code flickering in the distance. She wanted very much in that moment to know what it was like to lie wrapped in his arms in the dark, in silence, in the warm; to feel his body alongside her. To feel his hands on her.

As if reading her thoughts, his grip tightened.

'What did you mean, in the garden?' she asked.

'About what?'

'About baggage. From the past.'

He didn't answer right away. He still held her hand tightly, gazing at her. Then he said, 'It doesn't matter.'

'You didn't mean age? Not that you were older or wiser, something like that?'

'No, not that.'

'Because that doesn't matter to me, Alex.'

'No, I know . . .'

Something was escaping her here. She could feel it, but couldn't grasp what it was. 'You didn't mean business? You'd done something in business?'

He smiled half-heartedly. 'No. My company was taken over. I had to go. It was nothing I'd done,' he added. The last sentence was almost aggressive.

'You didn't want to stay on? They didn't offer you anything?' Looking at him now, she had a sudden conviction that she had seen a newspaper article about him. Just as he turned his head to see the wine waiter coming towards him, it lit a strong, abrupt memory: a picture in a paper. That same profile. Except that his hair had been dark. *Oh!* snapped a small voice inside her. *I remember now. I remember about you, and that company, and . . . something else . . .* His hair had turned white since then. And he had grown the beard.

She tried in vain to recall it.

The champagne came. The words and the picture vanished as abruptly as they had come. Alex grinned across at her as the cork popped and hit the curtains behind them, and the waiter apologised. She asked for the cork, because it would be a nice memento, stuffing it into her handbag self-consciously. With a great flourish, Alex toasted *the patter of tiny feet.*

Faith laughed, shaking her head.

Another couple across the room turned round to smile at them, and waved their glasses too, in congratulations. Although she had only taken two or three sips of the wine, Faith felt very light-headed.

They began to eat the main course in easy silence, when she suddenly said, more to make conversation than anything else, 'Tell me about your wife.'

Alex glanced up, fork poised half way to his mouth. 'Why?' he said.

She hesitated, thrown. 'I would like to know.'

'Why?'

'Well . . . I suppose I'm curious. And don't say "why?" again, for God's sake.'

He lowered his fork with the food untasted.

'How old was she?' she asked.

'When she died?'

'Yes.'

'Forty-one.'

'Oh, Alex. Was it an accident?'

He paused, looking down at his plate momentarily. 'Yes.'

'Oh . . .' Obliviously, she ploughed on, eating all the while she was talking. She didn't notice the change in his expression. The immobility. 'What did she look like?'

'Blonde, small . . .'

'That's all? What did she do? Did she have a job?'

He straightened in his chair. 'Do you mind if we change the subject?'

She glanced at him, saw his rigidity, and blushed. 'Oh, I'm sorry. I'm sorry, Alex.'

'That's all right. Forget it.'

'I just—'

'Forget it.'

This time, the silence was awkward.

The waiter came, cleared the plates. He asked if they wanted dessert; Faith said yes immediately, at the same time that Alex said no and ordered two coffees.

'Oh—well, then—' Faith began.

'Have what you want,' Alex said.

She asked for fruit, in an agony of embarrassment, and, when it came, took an apricot and some grapes on to her plate and sat looking at them miserably. *Damn it*, she thought. *My big mouth.*

'I expect you feel very tired,' Alex said, in a formal voice.

'Yes, I think I am.'

In a further ocean of quiet, he called for the bill.

TWENTY-FIVE

*W*HERE ARE YOU?'

Joz presses the phone close to her ear, hearing for the first time the note of unease in his voice. Since darkness fell, she has been sitting alone, savouring the absolute stillness. Images have invaded her; they possess her more and more.

Since leaving Thomas, she has dreamed of descending that make-believe stair to the garden. Again and again. The doors to the garden beckoning as if they contain the most valuable of revelations. Promise called from beyond the stairs and the garden doors. The stairs and the garden that the doctor showed her, in those first weeks in the clinic. Stairs, garden. Stairs. Garden. In the last twenty-four hours, she has found herself, both sleeping *and* waking, free-falling into the past.

She is full of bitterness: a bottle full to the neck, over the neck, spilling out of its mouth. Bitter liquid washing through every cell, every pore. She is far beyond being angry, or shocked. She has stopped trembling. She keeps seeing the day, and everything since stacked up behind it: scum stacking on a barrier in a stream.

My God, how you have lied to me.

The past . . . last night, she broke through to another country. It was a school in Suffolk, with a Georgian house as its centre. The art rooms were on the top floor. She was fourteen years old.

As she walked down the imaginary stair of her dreams, the treads became the worn linoleum of the school. Red swirling patterns along a cream-painted corridor. She turned into the art room, and saw Catherine Parker sitting by the window, writing a letter.

'Listen to me. Where are you? It's important.'

He is trying to pierce her silence now.

'People want to see you.'

Your step-father wants to see you.

Her heart contracted on that far-off day. The day in the school. The day that Catherine fell. Randolph came into the room, his bulk blocking the narrow doorway, his head bent to avoid the low ceiling. He was smiling broadly.

So this is your friend.

He is still talking on the telephone now, commanding her attention. She wrenches herself from the stuffy studio in Suffolk back to the present.

'I've rung to tell you something,' she says, ignoring his last sentence.

'Don't be silly, Cecily. You must listen to me.'

'No,' she whispers. 'It's the other way round tonight. *You* must listen to *me*.'

He laughs, on the other end of the line, not understanding yet what she has said. She has often objected before: asked for him not to ring, not to bully her, not even to speak. And yet he *does* ring, he *does* speak. That overbearing voice, rich and dark. He speaks for perhaps an hour, while she sits clamped in misery, unable to break free from him, not even understanding why she has no power to challenge him. The key lies in that voice. In the words he uses.

Even thinking of it now, as she sits in the dark in the strange house, is making her mind swirl. She fights to keep control of her memories. Memories dredged from dreams. Memories sewn into the ash-tree leaves beyond the window. *You belong to me.* The descending blind of words, cutting her away from any recollection. Drowning in his voice.

But he can't stop it any more.

It has come back.

Complete.

You must be Catherine.

Randolph held out his bear-like paw to Joz's friend that day. Catherine did not move an inch. She stared at his hand as if it revolted her. Joz thrilled at her courage: *no one* rebuffed her step-father. But Catherine did. She glared at him from the window seat, contempt and outrage mingled on her face.

'I know all about you, Mr Joscelyne,' she said.

'Do you?' He smiled. 'And what is it that you know, Catherine?'

'I know that you are very cruel to Cecily.'

He started to laugh, and stepped closer to them.

'And what's this all about?' he asked. 'Is it that I won't allow Cecily to come on your holiday?'

Catherine stood up. Joz had begun to cry. Randolph put his hand on her shoulder, where it burned possessively. She longed to wrench that hand away from her, as Catherine said she should. Catherine . . . the only one who knew. The only one she had ever confided in. The only one who had listened.

Catherine Parker. Catherine . . . short and round. A wing of thick brown hair. Round eyes. A defiant, cheerful little face.

She had told that round-eyed, bright face everything. She had cried, and told Catherine that she was afraid of going home at night.

And poor little Catherine Parker, on her own, had tried to come to her rescue.

'Cecily has been very upset lately,' Randolph said. 'And you're the one making her so.'

'No!'

It was the first time Joz had spoken that day. Catherine looked at her, kindly, sympathetically.

Cathy was such a tubby little girl. Only fourteen, and so unworldly. Their funny little games about horses and foxes. They were still children, despite their ages. And yet it was Catherine who stood up to Randolph. Catherine, her writing pad clasped in front of her, her mouth set in a rigid line of defiance.

Joz now lowered the phone, away from her.

So many walls breaking down, now that the first dam is breached. What do they call it? The veils that fall from the eyes. Dozens of veils are falling. She can see her way through. There is no more fog. She can see Catherine Parker clearly now, unafraid of her step-father. The only person that Joz has ever met who is not afraid. She can see Catherine's face so clearly. It makes her want to weep. She loved Catherine so much.

She was thin then. Thin when Catherine was her friend. When did she start to put on weight? In the clinic. When she left the clinic. Eighteen months later, she was two stone heavier. No longer the wraith. In the only way she could, she had become Catherine. Not Catherine's courage. But Catherine's size. All these years she had been trying to be Catherine.

Trying to confront her father.

Trying to tell him to stop.

'I know what you've been doing,' she says now, lifting the phone again to her mouth.

'Speak up.'

'I know what you've been doing.'

'But you can't know, little Martian. I've been spending all day with a charming girl. Taking her to lunch. She's a very nice girl. She's organising a show in Penbold Street. Grecian art. Her name is Chloe. She wants to marry a man called Guy.'

'Guy . . . ?'

What is he doing?

'She's very wealthy. But not very happy, poor dear. Quite an amazing situation. She's the mistress, and she's afraid that her boyfriend is cheating with his wife. Ironic, isn't it?'

'Why?'

'Why is it ironic? Oh come now, darling. Even you can see that.'

'No. Why look for her?'

'I found the other side of your triangle. I thought it was rather clever of me.'

'But you don't know anything about it.'

'Don't be silly,' he says. 'I know everything about everyone. Don't I? I know the chap who owns the company that this Guy fellow works for. Over dinner, he tells me that one of his wide boys hasn't turned in for work. Massive deal hanging fire. This person is chasing his wife across three counties.'

'No, no . . .' whispers Joz.

'Moreover, small world, James Fenshaw-Wright is the girl's father. She's been crying to Daddy. All girls do that, eh, Martian? You remember James?'

'No . . .'

'I know where you are. There was no need to ring me at all. I was about to ring you. You're a very naughty girl, Cecily, trying to get away from me.'

She closes her eyes. No more nightmares to act in. No more.

This is for her.

This is her place.

He can't have this.

'I was thinking what a nice companion Chloe might be for Thomas.'

Oh God.

Don't. Don't. Don't take him away from me again. You can't. I've found the place for us. The secret place. It's the only hope I have.

She squares her shoulders, takes a deep breath.

No more.

'You're right,' she says, making her voice level, deadened. 'I've done a stupid thing.'

She can almost see him smiling.

'I think we ought to get you back to Lewis. Just for a short spell,' he says.

'Yes,' she murmurs. 'You're right. I feel . . . very confused . . . I keep thinking about . . . hands, windows, I keep thinking I remember something . . .'

She hears the anxiety in the intake of his breath. It is almost like an electric current passing down the phone line.

'You sit tight, darling,' he says. 'I'll come and get you. I'll come and I'll take you to Lewis and you won't be confused any more.'

She smiles grimly at the phone.

Never has she hated him more than in this moment.

Slowly, she gives him exact directions to the house.

TWENTY-SIX

*I*N THE MORNING, it was as if the awkward conversation of the night before had never been. Faith came down to breakfast and Alex was already there, obviously watching for her. He jumped up, holding out her chair for her. She sat down into a pool of bright December sunshine.

'Did you sleep well?' he asked.

'Yes, thank you. Beautifully.'

He poured the coffee. She drank in luxurious silence, savouring its strong taste.

'Are you still in favour of walking?'

'Very much,' she told him.

'Fine.'

She smiled at him. He smiled at her.

They drove further along the coast that morning, to a more forgiving country, easier to the eye, sheltered from the wind. They walked along a river for a mile or so, occasionally stopping to remark on the birds or the boats. It was cold, peaceful.

'I'm sorry if I overstepped the mark last night,' Faith said, as they reached a stone outcrop and sat down.

'You didn't.'

'I did. I haven't any right to demand that you tell me. Except—' and she gave him a mischievous grin '—it's very frustrating.'

He picked an imaginary piece of dirt from his lap. 'It doesn't matter now,' he said. 'Don't let's dwell on it. I want to ask you something.'

You're lying, she thought. The idea was swift, and perfectly calm.

But whatever the lie, great or small, he wasn't ready to part with it yet. And she could honestly not see a single way of forcing the man to reveal something he wanted hidden. Or why she should.

The only thing she was really sure of was that that particular part of the past was painful. She knew what that meant. She knew how that felt. And she was almost mortally afraid of cutting through to that secret, watching someone else's blood flow. She was having trouble enough finding a place to put what she regarded as her own failings with Guy. She was the last person on earth to point the finger at Alex and demand what he had done that made him feel so bad.

Except that I want to help you.

More than that.

I want to know everything about you.

Everything.

She gazed at his profile now, as he sat looking out at the grey-silver river, the banks of bare trees opposite. He had a strong-featured face. High forehead, deep-set eyes, high cheekbones. And that white, thick hair and white-grey beard. His hands, folded on one propped-up knee, were large and the fingers square-tipped and long. She reached out now and placed her hand on top of his.

'You look like Neptune,' she said.

He began to laugh. 'Is that good? Isn't he supposed to have green skin?'

'And seaweed in his hair.' She laughed, too. 'I had a book when I was small. Neptune sitting on a rock and gazing out to sea, and the waves looking like seahorses. You look like the picture.'

He held her hand, examining it, turning it over so that he could see the palm.

'What a long life,' he said.

'Have I?' She looked.

As her head was bent, he said, 'Will you marry me?'

She looked up, shocked. 'Sorry? What?'

'Marry. Will you marry me?'

'I—'

'I would like us to be married.'

'But . . .' Her brain was working nineteen to the dozen. 'We hardly know each other.'

He pressed his thumb gently into her palm, working it in a circular motion that was not quite comfortable. But she didn't withdraw her hand.

'I can't bear you to be alone in that house, and I can't bear to *be* alone,' he said, eventually.

'But—' She tried to choose her words carefully. 'That isn't a good enough reason, is it? Do you think it is?' She was watching his thumb, not daring to look in his face. 'We might want company, but hate each other's.'

'I don't think so.'

'But we can't be sure! My God.' She smiled. 'You must be quite crazy. I've only known you a week . . . two weeks . . .'

'But you came down here with me.'

She looked up then. 'Yes, I did.'

He cupped her face gently. He gave her a kiss of such lingering intensity that she felt rather disorientated, the trees and the river shifting and refracting as she opened her eyes.

'I want to look after you,' he said. 'You and the baby. I want to protect you.'

She drew down his hands. Her own were shaking slightly, and for a second they made a fumbling duet in their laps, he trying to hold on, she trying to extricate herself. 'I'm not sure I want to *be* protected,' she said. 'I just want—I thought I wanted—to be left alone. I want to get *out*. Out from under this stone. The past . . . you understand?'

He did. She saw it in his eyes.

'I felt I couldn't breathe with Guy,' she continued. 'And I still felt that I couldn't breathe after he had gone.'

'And you feel the same way with me?'

She thought about it a second. 'No,' she said, truthfully. 'Strange, but with you is the only time I *can* breathe.'

'Faith—'

She held up her hand to stop him. 'No, no. I haven't finished. Everything is wrong; I'm off balance, I'm not *straight* . . .' She shook her head at her own inability to express herself. 'I can't explain,' she said.

He was watching her closely; he hadn't moved a muscle. 'Do you think I can bear to think of you, in that house, freezing through this winter?' he asked eventually. 'No heating, no comfort . . . trying to shop and make fires and cook, while you get to seven, eight months pregnant? Bringing in coal from the bunker with that ridiculous little bucket and spade of yours? What are you playing at? Orphan Annie?'

She laughed. He was right. But, this time, Alex was not laughing in return.

'It isn't funny, Faith,' he said. 'It's not good for the baby.'

She became suddenly serious. 'Are you saying you want to marry me to get me in the warm?'

'Don't be ridiculous.'

'That's what it sounds like.'

'Oh, for Christ's sake, if I wanted you to be warm, I'd just pay for the bloody central heating to be put in and be done with it.'

'Would you? I see.' She had bridled somewhat at this image of him blithely waving his magic wand of money over her.

'You *know* that isn't all,' he said, seeing her expression.

'I feel I'm being bullied, Alex.'

'You really are the most *exasperating* woman,' he cried, standing up, shoving his hands into his pockets.

'I've been told,' she said.

'Don't give me that wounded-fawn routine,' he snapped.

It really hurt her. She sat stiffly, as if he had slapped her, blood rushing to her face.

'I'm sorry, I'm sorry,' he said, immediately. 'God, I . . . It's not charity. It's not to spite Guy. It's not even to save you from Guy, or to save the baby, or to save me losing sleep over that bloody house of yours. It's because . . .' He turned round to her, took the two steps that separated them, lifted her to her feet, and told her, 'It's because I want you. Because I love you.'

'After ten days . . .'

'I do,' he whispered.

She looked down at their now-clasped hands, frowning. 'Alex, I don't want to get married,' she said. 'Even if I did, I'm not divorced.'

'Surely that's a formality.'

'Well . . . yes. But *I don't want to get married.*'

'Live with me, then.'

She glanced up. 'You're very persistent.'

'Come and live in my house. Let yours be renovated. You can have a separate room . . .'

She put her head on one side. 'I would need a studio.'

'You can have one. I converted the attic last year. I put in Velux windows. Come and look at it, at least.'

'I keep odd hours.'

'So do I.'

'I don't like Pink Floyd.'

'I'll only play it in the workshop.'

'I don't want—'

'. . . to be married. I know.' He held up his arms, like a puppet, with the hands hanging limply down. 'No strings attached,' he said.

'None?'

'None.'

Is there such a thing? she thought. 'I'll come for the guided tour,' she said. 'But . . . no other promises.'

TWENTY-SEVEN

$\mathcal{A}$s Randolph stood at the door of his London home the wind blew snow, heavier now, over the doorstep.

The woman at his side—pale, tall with luminous dark eyes and hair scraped back unflatteringly from her face—clutched his arm. If she felt him automatically stiffen at her touch, she did not seem to register it.

'You will find her?' she was saying to him, her voice quavering. 'I can't tell you—how important it is to me—'

Randolph smiled. He patted the hand on his arm. He looked down at her from his aristocratic height. 'On the contrary,' he murmured. 'You *have* told me. You've told me in tremendous detail. And—' He removed the hand. 'I shall do my utmost for you. I'm sure it's a terrible misunderstanding.'

On the very point of going, and having held her composure this far, the woman abruptly broke down. She fumbled through her handbag for a handkerchief. 'It's the house, you see,' she said. 'I'm so worried about losing the house. I've got business loans with the house as security. It's my home; I'm divorced; I've got two children at school; if we lose the house . . .'

Randolph made a soothing noise, somewhere between a hum and

a cough. As she blew her nose, he told her, 'I'm quite sure it's a mistake. Cecily must have paid you and the cheque has gone awry somehow. I shall find out today, at once . . .'

'They're so ready to help you, these banks, when things are going well, and they come down so hard when you start to fail,' she said. 'It's not as if I've done any bad work. It's just these four big contracts, three of them Miss Joscelyne's. And there's four thousand pounds I've spent on fabrics. She wanted silk; I mean you don't get that kind of silk, in that quantity, for less, and the colour, it was made especially, and she assured me, she *promised* me . . .'

'Quite, quite.' Randolph gave her a patrician smile as he ushered her, now rather forcibly, over the step. 'And if I can't contact Cecily, I shall write you the cheque myself.'

The woman hesitated, her eyes full of tears, the handkerchief pressed to her mouth. It evidently had crossed her mind to stay, and demand Randolph's cheque on the spot. But her nerve seemed to fail her.

'Thank you,' she said at last, going down the first two or three steps, her glance trailing back to the opulent interior of the house. 'You've got my number? If you could ring . . . ? I'm at home all Christmas . . .'

And her face squeezed in a final terrible expression of grief at the word *Christmas*.

'I will, I will,' murmured Randolph, and shut the door.

Ruth was standing on the first step of the immense staircase as he turned back.

Her face was set in a blank mask. She lifted her hand and beckoned him. 'Will you come into the drawing room,' she said. It was an order rather than a request.

He followed her.

She was wearing an old sweater and skirt. A scarf was secured at her neck with a pin that was not quite fixed straight. When she turned to look at him, he looked away. He could not bear to see her untidy. It offended him.

'How many now?' she asked softly.

'How many what?'

'Clients. How many clients of hers have rung here?'

'Well, Merrion-Walsh was bound to ring. She is known for becoming manic within an hour . . .' He began his broad, vacant smile.

Ruth turned from the fireplace and walked to the window. Her profile was pinched. She began stroking the sill, over and over. 'This morning I got a phone call,' she told him. 'From a newspaper.'

'Which one?'

'They asked me if it were true that my daughter had committed murder.'

Randolph sat forward on his seat, one hand gripping the edge.

'They seemed to know about Cecily's business,' she went on, in the same monotone, 'so I imagine someone like Merrion-Walsh—'

'If she's done this, I'll ruin her,' Randolph said.

She looked up at him. 'Like the others?' she said. 'Guess how much the paper offered me.'

'I can't imagine.'

'A hundred thousand pounds.'

Randolph began to laugh.

'Yes,' she continued. 'Hardly very much, is it? When one thinks of the scandals at one's fingertips.'

He stopped laughing. He felt the balance of power in the room shift and tremble. Ruth was looking at him frigidly.

'They told me an interesting story,' she said. 'They told me about this Treasury scandal, and asked if I knew who the third man was.' She smiled slowly. 'Of course, I told them I didn't understand,' she said.

Randolph had paled. He leaned backwards almost hesitantly, as if the back of the chair were capable of burning his skin. Then he propped his head on one hand, holding himself very still, watching her.

'It's a great mistake, you know,' she said. 'To think that you're invincible. There are only so many enemies one person can make. Only so many fortunes one person can steal.'

This time, Randolph flinched. Ruth smiled, turning away to look again out of the window, at the flakes of snow rushing diagonally across it. 'All this time,' she said, as though thinking aloud, 'I imagined that I really knew nothing at all. But, when I come to think of it, I suppose I know enough to merit *several* hundred thousand pounds, actually.'

'What . . . exactly . . . is this leading to?'

'I really think Cecily should be found, don't you?'

Randolph clasped one hand over the other, as if tempted to hit her, and afraid to stand up to try. 'Yes,' he said. 'I'll go and get her.'

'Good.'

'I'll take her straight to Lewis.'

Ruth walked across to him. He saw, when she stood very close, that she wasn't afraid of him.

'Why now?' he said.

'I am very tired,' she replied. Her voice was thin and very slow. 'Tired of turning my blind eye, Randolph. And that horrible man on the telephone today . . . that made me feel so filthy . . .' She gave a protracted sigh. 'He told me about a woman in America—I'd never even heard her name—and some story about her husband and you . . . and a business in Ireland, and . . . so many terrible things,' she whispered. 'Why do people . . . never stop talking when you ask them . . . ?'

Randolph's glance fell to a point in the carpet, where two nymphs sported in permanent leafy luxury, on a bank of green and gold. He stared at a flower held in the hand of the woman on the left, as if it held the answers.

'I'll find Cecily,' he said.

'Bring her home.'

'I'll take her to Lewis and Burne-Vaughan.'

'No,' she said. 'I'll take her. Cecily and I will be going away. For a long holiday.' She fixed him with that new, weary look. 'I think you'll agree that would be best.'

He didn't answer immediately. Then, flushed, he replied, 'She won't come with you. She won't listen to *you*. She only listens to me.'

Ruth sighed deeply. 'Yes, she has been listening to you for a very long time,' she said. 'Too long. And that is entirely my fault.'

'You can't—'

For the first time, Ruth raised her voice to him. She cut through his sentence: 'Oh yes,' she told him, 'I *can*. I've come to it very late, haven't I, Randolph? I've come to it after my daughter is lost. I've come to it twenty years too late, probably, and that has been my weakness . . .' She began to shake. He saw her hands trembling uncontrollably, and the way she immediately clasped them, to stop them in the face of his contempt. She raised her face and looked him in the eye without flinching. 'But . . . What is it they say, Randolph? What is it?' Tears formed in her eyes, but she did not shed them. 'That silly phrase . . . better late, isn't it? Better late . . . than *never.*'

She turned back to look at the window.

The silence in the room, for almost a minute, was complete.

'When I was young, I thought the world was a beautiful place,' Ruth murmured. 'Hard to believe one was once that naive.'

She walked past him.

Against the window, flakes of snow adhered to the glass, slipping slowly down as they dissolved.

TWENTY-EIGHT

*J*OZ STOOD AT THE WINDOW, WAITING.

It was dark now, the early dark of December. The radio in the kitchen was just playing the theme of the five o'clock news.

He would come.

She hugged her crossed arms to her. She was wearing a sweater of Faith's that clung to her; she had found it in the drawer when it began to get too cold. She looked down at her feet, incongruously still in their Italian leather pumps. There was sand on the floor, and one of the cement bags had split. She had walked the dust through; it was everywhere now. In the living room, in the bedroom. It ground under her feet, as irritating as spilt sugar.

The phone rang.

She jumped for it in the darkness, hitting her knee on the corner of the couch.

'Yes . . .'

Don't let it be him. Tell me he's on his way. Please God. This once. For me.

The line crackled. 'Miss Joscelyne?'

'Yes.'

'It's Webber Brothers. The tilers.'

'Oh . . . yes. Yes.'

'The blue isn't in. We can't get it before Christmas. But we got the terracotta, the rope. Was it ninety?'

'Eighty.'

'Ah . . . and you want these delivered—'

'Tomorrow.'

'Right . . . There'll be a charge.'

'That's all right.'

'OK. Give us directions, then.'

She did. She told them about the causeway and the unmade road. They rang off.

Cold enveloped her.

She went to the fire she had made and struck a match. The paper was damp. She sat thrusting more and more rolled-up sheets into it, until at last it caught. The hearth was scattered with spent matches.

She stared into the first light blue wreaths of flame. She thought of Catherine Parker. In the last eight hours, Catherine's face had been looking into hers. Fourteen. Curious. For it to have been buried for so long, and to have been so intractable, so hidden. It had only been through that little door to the garden, down the long slope of imaginary green grass. It had only been a thought away. A word or two away, all this time.

Randolph had always said that he loved her. He took her to parties when Mother was ill with one of her undefined sicknesses. He would claim she was the prettiest girl in the room. At ten, at twelve, she would accompany him, feeling incredibly grown-up on his arm.

She had these party shoes. Black patent with a bar strap. She could never fix that strap. Randolph would come and fix it for her.

Randolph would come.

She got up abruptly, and began to walk around the room, following her own track unconsciously, like an animal in a cage, tracing the same unerring line. Catherine Parker said she went to bed at half past eight. She never went to parties, except those in the afternoons. She never went anywhere alone, at night, with her father. She never saw him in her room. She never did things for him. Never combed his hair, or manicured his fingers; was never made to stand still for hours; never had to learn songs. Or listen to lies. Catherine had escaped all that.

Catherine had sat with her on the bench under the beech tree. They were watching the Seniors play tennis. There was a tournament, and then a Parents' Evening.

Catherine was going to Wareham that summer, to a house her grandmother used to own, that was now her mother's. The family had been spending weekends there for as long as she could remember, she said. She described the things they did—the shopping, the beach, the barbecues. Described sharing a bunk room with her older sister. Described her younger brother's snores. Described her parents' laughter on the porch, a sound that lulled her to sleep. A sound of perfect security.

Joz had told Catherine, then.

They could see Randolph's car edging into the gravel drive, across the playing field.

'It must be very exciting, where *you* live,' said Catherine. 'I wish exciting things happened to me.'

So she had told her.

Their eyes were fixed on Randolph and Ruth making their progress across the grass. Ruth passing her handbag from one hand to the other. Randolph three paces in front.

Cecily had told Catherine what exciting things she did, at home.

'It doesn't matter,' she had explained. 'You see . . . I help him. He says so. You have to help your father.'

'I don't understand,' Catherine had said. By now, Randolph was only twenty yards away.

'It's nothing to do with me, any more,' Joz had said. 'I go somewhere else. I go *outside*.'

Catherine had stared at her, frowning, mystified. Only later did she grasp what Joz had meant; later, in the next week, in their whispered conversations. *Outside*—you floated above the ground. Above whatever was happening below. You flew through the windows; you lay on the ridge of the roof, deep in the blackness between the stars. You were not *there*.

On the following Wednesday, as they were going in to prayers, Catherine had linked arms with Joz, smiling. 'Why don't you come with me for the holidays?' she had asked.

'Won't your mother mind?'

'Why should she? One more won't make much difference.'

Joz had told Randolph that night. Been all excitement. Randolph had protested that he didn't even know Catherine's family. He said that she couldn't leave him. Not for a whole six weeks.

'Come and meet her,' she had said. She never guessed for a moment that Randolph would object. At the bottom of everything, after it was all done, didn't he really love her? Didn't he really want the best for her?

But Randolph and Catherine had understood each other the second they met. The second that Randolph dipped his head to avoid the low doorway, and walked into the art room with his hand extended. In that second, disgust crossed Catherine's face. Randolph saw it at once.

And that was the end of them.

In Faith's living room, now, Joz stopped walking.

She had heard a car in the lane. She looked through Faith's window, at the low curve of the drive. Headlights picked out the hawthorn in a bitter halogen stream. In the next moment, they flooded the room where she stood. He must have seen her, behind the glass, picked out as though by arc lights, on her private stage.

Here I am, Randolph.

Come and get me.

She grabbed the coat—Faith's coat—from the back of the sofa.

He killed the engine and got out.

'This is it?' he said.

She rushed to the driver's door, impatient while he slowly locked the car. He was wearing a thick coat, dark and velvety. As he got out, he smiled at her. 'You are really a very naughty child,' he said.

'Yes,' she said, automatically.

'Are you packed?' he asked.

'Not quite.'

'I'll wait in the car.'

'No,' she said. He glanced at her, eyebrows raised, questioning.

'Come and look at something,' she said. 'I want to show you something.'

He hesitated, then shrugged his shoulders. She reached for his hand, fighting down the distaste.

I remember. You see? I remember everything.

That long-ago room with Catherine, and her, and Randolph. That muggy early-summer afternoon. Below the art room was a flagged terrace, and the place where the tutors and visitors parked their cars. Randolph drove an MGB then. It was racing green, catching the sunlight.

Catherine had begun to talk. Flushed in the face, her voice steady. Randolph's amused little smile had shrunk, and then vanished. Catherine told him, clearly, what she was going to tell her parents. How Joz was invited to stay all summer. She said that her parents would take Joz away from him.

Randolph had stepped forward and suddenly grasped Catherine's wrist. She gasped, trying to shake him off, flinging her hand around ineffectually. His fingers were tight, perfectly encircling her arm.

'You won't do any such thing,' he had said.

'I will, I will! She's only little. You're a bully, a bully . . .'

Catherine was heavy. Too heavy.

That was the problem.

She stumbled, and caught the back of her knees on the low window sill. The window was wide open. She fell backwards, the upper half of her body wedged for a second outside. She wriggled, her eyes widening. Time hung suspended, Catherine half in the shade of the room and half in the brilliant light of the sun outside. Her free hand skittered along the pane—Joz heard her nails on the glass—searching for the window frame. She found it. Joz began pulling at her friend's legs, frantic.

'I'll tell them, I'll tell them,' Catherine was saying.

Randolph placed one broad, big hand in the centre of Catherine's chest. She fell backwards, her feet coming up, as neat as a doll propped permanently into a sitting position, the bottom half of her rising as the torso was pushed down. The expression on her face was one of almost comical disbelief. It was so sudden.

Joz squealed and shouted. 'Catherine!'

The other girl's legs were wrenched from her grasp. At Randolph's shoulder, she saw, for a terrible moment, Catherine's hand holding the frame, her fingertips white. Then she dropped. That hand scrabbled on the wall as she went down.

It was forty feet to the paved terrace below.

Hands. Trees. Falling.

Randolph had turned towards her.

'Oh,' she was crying, hysterical. 'Oh, oh . . .'

He had advanced on her, and pushed her to a sitting position. She almost fell down, terrified that he would shove her through the same window. Randolph himself was shaking.

'That was a silly thing to do,' he said.

She had gaped at him. She saw the savage determination close over his expression.

'Me?' she had echoed. '*Me?*'

His hand had tightened on her shoulder. The voice began. That rolling, insistent voice. 'A terrible, wicked thing,' he said. 'I don't know what we are going to do about this at all . . .'

'No!' she had screamed.

She had rushed to the window, hanging out of it. There was already a small group of people below, rushing to Catherine's body. They looked up at her. She could still see the horror etched on their faces.

She had held out her arms, as if she could snatch Catherine from the ground. 'I didn't do it!' she had screamed. 'I didn't! Catherine . . . Catherine . . . Catherine . . .'

She led Randolph now down the path, a weedy strip of tarmac in a forest of grass and thistles. Overgrown roses scratched at them as the ground sloped away. *Now* they could hear the sea, talking on the pebbles and sand below, whispering and rolling as it drew the stones back with every wave. The snow was three or four inches deep: it gave a little light, showed her where she knew the rotted gate stood permanently propped half-open. There was a deep rut past the gate, a scoop of track. Hawthorn bent over their heads. As they emerged from the shelter of the trees, the wind suddenly tore up the side of the cliff.

'Be careful,' she said. 'It's very steep.'

The path was a series of rough hairpins that quickly fell out of sight; shoulders of rock could be seen, silhouetted against the lighter shade of the water.

'You have to grab on most of the way,' she said. 'It takes about ten minutes. Longer to come back.'

'Far enough,' he said.

'Don't you think it's wonderful?'

'Not particularly. Darling girl, it's absolutely freezing.'

'Yes,' she said. 'It's very cold.'

He was always acute to the changes in her voice. It was one of the things he liked so much about the phone. He liked to hear her worried and afraid. He liked to hear her submission. Ruth would sometimes look at him, dare to look at *him*, with a face of disgusted pity, a long way past frustration: a grown woman's private knowledge. But Joz never did, because he had never let her grow. He had stopped her at eight, perhaps nine—stopped her dead in her tracks. She never matured past that terrified point of dependency, for fear of offending him; and even if there had never been a Catherine Parker, Joz would still be helpless inside her head. He turned her to him now, on the edge of the path. The sea below them glittered through the gloom.

'You're not very well, Cecily,' he said. 'Don't you feel very poorly? You need a long rest.'

'Do I? Isn't here the right place? I was sure that it was.'

'No, no, no.' He stroked her shoulders. 'Somewhere else, Martian.'

Joz retreated from the present. Back down the stairs to the garden.

You are walking down the garden now, Cecily. It is a very beautiful garden . . .

The doctor's voice surrounded her.

It is full of flowers. There is no one in the garden to hurt you. You are alone and feeling very relaxed and very peaceful. At the end of the garden is a stream of clear, deep water. You may sit by the stream, or walk through the stream, but you will pass over the stream and into the land beyond. Here, in this lovely place, you can see for miles. You can see what

*is past in every detail. I am here with you. I am beside you. Nothing can
hurt you. You are walking past the stream and deeper into the past. You
are fourteen now. You are thirteen. You are twelve.*

She had showed the doctor the past in all its miserable detail. But
he had never asked for a description of the present—what was then,
to her, the awful present. Randolph's word had been accepted. It tied
in with what the teachers said: that Cecily seemed to be a very with-
drawn, moody, sometimes angry little girl, who formed intense rela-
tionships, usually of dislike and envy, but, with Catherine Parker, of
clinging, possessive friendship.

Randolph had told them that Cecily wanted to spend the summer
with Catherine and that Catherine did not want her company. Even as
he had walked into the room, he said, the girls were arguing. Before
he knew what was happening, *before he could stop his daughter*, Cecily
had pushed Catherine through the open window.

It was all very tragic. Randolph had wept, Ruth had wept. Cecily
had not wept. She remained silent, words and feelings and thoughts
welded by unbelievable horror to the inside of her skull. She was
admitted to a psychiatric clinic. For eighteen long months.

She looked at her father now.

'Am I going back to hospital?' she asked.

'Just for a little while.'

She glanced down at the sea. 'Thomas and I are going to live here,'
she said.

'No,' he told her. 'It's all in your mind, Cecily. It always was. You
can't have Thomas. He is your brother.'

Faces rushed up through the shadows. All alive, all reaching for
her, all extending their arms to hold her. Piers Hammond. Mark Estwood. All those before. Perhaps twenty. Perhaps thirty. Like avenging angels, their moment come, they flocked about her, beating their
wings against her face.

'And you are not my father,' she replied.

Randolph lifted his hand, as if he could push back the wind that
was sweeping up the steep side of the cliff. Ice stung Joz's mouth.

'All those terrible things,' she said.

'Cecily, listen to me.'

'The world is falling down,' she said. 'Isn't it? It's going wrong. Can't you fix it?'

'It's nothing.'

She sighed deeply. 'I fixed a lot of things, didn't I?' she said. 'I was a very useful and good girl. I got presents. I was *good*. Want me to fix something for you now?'

He was shaking his head. 'You're wrong . . .'

'The word *belong*,' she said.

A sound came out of him: a kind of smothered cry of surprise. The wind snatched it away.

'It isn't a very long word, is it?' she continued. 'Not even a sentence. Said in your voice. Just you, and the word *belong*. *You belong to me*. That was it, wasn't it?'

'No . . .' he said, but there was no strength in his denial.

'Do you know what happens,' she asked him, 'when you know the password to the fortress? Didn't Doctor Lewis tell you that it might not work forever?' She realised that she had begun to cry: wrenching sobs that tore her apart. 'What did you know about him, Randolph, to make him do such a terrible thing to me?' she wept. 'To put me inside this place? Don't you understand . . . it doesn't work for always. You can't always keep the lid on the boiling pan forever. It blows. Steam inside. It blows.'

'Cecily. Darling . . . you're very sick. Your memory is very sick.'

'No. It's like Jericho. You play the right note. Just one note. And all the walls come tumbling down.'

She was sure that he turned white in the darkness. But she would never know for certain. He looked behind him, as if trying to see the way back from the edge of the cliff. The blackness of the sea rolled beneath them.

Darkness, all-consuming, swept over her. She had a fleeting sensation of drowning.

The real world left her forever.

She reached for him, her hand flat, the palm facing him.

'Don't you see?' she asked him. 'Don't you see what it means? I remember . . . *I remember* . . .'

TWENTY-NINE

*T*HERE WAS A FESTIVE ATMOSPHERE in the car as Alex and Faith
drove back the next day.

They were singing carols and playing I-Spy at the same time, so
that the carols came out something like, *It came upon the midnight—
fence, farm, fly, flies, fiver, fumb—that glorious song of old—*

'Fumb?' said Alex. 'What's a fumb?'

Faith held up two thumbs. 'Dis is fumbs,' she told him.

'Wrong, then.'

'Foible?'

'You're getting desperate.'

'Fantasy. Fantail. Fidel Castro.'

'Give up?'

'I give up. What was it?'

'Feet.'

'Feet? *Feet?*'

'The things at the ends of your legs.'

'Ah, that's not fair . . .'

'H.'

'Cheat.'

'H.'

'Hedge, horse, hawthorn, hou—'

They were turning into the drive. Alex shouted, 'Right!' Then they saw Faith's garden. The Range Rover lurched up the remaining incline.

'House . . .' Faith murmured. Then, 'My *God*. What is this?'

Alex turned off the engine and sat staring through the windscreen. As Faith turned back towards him, questions racing across her face, he murmured a single word: 'No.'

Faith leaped out of the car.

'Be careful,' he called.

He got out after her and tried to catch her up as she ran towards the steps. She wheeled around to him. 'What's happened?' she demanded.

'I don't know.'

'You ordered all this?' she said. 'What you were saying in the hotel . . . about renovating . . .'

'No, no.'

'Well, *I* didn't!' Her eyes ran over the piles of bricks, pipes, sand, hardcore. Over the two vans parked close to the rear. *Parker's* said one, in red lettering. *The Conservatory Specialists*. The other was blank, but its back door was open, revealing tiers of screws, nails, power tools, wire.

'What the *fuck* . . . ?' Faith muttered under her breath.

Alex was level with her now. She fixed him with an accusing glare. 'If you know anything about this, if this was meant to be some sort of present, I promise you—' she began.

'I don't. I really don't,' he objected.

She looked at him narrowly. 'You know *something*,' she said.

'I'm hoping to Christ that I'm wrong,' he replied.

Cecily Joscelyne came out on to the porch.

'Hello!' she called cheerily.

She was wearing a track suit. Her hair was limp, unsprayed, unbrushed. She waved to them, standing across the doorway.

Faith strode round the side of the house, up the steps. Joz did not move.

'What are you doing in my house?' Faith said.

Joz held up one hand. '*My* house,' she said sweetly.

'Your . . .'

And she saw the way that Joz was looking at Alex. She wheeled around. He was coming up the steps, his face ashen.

'You'd better tell me,' Faith said. 'And it had better be damned bloody good.'

'Don't get upset,' he said.

'Don't get *upset!*'

He waved his hands ineffectually, not daring actually to touch her, pull her away. 'I really don't know,' he protested. 'At the hospital—'

'I offered him two hundred thousand pounds. He didn't refuse it. I think it's a terribly good offer,' said Joz. 'So would anyone. A terribly *generous* offer.' She sighed and shook her head at the wall behind them, the wall of the living room. Through the window, Faith glimpsed her easel, her sofa, her chair, piled into a corner, one on top of the other. Fury ballooned inside her, choking her.

'Considering the amount it will take to renovate,' Joz was saying.

Faith almost hit her. 'This is *my* house,' she said. 'It isn't for sale. I mean, what's going on here? I go away for a couple of days, and . . .' She gasped, staring from Joz to the window, from the window to Joz. 'I don't want your money. I want my house.' And then she tugged unconsciously at her hair, a residue of childhood, a gesture of frustration when she couldn't make herself understood. 'I haven't sold it to you. Don't you understand? What's happened here? I *own* this place!'

'I offered two hundred thousand—'

Faith slapped her fist hard against her thigh. 'I don't *want* your bloody money!' she shouted. 'I want my house! You've got no right—'

And she caught a look in Joz's eye. It was a vacant, untroubled expression. She had her head slightly to one side, listening, as though trying to understand a subnormal child. Her face showed nothing but this blank, almost drugged, sweetness.

'You're insane,' Faith whispered. 'You're out of your bloody *tree.*' And she pushed Joz to one side. She already had her key in her hand, and she held it out for the familiar lock.

But it wasn't there.

There was a faint scar on the woodwork of the frame, and a new

Yale was in place of the old keyhole. Faith's hand hovered impotently, the old iron key circling over the new brass.

'What have you done!' she said, disbelievingly. 'You changed the *locks!*'

Her heart began to pound ominously in her throat. She had a moment of hysterical despair. She turned, ran down the steps, and around the side of the house. She almost tripped as she came around the corner. The old broken paving stones of the patio had been prised up and stacked in a pile. Swerving, she ran to the back door. She could hear, now, voices inside. Men's voices.

She looked down at the lock.

It was the same as the front. Changed.

Wildly, she began banging on the door. 'Let me in!' she shouted. 'Let me in!'

Almost immediately, a face came to the kitchen window. The man stared at her, turned round to say something to someone at his back, and then turned back to her, smiling slightly, shaking his head.

She pressed her face close to the glass. 'Please . . . please . . . it's my house,' she shouted. 'Can you open the door? There's been a mistake here! Please, *please!*'

He only went on shaking his head, shrugging his shoulders. His look said, *I would like to. But I can't.*

She couldn't fathom it. It was like some nightmare. She turned to see Alex and Joz emerging by the pile of flagstones. Joz was still smiling.

'They won't let you in,' she commented. 'I told them about you. I said you might come round.'

'They . . . know about me? What are you talking about?'

Joz laughed a little, as though embarrassed at having to explain herself. 'I told them the previous owner might make a fuss,' she said. 'I told them you might not like me ripping the place to pieces. People get very funny about houses, don't they?' she added conversationally.

'The previous . . . !' Faith really felt as though she were going mad. She looked at Alex. 'Tell me this isn't happening,' she begged.

'Of course,' Joz was saying, 'provided you throw enough money at these people, they will be quite compliant. Don't you find that with tradespeople?' She crossed her arms with quiet satisfaction. 'They said they couldn't come out before the New Year. Ridiculous, isn't it? And yet . . . all change for a little extra boodle. Same old story.'

At that moment, Alex grabbed Joz's arm. She looked down at his hand as if some giant insect had just bitten her: a look of surprised disgust. It seemed as if it had not occurred to her that either of them should be angry, that this reaction was disgraceful, *unseemly*.

Faith saw the look. The thought flashed in her head, *I'll kill you.*

'All right,' Alex was saying. 'All right. This has gone too far. I don't know what you're playing at, I don't know what the game is this time, but I'm warning you, I told you in the hospital—'

'Oh, *puh-leese*,' Joz said.

'I warned you. I told you to leave her alone. Give Faith the new keys, get your things. If you go now, we won't say anything else about it.'

'Oh, won't we?' yelled Faith. 'The hell we won't!'

Joz pulled herself free of Alex's grip. 'Two hundred thousand pounds,' she said evenly. 'It's in Faith's bank account. As of yesterday.'

'It's . . .' Faith's voice trailed away. For a second, she thought she was going to faint. Her feet no longer felt as if they were touching the ground. She was dropping through a hole in the earth; behind her back, she heard the muffled conversation of the builders in the kitchen, eager spectators at this lunatic game.

'Faith,' said Alex.

He rushed forward, caught her as she was going to fall.

'Come home,' he said.

'Get your fucking traitorous hands *off* me,' she retorted.

'Oh dear,' murmured Joz, beginning to laugh.

Faith pointed a finger at her. 'And *you*,' she shouted. 'I'm going to the police, they'll get you out of here, they'll break down that door, and—'

'I think you'll find they won't,' Joz remarked.

'Faith—come home,' Alex said. 'Let's get this sorted.'

'Get *off*.'

He shook her slightly, lowering his voice, turning his back so that Joz could neither see his face nor hear what he was saying. He looked deep into Faith's eyes, an inch from her face, forcing her to listen to him.

'Come home,' he repeated. 'Please, darling . . .'

She passed a hand, trembling, over her eyes. He put his arm around her.

'Trust me,' he whispered. 'Trust me.'

THIRTY

$\mathcal{W}$HEN THEY GOT INTO ALEX'S HOUSE, they walked into the drawing room, with its stunning view of the sea.

'Sit down,' Alex said, drawing forward the wing chair.

'No.'

'Now, Faith . . .'

She took a deep breath. She hated that *I-can-sort-this-all-out* tone. It was the one that Guy used whenever he was trying to pull the wool over her eyes.

'What we'll do is—' he began.

'No,' she said. 'Listen to me, Alex.'

He stopped mid-floor, his hands still resting on the back of the chair.

'Cecily Joscelyne.'

'This isn't my fault,' he said.

She waved her hand. 'I don't want to hear that. I want to hear what hold she thinks she has over you.'

'She hasn't.'

She let the statement hold between them for a second. It sounded hollow.

'Tell me,' she said. 'Not half the story. *All* the story.'

'There really isn't anything to tell.'

'For God's sake, Alex! She's blackmailing you?'

He gave a short derisory laugh. 'No.'

'What is it, then? Something she knows that I don't know.' She thumped her fist against her leg impotently. 'She said, *in the hospital*. You talked to her in the hospital, and some subject came up—something you don't want to talk to me about . . .' She stopped, realising. 'Your wife.'

He shook his head.

'Tell me what it is about your wife.'

They looked at each other. After holding her gaze for a second, he sat down on the chair. She remained standing.

'I'm sure, if you cast your mind back, you'll remember,' he said, wearily. 'Or perhaps you won't . . . these things seem so important to the people involved. It's as if no one will ever stop talking about it. Then, six months later, they can't recall what it was. They think they know your face. They *think* . . . but they don't know . . .'

She let him talk. All the time, as she watched him, she thought of ridiculous details, as though to defer the impact of what was coming. She thought how much she liked that unconscious gesture of his hands, as he spread his fingers in a too-wide expression as he spoke, like a toddler spreading his hands wide to catch a ball. Or that slight mark on the side of his face, underneath the ear, the nick of a childhood injury . . . She thought, with an infinite sadness, *I don't want to lose this*.

'Eight years ago, a foreign company made a bid for Robertson Hall,' he said, 'the company I'd built up since I was twenty. I didn't want the merger, but some of the Board did. About the same time, Piers—I told you about Piers?'

She gave an infinitesimal nod of her head.

'He started with Cecily. Her step-father is a shareholder. On Robertson, and a dozen others. Very influential. Knows a lot of the Government people. He wanted to accept another bid. This rumour went around that there would be some investigation of the company unless we took the rival offer.'

'What has this to do with that?' Faith tossed her cocked thumb back in the direction of her own house.

'I'm coming to that,' he said. 'I suspected that Randolph Joscelyne had some sort of leverage with the Board; he had interests in the other company—'

'Isn't that illegal?'

Alex gave a cynical laugh. 'He took a dislike to me, wanted me off the Board . . .'

'But it was *your* company,' Faith interrupted.

'Not for much longer. It was *personal*. I couldn't bear him.' And he glanced away, towards the corner of the room, thinking aloud. 'The funny thing was, Piers had had a run-in with him, too. Piers handled some stocks of his that dived. Not Piers's fault. Just the market. But Joscelyne took it *personally*.'

Faith frowned, puzzled. 'This has some connection with Cecily?'

He said nothing.

'You're not saying Cecily had the affair with your friend to—what would you call it?—to *avenge* her stepfather? Because he took a dislike to Piers? That's ludicrous!'

'Is it?' Alex said. 'Have you ever met this family?'

'But, my God . . . no one has an affair for *their father* . . .'

No one has an affair to please their father.

Not unless they're sick.

She shook her head, as if to clear it of this outlandish idea. 'Did you take the offer?' she asked. 'To leave the Board?'

'No.' The reply was firm. His face clouded. 'He reminded me of her,' he murmured. 'His massive, great booming voice, totally . . .' He searched for the right word. 'Theatrical. He manages theatres, that's where he made his money. But he carries it on everywhere he goes. The room has to stop when he walks in. Everywhere. It's an entrance. The king has come. He doesn't like it at all, you know, if you carry on talking, don't look up . . .' He gave a rueful little smile. 'It irritated the hell out of me, I can tell you,' he said. 'This sod turning up to shareholders' meetings, Board meetings, acting the lord of all he surveys, questioning building designs he knew nothing about, planning rights . . . *Christ*.' Alex ran his hand through his hair.

'Anyway, the Board split. There were these undercurrents; it was like captaining the *Titanic*. One day someone would be supporting me, the next . . .' He paused, looking out of the window. 'I always felt there was a threat in his dislike,' he said slowly. 'As if he could harm me. Not by anything I could see. But something invisible. The icebergs under the water, you understand? He would drop a hint about someone he knew. He knew everybody. He would regurgitate private conversations that he somehow had got to know about . . . I never quite figured that out . . . He was one step ahead of the game, and sometimes would let you know it. Not in technical expertise, not even particularly in the amount of money he controlled, but in *people control* . . .' He paused. 'They say he made over four million out of it,' he said.

'Good God,' whispered Faith.

'It wasn't the first, either. And she . . . Cecily, always *there* . . .' He shook his head. 'I think they're *both* sick.'

Faith sat down, carefully, on the arm of the chair opposite him.

'I'm still waiting,' she said.

'I know,' he responded.

He leaned back in the chair, closing his eyes for a moment. Then, opening them, and looking directly at her, he went on: 'I had this divided Board, a cash problem; the Bank turned on me—out of the blue—' He clasped his hands together tightly. 'This was my company. I started it in a railway arch lock-up in Clapham, it made a profit of a hundred and twenty million that year, and they were literally taking it from under my nose, stealing my . . .'

'Tell me,' she said.

There was a long silence, in which Alex gave a tortured, prolonged sigh. 'The rival company had a Far East operation. Wanted to drive roads through parts of Nepal. I thought of taking over out there, starting again. I thought, in five years, I'd have enough influence to move something on that Board again. I knew they were trying to shunt me out, but . . . I came home to talk it over with Clare one afternoon. Randolph had been in that morning, the usual crap, the raised eyebrow, that bloody *look* of his. All very gentlemanly. Got my fucking back up as usual. He had this thing of referring to my background, I grew up in East London.'

Faith raised her head. She knew how that felt. She flashed a momentary sympathetic glance.

'I imagined Clare and I flying out the next week to India, changing everything, selling the houses, living there. She'd been down lately, too. We both needed it, I thought. I got home . . . I think . . . I think, looking back, I was out of my head that day . . . I was angry; I charged in the house . . . Clare was sitting in the kitchen . . .'

He put his head in his hands.

'Tell me,' she said.

'It was in the newspapers,' he said.

Faith clenched her fists, trying to keep control. 'What has it to do with me?' she asked, thinking aloud. 'How did it . . . why has it got anything to do with some crazy woman breaking into my house?'

'In the hospital,' he said, 'she said that she wouldn't tell you who I was, what I'd done, if I got you out of the house. She wanted the house. What for, who for, I don't know. She just wanted the house.'

Faith stared at him in horror. 'You took me to Cornwall, and gave her the key,' she whispered.

He dropped his hands immediately. 'No!' he said, standing up. 'I gave you the key, remember? It was hanging in the back-door lock. As for Cecily Joscelyne, I told her she was crazy—'

'You took me away, and let her in!'

'No!'

'What did you think—that I wouldn't mind? That I'd—' And the realisation suddenly hit her. 'That I'd *marry* you, and never want to go back to the house anyway? Are you that *stupid!*'

'No! No!'

'I don't believe this is happening,' moaned Faith to herself.

Alex made a move towards her, thought better of it, lowered his voice, trying to stay calm. 'The only thought on my mind that morning was you,' he said. 'I woke up early, I wanted to see you, I thought of the hotel, I went to the house. It didn't surprise me when it was locked, but I felt frustrated, and wandered round the back and—well, it was open. There was no sign of Cecily. No sign of anything being disturbed.'

'How convenient,' Faith said.

He shook his head. 'How can I convince you?' he said. 'I'm not in league with that *lunatic* up there.'

'Where was she then, when you took my clothes that morning?'

'How do I know? In town getting a bloody locksmith, probably. Ordering builders. Christ!'

'So all this work, all these deliveries, have happened in the last twenty-four hours?'

'They must have done.'

She laughed. 'What the *hell* do you take me for?' she demanded.

He strode forward. She jumped from the arm of the chair and took several steps backwards, holding her hands out in front of her as if to ward him off.

'Don't touch me,' she warned.

'Oh, Faith, please. Please!'

'And in the hospital?'

'She told me she'd give you two hundred thousand. I told her she was crazy. I never thought for a second she meant it.'

'Why didn't you tell me?'

'In the state you were in?'

She stared at him. She didn't know *what* she believed, *whom* she believed any more. 'And what was it?' she asked.

'What was *what*?'

She almost screamed at him. 'What was it she was blackmailing you with, for God's sake!'

'She couldn't blackmail me,' he repeated. 'I just needed time. She didn't have that kind of hold over me. I only hadn't told you because of . . . time.'

'The day in the garden, the day when I went to hospital . . .'

'I was going to tell you. I wanted you, but I wanted to tell you first.'

'But she thought—'

'She couldn't blackmail me, force me to give her your keys or get your house, or marry you to get you out of the way—all those things you're thinking—*because I was going to tell you* . . .'

'You wouldn't tell me in Cornwall,' she said.

His strength flooded out of him. He had the sudden appearance of a deflated toy, shrinking from the inside. 'I couldn't,' he said. 'I was frightened to death. That there would be a scene. Like this,' he added, almost mournfully. He looked back up at her, shaking his head. 'But I *would* have. I promise you, Faith. I would. After all, it used to be public knowledge—'

'Except that people forget,' Faith said acidly, repeating his words. 'Six months later, they can't remember. That's what you just said. Were you hoping I wouldn't remember?'

He looked at her, frozen. 'Yes,' he said.

She turned away. 'Oh, Alex.'

This is so like Guy, she was thinking, her heart a cold stone in her chest. *Lies.*

'I was hoping we would have the chance to get to know each other better,' he was saying. 'From the first moment I saw you, the morning you moved in, I thought, here is someone special, don't rock the boat, go slowly. The first time since Clare; I didn't dare to breathe . . .' He held out a hand towards her, a hand that she didn't see because her back was turned. She put her own hand to her face and angrily brushed away a tear.

'Things happened so quickly,' he said. 'You feel that, too? Don't you? They were happening so quickly.'

She wanted to turn and say yes, and put her arms around him. But she could not.

'What is it you were hoping I wouldn't remember?' she asked. 'What is it that Cecily Joscelyne thought she could bargain with?'

There was utter silence.

'What was it, Alex?'

'I love you,' he said. 'I want to care for you.'

'What is it?'

'Will you promise, when I tell you, just to . . . take some time . . .'

'What *is* it!'

At last, she turned to look at him, and thought, with horror, that she had never seen anyone look so guilty.

'That afternoon, when I came home,' he told her softly, 'I killed my wife.'

THIRTY-ONE

$\mathscr{S}$HE GOT IN THE CAR AND DROVE.

At first, it didn't matter where. She shoved the gear into fifth and sheared down the causeway road, gravel scalding the side of the car. When she reached the tarmac, the long winding grey thread through the heathlands and the hills, she put her foot down. Seventy, eighty. Pale colour was flooding the winter sky in her rear-view mirror, over the sea. Winter sunset.

At Tollard, she parked on double yellows and ran into a phone box.

She dialled the solicitor who had handled the house sale, the solicitor in London. The number rang a dozen times. She glanced, despairing, at her watch. It was half past three in the afternoon.

'Hello, Wimbards.'

There was a tinkle of glasses, and voices, and music in the background.

'That's . . . Wimbards, the solicitors?'

'Yes.'

'Mr Ackland, please.'

'I'm sorry, he's not here. He went on holiday yesterday.'

She suppressed a frantic groan. 'Is there someone else I can speak to? It's very urgent.'

'Well . . . who shall I say is calling?'

'Faith Mary Collins.'

'Hold on a moment.'

Faith pressed her head against the glass of the kiosk. She noticed, along the village street, red ribbons fluttering above a doorway. The pavement was packed, and, for a second, she couldn't think why. Then it struck her. It was Christmas Eve.

On the way home, she and Alex had planned to come in and shop. It was just as if that conversation had been wiped away, erased from her experience. It was like looking back on a foreign country: at strange people, acting on a blurred screen. And it was only four hours ago.

She began to cry. Huge, choking sobs. Someone—a woman passing close to the kiosk—stopped briefly, staring in at her. Then hurried on. The afternoon was darkening; beyond the red ribbon decoration, the lights of a shop front were suddenly switched on. The tears poured out of her.

'Hello? Miss Collins?'

It was a woman's voice. Not the same one.

'Miss Collins?'

'Yes, I'm here.'

'This is Catherine Jamieson. I'm Mr Ackland's colleague. How can I help you?'

Faith tried desperately to get her voice under control. 'I'm sorry,' she said, finally. 'I've just realised. I've interrupted your Christmas party.'

The woman laughed. It was a rich, well-modulated laugh. 'You've done me a great service,' she said. 'I'd just been poured my second warm sherry by a man who did his own conveyancing.'

Faith dredged up a smile. There was a real world operating somewhere. Somewhere down this phone line. Reality. People were looking forward to the holidays. Their lives orderly and organised. She felt like crying, *For God's sake, come and help me. I've woken up in hell.*

'I've got a terrible problem,' she said. 'Someone has got into my house while I was away, and changed all the locks, and they say it's theirs.'

There was a split second of stunned silence.

'Did this person break into the house?'

'No . . . I was ill, I went to hospital. I left the back door unlocked . . .'

'I see.'

'She offered a friend of mine—' *A friend? Never mind. Pass on that now.* 'She told him she would give me two hundred thousand pounds for the house, and it's not worth half that, and she's already put the money in my bank—'

'Did this friend have power of attorney to act on your behalf?'

'No, no.'

'Are you the sole owner of the house?'

'Yes. Mr Ackland completed the sale a fortnight ago. He has all the papers . . .'

'Was anything written down? Any form of agreement or contract between you and this woman?'

'No! *Christ.* She's . . . sick, somehow. She can't even seem to see that she's done anything wrong.'

'All right.' Again, the warm, sweet tone. It was reassuringly calm. 'All right. We can do something for you. It's a summary procedure, a court order. We can get her out.'

'Today?'

'No . . . not today.'

'She says the police won't help me.'

'Not right now. We have to get a court order to move her out. The police will help if she won't move out after the week is up.'

'The *week!*' So it was true. 'I can't get her out for a week? And it's my own house?'

'I'm afraid not . . . Look, can you come in right now? I'll see what I can do.'

'I'm in Dorset. The house is in Dorset.'

'Oh . . .'

The tears came pouring out again, despite Faith willing every fibre of her being against them. 'She's tearing the place to pieces. I've got nowhere to go. Nowhere to live. She's got builders in.'

'On Christmas Eve!'

'You don't know this woman,' Faith whispered.

'I don't think I want to,' came the swift reply. 'Is she a friend of yours?'

'She's my agent. My business agent.'

'Dear God.'

'I don't know . . . what can I do . . .'

'And—excuse me, but this other person, this man friend of yours, she *told* him what she was intending to do?'

'He didn't believe her.'

'And didn't warn you?'

'No.'

Alex, Alex.

'Is there any way you can get here before, say, five?'

'I don't know.' Faith tried a lightning calculation, and failed. 'I might.'

'Right. I'll stay on here until you arrive. We'll sit down and I'll tell you what we can do. Meantime, I'll ring round. There may still be people at court.'

Faith found she couldn't speak at all. Only one person in the world to trust. A woman she had never met, in a city she didn't particularly care to see again, at the end of a journey she didn't want to make.

'Miss Collins,' said Catherine Jamieson.

'Yes . . .'

'Don't lose hope. However bad this seems, we will sort this out. You can count on that.'

'Thank you,' Faith whispered. She wiped the tears from her face with her free hand. 'I'll be there as soon as I can.'

'Don't rush. Drive carefully.'

'Thank you.'

She put down the phone. Looked at the cheerful street, now almost dark. Picked up her car keys.

'Thomas?'

'Hello, mother.'

'Hello, darling. How are you?'

'I'm fine, mother. Is there something you wanted?'

'Are you working?'

'Of course.'

'Oh . . . I'm sorry. I won't be long.'

In London, Ruth looked at the drink she had poured herself. A large, neat brandy. She hardly ever drank. But tonight, the world was disintegrating. She had spent all that day cancelling their customary Christmas Eve party. 'Is everything all right?' people had asked. Their voices held a smugness, a curiosity, just below the surface. 'Yes, of course,' she had lied. 'Randolph is unwell, that's all. I'm so sorry to disappoint.'

Disappoint.

Yes, they would be disappointed. Disappointed that they hadn't been here, in person, to witness their disgrace.

That afternoon, the police had called. They, too, wanted to see Randolph. Something about a Government contract. The Treasury . . .

She gripped the phone now, hard. 'Have you seen your father?'

Thomas closed the computer file he was working on and sat back, looking at the blank blue VDU screen with its little white menu box in one corner. 'Randolph?' he said.

'Yes, he . . .' Ruth couldn't speak for a second. Instead, she took a long swallow of the brandy. 'I thought he might have come to see you,' she said. 'He's looking for Cecily. We can't find her, and now—'

'Why would he come here, looking for Cecily? Why would Cecily be here?'

She didn't reply for some time. Then, down the miles of phone line, he heard a distant, fragile, disjointed whisper.

'I don't know,' she was saying. 'I never knew. I swear, I never *really* knew.'

Faith reached London at a quarter past five.

She spent half an hour with Catherine Jamieson, among the debris of the party. Catherine was a mild, tall, beautifully calm woman, with a wing of almost black hair that she kept pushing behind one ear. She told Faith that the court order would be issued in two days, and that Cecily Joscelyne would have to vacate by the second of January.

On the doorstep, she kissed Faith on the cheek and hugged her. London was emptying: traffic sped, instead of crawled. They stood on the corner of New Bond Street and watched for Catherine's taxi.

'I've kept you from your family,' Faith said. 'I'm sorry.'

Catherine merely smiled. 'You've kept me from my mother-in-law,' she said, shrugging. The taxi pulled up. As she opened the door, she gripped Faith's arm. 'Where are you going now?'

'Oh—that's OK. I've got a friend.'

Catherine grinned broadly. 'I hope more reliable than your other friends.'

Faith smiled back. 'Oh . . . yes. Yes.'

'Good.' At the last moment, she scribbled a phone number on a notepad. 'Here's my phone at home,' she told Faith. 'Any problem, ring.'

'Thank you.'

Faith watched the taxi accelerate into the traffic. From the back window, Catherine Jamieson waved.

Faith turned away.

A friend.

What friend? There *was* no friend. She had made it up. She didn't want to weigh Catherine down with anything else, have her worrying all the way home. There was nobody Faith could call, there was nowhere to go. Feeling her car keys in her pocket, she walked woodenly back, got in the car, turned the ignition over, reversed, turned on the heater to clear the windscreen of frost.

'Help me,' she whispered.

She turned into Piccadilly, and drove towards Hyde Park Corner. She drove without thinking, without seeing, through Knightsbridge, Sloane Square, Belgravia, Westminster. She lost track of where she was, took no notice of road signs. The inside of the car was curiously comforting, warm and fugged with her own breath and condensation. There was no need to think in here. Not for a while. The engine droned on, through dark streets and past store windows festooned with tinsel, fake forests, gauze fairies and angels, Victorian gowns and fur tippets, seas of captive poinsettias. The wipers described an arc in the glass, clearing the still-sleety drizzle that fell as a fine curtain across London.

When she got to the river, it surprised her. She had almost gone in a circle. She drove up Millbank, the river shifting and glinting on her right-hand side.

Guy said he lived near the river.

She shook her head. Useless to think of Guy. What could Guy do? Nothing. They were all powerless. Nothing could get Cecily Joscelyne out of her house for nine days. Nine days of waiting in this vacuum. Guy would thunder and rage. She sighed. There might be a kind of comfort in that. Thunder and rage against all this staying-calm and being-reasonable farce. For a moment, she longed for Guy, quite unexpectedly. She longed for him to put things right in his old, clay-footed fashion; to bluster and fume on her behalf. She wanted a Spartacus.

'If you break down the door, you'll be committing criminal damage,' Catherine Jamieson had said. 'If you lay a finger on her, it's assault. It's not as if she broke into the property. She walked in. You left the keys.'

'But she's changed the locks. Isn't that damage?'

'We'll get her to put everything straight. Everything how it was before. But not now.'

Inside the car now, Faith, remembering, began to laugh. *Put it back how it was before.* It was absurd. Rip out Cecily Joscelyne's conservatory and put back the broken paving stones. 'God,' she muttered, and the laughter gurgled up, smothering her. It was a dreadful sound, had anyone been there to witness it. Frightened, choking.

She saw a lay-by loom ahead, and pulled sharply into it. She rested her head on the steering wheel, breathing heavily. Her hands and back ached miserably; her throat was dry, her mouth felt as if it had been coated in sand.

There was a tapping at the passenger's window.

She sat up. A man's face smiled in at her.

She froze for a moment, then saw his uniform. It was some sort of livery. She glanced out of the window in front of her, and saw the lights of an hotel, the cream foyer basking in warmth, the gold-and-black engraved glass doors. She wound down the passenger's window.

'Can I help, madam?' the commissionaire asked.

For a moment, she was about to ask where she was. Ask how to get back to the M3, to explain that she was lost. Then, abruptly, she thought, *What the hell for? Where am I meant to be going? Home?*

'Can anyone park this for me?' she asked.

'Of course.'

She got out.

In the brighter light, she was suddenly aware of how travel-stained, how crushed she must look. A man turning in at the hotel door gave her a superior glance of disapproval. *Fuck you*, she thought. She drew herself up straight.

What the hell, I'm rich. And she gave a sour little smile. *I've got a fortune in the bank.*

'Madam's luggage?'

'There isn't any,' she said. And she tossed him the keys of the car.

She walked straight to Reception. The young man behind the desk, superbly smart in a dark frock coat, acted as if bedraggled young women towing a handbag and no other baggage on Christmas Eve were the most natural thing in the world. He gave her a dazzling smile of utmost charm.

'May I help you?'

Faith pushed back her hair.

'Yes,' she said, in a clear voice. 'I want a room for nine days.'

'We have a single . . .'

'No single. A room. A proper room.'

'I'm afraid there's only two left. Two suites. The Pemberley and the Excelsior.' Out of the corner of her eye, Faith saw a couple descending the stairs. They were dressed for the evening: black tie and ball gown. She glanced back at the receptionist. 'Our Christmas Eve dinner,' he explained. 'I'm sorry, there are no tickets remaining.'

'Good,' she retorted. 'This Excelsior. Is it quiet? I don't want to hear the bloody "White Christmas Waltz" at two in the morning.' She stopped herself from saying that she didn't want to hear anything, any human voice, any laughing, any carols, any choirs.

'The fifth floor, madame.'

'Good. A spa bath?'

'Yes, we have a spa bath in the Excelsior.'

'Fine,' she said, taking up the pen to sign in. 'Give me that.'

'We have a programme of Christmas events,' he offered, as she wrote. 'In the morning, we have breakfast from Room Service, we have a Christmas brunch from eleven to three, we have the choir of St Saviour's, with handbell ringing . . .' The words died on his lips. She was fixing him with a look that could have melted concrete.

'As madame wishes.'

'Too bloody right,' she muttered. She signed her name in huge, flowing script.

Faith Mary Collins.

Homeless, alone, and pregnant.

She underlined her name, thinking, *Faith, don't cry now. Don't look a fool in front of all these people. Give it five minutes,* she told herself. *When you've locked your door, you can howl all you like.*

And, taking her key, she walked resolutely to the lifts.

THIRTY-TWO

*J*OZ WAS STANDING ON THE WRECKED PATIO, staring out to sea.
It was a bitterly cold, beautiful night. The snow had stopped an hour ago; the sea was a sheet of perfect, undisturbed grey.

She put her hand to her face, and wiped away the traces of tears that were literally freezing to her face. Curious, she considered. Curious. She hadn't cried in she didn't know *how* many years. Not since she was five or six.

Nearly five. When Daddy died.

Six. When Randolph came.

What on earth did weeping achieve? Ineffectual drops of water. Some physical agency of clearing the eye. Some primitive reaction to fear, programmed to respond on a twentieth-century lens.

She knew that she would never need to cry again. The past—all those descending veils—could no longer hold her. She looked along the coast—to the inlets and small islands, some no more than thumbnail-sized discs now in the dark water, and the lights of the town twenty miles to the east. None of it seemed to matter.

She had no urge to go anywhere. She felt removed from life. The rest of the world had no interest for her: it was all just so much noise, so much shape and nagging colour.

She had never really known what the world was for. Sometimes, when she saw someone getting married—and here her face creased in a frown of passing despair—or when someone had a baby, or the television showed people in various dramas, she would wonder what it meant. Why people had arms and faces and why they wept and argued. She had always looked in on them like a vaguely distracted shopper staring at a window display.

When Thomas came . . .

When Thomas came, she would feel different. Everything would be different.

She would be alive at last.

She was unaware that she was pulling at the clothes she wore—tugging at the front of the thick sweater, just as the dying clutch and wring the bedclothes as if they are being smothered. The sweater was pulled out of shape now by her relentless fingers, but she stood with a smile on her face. From now onwards, she had nothing to look forward to but happiness, no one who could tell her any more that she didn't deserve it, or had some other last job to do, some other last trick to pull, some other place to be.

She was free.

She sighed. She was very tired.

In the background, the radio was transmitting *Shades in the Sun*. It was one of the musicals that Randolph had staged, fifteen years ago. It had gone to Broadway. It was a great success: a wild, dizzying time when people came to the house and Randolph set her free for a while, because he had what he wanted.

Free of Randolph. *To be free of him.* She had committed every crime asked of her. Little, wounding things. Bigger, more savage transgressions. She had done them all without flinching.

For him.

She glanced back at the house. It must have been a terrible shock to him, to realise how much she could want something. *This* thing. How peculiar it must have felt to him, the worm in the child turning.

What was that phrase? One of those Asian men, one of those he used for that takeover deal . . . he had taught it to her. She had thought it wildly ironic at the time. So ironic that it made her laugh, that he should say it to her, and then break himself on Randolph's burning wheel.

Bend like the willow, or break like the oak.

Randolph had never learned to bend. If only he had bent just a little, just a fraction; if only he could have stepped back and said, *This isn't right. Not this time.* But no. It was beyond him. He couldn't say that, could he? He always said that she belonged to him. And he meant, *belonged.*

Belonged in every second, from the moment she awoke, belonged in every thought, belonged in every drop of blood, in every cell of her body. She had been so much more than a possession to him. She had been an echo of him. She breathed because he breathed. He had often told her that. He told her that without him the family would have suffered. Lived in a two-roomed flat, dragged down by poverty. *How would your mother have managed?* he would ask her. *Can you imagine how it would have been?* He had saved them, he said.

In time, she had felt that it was true, and that she *was* him. She carried his traits, looked like him, walked like him, acted as he did. She forgot where she ended and he began. When he was not there, she didn't know how to act. He told her that. He told her all the time. She carried it out. She had never played a note of music when she was alone. She had never made any important choice without him. She had been incapable of it.

Except the house. When she had bought the house—that only, first, strangling frisson of freedom that terrified her and was over in an afternoon in those Eighties days of settling a house contract in hours—and only when she had bought the house had she ever done anything without his instruction. As a reward, he had descended on her harder than ever. The phone rang to wake her and to put her to sleep. She had had so many plans when she bought that house. She had actually believed, for a day or two, that she might be able to break free from him. Randolph soon told her how stupid that was. And she *saw* how stupid it was, almost at once. The materials she brought home to make curtains rotted on the floor. She never got further than the builder's built-in kitchen. She never put a painting on the wall, a book on a shelf. Even the dog . . .

She didn't know what to do with her feelings unless Randolph told her.

It was only with Thomas that she ever felt . . .

Bend like the willow.

. . . alive.

She walked back into the house. The kitchen units had been stripped out. They stood in a ruinous pile, doors flung haphazardly on top of tiles, dividers, wire trays. She was going to take the wall down behind the sink, and extend out twenty feet.

'You got any drawings, love? You got planning permission?'

Or break like the oak. She looked behind her, towards the bedrooms.

For a moment, she swayed where she stood, pressing a finger to her temple. She kept getting that strange sensation . . . as if the inside of her skull had been scoured and her aching head filled with cotton wool. It was so hard to think. Ideas kept running away from her, twisting and changing. It would be all right when Thomas came. He would be able to set it straight. She had never asked him outright for anything before. But now he would be able to iron out her thoughts. Thomas was so calm, so self-possessed. She imagined him untying the scrambled lines inside her, laying each separate idea in a neat line on the ground, pressing them flat. Unwrinkled, untied thoughts.

What did I do wrong?

Thomas will tell me.

She walked over to the telephone. She had rung him perhaps twenty times in the last two or three hours. No reply. He must come home soon. A little while ago—it must have been about seven o'clock or so—she had wondered, with a sudden flash of panic, if he had gone into London, to see Ruth. She dialled the number of her mother's house, and, as she waited for Ruth to answer, her breath came in ever shallower waves, until she was literally gasping. Ruth answered: Joz held the phone in her hand, listening to her mother's voice.

'Who is it? Randolph . . . is that you? Cecily?'

She had put the receiver down, gulping great draughts of air, one hand pressed to her throat as if she could pull a channel of oxygen clear of the flesh.

It passed. But she kept looking at the phone, wondering if Thomas had been in that London room.

You must come here, Thomas.

You must tell me what to do.

You MUST.

Raising her eyes, she saw Faith's canvases to one side of the chimney breast, where she had piled them. Faith Collins . . . It was a pity she didn't understand. Faith had everything . . . talent, a child, two men who loved her, a home, money. Two hundred thousand pounds, and the advance on the contract. She could buy another house tomorrow. She could walk away, and it wouldn't leave a mark. She knew how to get love out of people, to make them want her. She knew how to *do* that. She had everything she needed, and more.

Joz put her hands over her face.

And yet Faith still came here, ranting and raving at her on the doorstep. Demanding. Waving her hands in her face. She had wanted to snatch the house back, when Joz had paid so dearly for it.

Slowly, Joz pushed her hands back over her hair, and stood up. She had to see to Randolph. A prolonged, vocal sigh came out of her—something between a breath and a moan.

Or break like the oak.

What was she asking people to do? Just to give her a little space. She was always running round after other people. When it was not Randolph, it was the clients he brought to her. Furnishing their homes, tracing the papers, the fabrics, the colours, the shapes, the paintings, everything, right down to the spines of the leather books, just the right shade of red, of gold . . . She pulled a disgusted face in the darkness. No more. Everything . . . running after Randolph, after his needs, after his targets like a frantic missile, heat-seeking secrets. Running ever faster, to pander a fathomless need. She was always running . . . after people like Faith Collins, trying to flatter and fix them, trying to mould them to what was wanted.

Randolph most of all.

He had fallen the same way . . . hands scraping, a second, for purchase on the stone. Ironic. And quite perfect. Face turned back towards her, a descending disc of pale skin swallowed up by the darkness. Eyes fixed on hers. Fitting, wasn't it? It made a neat, finished circle. Watching, just those few brief seconds, she had felt nothing but the utmost exhilaration. *Done, done!* She wished that she could replay the moment interminably; wished that it were recorded on film. To play again and again and *again* . . . The justice in that movement was exquisite and total. To have repaid Catherine, in exactly the same way . . .

Joz passed her hands down her arms, feeling the frost on her clothes. Funny, how hot she felt. The house was icy—she could see her breath—and yet she could feel the heat radiating from inside. She was full of warmth, as she had never been before. So many better things were going to happen.

When Thomas comes.

Break like . . .

She switched on the kettle, and looked down again at the tray that she had laid two hours ago. China and white linen. Cold meats arranged almost artistically with a heart of endive and a spoonful of mayonnaise. Randolph would have liked a little Parma ham. A pity. He would have to have what he was given, what she could spare.

It was the other way round now. The knowledge of it ran down her spine like a chill. She didn't belong to him any more. No, no. The other way around. Now, *he* belonged to *her.*

She would teach him exactly what misery it was to be possessed.

She poured the boiling water into the teapot and its accompanying hot-water jug. Taking a last look at the still life of food, she picked it up, and walked, in the darkness, down the hall.

'Randolph?' she called.

She pushed the door open with her foot.

Randolph was sitting in the bed, his eyes open, his bulky body propped high on pillows. He looked like a Roman Emperor. Joz had pulled the sheets up to his chin, but one side had fallen down. He wore it jauntily, like a toga. It rather suited him. She ought to get him a laurel wreath from the garden, she thought. There was a holly bush out there. She could make him a crown of holly. As saintly as Christ in his sheet toga and bare feet and serious, averted expression, and his crown of thorns. Pondering some private spiritual experience. The meaning of life, perhaps. She smiled broadly at her own silent joke.

It was the first time he had been in her bedroom and not told her what she could do and what she could not do. She put the tray on the bedside table, and considered him, smiling.

'Don't pretend to be asleep,' she said.

Randolph did not move.

'There isn't any use pretending,' she said, as she leaned over him. 'Not any more.'

In the kitchen, the faint introductory note of the next song sounded.

THIRTY-THREE

*O*N CHRISTMAS MORNING, at eleven o'clock, there was a knock at the door of Faith's suite.

She was lying on the enormous bed, dressed only in the T-shirt and leggings that she had been wearing when she arrived yesterday. The coat and sweater and shoes lay in a pile on the floor. She was lying with the TV remote in one hand, flicking through the channels.

The knocking was repeated insistently.

She knew that she had put the Do Not Disturb sign outside. She turned away, pressed the volume switch. *Dumbo* was on the next channel. She watched intently, as if the little cartoon with its mother and baby and absurd mouse could smooth out her own situation.

'Faith!' said a voice outside.

She shot to her feet. Guy's voice.

'Faith! Please!'

She shifted from one foot to the other. She didn't want to see him—or anyone. More importantly, she didn't want to be seen like this: in the floor-length mirror opposite, a woman with straggling hair and a pale, unmade-up face stared back. She looked like Tenniel's drawings of Alice: a head that looked too big for the body, hair and eyes dominating. Small precise hands clasped in front of her.

'Faith . . .' And he began to pound with his fist now.

She went to the door, shrugging in defeat, and opened it.

Guy walked straight in. 'Christ,' he said. 'This must cost a packet.' And he gave a low whistle.

Faith looked at him, one hand on her hip.

'I'm fine, thanks,' she said. 'And how are you?'

She closed the door.

'Well,' he said. He sat down in a chair facing her. She ignored him, and walked as far away as she could get, sitting on a low, apricot-coloured couch that faced the window. 'Well,' he repeated, 'aren't you going to ask me how I found you?'

'No need,' she replied drily, 'because you're dying to tell me.'

'You might act surprised,' he said.

She gave a short laugh. 'I did *surprised* yesterday,' she snapped. 'It was an Oscar-winning *surprised*. More like *stunned*, in fact. But I can do *pissed off* for you, if you like.'

Guy laughed. 'That's my girl,' he said.

She crossed her arms and looked away, out on to Hyde Park, which was empty and impossibly quiet. 'Go on, then,' she said slowly. 'How did you find me?' She glanced at him from the corner of her eye. 'And—if this isn't getting boring for you—where is Chloe?'

'I don't know,' he said.

'You don't *know*? Guy, it's Christmas Day.'

'She went out to a party last night, and she didn't come back,' he said.

'What party?'

'I don't know.'

'Just a minute,' Faith said. 'Just go back a minute. How did you find me?'

'Catherine Jamieson.' He produced the name with a flourish, like a magician pulling a rabbit out of a hat. 'I rang your house, was told it was *sold*—' Here he raised his eyebrows and grinned. 'Rang Richard Ackland, not home, answerphone, Catherine Jamieson's number for emergencies . . .'

'And you thought this was an emergency?'

'Of course it is.'

'And she gave you my number. Well, thank you Catherine.'

'I told her I was your husband.'

'All the more bloody reason not to give it to you. I wouldn't be here if I wanted to see my *ex-husband*, would I? Just wait till I speak to her.'

'Look, don't blame the woman. When you rang her last night, you told her that you could be reached here *if anyone wanted you*.'

'I didn't mean you.'

'Ah. Who did you mean?'

'Forget it.'

'Your knight in shining armour?'

'Just forget it.'

Guy got up and walked across the room. He stopped in front of her, then squatted down so that his face was level with hers. 'What's going on?' he asked, gently. 'Why did you sell the house? Why didn't you tell me what was going on three days ago?'

She marvelled at him for a moment. He looked so fresh—pressed, clean, neat and handsome. More like an advertisement for some expensive aftershave than a man whose partner had just deserted him. He was just absurd: so untouched, untroubled. She shook her head. 'You really are something,' she murmured.

'Why?'

'Look at you. Mr Clean and Tidy.'

'What have I done now? I've had a shower and a shave, so what?'

'Never mind.'

He gave her an *aren't you peculiar* smile. 'What is it?' he asked. 'Come on. Tell me.'

'Guy . . . please. Just go away. If I'd wanted you, I'd have rung you last night. Really. Just—'

'No,' he said. 'No, hold on here. It doesn't make sense. I thought Catherine Jamieson was joking. I said, *The Parke Helena*? What the hell's she doing in there?'

'And what did she say?'

'Nothing. Well, next to nothing. She hummed and hahed a bit, said you were in a difficult situation, wouldn't tell me what—I told her I wanted to help you, wanted to contact you—'

Faith gave him a weak, watery smile. 'You could bully for England.'

He put his hand on her knee. 'What is it?' he said. 'What happened?'

Looking at his concerned face, Faith felt her resolve crumble. Tears sprang to her eyes and promptly ran down her face with the forced fluidity of a tap. She rubbed at them, half-laughing, and then dissolving into real sobs. It was helplessness more than anything else. Helplessness and frustration and the damned feeling that Guy would be thinking he had been right all along. That she couldn't function without him.

He sat alongside her, and took her in his arms, whispering, 'Come on now, tell me. Come on now.' She didn't want to look up at him. She was sure that she'd see that smug expression on his face, the *I told you so* look. She managed, eventually, to surface for air, and blew her nose on a tissue from a satin-padded box on the table at her side.

'Look at this,' she said. 'They must expect people to weep regularly.'

'It's for when they get the bill,' he said.

She smiled.

'Well, are you going to tell me? Do I have to shine a light in your face?'

She wiped her eyes, and took a deep breath. 'Did you ask who it was, in the house?'

'No . . . just some woman. She sounded excited. I said, "that was quick," something like that, and she laughed. She said, "Oh yes, I just had to have it," and laughed again.'

'God. She is sick.'

'I thought she must be, to want that place.'

'I mean, really sick. Insane.'

'Why?'

'Do you know who it was?'

'No . . .'

'Didn't you recognise the voice? It was Cecily Joscelyne.'

This time, Guy rocked back on his heels for a second. 'That family gets around,' he commented. 'Heard the news?'

'No. Why?'

'Never mind. Just another Cabinet scandal.' Then he asked, 'Wasn't she the one who went to the hospital?'

'The same.'

'She didn't mention anything.'

'Didn't she, though?'

'You've lost me.'

Faith sighed deeply. 'I didn't sell the house to Cecily Joscelyne,' she said. 'I went away for a couple of days, and when I got back she'd walked in, and changed the locks. She's put two hundred thousand in my bank account and says she told Alex all about it. I can't get her out until January the second.'

Guy stared at her, his mouth working soundlessly for a second. 'You're joking,' he said.

'If I am, is it funny?'

'Bloody hell. You mean . . . she broke in?'

'No. We left the place unlocked when we went to the hospital.'

'And she told . . .'

'That she wanted the house, and would give me the money.'

'When did you come home?'

'Yesterday.'

'They kept you in hospital until yesterday? Why?'

Faith looked away, squeezing the tissue into a ball, and throwing it into the wastebin. Guy had gone to London when he heard she was being kept in overnight. 'I went away with Alex,' she said.

He said nothing in reply for perhaps almost a minute. She could see his brain working overtime, turning the problem this way and that.

'I rang you at midday the next day,' he murmured, finally. 'There was no reply.' Then, a light seemed to dawn on his face. 'He's in it with her,' he said. 'He must be.'

'No. He says he just didn't believe her. He thinks she's crazy.'

'Well, of course she's fucking crazy,' Guy said, calmly. 'But what . . . what's it to do with him? Why did she offer the money to him?'

'It's complicated. I don't want to go into that.'

Guy's glance narrowed. 'And why didn't you stay with him? Right next door. That's the obvious place. Why aren't you with him?'

She shook her head again. 'That's nothing to do with it,' she said.

He looked over her from head to foot, as if the answer might be written on her somewhere. Then he grabbed her wrist, almost fiercely. 'He thought it was his baby and it isn't,' he said. 'He dumped you.'

'No, no. It's nothing to do with the baby. He didn't dump me.'

'You dumped him?'

'Oh, for Christ's sake.'

'Well, what then?'

'It's just . . . I can't tell you. I don't even know myself . . .'

'Some nice bloke. Leaving you alone at Christmas.'

'I left *him.*'

'Because he dropped you in the shit.'

Faith's temper broke. 'Some people don't act as *you* would act,' she retorted hotly.

'Oho,' he said. 'Touchy, touchy!'

'Oh, sod off.'

'Feet of clay, then?'

'It's none of your business.'

'But it is. If it affects you, it is. I've told you that already. When are you going to believe me?'

She got up abruptly and walked to the window. Standing there, she had a desperate and violent urge to open the window and jump. It was nothing more than a flash, a feeling of longing to float, to fall, to fade to oblivion. To be released.

'Don't like the sound of this Alex,' Guy said, in a self-satisfied, almost happy tone. 'Didn't like him from the minute I set eyes on him.'

'I gathered that,' Faith whispered. 'Anyway . . . it's finished. Not that it ever got started . . .' And she had a piercing moment of longing for Alex. Lately, whenever she felt at her worst, she had had this reflex reaction to go to him. She felt instinctively that she could trust him. The irony of it now hit her with seismic force.

Guy is right, she thought miserably. *I just get it wrong all the time. Trust a man who murdered his wife. Trust a woman who steals my home. Some judge of character I am . . .*

Guy had walked up behind her, and now put his hands on her shoulders. 'Poor Fay,' he said.

She sighed, crossing her arms. But she didn't shake him off. Instead, dropping back into life from a thousand years ago, she leaned her head on his shoulder while she stood with her back to him.

'How are you feeling?' he asked. 'How is the baby?' His tone was tender.

'We're OK.'

'No pain?'

'No.'

His head touched hers. 'It was unbearable,' he whispered.

She turned to look at him. But she saw at once that this was no game. It was not said for effect. Guy was staring out at the landscape of the Park. And, as she looked at him, he tore his gaze away and kissed her, very lightly and softly, on the lips.

He put his arm around her shoulder. 'It really never got started?' he asked.

'What?'

'With Alex.' She looked away from him, and he looked at her sorrowfully, so much so that it was almost comic. 'That's some torch you're carrying,' he said.

She pulled him to the couch, and he sat down close to her, still with one arm loosely about her.

'He told me something,' she said, slowly. 'He owned Robertson Hall Construction, and—'

Guy straightened up as if an electric current had been passed through him. 'Never!'

'He—'

'He's *the* Alexander Hurley? Hot *shit*! The bugger.'

'You know him?'

'Everybody knows him. But—' Guy paused, brow furrowing. 'Christ. He looks twenty years older. He used to have this black—I mean, really dark, coal-black—hair. Flash suits, string ties, very smoothie looking—hot *shit*. I thought he was dead.'

'Dead?'

Guy was gripping her hand now. 'I thought he must be. I always reckoned he'd come straight back when they finally let him go—brazen it out. Get the company back.' He shook his head thoughtfully. 'Who'd have credited it. Alex *Hurley*. When did he get out?'

'Get out? From where?'

'Prison.'

Faith slumped back, never taking her eyes from Guy's face.

'You did know?' he asked. Then he saw her expression. 'You didn't know.'

'Yesterday. He told me yesterday.'

'Nice guy, eh?' He couldn't stop shaking his head. 'Well, I thought he'd snuffed it,' he muttered. 'His wife. Must be six years ago. No. Eight years? But surely you recognised him when you first met him? It was in all the papers.'

'Did you?' she asked.

'He's aged. My God . . .' Guy gazed into the middle distance.

Cold, absolute cold, had invaded Faith. It was utterly unlike the sensation of yesterday, when a kind of panic had set in, and her only thought was to get as far away from Alex as quickly as she could. It had been one last straw breaking the camel's back. One more thing she could not handle. And, as she went back along his drive to get her car, she had looked back at him just once. He had been standing on his doorstep. He hadn't called her back. As she had got to her car, he had gone inside and closed his door. A kind of blind grief soaked her, drowned her.

This was a different feeling. No raging, no panic, no running. Just cold.

'Tell me what he did,' she said.

'I thought he told you.'

'He told me that he killed her.'

'He shot her.'

'Oh, God . . .'

'He always claimed there was a struggle. But it didn't hold up. Shot her clean through the heart. He got life.'

'Life? But he hasn't *done* life, surely!'

Guy shrugged. 'Search me.'

Faith leaned forward, resting her head in her hands, her fingers pressing into her cheekbones. 'Even now, I can't believe it,' she said.

'He pleaded guilty,' Guy said. 'I remember that much.'

'Yes,' Faith murmured. 'Guilty . . .'

'Wait till I tell them I found Alexander Hurley.'

'Who? Tell who?'

'Well, everybody—'

She caught his wrist in one hand. He had been gesturing expansively, as if the *everybody* encompassed the entire world. 'Don't talk about this,' she said. 'Please, Guy.'

He lowered his hand. 'You can really pick 'em, can't you?' he said.

She looked at him directly, half-smiling despite herself. 'Yes, I can pick 'em,' she murmured.

He leaned forward, ready to kiss her. Then paused. She gazed at him.

'Funny how things turn out,' he said.

'Hilarious.'

His eyes ranged over her face. 'You're so very pretty,' he said.

She was shaking her head violently, *no*. His voice was low, almost monotonous. Then he wrapped both arms around her and kissed her so hard that she hadn't time to breathe. She felt, for a second, ludicrously like Mrs Robinson in *The Graduate*, swallowing smoke while Benjamin fumbles. She tried to push him away, and then the familiarity of him caught her. The Guy smell—expensively clean; smooth and sweet, like a baby. And she thought, *Guy's baby*. It was a visceral, unintelligible response. She allowed herself to be pushed back on the couch, folding her arms around his neck, her whole body loosening.

'Remember this,' he was saying. 'Don't you miss this?'

He had got to his knees on the floor alongside the couch. She lay with her eyes closed, thinking of their first lovemaking, their last lovemaking. The first in a car after a party, hamfisted and funny, and Guy running up the steps of her flat afterwards, laughing, her handbag outstretched in his hand, apologising. Then asking to use the telephone, saying his car wouldn't start. Waking at ten the next morning with this same mouth that now was intent on arousing her, doing the same, the same . . .

And the last time. Quick and terrible. His turning away. The eloquence of that turned back. That was the time that their baby was conceived.

She ached for the old security of his arms. Whenever they made love she had always felt that *this* time it would alter things. *This* time she would lie next to a Guy who genuinely meant what he said, and whose gaze did not glide over and past her the moment the lovemaking was over. He would never again be a Guy preoccupied with his schemes or his stories. He would listen, he would look. He would *feel*.

He was whispering as he touched her. Something about never leaving her alone. A warning bell rang abruptly, loudly, in her head. She sat up, pushing him back. He reverted to his half-crouching position on the carpet, looking puzzled.

'What's the matter?' he said.

She wriggled, thoroughly embarrassed, back into her sweatshirt, which was over her shoulders but not over her head. 'I'm sorry, I can't do this,' she murmured.

'Why the hell not?'

She glanced at him.

'Sorry,' he said. 'All right.' He stood up, running his hands through his hair, looking both rebuffed and mildly amused. *That's a first*, his look said.

Isn't it, she thought.

A kind of ache ran through her. Not of pain. Not as tangible as that. A wave of muted, deep regret, of familiarity slipping away. 'Excuse me,' she said.

She got up, and went to the bathroom. There, with the door firmly closed, she stood with both hands on the cistern of the toilet, looking at herself in the mirror suspended over it. She wondered how much longer it would be before the promise she had made herself came true and she would be able to forget him entirely. She turned to the wash basin and splashed cold water on her skin, dried it scrupulously with the towel, and then fixed her make-up so that she looked half decent. 'Come on,' she whispered.

When she came out of the bathroom, he spoke immediately. He was sitting on the bed, propped up on the sumptuously thick pillows.

'I've been thinking,' he said.

She sat down on a chair and looked at him.

'Why don't you just take the money?'

'What money?'

'*The* money. *Her* money. The two hundred thousand.'

'The—' She gave an enormous, disbelieving sigh of frustration, slapping her hand against the arm of the chair. 'Because I don't want it!'

'Ah . . . but wait a minute. Wait a minute. Think a minute. Suppose you took the money, let her have the house. Agree to it all. You could go and buy a better house.' He took a bite from a cold croissant on the breakfast tray. 'You're better fixed than me, at any rate,' he told her. 'I guess Chloe will throw me out when she emerges. Dearest Daddy paid for the flat.' He grinned sheepishly. 'So I haven't a penny to my name.'

'But—where did the profit go from our house sale?' Faith asked.

'Into the car.'

'What car?'

'My BMW.'

Faith faintly registered the silver car he had been driving the last time she saw him. 'You spent all that money on a *car*? *All* your half of the profit from the sale?' she said.

He didn't bother to confirm it. Instead, he spread marmalade on the last bite of the croissant, and picked up the covers on the remaining plates, clicking his tongue against his teeth. 'What a waste of good bacon,' he remarked.

Faith stared at him.

He suddenly held up a finger, obviously remembering something he had meant to ask her. 'You haven't got my Filofax?'

'Your . . . ? Don't be ridiculous.'

He shrugged. 'Left it somewhere. Bloody nuisance. Spare keys, the lot. I've had to cancel my credit cards.'

'It's typical of you. Did you leave it at the hospital?'

'Who knows?'

'The house?'

'Could be.'

He looked at her, but she glanced away. Talking about the house had reminded her of the one thought that had been uppermost in her mind since yesterday. 'I keep thinking of her going through my things,' she said. 'I don't care about the clothes. But Mum's bits and pieces I've kept . . . and the photo frames. If she broke those . . .'

Some years before, Faith had made frames for her parents' photographs. They were ceramic, sculpted and painted; and Guy knew how long, and with what effort, it had taken Faith to finish this labour of love.

She thought, for one terrible second, that he was going to come over to her. *Don't move a single muscle,* she thought. *I can't go through telling you no again.* There was silence for more than a minute, while Guy watched her, while he picked at the linen of the throw on the bed.

'I still think you should take her money,' he said.

Faith sighed. 'Cecily Joscelyne has had some sort of breakdown,' she said, with desperately forced patience. 'When she recovers, she's going to find herself two hundred thousand pounds poorer with a liability of a house on her hands. Even if she signs a contract I doubt if it'd be legal, in her state of mind. Then there's her family. When they find out what she's done, you can bet your bottom dollar that they'll kick up a fuss. So . . .' She looked at him levelly. 'I'm going to do what Catherine Jamieson says. Cecily can foot the bill for this hotel as . . . What do they call it? Reasonable expenses?'

Guy gave a great sigh. She didn't think he accepted a word of what she had just said. He would always think he could find a wrinkle, an angle. He had the utmost faith in his own ability. In another life, he had been an avalanche, smiling as he swept all before him, crushing a few unimportant bodies on the way.

'Why don't you ring Chloe?' she said. She was trying valiantly to be constructive. 'I'm sure it's a misunderstanding. You could patch things up. I know you could.'

He laughed. 'Why don't you ring Alex?'

She cast about her for a sensible-sounding reason, then came out with the truth. 'Because I'm frightened to,' she said.

He nodded. 'There you go, then. That's the reason.'

'Oh, Guy.'

'Something funny?'

'No, not really. Something sad.'

He smiled. 'What a pair we are.'

'Yes,' she agreed. 'Pity it's not a matching one.'

He rubbed a hand across his eyes. 'Can I ask a favour?' he said.

'Yes . . .'

'Can I stay with you until I get fixed up with something?'

She stared at him, then started to laugh. 'You never give up, do you?'

He smiled broadly. 'I'll sleep in the bath,' he said. 'I mean it. I haven't anywhere to go.'

'You could go back to Chloe this minute.'

'No,' he said. 'There's someone else.'

'You . . .'

'Not *me*. Her. She's seeing someone else.'

'Since when!'

He shrugged. 'A week. Recently, I think. Can't be sure.'

'But . . .' This time, it was her gaze that reverted to the apricot couch by the window.

'That's not why I came here,' he said at once.

She struggled with her reaction for a second.

'Try me. Even now,' he said. 'I didn't come here because Chloe's got anyone else. I came here because I care about you.'

'All right,' she said. 'OK.'

'Pax.'

'Yes, all right.'

A flicker of hope crossed his face. He swiftly erased it before she could see it. Faith had risen to her feet, and began absently tidying the breakfast tray, picking up the teaspoon and knife, extricating them from the crumpled napkin.

'You can't stay with me,' she said.

'The hotel won't mind.'

'No. I'll mind.'

He walked over to her, and lifted her chin with one finger.

'Let's get out of here,' he said.

'Out? Where?'

He shrugged. 'The house.'

'*My* house? You must be joking.'

'Why not? Might be *vair-ee* interesting.' He took a coin from his pocket and began, like a conjuror, flicking it from palm to finger. 'Heads we go, tails we stay.'

'Guy . . .' She felt intensely weary—defeated, almost—in the face of his buoyant insistence.

He paused. 'Come on,' he said. 'This I have just got to see. We won't barge in. We'll just knock on the door. Ask for your stuff. See if my Filofax is there.' He grinned. 'I'd like to see her face.'

'No.'

'Call. Think of her, running her fat little hands over your letters, and paints, and—'

'Catherine said . . .'

'*I'll* call, then. Heads.'

He tossed the coin, and it landed on his palm. He smiled, held it out to her. 'I win.'

Faith sighed. 'You're crazy.'

He came up to her, put an arm around her. 'You really want to stay here and listen to "Silent Night" on the handbells?'

'Yes.'

He stroked her shoulder. 'Or is it just an excuse to have another lunge at my body?'

She looked at him steadfastly for a second longer, then picked up her coat.

'You can just ask her for the frames,' he said. 'You never know, she might have calmed down by now. She might even have left.' He was propelling her gently towards the door. 'Cheer up,' he said.

THIRTY-FOUR

As ALEX WALKED UP THE HILL, he felt as though he were climbing a mountain.

Everywhere he looked in the last twenty-four hours, he saw Clare's face.

That afternoon, re-lived so often, had not disturbed him for some time. His solitude had guaranteed an uneasy peace. He had wanted to be more than simply alone: he had wanted to resign from the human race. When he had first come out of prison, he had never returned the occasional messages left on the phone. His life had divided itself into two totally unconnected parts—the before and after of Clare's death. Before and after that single afternoon. He had felt that he was a different person, and that he had emerged into a different world. He had had the house built as far away from people as he could manage. And then . . . changing everything . . . came Faith.

He got to the top of the hill now, and looked about him. It was a cold and cloudy morning. The thin snow was dry underfoot.

He had come up the back of his own property, skirting the cliff edge, an acre of rough pasture. From the fence at the very top, you could see the Needles on a fine day. He stood here, hands plunged deep in his pockets, staring out to sea.

Clare's face.

That afternoon.

Clare had been sitting at the table in the kitchen. She had papers and letters spread in front of her, and a box. He had recognised it at once, even as he came charging in, already talking, as her father's strongbox: the one they had taken from his house when he died, and through which they had sorted to find his insurances, his will.

Alex had been worked up to a fury over Randolph Joscelyne. If he had been in any kind of normal mood, he would have remembered the gun.

Clare's father had served in the Second World War and he had kept his service pistol. When they first found it, seven or eight years before, they laughed over it, marvelling at its polished and clean condition. It had been wrapped in a piece of chamois leather in the bottom of the box.

'What are you doing?' he had said, flinging down his case, taking off his jacket.

Clare didn't reply.

He had walked to the sink and poured himself a glass of water. Standing with his back to her, he had been thinking only of Randolph—the way the older man had warned him to give in, to give away his own company.

'I've been pushed out by that bastard Joscelyne,' he had said. And, as he turned, he was adding, 'How would you like to live in India?'

Clare had taken the gun from the box and was holding it to her head.

Everything had happened in slow motion.

He had jumped forward, and put his fingers round her wrist, and pulled the gun down. He remembered being faintly surprised that it was so easy, that she didn't resist him more. He had got the thing out of her hand and stepped back, staring from it to her face.

She had been crying, and her head had been making a slight nodding motion. She did that when she was emotional, he had noticed it first one afternoon when they had been to a friend's wedding. Her father had Parkinson's disease and the ghost of his shaking hands superimposed itself whenever he looked at her face. She was afraid of it, too. He knew that without ever having to ask her.

And Clare had been shaking then. Her left hand had leaped gently on the table top, as if beating a ghastly silent rhythm to the scene.

'What . . .' He stumbled over the words. 'What in the name of God are you doing?'

They had looked at each other for perhaps thirty or forty seconds, while pictures of Randolph and the boardroom and documents he had been signing that morning, and about which he had been furiously thinking as he had driven home, jostled for space in his head with pictures of his wife with a gun pressed to her forehead.

He had tried, in those few short seconds, to make sense of it. He knew that she had been distracted lately, perhaps for two or three months. He knew that she had always seemed tired. He knew that she had been on edge: bright—blindingly bright—on some mornings, and silent the next. But the truth was, he hadn't given her much thought. He had been too busy.

Standing now on the hillside, Alex's face creased in grief.

When he was first in prison, that single thought had been enough to drive him mad. *Too busy.* If he hadn't been *too busy*, he could have saved her life, his own sanity. He had sworn to himself that, if ever he were free again—and, inside that place, it had seemed as laughably remote as walking on the surface of the moon—he would never work in business again. He would never again live in London. He would go somewhere where there was time, always time, for everything. Where no one knew him.

Alex walked slowly on, and reached the fence that divided Faith's property from his. He lifted the rough and lichened wooden stake out of the soil, and crawled under the wire. He wanted to see her house.

He came over the brow of the hill and saw it, marooned in its bleached sea of grass. There, too, was Cecily Joscelyne's Mercedes, an exclamation of red in the rough drive.

And there was another car.

Alex frowned as he gazed down at it.

A C-type Jag. Very rare. Obviously lovingly restored. He tried to

make out its details. He could only see the bonnet and part of the roof;
it was parked close to the front porch.

Whose is that? he wondered.

Who would come and see her, here? What would they be saying
to her? Had they helped her invade Faith's home? Did they approve?

His first instinct—the same one that had brought him out of the
house that morning—was to go down there straight away. He had had
a vague idea of trying to making Cecily see sense, though instinct told
him that she was already way beyond that. He had thought he might
tempt her out of the house—maybe say he would take her for a drink,
though his stomach recoiled at the very idea—then somehow get the
keys from her . . .

It was all *Boy's Own* stuff.

He would have stormed the place once. Once, in another lifetime, on another planet, when he had been so utterly sure of himself.
Grabbed a gun from a woman's hands and demanded to know what
was going on. Absolutely *one hundred and ten per cent sure* that he
could set things straight.

Like Guy.

He'd seen that same *fixer* look in Guy. Himself, twenty-five years
before.

But he hadn't fixed things, hadn't put them right, with Clare. He
hadn't even known there was a problem until two minutes before she
died.

'What the hell are you doing?' he had demanded of her.

He'd turned the gun over in his hands. He'd never even touched
such a thing before. He had held it gingerly in front of him, not even
holding it securely, but balancing it in his hand, his index finger curled
around the barrel and his thumb slipping on the stock.

'What are you doing?' he had repeated. 'What in God's name is the
matter?'

Clare had stood up suddenly and lunged for the pistol, making a
low sound in her throat.

He had realised then that she was out of her mind, and the thought
telegraphed—*someone's died, or she's been told she's got an illness*—and
a spark of dread and compassion had ignited in his chest. She'd missed

in her first grab for the weapon, and he'd held it aloft. His thumb came slipping down on to the trigger, and he had thought—rather calmly, looking back—*I better watch I don't fire this damned thing.*

By that time, he was back at the sink, facing into the room, and she was coming for him, around the table. He had brought the gun down and was holding it out, trying to tell her, by showing her the pistol, how stupid it was to handle anything like this—

And then—

The explosion was tremendous.

It lit the room for a second, the light piercing his image of her. She had raised both hands, like someone glorifying God. She tipped back her head. In her eyes he had seen something like thankfulness, just for a split second.

Alex, now, shut his eyes.

She was probably dead before she slumped to the floor. The hole in her chest was remarkably neat and clean for the first few moments. He had looked, just once, at the gun, and then placed it carefully on the table. He had bent down and felt for a pulse in her neck.

It was just as if it were happening to someone else. Some stranger, projected on a screen in front of his eyes. He'd watched scenes like that before—for entertainment, in films, he thought. Quite lucidly and disinterestedly. It could have been anyone: that man, standing over a woman's body. Anyone.

But it was him.

He had phoned for an ambulance.

The woman on the other end of the emergency line had asked him why, and he had said, 'You'd better get the police, as well. I've shot my wife.'

He had sat at the table until they arrived. He had gone to the door and let them in, and all the time he was hoping that they would come in, take one look at her, and say, 'It's all right, Mr Hurley. It was just a little game. It was like in the films. It was only acting. She's just asleep.'

He really thought that she might be asleep.

Sitting at the table, he had watched her, waiting for her to sigh as she usually did when she woke up, open her eyes and stare at the ceiling, a half-smile on her face. He was so used to seeing that profile, and he was waiting for it again. It had annoyed him slightly when the police hammered on the door. They made such a bloody noise about it, and it had been so blissfully silent in the kitchen.

Another minute and she would have woken up by herself.

It was the police who had first looked at the papers that Clare had spread in front of her. In all the time that he had been sitting there, he had not even glanced at them.

The first letter began, *My darling Clare.*

There had been about twenty others, going back three months. The first was dated just about the time that people began withdrawing their support in his company—people Alex had known for years, and counted as friends.

The last one, dated the previous day and patently received that very morning in the post, had spoken about finishing the love affair. Very cruelly, even crudely.

And it was signed—as all the others were signed—*Randolph.*

THIRTY-FIVE

*G*UY AND FAITH ARRIVED AT THE ISLAND in mid-afternoon, just as the light was beginning to fade.

As they began to cross the causeway, Faith grasped Guy's arm. 'What is it?' he said.

She was looking directly ahead. 'Let's go back,' she said.

He laughed. 'Back?'

'I mean it,' she told him.

Guy looked across, and saw that she had turned a truly deathly shade. He stopped the car at once, and she sprang out, leaning on the bonnet, taking deep breaths of air.

Gulls rose from the reeds with keening, offended cries. She watched them circle. They drifted out across the water, and then turned in towards the house. The sea was ice-grey, the land dark green. Every detail had been drained from the landscape.

'What's the matter?' Guy said, coming round the car to hold her hand.

She took it away, and crossed her arms. 'I've got a bad feeling,' she said. 'A really bad feeling.'

'It'll be no problem.'

She turned to look at him. 'How can you be so sure?'

He smiled, and guided her back to the passenger door, opening it for her, and pushing her gently into the seat.

'Leave everything to me,' he said.

She hesitated, looking at him as he went back around the front of the car. He gave her a grin and a mock salute. Through the tinted glass, his face was just a series of light and dark shapes in the fading light.

She heard his shoes scrape on the road surface as he opened the door.

For a reason she couldn't fathom, it made her skin crawl.

THIRTY-SIX

$\mathcal{A}$LEX DID NOT KNOW HOW LONG HE HAD BEEN SITTING on the hill above Faith's house.

He only knew, as he moved now to get up, that it must have been some time. He was stiff from the cold and the hard ground. He brushed the grass stalks from his trousers, and, as he lifted his head to straighten up, he saw a flash of movement below.

A car was coming up Faith's bumpy drive. Its headlights were on. Silver, a BMW. He frowned and stared hard at it. *This is becoming a real house party.*

Fury stirred in him on Faith's behalf. Cecily Joscelyne was intent on filling the place with people, it seemed.

He took a step forward. He could at least stop any more strangers coming in. He had an idea that he could run down there, and tell them that what Cecily had done was criminal. That Faith had not sold her the house. Perhaps even the kind of person that Cecily Joscelyne counted as a friend would have at least a fraction of decency. They might even persuade her to go, if they knew the truth.

He started to walk, keeping his eyes on the car.

It killed its headlights, and, at the very same moment, the light that had been bleakly shining in the kitchen, at the back of the house, went out.

Alex stopped a second. Was this someone Cecily *didn't* want to see?

Then his heart turned over. It did a sluggish little dance in his chest, somewhere between pleasure and disappointment. Faith was getting out of the car. And Guy.

They stood in front of the car for a moment, looking at the house. Then they walked forward, Guy striding purposefully in front, Faith bringing up the rear. Alex saw the hesitation in her step, then saw Guy turn and say something to her and hold out his hand. Faith took it reluctantly, and they disappeared, walking up the steps to the porch.

Alex stopped dead in his tracks.

Faith had gone to Guy.

And Guy had come to the rescue. Every angle of his body, the way he held his head, the squared look of his shoulders, announced that he had this situation under control.

A wry smile came to Alex's face. Then, rapidly following it, a twist of both sadness and apprehension.

Turning, he started to walk away.

THIRTY-SEVEN

$\mathcal{A}$s Guy approached the door, Faith began to say, 'The locks have been changed,' but Guy pressed his index finger to his lips, motioning her to be quiet.

They could hear a faint sound inside.

'She's talking to someone,' Faith murmured.

They listened for a few moments longer.

The voice stopped. They heard the slight note of the telephone receiver being replaced. Then, curiously, the whispering resumed, in a kind of sing-song voice, like a teacher leading a nursery rhyme. They heard Cecily move, and the light in the kitchen, which had gone off as they arrived, came on, but only for a second. Standing there in the dark, they stared at each other while the light went on, off. On, off.

'What's she doing?' Faith whispered.

Guy stepped back from the door. He gauged it for a second, and threw his weight at it.

'No!' Faith cried. She clutched at his arm, and he shrugged her off. 'You promised,' she said.

The lock did not give, but a panel did. It was little better than chipboard, and it splintered down its length. Guy pounded at it, but it refused to go any further. In frustration he returned his attention to the lock, stood back, and began kicking at it. This time it was the door frame itself that gave way. A piece of wood flew off, and he returned to forcing his shoulder against the door. All the time, Faith was whispering, 'No, no,' ineffectually under her breath. With a crash, Guy tumbled into the room beyond.

Faith followed.

It took a moment for their eyes to adjust. Faith swung her head from left to right, trying to find Cecily in what appeared to be total chaos. The furniture had been pushed back to the edges of the room; clothes and papers had been flung on to the floor. The curtains were half-drawn, making the farthest left-hand corner completely black. There was sand and cement trampled into the carpet; boxes of tiles, pattern books, and tins of paint were stacked closest to the door.

'My God,' Faith whispered. She reached for Guy without looking at him. 'Let's go,' she said. 'Just let's go . . .'

Guy was searching for the light switch. He stumbled over the pattern books, cursed, and jabbed at the switch. Nothing happened.

'It goes off,' said a voice.

Faith and Guy turned in its direction. Cecily was walking, apparently quite unconcerned, as if on an afternoon stroll, from left to right across the room, towards the kitchen. At the kitchen door she stopped, reached inside to the light switch, and turned it on.

'On and off,' she said. 'I haven't any bulbs.' She flicked the switch. Light alternately flooded into and out of the room, on to her profiled face. Cecily shrugged, smiled, and turned away, the kitchen light throwing a long triangle of light into the main room. 'On and off, on and off. It goes on and on, then I have to put it down. It rings on and off even when I've put it down. And then the lights are the same. It's *so* annoying.'

Guy glanced at Faith. He put his index finger to his temple and tapped the skin. *Crazy.*

Faith, however, was not looking at Cecily. She had turned towards the hallway, her head up. 'What on earth is that smell?' she said.

Cecily had begun to talk again. She was standing in the centre of the living room, surrounded on all sides by shreds of paper. It looked, now that there was some light, as if she had been drawing.

'I've got a perfect room,' she was saying. 'It's divided into two. Do you ever dream of rooms for yourself? That's how it began, you know. I dreamed of rooms. And gardens. I always dreamed of the same lovely place. I would wake up and wonder where it was. I had the feeling it had been given to me once, and yet I could never quite reach it. A place where you felt right. Secure . . . You can make Georgian windows. Pale yellow drapes and a pale yellow linen sofa on three sides, lots of cushions. A piano. Do you play? Thomas can. A piano. And, on the opposite side, the fireplace. The centre of the room is flagged. It leads straight to the doors to the garden.' She smiled at them both. 'There are doors to a lovely garden,' she said.

Guy took a pace forward. She turned a look of attentive sweetness on him.

'Miss Joscelyne,' he said. 'Do you know who we are?'

'Guy,' said Faith. 'Leave her alone.'

He waved the remark away, advancing on Cecily with his hands on his hips. 'You do know that this house isn't yours?' he said.

'Yes it is,' Cecily replied.

'No. It belongs to Faith.'

Cecily looked over at Faith, who was nursing a desperate desire to run. Something terrible, nameless, seemed to be advancing on her. As Cecily noticed her for the first time, Faith's mouth went totally dry. Cecily stumbled across the room, holding out her arms, pinning Faith against the wall; there was nowhere for Faith to go.

'Faith!' Cecily cried.

Arms enveloped her. The smell of sweat and perfume. Faith held her face away in gagging distaste as Cecily hugged her; it seemed Cecily had not washed in several days. Over the other woman's shoulder, Faith motioned Guy to help. He had an incredulous smile on his face.

Cecily stepped back, grasping Faith by both arms, and began pulling her. 'Come and see what I've done,' she said.

'No. No, I—'

'Do you know where he is?'

'Who?' Faith was trying to dig her heels in.

'He'd like this so much,' Cecily said. She picked up a piece of paper from the floor. 'Look, look. As you come in the door, there's a dog-leg stair. I want to put a stained-glass window—just two feet high, but it would be about seven feet long—in the aperture as you go past the roof joist. It's facing east. The sun in the morning, you see? What do you think of the design? Green. I'm even making a model of it.' She smiled hugely. 'Can you believe that I'm making a model! There is a lot of green in it. I always imagined green . . .'

Faith was trying to get Cecily's hand off her elbow. The fingers were digging into her skin, the nails already making deep marks in her flesh. The two of them stumbled now as they stepped further into the darkness of the corner, Cecily dragging Faith, who lost her balance temporarily. There were tools on the floor—wire, a hammer, screws, tubes of glue.

As Faith stumbled, it broke the spell of disbelief that had enchanted Guy. He grabbed Cecily's arm; as he did so, he snatched the paper out of her hand.

'You fucking woman,' he said, in a voice of contemptuous calm. 'Can't you understand? We're not bloody *interested*.' And he tore the drawing in two.

Cecily froze.

In the silence, Faith thought that her heart would surely climb out of her throat. She was terrified, all the more so because Guy seemed to be finding this funny, finding it ridiculous, and now some sixth sense was roaring through Faith, screaming, *It's not funny. Be careful. It's not funny* . . .

Cecily watched the two fragments of her drawing flutter mid-air for a second. Guy had thrown them at shoulder height behind himself. One piece snagged against the closed curtain and fell in stops and starts to the floor, as if it were hanging to each thread, a last gasp before dying.

'I've been looking for the perfect room, in the right place,' Cecily said. 'For him.' She began to shake her head, left to right, right to left, left to right, excruciatingly slowly. 'And he will. He *will* come.' Cecily's body drooped momentarily. Faith thought that she was sitting down on the floor.

'Guy,' Faith hissed, desperate. 'Let's go. Please. *Guy!*'

All she saw next was a black arc, drawn suddenly against the curtain cloth. Guy at its furthest point, Cecily at its beginning. An overhead arc, sweeping down. There followed the most sickening sound that Faith had ever heard.

She glanced down. Something wet had landed on her clothes—on her right thigh. A spray of freckled colour.

She looked up again, and saw Guy stumbling backwards. He landed against the curtains and crashed, holding one arm up, obscuring his face, through the window. Glass sharded in all directions, and Guy disappeared for a moment, the curtain neatly folded over him. The window frame was aluminium, and at hip height. The top half of his body sagged out through the broken pane. His head and shoulders and upper torso became invisible in the darkness outside. Only his legs remained, wrapped in the sickly grey-green drape, thrashing weakly up and down. His left foot described a perfect half-circle on the ground, and came to rest on the sill, drawn up like a child's. He might have fallen asleep, curled up with the curtain for a comforter.

'Guy!' Faith screamed.

She took the first staggering steps towards him and Cecily stepped out in front of her.

'You haven't seen him, I suppose?' she asked.

Faith stretched out her hand to Guy, trying to reach past her.

'He ought to come. He really should,' Cecily said, and she raised her arm.

It was then—only then—that Faith saw the hammer. The head was neatly tipped with red, as if it had been dipped in paint. But there was more on the handle, and, she saw now, with horror, more on Cecily's face and neck and upper chest.

'What have you done?' Faith whispered. She stepped to the side, her eyes fixed on the other woman's bland, expressionless face. Guy was making a low, rattling sound in his throat.

'I wouldn't do that,' Cecily said.

'I've got to help him.'

'I wouldn't do that.'

'But he's—you've hurt him—I must—'

'No.' The hammer was swinging gently in her grasp.

'I'll just look,' Faith blurted out.

'He's in the way.'

Faith's eyes strayed, agonised, for one moment to Guy's inert form. Glass lay all around him. He was actually lying on shattered fragments, where his body was looped over the frame.

'Yes,' Faith agreed. 'But . . . if you like, I could move him out of the way, couldn't I?'

Cecily moved close to her.

Panic pulled at every muscle. Faith's first instinct was to run, to get the hell away. But the sight of Guy held her back. If she left him, this crazy woman might do something else, something *worse*, to him.

Guy groaned. The curled-up leg began to twitch repeatedly.

'I've *got* to get him down,' Faith said. She stepped past Cecily and pulled back the curtain. Guy's head and shoulders hung out through the glass. One hand was drawn across his chest. She took hold of that arm, and pulled, bracing her feet on the floor. 'Please, *please*,' she whispered. All the time, the skin on her back and neck prickled with the expected blow from behind her.

With the second or third pull, Guy's body came towards her, turning slightly on its side as he came back through the gap. He was heavy. As his whole weight came tumbling through the broken window, Faith put out her arms to try to cradle him and break his fall. His forehead slammed against the window frame.

'Oh God, oh God,' Faith sobbed.

The right side of his face was thick with blood, which was pumping down on to his clothes as she tried to get him upright without falling. It had run into his right eye, but that hardly mattered. The eye, the right temple, the right side of the skull were a mass of shattered bone.

'No . . . oh, no,' she said. She found that she was weeping. With a final tug, Guy's whole body came crashing down on to the floor, his legs buckling beneath him. He ended in a slumped position, Faith desperately pulling at his feet to try to straighten them. She reached for his head, then pulled back.

'I've got to ring for an ambulance,' she said, scrabbling to her feet, looking around for the phone.

Cecily pushed her. For an instant, Faith was convinced that this was the blow she had been anticipating. But she was wrong. Cecily had merely shoved her with her hand. Nevertheless, Faith was sent back four or five feet.

'No, no,' Cecily said. 'I can't allow it.'

'You—can't—!' Faith felt like screaming. She was sure, in another second, she *would* scream. She would start to scream and never stop. She tried to bring her voice under control. Every scrap of victim advice she had unconsciously collected in her head for years came tumbling into her mind. *Keep very calm. Don't run, and don't shout. Don't beg. Talk very quietly. Listen to what they say. Reason with them.* 'Where is the phone?' she asked.

'No, no, no,' murmured Cecily.

'The phone . . .'

'No, no, no . . .'

Faith looked round for something to throw. Something as heavy as the hammer. Anything. By the window, Guy started, horribly, to cry out. It was a guttural, rasping, primitive noise.

Faith looked back at Cecily. 'Please,' she said. 'He needs a doctor. He's got to get to hospital.'

Abruptly, Cecily sat down on the sofa that she had wedged to one side of the fireplace. She stretched her legs in front of her, the hammer still in one hand. 'That reminds me,' she said brightly. 'How *are* you?'

Faith stared at her. She felt herself begin to shake: a feeling over which she apparently had no control, like being caught in an earth tremor. 'Please,' she whispered. 'Where is the phone?'

Cecily at last looked down at her hand. A look of surprise crossed her face. She dropped the hammer and wiped her fingers, with a moue of disgust, down the leg of her trousers. 'I can't let you use the phone, I'm afraid,' she said. 'I would like to let you, but I can't. I'm expecting a terribly important call.'

Faith closed her eyes.

'Important call,' Cecily repeated.

Please, Jesus, Faith thought.

Please, Jesus. Help me.

'I've got something else to show you,' Cecily said.

Faith opened her eyes; Cecily had crossed the room silently in her bare feet, and was at her side, pulling at her. 'Come and look,' she said.

She began to walk past, and Faith's eyes immediately flickered to the door. But, just as she was ready to move, Cecily stopped, turned, and gripped her firmly by the elbow.

'It wasn't me,' she said. 'That's the really amazing thing. All those years, he told me that *I* did it. And I believed him. Can you understand that? To do that to a child? He told me it was *my* fault.'

'Who?' asked Faith, confused. 'Guy?'

Cecily laughed. 'My step-father.'

'I'm sorry, I don't—'

'He lied to me. All that time. Don't you think that's very cruel?'

'Well . . . yes, of course. It's cruel.'

'Do you know how old I was when they got married, when it began? Six.'

'I see . . .'

'Six.' She wiped her hand across her face, leaving a sticky trail of Guy's blood on her skin. 'Yes, don't you think that's dreadful? He had me taken to a clinic, you know.' She looked past Faith, into an impenetrable past. '*You belong to me,*' she murmured.

Guy was stirring. Out of the corner of her eye, Faith saw his hands move—fluttering briefly in mid-air, then groping slowly on the floor about him. She looked back at Cecily.

'You see,' Cecily said, 'it wasn't my fault, all those things. I was lost from the day he first came to the house. *Six years old.* He could see it in me, I suppose. My father had been so sweet; Ruth was so helpless. We were like cannon fodder, you know?' Her hand passed over her hair abstractedly. 'Have you ever heard that poem, the one they always read to you in English class when you're ten or eleven? *Anthem for Doomed Youth.* I can remember the first time I heard that, in school. Sitting in my row. It was like us. I thought, as soon as I heard it, of Mother and myself. *What passing bells for these . . . only the monstrous anger . . .* You know how you can see how it will be with some people the moment you meet them? I think he saw that in us. That we were *usable.* We could be made to . . . do things. He could see that he could . . . do those things . . . He sees that in people. Sees who can be used . . .'

Guy was moving, his fingers splayed, his hands ahead of him. Faith realised that he could not see. But he could hear. He turned his head in the direction of Cecily's voice. It was all Faith could do to stop crying out.

'I wrote letters,' Cecily was continuing. 'I made phone calls. I found things out. When Thomas first started seeing Anna, he told me that I could stop it. He told me she would break.' She nodded. 'He saw that in *her*; saw she could be broken. He said that if I wrote the letters, found things out about her to use against her, that she would break and stop seeing him. Thomas doesn't like people to make a fuss. And she would make a fuss, you see? She would insist on going back to stay with her mother—if I went there, and got some of her things from the house—and it frightened her mother a bit, so that Anna would have to go home again . . .' She bit her lip, and then began scratching at the corner of her mouth. 'She had a heart attack, you know.'

Faith tried desperately to concentrate on what she was saying. 'Anna had a heart attack?' She was wondering who Anna and Thomas were.

'No. Her *mother* had a heart attack.'

'When you visited her?'

'Yes . . .' Scratch, scratch, scratch.

'That must have been terrible for you,' Faith said. She winced. Cecily's finger had torn a red line in the edge of her cheek.

Cecily looked at her. 'I think I started to remember that day,' she told her. 'I started to remember the trees outside the room. And the doctor's voice . . .'

'I see,' said Faith.

Guy was crawling towards them. Faith longed to stop him, to warn him that he ought to keep still. She was already hoping that, if she listened carefully enough and for long enough to Cecily, she could get her in some other room, perhaps *lock her* in some other room, *or outside* . . .

'He never leaves you alone. Never. *Never*,' whispered Cecily. 'Just one night. If he had ever left me alone, just for a little while . . . but *never . . . never . . .*'

It was all Faith could do to suppress her tears. Past Cecily's unfocused gaze, she could see Guy's face was almost obliterated by blood; just that small peak of hair showed at his parting.

Abruptly, she took Cecily's hand. 'Weren't you going to show me something?' she asked.

Cecily gave her a smile of terrible pleasure. Her face lit up. 'That's right,' she said. 'Of course! How dreadful of me. You must have been so looking forward to it. Come with me.'

They advanced, hand in hand, down the narrow hallway. Faith dared not look back, but she prayed that Guy would take the chance to get out of the door.

Don't be a hero this time, she prayed.

You can't solve this one. Get out.

They were at Faith's bedroom door.

Smiling, Cecily opened it, and ushered Faith inside.

Alex had gone back to his house, but he could not settle.

He began slowly walking the length of his living room, with its view of the sea. The light faded and the coast emerged as one thin band of lighter colour against the dark. He stopped at the window.

He was trying to imagine what was going on in Faith's house. Every time he put his mind to Guy and Faith and Cecily, the picture would not lie straight. He could not imagine them sitting down and talking this through. If Faith had gone there hoping that Cecily would be civilised, would see the error of her ways, she was surely wrong.

And he kept thinking of Cecily's face next to Faith's. Faith, trying to reason. Cecily Joscelyne . . .

His brow furrowed.

What would she do, if driven?

He tried to think why she should want the house, *that* house. He tried to tie Guy into the equation, acting as broker between them. And still it came out all wrong.

Still it fell to pieces in his head.

He went to the kitchen, and poured himself a drink from the bottle of Scotch that he kept, not socially in a cabinet for guests, but hidden in a cupboard for himself. Every now and again, a glass would calm the demons that stalked him. Not for ever, of course. Not even for a night. But perhaps for an hour. He would forget Clare's face, and stop feeling guilty. Guilty as hell. Guilty to the depths of his heart.

The charge had been altered to manslaughter. His own state of mind. The letters on the table.

In the end, he had got nine years. He was released in just over six.

But it wasn't enough. He felt that there couldn't be enough time in eternity to put that particular nightmare right. To lift Clare from the cold floor, to tell her that he knew what Randolph Joscelyne could be like, and that they could start again. He knew without a shadow of a doubt that he could have forgiven her. If only she had let him try. After all, he had never felt that Clare *belonged* to him, or owed him anything. He had never felt, from the beginning, that because he was married to her he was in possession of her.

Standing now at the kitchen sink, draining the Scotch like medicine, grimacing as it burned his throat, he looked at the last traces of the liquid in the tumbler in his hand. Quite suddenly, the fact that he was standing alone, drinking hard to obscure unwanted thoughts, disgusted him.

He didn't want to live in this heartbreak any more. He wanted to climb out of it, back into the living world. For the last few days, he had felt as if Faith Collins could help him do that. He could take the slim hand offered to him as he tried to get his head and shoulders above the pit into which he had flung himself. Out of the blackness, into a little light.

What was she doing, out there, in that house?

He put down the glass.

What was Guy doing?

And . . . *Cecily?*

Striding out into the living room again, he picked up the phone and dialled Faith's number.

THIRTY-EIGHT

*J*UST AS CECILY OPENED THE BEDROOM DOOR, the phone began to ring. She stopped, a smile immediately lighting her face. 'I must answer that,' she said.

Faith gripped her wrist. 'No,' she said, thinking of Guy, willing him to have reached the door and found his way free. 'You were going to show me something important . . .' But she really didn't want to know what was beyond this particular door. Something inside there smelled sweet and rancid, disgustingly insistent on the air.

Cecily wrenched her hand away. 'I've got to answer that,' she repeated, and began to run back along the hall.

Faith had only that moment to think.

There was no use trying to get out *past* Cecily. And there was no way out through the bathroom opposite—no window large enough. There was no door along this way—only the back door which was between the kitchen and the living room, and that again was back in the direction that Cecily was heading.

But in the bedroom was a window large enough to get through. She grabbed the door-handle, taking a last desperate look at Cecily's retreating back as it disappeared into the semi-darkness of the living room. The phone stopped ringing.

Once on the threshold, Faith had to stop, clamping her hand over her mouth. She could see that there was something lying in the bed—a shadow—a *person*. Reaching behind her, eyes fixed on the shape, she fumbled for the switch. At the same moment, in the living room, she heard Cecily's voice raised: 'Don't you *do* that!'

Guy, she thought.

And switched on the light.

Randolph Joscelyne lay slumped slightly to one side in the bed, the sheets pulled up around him. His whole upper torso was badly bruised—blooms of discolouration. His skin tone was grey, turning to blue. His eyes were fixed somewhere close to her, and his expression was one of great surprise. Not horror or pain. Just enormous, even rather amused, surprise.

Just for a second, she thought he was alive.

Just for a second.

'Oh Jesus Christ,' she breathed.

She thought she might be able to contain even this—to go forward past him to the window, holding in the cry that seemed to be lodged in her throat. She took one step, shielding the sight of him with one hand pressed to her face, the other still over her mouth.

Then she heard Guy screaming.

She turned back, ran through the door, up the hall. Pinpricks of light flickered in her sight. *Don't faint now. Now is not a good time to faint.*

There were no words in Guy's shout. Just four or five wire-taut pitches of sound that were being beaten out of him. As Faith got to the doorway, she saw Cecily standing over him, kicking at him in a silence that looked like mime: only the connections of each blow brought this animal response from the body at her feet.

Guy was lying close to the outside door. He had managed to pick the telephone from its hiding place, behind the boxes. The red cord snaked over the strewn carpet. He was lying on his side, holding the receiver in mid-air, as if every atom of his being depended upon keeping hold of it. His face was turned down towards his body, and his

YOU BELONG TO ME

other arm was raised in a vain attempt to protect himself. Cecily was aiming the kicks at his head.

'No!' screamed Faith.

As she ran forward, Cecily forced the receiver out of Guy's hand. His arm fell away in one last weakly grasping arc. Cecily put the phone to her ear.

'Thomas?' she said. 'Thomas?'

Faith ran to Guy, knelt down next to him, and pulled his head and shoulders up into her lap. Blood soaked her, but she did not notice it. His head rolled loosely, his body totally inert. As she watched, only his hand had any life: it groped for her, and she caught it, pressing it to her throat, 'I'm here,' she said.

His mouth opened. There was no sound.

Faith stared up at Cecily. 'Help me!' she said.

Oh God, so useless. To ask his murderer to help, to actually ask her . . . and Cecily was oblivious to them both, standing with both hands clutching the phone, staring into nothing, her mouth working. Faith looked down again at Guy.

'It's so lovely,' Cecily was saying. 'It's what we said. It's what we said . . .'

Guy's faint grip vanished.

Faith looked at his face, felt his neck, looked at his hand. There was nothing left. She let his arm drop to his side. Blood was still seeping from the wound on his temple.

'Stop,' she whispered.

Cecily held the receiver away from her ear, then hurled it as far as its cord would allow. She turned to Faith, full of fury.

'He won't talk to me,' she said. 'That's *your* fault!'

Faith edged back, slowly, so that Guy's body rolled gently from her. Cecily was looking from side to side, her hands flexing. '*Your* fault, *your* fault . . .'

Faith knew that she had to run, that it might be the only chance she would have. Yet, as she tried to stand, her legs felt like water under her. Cecily was screaming in her face as though Faith's movements were hardly registering.

'He wouldn't even speak to me!' she was yelling.

Faith got to her feet. *If you try to touch me, I'm going to kill you*, she thought. And she started backing to the kitchen.

To the door to the garden. To freedom.

In his house a quarter of a mile away, Alex stared at the phone receiver in the palm of his hand.

But only for a moment.

The phone had rung twice in Faith's house before it had been pulled off the hook. There was a muffled, gasping reply that he couldn't understand.

Then, Cecily Joscelyne's voice, away from the handset: 'Don't you *do* that!'

His heart had seemed to stop as the line was then flooded with a man's cries.

Guy? he thought. *Guy?*

Then, Faith's scream. 'No!'

He had almost dropped the phone that second. Cecily Joscelyne's voice, throaty and close, swarmed down the line. 'Thomas?' she said. 'Thomas?'

He heard the sound of someone running, then a thud. Then Faith again—soft, pleading. 'I'm here . . .' And, loudest of all, closest of all, 'Help me!'

That was enough.

He never heard the rest. Cecily's description of the house, Faith's whispered *Stop*.

Because he was already out of his door and running.

Cecily followed Faith.

'I wish you wouldn't come when I'm busy,' she said. 'Don't you see? I'm just very busy and I haven't *time*, and you just . . . you just come in here and get in the *way* . . .'

'Don't come any nearer,' Faith said.

They were in the kitchen. The light seemed unbearably bright to Faith; she narrowed her eyes against it. And saw the hammer again in the other woman's hand.

'I wish . . . people would . . . when I try to *tell them* . . .' Cecily muttered.

'Don't come any closer.'

'I . . . just . . . wish . . .' Cecily was breathing hard, dragging air, her eyes widening. She was holding the hammer wrongly, Faith realised. With its head pointing back.

Faith looked desperately around herself. She had a block of kitchen knives. Somewhere. Somewhere, *somewhere, for Christ's sake!* But they were not on the draining board where she had left them. *Where did I put them?* She gazed about wildly, seeing the familiar shapes and objects and yet not seeing them, not being able to put a name or a purpose to them. *Think. Oh, sweet dear God, help me think.* In the drawer under the sink was the cutlery. Yes. *Back up to it. Don't let her see.* There would still be a breadknife there. And a grapefruit knife. And meat skewers . . . 'Please,' she heard herself say, 'stop.'

Don't make me.

To her profound amazement, Cecily did stop. She came to a halt like an automaton, on command. Within two or three feet of Faith, she shrugged, her hands extending each side like a doll. 'I think . . . what *do you* think?' she said, blankly. 'For the room? Would you do me a painting?'

'A painting,' Faith repeated. Hysteria climbed into her voice. 'A *painting . . . ?*'

'I don't want it too bright . . .'

Faith's hand trembled at her own back, finding the cutlery-drawer handle. She pulled it open, searching blindly with her fingertips. 'I'll do a painting for you,' she said. 'I'll do it now.'

Cecily considered. 'He'll be here soon.'

'Tell me what you want, and I'll go away and do it.'

'Tonight?'

'You can see the first sketch in the morning.'

'The morning.' Cecily's fist clenched halfway up the hammer's wooden handle.

'What would you like?' Faith asked, frantic now. 'What do you think? Matisse is good . . .'

'No . . .'

'Manet, then. Manet is . . . Manet is nice . . .'

'No, no, *no* . . .' Cecily's voice rose to a shout.

'I know.' Faith's tone broke. It came out more of a sob. 'You could . . . you could always have . . .' She was searching her memory wildly for green gardens. 'You could have . . . let me . . . let me think . . .' Tears began to course down her face. 'There's . . .' The most vibrantly green painting she could think of at that moment was a Sisley: *Avenue of Chestnut Trees.*

No trees. God. No trees.

'There's, perhaps, Klimt . . .'

Cecily glared at her as if she had suddenly sworn. 'What are you doing?'

Faith tried to steady her voice. 'It's called *Island on the Attersee.*' But she was openly weeping now. 'You'd like it very much. There are no trees. Or there's *Field of Flowers* . . .'

'You're crying,' said Cecily. She watched Faith for a second, then a sigh of intense sadness broke from her, and she clasped both hands in front of her. Guy's blood was drying on her skin, on her clothes. She glanced down at Faith's left hand, held before her. 'You've got a wedding ring,' she said.

Faith did not reply. She couldn't have said a single thing. The connection of the ring to the dead man in the other room was too enormous. It seemed to her that the lifeblood of the two of them—not just Guy's—was seeping into the very ground on which she stood.

Cecily raised her glance to Faith's face.

'I don't know what you have to do to make them love you,' she whispered. 'You see . . . Randolph never told me.'

THIRTY-NINE

$\mathscr{A}$LEX CAME RACING UP THE DRIVE IN THE DARK.

The breath was tearing in his chest. He hadn't run anywhere, like this, since his twenties. He was out of condition. He damned himself with every step. Even his twice-weekly jog couldn't have prepared him for the upward drag on the snow-slicked surface.

'Hurry up,' he whispered. His leg muscles were screaming defeat. 'God,' he kept saying. A whip to speed. An incantation. '*God . . . God . . .*'

He came around the corner of the drive, past the low-sweeping hawthorns of the gate; two black shadows crouched like dogs. He gasped for breath. Now he could see the roof. Now the porch. Now, a faint light in the house.

The C-type Jag and Guy's BMW and the red Mercedes were all still parked. The sight slowed him for a second. Who was the fourth person—the person who owned the Jag? Why hadn't he heard *their* voice on the phone?

He shook the thought away. There was no time for it. He would just have to expect some other barrier—the barrier posed by the invisible fourth, who must surely be on Cecily's side.

He slowed to a walk, gulping air desperately. He edged off the gravel, and on to the thick grass, watching his footing as best he could. The last thing he needed now was to fall on the rough ground and break his bloody leg.

He went around the side of the house, and along the back. Shapes loomed, and he side-stepped them. Building materials. A wheelbarrow. A skip. Then, half-way along, his feet ground on fragments of glass. He stopped.

The window had been broken, and the curtain beyond it was fluttering lazily back and forth in the steady breeze that blew into the room beyond. Alex could hear two female voices off to the left, in the kitchen. They were talking too low for him to catch distinct words, and he drew closer to the window, looking down at his feet, wincing at the prongs of glass piercing even the thick rubber of the soles of his shoes.

He put his palms flat on the intact panes of glass to either side, and leaned in.

Guy was lying on the floor in a triangle of light spread from the kitchen. He was on his back, his arms by his sides, his head turned away from Alex. No detail could be made out in the gloom, but it was clear that he was injured. Perhaps worse.

Alex drew back, grimacing.

Where was the fourth person?

He edged along the wall until he was outside the back door. As he got to it a thought flashed into his head: *I should have called the police. And an ambulance.* It had been obvious from the phone call that Guy was hurt.

'God damn it,' he muttered. Faith's terrified voice had wiped everything else from his mind. His only idea had been to get to her as quickly as possible.

'I can't help you,' said Faith.

He leapt, there in the darkness. She was so close she might have been at his side. He swung his head around. The house extended into the garden here, so that the back door was set in a right angle. He could see the patch of light on the ground, cast from the kitchen window. But he could not see in. It sounded from Faith's voice as if the window were ajar, and she standing very close to it.

He tried the handle of the back door. It was old, and slipped in his palm. It shifted with a slight but distinct click, the kind of sound that would never be noticed in the normal course of a day. Tonight, it seemed to him that it had all the impact of a pistol shot in the silence of the garden.

Where in hell was the fourth person?

Cecily was talking now. Saying something about getting married. He caught snatches of her voice.

'. . . at the wedding . . . I remembered afterwards . . . stopping the car at the next lights . . . branches overhead . . .'

An expression of violent disgust came to Alex's face. In one quick movement he pushed down the door handle and stepped inside the house, leaving the door open. He took the two or three paces to the entrance to the kitchen.

Cecily had her back to him.

Faith was facing him, though looking down, to one side. He could see that her right hand was behind her.

He hesitated just a fraction, thinking . . . *the fourth* . . . then he lunged forward, reaching out to try to grab Cecily by the neck from behind. To his utter amazement, the moment he touched her she collapsed, sagging to the floor. That split second of hesitation must have been enough to warn her—enough to betray the sound of his foot on the floor. He found himself falling over her. She slithered through his scissored arms and fell sideways across his feet, and he lost his balance completely. He had time to think, *they teach you that in self-defence . . . don't resist the attacker from behind . . . go loose and drop . . .*

God damn you, he thought. *You quick bitch.*

He fell forward, planting his open palms flat on the floor to stop himself, and found himself staring into Cecily's upturned face. It was spattered with blood. She was smiling blankly.

At once, an explosion of pain hit his right knee. Blades of agony telegraphed upwards. 'Christ!' he yelled. He fell to his left. 'Oh Christ!'

And he thought, *they must be here. The other one. The fourth.*

Cecily was moving, on hands and knees, out from under the weight of him. He squeezed his eyes shut, fumbling with both hands around his knee to locate the pain, and, in that same second, there was another terrible blow to the side of his body.

The air went out of him. Pain in his ribs, pain under his ribs. He brought his arm to his side. He opened his eyes and saw her crouching, still smiling, a hammer in her right hand.

You? Only you?

On the other side of the kitchen, Faith was scrabbling wildly in the drawer behind her. She was weeping and whispering frantically; then she turned. Ludicrous things fell out of the drawer as she brought her hand up: pastry cutters in childlike blue and yellow and red plastic rings, a cut-out voucher from a cereal packet. She tore them away, cursing. Then she held up the knife.

It was black-handled. The kind that is supposed to last a lifetime. Its edge was serrated into sharp points.

'Get away from him,' Faith said.

The other woman looked at her, eyes round. She got to her feet.

'Drop the hammer.'

Cecily looked at the weapon in her hand. Obediently, she let it fall to the floor.

'Step . . . step back from him . . . Go out of the kitchen . . .' Faith's voice was helplessly wavering.

Alex tried to get up.

Cecily suddenly reached forward, grabbing the knife. Her fingers closed over the blade, level with Alex's upturned face. He saw, with horror, the flesh fold around the steel, saw the blood leap from the cut. Still the fingers closed.

Faith gave a little cry, of terror and disgust, staring down at the knife, her gaze flickering between the blade and Cecily's hand and arm. She cried out, throwing the knife away from her. The force of it tore the blade backwards, and it was wrenched out of Cecily's grip and on to the floor.

Instantly, Alex grabbed it. Crouching at waist height to Cecily, he brought the blade up, its tip aimed directly towards her.

All that filled Alex's mind was to stop her. Just to stop her, *to stop her hurting Faith.* His hand moved without command, with its own blind desire.

And then—there in the same room—was Clare.

Clare on another smooth tiled floor. Clare in a hands-raised, plunging attitude. He saw immediately the way the knife would go. Straight up, into Cecily's stomach and chest. He saw how her hands would reach and fumble in an attempt to pull the blade away. He heard how she would sound, the noise of her breath in her throat. That sound of the last air trailing in and out.

Clare . . .

He dropped the knife.

'You can't do it,' Cecily exclaimed triumphantly. 'You can't do it, can you?' Then her voice froze.

Just for a moment they crouched opposite each other, like children involved in some private game. Alex saw bewilderment register in her face. And she eased forward, sighing.

He was sure that it was another trick. Despite the agony in his leg, he leaned to one side, trying not to touch her as she came at him, the smile still plastered to her mouth, the puzzlement still fixed in her expression.

She hit the cupboard that had been behind his shoulder, catching it full in her face. He heard a bone in her neck wrench, like two pieces of dry stone grinding together.

Then she fell to the floor, face down.

The black-handled knife was buried in her back.

And Faith was standing over her.

POSTSCRIPT

$\mathscr{T}$HERE WERE LILIES AT THE DOOR OF THE CHURCH. Faith stood in the shade, with Sam sheltered in the crook of her arm. It was a hot summer's day in the last week of August, and, at eight weeks old, Sam was fast asleep, seemingly drugged by the heat.

Faith and Alex were watching the wedding photographs being taken.

'She's a very pretty bride,' Faith said.

'Too chocolate-boxy,' Alex replied. 'All that froth.'

'Sssh!'

They smiled at each other.

The photographer was grouping the immediate families. Chloe's mother wore a hideous shade of fuchsia pink; the men were plainly stifling in morning suits. Ruth Joscelyne alone managed to look serene. She was standing very still where she had been put, on the left arm of her son. There was an almost glacial dignity in her bearing. As Faith watched her, she realised that she had never looked once at Thomas.

'Not as good as ours,' Alex whispered, in Faith's ear.

She smiled up at him. 'Registry Office, pub lunch and an evening of Sam's colic?' she replied. 'No contest.'

He squeezed her shoulder, grinning.

They stepped out into the sun.

Just as they drew level with the families, Chloe moved out in front of them, holding out her arms.

'Just a one-minute cuddle,' she said. 'He's so *adorable.*'

Thomas caught Faith's glance as she slipped the sleeping child into Chloe's grasp. He walked over to the group. Chloe was smiling as Alex unwrapped the shawl from Sam's legs. 'He's such a beauty,' she was saying. 'I want half a dozen, all the same.' She put her face close to Sam's warm, smooth cheek. 'Oh, I wish you were mine, all mine,' she whispered, and her glance met Faith's for a second, as she held Guy's son.

Thomas drew Faith to one side. 'I'm very glad you came,' he told her.

Faith did not know what to say. Receiving the embossed invitation a month before, only two days after they themselves had been married, her first reaction had been to say that it was impossible.

'Can't you see?' she had asked Alex, aghast, across the breakfast table. 'I mean, what would it *look* like?'

Alex had considered the card for a moment, then passed it back to her. 'I think it's a great compliment,' he said. 'A sign that they don't bear any grudges. You remember what he told us. He said, *Cecily was always a very sick girl.* They knew that.'

'I don't know . . .'

'I think it would be a mistake to refuse,' he told her. 'After all, they weren't the only injured party.'

She had bitten her lip. Alex was right. If the invitation was an olive branch, its acceptance was also a mark of peace. And the Joscelynes were not the lions they had been a year ago. Ruth had sold the London house after the Treasury scandal blew. She had moved into a small flat near Thomas, in Cambridge. Lawyers were still fighting over Randolph's tortuous estate.

Nevertheless, Faith found it terribly difficult, now, to look into Thomas Joscelyne's eyes. They were so flat calm, they were almost disturbing. As if he had shut the world away. Very cold eyes; as cold and icy calm as he was. She kept remembering Cecily's voice. Its inflection of pathos as she stared at Faith's hand.

You've got a wedding ring.

Faith looked across at Thomas now. You would never know the year he had lived through, she thought. There wasn't a sign of it in his face. Did he ever know how much Cecily had loved him?

She recalled how horrified she had been when she found out that Thomas was Cecily's *brother*. It had added an extra dimension to Cecily's sickness. And the murder of that poor teenager. How they had all covered up for her, especially her step-father. All that love she had been given, all that protection . . . and still she went to waste. All that concentrated effort to cure her.

And yet . . . Joz had been so pitiful. That night at Christmas was scored into Faith's memory. Joz standing in the harshly lit kitchen, wounded confusion on her face, belying the voice. Sometimes, lately, in the deep security of a quiet evening, with Alex's arms wrapped round her, and Sam sleeping at their side, Faith wondered about Randolph Joscelyne, and that last confrontation above the sea. It was a picture that would not leave her: Joz stretching forward to send him to his death . . .

But Alex brooked sympathy neither for Cecily nor for Randolph. 'They deserved each other,' he said. And that was all.

'I wasn't sure this was the right thing to do—to come,' she said, still feeling deeply awkward at Thomas's side.

Thomas smiled. 'But I am,' he replied.

She nodded. She felt suddenly short of breath, as if his presence alongside her were almost suffocating. *It's the heat*, she thought. *It's so hot.*

'We . . . sold the house,' she said, a shade too brightly, too quickly. It sounded at once as if she were desperate to change the subject. 'That is . . . I thought you might like to know.'

'Really?' he said. 'Good. I expect you are glad to be rid of it all.'

She almost replied, *Are you?*

He would love it here. It's so lovely. It's what we said, it's what we said . . .

He was looking away, across at Chloe and Sam and Alex. Chloe, still laughing and cooing at the baby, was calling to them both.

'Excuse me,' Faith almost said. 'But what, exactly, did you ever promise your sister?'

Almost. Almost said. But not quite. The moment evaporated into the heat of the dying afternoon.

Perhaps he never promised her anything.

Faith and Alex had learned of Cecily's background not only from the newspapers, but from Ruth, who had visited them in hospital. 'I hope, in time, that you will forgive my daughter,' she had said. 'And my husband.'

'What do you think she meant—*and my husband?*' Faith had asked Alex, when Ruth had gone.

'She's distraught,' he had replied. 'You could see the way she was just holding it together. It doesn't mean anything at all.'

She and Thomas had left the shade of the trees. Side by side, they reached Chloe and Alex.

Faith held out her arms and took Sam back, smoothing a hand protectively over his head. Sam had the same thick dark hair that showed in her own baby photographs; but he had the peak on the forehead, a wayward strand that would not lie down, that belonged only to Guy.

She kissed her son's forehead, holding his small body close to hers, feeling an anxiety that did not quite have a name. Alex was already holding her elbow.

'Shall we get to the cars?' he asked.

'Yes,' she said.

Thomas and Chloe were drawn away by other guests. As they got to the path, Alex and Faith turned to take one last look at them.

Chloe was holding her arms up to Thomas, asking to be kissed. Obligingly, he bent down to her, rather stiffly in the sunshine, his dark head covering her blonde one. She hung on afterwards, laughing as she gazed up into his face.

'You are Mr Joscelyne,' they heard her joke, waggling her ring finger under his nose, 'and I claim my five pounds.'

Thomas was disengaging Chloe's hand from his neck. 'And you are Mrs Joscelyne,' he replied, 'and you belong to me.' A shadow crossed his face, and he seemed to hesitate a fraction, listening to some inner echo that only he could hear. He straightened up, and looked around him with a patrician, superior expression: just like an actor taking centre stage. And, for that brief moment, Faith thought *Randolph Josce-*

lyne. Then Thomas turned away and Chloe followed him, lifting her dress clear of the grass as she hurried to match his pace.

Faith stopped walking.

'What is it?' Alex asked.

She looked at the couple for one moment longer. The sunlight was playing over them, and the first green shadows of the trees.

Faith shrugged, and turned away.

'Nothing,' she replied softly. 'It's nothing at all, I'm sure.'

www.ingramcontent.com/pod-product-compliance
Lightning Source LLC
Chambersburg PA
CBHW030317200626
46816CB00006BA/1825